Martin A. S. Hume

Sir Walter Ralegh

the British dominion of the west

Martin A. S. Hume

Sir Walter Ralegh
the British dominion of the west

ISBN/EAN: 9783337387440

Printed in Europe, USA, Canada, Australia, Japan

Cover: Foto ©Andreas Hilbeck / pixelio.de

More available books at **www.hansebooks.com**

SIR WALTER RALEGH

THE BRITISH DOMINION OF
THE WEST

BY

MARTIN A. S. HUME

AUTHOR OF
THE COURTSHIPS OF QUEEN ELIZABETH
THE YEAR AFTER THE ARMADA
EDITOR OF
THE SPANISH STATE PAPERS OF ELIZABETH

With Photogravure Frontispiece and Maps

NEW YORK
LONGMANS, GREEN & CO.
91 AND 93 FIFTH AVENUE
1897

'TO HER WHO IS THE FIRST, AND MAY ALONE

BE JUSTLY CALLED THE EMPRESS OF THE BRETANES.'

Sir Walter Ralegh.

PREFACE

IT is fitting that a series relating the lives of those who have reared the stately fabric of our Colonial Empire should begin with the story of the man who laid the foundation stone of it. The prescient genius of Sir Walter Ralegh first conceived the project of a Greater England across the seas, which should welcome the surplus population of the mother country to industry and plenty, and make of England the great mart for the products of its virgin soil. Others before him had dreamed of North-West passages to tap the trade of the teeming East; of gold, and gems, and sudden riches, to be grasped in far-off lands; but to Ralegh and his brother Sir Humphrey Gilbert belongs the more enduring honour of a nobler ideal—the planting in savage lands of English-speaking nations, ruled by English laws, enjoying English liberties, and united by links of kinship, and allegiance to the English crown. To them, more than to any other men, is it due that for all time to come the mighty continent of North America will share with England the cherished traditions and the virile speech of the race to which Ralegh belonged. To measure the greatness of the world's debt to him it will suffice to compare the sloth and poverty of the Southern part of the continent with the riches and activity of the North.

Through all the stirring career of Ralegh, splendid favourite, successful soldier, statesman, poet, historian, philosopher, chemist, admiral, explorer and privateer, there ran, like a golden thread, shining brightly amid the dross that surrounded it, the inextinguishable resolve that the arrogant claim of the Philips to the exclusive possession of the western world, by virtue of a Pope's bull, should be resisted to the death; and that in order to make this resistance effective England must be supreme upon the sea.

To this ruling principle he devoted his talents, his fortune and his life; he was the apostle and the martyr of a British Colonial

Empire; and this is the phase of his multitudinous activities in which the present short
biography is intended to regard him.

His commanding personality, and the strange
vicissitudes of his fortune, from the first impressed the imagination of his countrymen;
and his life has been written so often, and so
thoroughly, that there is little fresh material
to reward the research of more recent inquirers.
In 1733, before the modern methods of his-
torical investigation were possible, Oldys, with
marvellous industry, collected every fact then
obtainable respecting the life of his hero; much
of his information being derived from sources
not now easily accessible. In 1867 Mr
Edwards, with equal thoroughness and erudition, ransacked State-archives, official documents and private muniment rooms, for such
information as they contained on the subject.
To Oldys's *Life of Ralegh*, in the eleventh
edition of the *History of the World*, and to
Edwards's *Life and Letters of Ralegh* all subsequent biographers must perforce be indebted, either for direct information or for
the indication of original lines of research.
To a lesser degree acknowledgment is due to

the works of Southey, Tytler, Sir Robert
Schomburgk, Mr Stebbing, and especially to
Dr S. R. Gardiner.

But however well gleaned a field may be,
there is always some stray grain still to be
gathered; and another Life of Ralegh would
hardly be justifiable, unless it contained some
new contribution, however humble, to the
knowledge of the subject; some fresh fact,
however small, which should aid us in arriving
at a just judgment upon the extraordinary,
and sometimes problematical, circumstances of
Ralegh's career. It has always been known
that he was deliberately sacrificed to the
importunities of the Spanish Ambassador,
Gondomar, and many reasons have been
suggested for the Spaniard's apparent animosity. Dr Gardiner has to some extent
lifted the veil, but the exact process and
reasons of Ralegh's ruin by Gondomar have
hitherto never been set forth in Gondomar's
own words. It will be seen in the course of
the present volume that it was no private
revenge, it was with no desire to inflict
punishment for the injury actually done on
the last Guiana voyage, that led Gondomar to

hound Ralegh to death, for he was practically
condemned before he sailed, but to serve as
an object lesson to England that all South
America, at least, belonged to Spain. The
reason why the weak King allowed Gondomar
to hector him into judicially murdering his
most distinguished subject is also clearly seen
in the Spanish papers utilised for the present
volume, to have been a pusillanimous desire to
curry favour with Spain at any cost, and to sell
Ralegh's head at as high a price as he could
get for it. Gondomar's letters at Simancas
and in the Palace Library at Madrid place this
beyond doubt, and furnish also several side
lights which help to elucidate other disputable
points. They have likewise afforded me an
opportunity of including in the present work
two important letters from Ralegh to Lord
Carew which are not contained in Mr
Edwards's collection.

MARTIN A. S. HUME.

LONDON, *June* 1897.

d

CONTENTS

XV

CONTENTS

CHAPTER XVII

LIST OF PLATES

Sir Walter Ralegh

CHAPTER I

DEVELOPMENT OF ENGLAND'S MARITIME POWER— ANCESTRY AND PARENTAGE OF RALEGH

THE most striking development of national thought in modern times has been the almost sudden quickening of the imperial instincts of our race. There has been little excitement or shouting about it ; but the stream of conviction flows swiftly, and with ever-growing potency, that the stately confederacy of nations we call the British Empire has a future before it even more splendid than its glowing past, and that all its citizens from the highest to the humblest may with reason hold their heads higher as they claim their share in the glory of their common birthright. It was not always so. For many a long year we were so busy garnering the results of empire that we had almost lost sight of the means of retaining it. Over-prosperity, per-chance, had softened our muscles and thickened our brains, and we were content for a time to continue

A

to reap without sowing; but the national awakening came in good season, and has braced us with the knowledge that the responsibilities of empire must be boldly faced if. the pride of empire is to be preserved.

We know now that Britain must be undisputed mistress of the seas, or meekly take a secondary place amongst the nations; and there is no divided counsel, no wavering faith amongst us as to the fulfilment of our duty. Our insular position has intermittently brought the fact home to us ever since we were a united nation. Every hundred years or so, the conviction grows irresistibly great, and leads to effective action; but only if the material elements of effective action have been evolved during the period of quiescence. If during that period wealth has not increased, science has not advanced, practical seamanship has not improved, or the physical development of the race has decayed, then no amount of popular enthusiasm, however dire the need, will conjure up a great navy as by the touch of a magician's wand. Great navies, like great · empires, are things of slow growth, depending for their very being upon previously existing material, and experienced knowledge. The great Portuguese African and American possessions sprang from the patiently accumulated elements, material and scientific, gathered at the instance of one enlightened prince from all quarters of the known world, through a long series of years. Seamen, navigators, cosmographers, astronomers, mathematicians and naval architects were all bribed to surrender their observation or their learning to the man who slowly built up a navy with the deliberate intention of founding a colonial empire for his country. But valuable as may have been the services rendered to Prince Henry's great plans by the wise men from afar, the ultimate success of his efforts, and of the subsequent triumphs of Columbus, depended mainly upon the existence of a school of fearless mariners who knew the sea and loved it, and the invention of the caravel, a form of craft, finer in line, handier in working, and swifter in pace than had ever been seen before.

The great naval renaissance in England, during the reign of Elizabeth, sprang from exactly similar circumstances.

During the lifetime of the great Queen the sceptre of the seas passed from the hands of Spain into the powerful grasp which has held it ever since, and the dramatic completeness of the transference is rightly looked upon as one of the greatest marvels of that virile age. But wonderful as it seems when regarded from a distance, the causes are perfectly clear. The Queen personally did but little for it, except in so far that her national policy gave all Englishmen pride and faith in their country, and that she honoured success when it came.

The Spanish Armada was not beaten by fighting

but by *not* fighting. It was the fact that they could not get at the swift, handy craft of the English which turned the proud confidence of the Spaniards into dismay and panic. It was the superior build of the English ships, and the greater efficiency of the English seamen, which gave Spain her deathblow upon the seas; and these circumstances arose from causes long anterior to the date of the armada itself.

The foundation was laid by Henry VIII. He knew that Columbus had offered to discover the new world for England, and had been repulsed by the cautious Henry VII. He knew that the Cabots had failed to reach Cathay by the west, and that if he was to secure his share of the spoils of the Indies—for it was no question of a colonial empire for England yet—he must have larger and stronger ships. He was rich, clever, and ambitious, and set about improving his navy. The royal dockyards were refitted : navigators, shipbuilders and cannon founders were brought from the English west country, from Genoa and from Portugal; and before he died he had the satisfaction of knowing that some of the finest ships that sailed the seas flew the flag of St George. An eye-witness of the attempt of Francis I. with his fleet of three hundred sail to attack the Isle of Wight in 1544 echoes the impartial foreign opinion of Henry's navy at the time. The English had only sixty ships to five times that number of

Frenchmen. But amongst them were the *Great Harry* and *Mary Rose*, of nearly a thousand tons burden each, and there were many of those wonderful vessels 'such as had never been seen before which would work to windward with sails trimmed fore and aft'; invented by 'Mr Fletcher of Rye': and the English were so little dismayed, that great Harry, the King, had himself come down to see the victory of his beloved fleet. The watchword on board was 'God save the King,' and the answer was 'Long to reign over us.' 'You may believe me,' says the eye-witness, 'that one English ship was worth more than any five Frenchmen. It was truly a pleasant sight to see them anchored all in a line.'

The French did not enjoy the sight so much as the onlooker, and decided to leave great Harry's ships alone.

Then a period of quiescence came, and England's navy was allowed to rot in harbour. Somerset and Northumberland were too rapacious, Mary too poor, to spend money on the fleet; and in 1555 the Council was obliged to confess to King Philip that the English navy was unfit to put to sea. Even he saw that, at all costs, this must be remedied, and wrote to them that—'England's chief defence depends upon its navy being always in good order to protect the kingdom against aggression. The ships must not only be fit for sea, but instantly available.'

When Elizabeth came to the throne, the merchant
navy of England engaged in lawful commerce
amounted to no more than 50,000 tons, and the
royal navy in commission consisted only of seven
cruisers, the largest 120 tons, and eight armed
merchant brigs. The navy was a mere skeleton;
but the material was being formed in this period
of depression from which England's future maritime
greatness was to be built. The constant wars
between Charles V. and the French kings had
caused the English Channel to swarm with Spanish,
Flemish and French privateers. Some bore letters
of marque, some were mere pirates, but whatever
they were, the sight of their easy gains and their
adventurous lives fired the young English west
country seamen, into whose ports they came. There
were no sailors better than the Cornish and Devonshire men. Their voyages were the longest and
roughest; for Falmouth, Dartmouth, Exmouth, Plymouth, Bideford and Bristol well nigh monopolised
the over-sea traffic, excepting that with France and
Flanders. The abolition of the fasts of the Church
had immensely decreased the demand for fish, for
the consumption of anything but flesh was looked
upon almost as a sign of Papistry, and it was an
easy step for the English sailors to take up such
a profitable trade as piracy in exchange for fishery.
Vessels of all sorts passed into the business; younger
sons of county families, and even sober merchants,

were attracted by the gains; and soon anarchy reigned on the seas. The race was with the swift, the battle with the strong; and only the swiftest and the strongest survived. The stauncher, the handier, the quicker a vessel was, the greater was its chance of success, the bolder, and more hardy the men, the greater was their gain; and out of this welter there arose such a race of seamen and shipbuilders as the world had never seen before. In the struggle for the survival of the fittest, Devonshire and Cornwall carried off the victory; and when the supreme effort had to be made, which was to establish the sea power of England for good and for all, the stout hearts, the keen eyes, the matured experience of these scourges of the sea, were ready to fight their country's battle.

The national policy of Elizabeth in adopting the reformed faith, and keeping Spain at arm's length, her aid of the revolting Netherlands, and of the Huguenots in France, had naturally led to a recrudescence of the persecution of English Protestants who fell into the hands of the Spaniards. The English sailors were of course those who suffered most, and their kinsmen at home at Plymouth, Falmouth, or Exmouth, gradually concentrated most of their attacks upon Spanish shipping. There were few country gentlemen on the Devonshire coast who had not a swift cutter or two at sea, on the look out for plunder or revenge; and the talk at the firesides

of cottage and manor house alike, was all of daring
and profitable adventure, and of the improvement of
shipbuilding which made it possible. These must
have been the topics which from his earliest child-
hood filled the eager ears of young Walter Ralegh,
His father, Walter Ralegh of Fardell, had been thrice
married, and had a large family—four sons and two
daughters, Walter being the second son by the third
wife, Katharine Champernoun, widow of Otho
Gilbert.

Wonder has been expressed by Ralegh's biographers
as to how, or when, he acquired his skill in maritime
affairs, since he is not known to have had much
practical experience in seamanship before he appeared
as a naval commander of accepted authority. But,
apart from the marvellous versatility, which enabled
him, as one of his contemporaries said, to do each
thing as if he had been born especially for it, love
of the sea, and all that belonged to it, must have been
in his very blood. Champernouns, Gilberts, Gren-
villes and Carews—men whose names ring across
the ages like a trumpet-blast in the ears of Englishmen to this day—were all his kinsmen. His mother's
cousin had been that Sir Peter Carew, 'the prettiest
man, and the finest seaman in England,' who had
commanded the *Mary Rose*, and was drowned in her
when she capsized off the Spit at the time of Francis
I.'s attempt on the Isle of Wight. Sir Arthur Champernoun, his mother's brother, was the Vice-Admiral

of the west country, in command at Plymouth; and
his Champernoun cousins were, almost to a man,
hardy sea-rovers, gentlemen of long lineage and
noble blood, sailing their own ships, carrying their
lives ·in their hands, now searching for the north-
west passage to Cathay, now swooping down and
plundering Spanish settlements on the American
coast, or carrying thither cargoes of negroes from
Guinea for legitimate trade, now standing off the
Azores to await the coming of the homeward bound
silver fleet with King Philip's doubloons on board.
There was short shrift for them, they knew, if they
were beaten, but they took care usually not to be
beaten. The Queen repudiated them and called them
hard names in public; but she was quite willing that
they should continue to weaken and terrify her enemy,
and enrich herself, so long as no responsibility rested
upon her. Sir Humphrey Gilbert was Ralegh's half-
brother, many years older than himself, and to him,
perhaps, rather than to his greater brother, should be
given the credit for the first projecting of an England
over the sea; though in his case, as will be told, the
project was never effected, as it was by Ralegh.

Of the youth of few Englishmen of the first
rank is so little known as that of Ralegh. Such
stray hints as exist are mostly scattered by way of
illustration in his own writings, and have been
carefully pieced together by successive biographers.
But, withal, the result is almost a complete blank

until he emerges into the full clearness of day, already an acknowledged man of light and leading.

The family of Ralegh was an ancient one, although before the date of Walter's birth it had become somewhat impoverished. Walter Ralegh, the father, had ceased to live at his picturesque manor house of Fardell, on the borders of Dartmoor, two miles from Ivybridge, aud occupied a solitary thatched farmhouse called Hayes, standing—as it still does—in a dip on the edge of the downs, about two miles through the wood from Budleigh Salterton Bay.

The house, of which the elder Walter Ralegh had only the remainder of a lease, cannot have changed very much since the boyhood of the hero. It can never have been a grand or imposing residence for so large a family as that of its owner. The country gentry had lived like toads under a harrow for the last three reigns, except those few who had succeeded in grabbing some of the Church lands ; and young Walter Ralegh's earliest days must have been far from opulent. All that is known of his father is that he was a pronounced Prostestant. In the Catholic ' Rising in the West,' his religious opinions nearly caused a premature end to his career. It was early in 1549 that, when he was on his way from Hayes to Exeter, he overtook an old woman telling her beads. Considering that the whole country was in a religious ferment, and that the city of Exeter itself was surrounded

by the rebels, it argues more zeal than discretion
on the part of Walter Ralegh that he took the
old woman to task for illegally pursuing her Popish
practices.   She roused the congregation of the church
of Clyst St Mary, crying that the gentleman had
threatened to burn their houses over their heads,
unless they would leave their beads, and give over
holy bread and holy water.   The infuriated rustics
barricaded Clyst Bridge towards Exeter, and sent
a body in pursuit of Ralegh.   He took refuge from
them in a wayside chapel, 'whence he was rescued
by some mariners of Exmouth.'   No sooner had
he escaped from his assailants than he was met
and captured by another band who carried him to
St Sidwell's, where they imprisoned him in the
church tower until the turmoil was over, and the
'Rising in the West' had been crushed at the
bloody battle of Clyst Heath.   It is a fact which
appears to have been generally overlooked, that
amongst Lord Grey's force, which so ruthlessly put
down the rebellion, was a considerable number of
Spanish mercenaries.   This may to some extent,
perhaps, have deepened the feeling of hatred which
the people of Devonshire afterwards showed towards
the Spaniards.   In any case, the marriage of Queen
Mary to a Spanish prince was nowhere more unpopular than in the west country, although the
Catholics there were in a majority.   On the premature outbreak and collapse of Wyatt's rising, the

Carews and other heads of revolt in Devonshire saw the game was lost; and Sir Peter Carew was carried by Walter Ralegh's ship to France, where, during the rest of Mary's reign, he was chief of the little band of English exiles who sullenly refused to be reconciled to their Spanish king. Foxe, in his *Acts and Monuments*, tells a story of Katharine Champernoun, our Ralegh's mother, which proves that she, too, as became her ancestry, was as strong a Protestant as her husband. In the time of the Marian persecution, a poor woman, afterwards martyred at the stake, was confined for her faith in Exeter Castle. Her name was Agnes Prest; she was an illiterate, but steadfastly firm, woman, whose heroic adherence to her principles, in the face of great suffering, aroused the admiration of those who, like her, held to the reformed religion. To visit and comfort her was a brave deed, but Sir Walter Ralegh's mother did it. 'There resorted to her,' says Foxe, 'the wife of Walter Ralegh—a woman of noble wit and of good and godly opinions, who coming to the prison and talking with her, she said the *Creed* to the gentlewoman. When she came to the article "*He ascended*," there she stayed, and bade the gentlewoman to seek His blessed body in Heaven, not on earth; and said that God dwelleth not in temples made with hands.' And, says Foxe, when Mrs Ralegh 'came home to her husband, she declared to him that in her life she never heard any woman of such simplicity to see, to talk so godly and so earnestly; insomuch that if God were not with her she could not speak such things.   I was not able to answer her—I, who can read, and she cannot.'

CHAPTER II

THESE were the conditions and circumstances which surrounded the youth of Ralegh. We can only conjecture in the light of his after life the influence they exerted on his character. The younger son of an impoverished family of great descent, with all his kinsmen engaged more or less in the search for wealth and adventure on the sea, it is hardly wonderful that in after years the lustre of his genius should have been blurred by greed, arrogance and unscrupulousness. He was the child of his age, the same age that produced Bacon; when heroism and baseness went hand in hand; when that sweet persuasive Elizabethan English, which Ralegh managed in so masterly a fashion, could clothe wicked deeds with splendid sophistry, and black treachery could be hidden under fervent appeals to the God of faith and righteousness.

England had burst into a new life during the early

years of Ralegh's boyhood. The conviction of growing national potency was running riot through the
veins of Englishmen. It was a period of youth :
ignorance had burst its bonds, and a fresh era of en-
lightenment and intellectual beauty was dazzling men's
eyes. New worlds, enclosing untold wealth, unheard-
of wonders, were being discovered by the bold and
adventurous ; the limits of the universe, moral and
material, were extending in the sight of men ; and
Englishmen for the first time in their history realised
the fact that to their country, to their race, belonged
the coming heritage of universal greatness. But youth
and ambition are ever arrogant and unscrupulous, and
the Elizabethan age, with its noble ideals, its splendid
promises, its great ambitions, its exuberance and its
force, was a young era, and bore upon it the defects
as well as the advantages of youth. Of its virtues, as
well as its vices, Ralegh may be taken as the fairest
prototype ; and any attempt to apologise for, or to
minimise the more questionable side of his character,
would lead to the presentation of an imperfect picture
of the man, and the period which he illustrated.
Ralegh was, it is believed, born in 1552, and until his
sixteenth year lived upon the Devonshire coast, either
at the farmhouse at Hayes, or at a house in the city
of Exeter which is sometimes incorrectly claimed for
his birthplace. He was a great reader, and must have
listened many times to home-coming sailors telling
thrilling stories of their adventures on sea and land, of

their sufferings at the hands of the Inquisition, of the wonders of far-off countries, and of the boundless wealth of gold and gems to be won in the Indies by the bold and fortunate. Even thus young, he must have been eager for action. We are told by Anthony à Wood that he entered as a Commoner at Oriel, Oxford, in 1568, and stayed there for three years, looked upon 'as the ornament of the juniors ; and was worthily esteemed a proficient in oratory and philosophy.' This last may well have been true, but although his name appears as an undergraduate in the Oxford Register in 1572, he could not have remained at the University during the interval, and he certainly did not take a degree.

The first war of religion was raging in France, and Cardinal Chatillon, Coligny's brother, was at Elizabeth's court praying for aid and countenance for the Huguenots. The Queen, as usual, was diplomatic, and would not openly pledge herself, but was quite willing that her subjects should help the cause of Protestantism on their own responsibility. Gawen Champernoun, Ralegh's first cousin, had married Gabrielle de Montgomeri, the daughter of that Anglo-French Huguenot leader who had had the mischance to kill the King, Henry II., at the tourney to celebrate the peace of Chateau Cambresis. The connection, no doubt, deeply interested the family in the war, and young Ralegh must have left Oxford early in 1569, to join the forces of the

Huguenots under Condé; for in the *History of the World* he incidentally states that he was present at the battle of Jarnac, where Condé was slain, on the 13th March in that year. Whether he continued in France thenceforward until the autumn is uncertain, but his cousin, Gawen Champernoun, raised a body of one hundred western gentlemen later in the year to go to the aid of the Huguenots. They arrived two days after the disastrous battle of Montoncourt; but according to Ralegh's own statement he was present at the battle and retreat itself, so that it is probable that he remained with the Huguenots in the interval. Thenceforward, for five years and a half, nothing is known of him, except that he was engaged in the civil war in France. The experience was doubtless a valuable one in every way. His remarks upon tactics in the *History of the World* and in his other writings prove that his marvellously receptive mind had assimilated and stored up the most profound lessons of military, as well as naval, strategy; and whatever else the long and cruel campaigns in France may have taught him, he certainly emerged from them an accomplished soldier at the age of twenty-three. But to be a soldier alone did not satisfy his multitudinous mind. Even whilst in France he must have kept his name on the books of his university; perhaps with the thought of some day returning and taking his degree. This he did not do, but in February 1575 entered as a member

B

of the Middle Temple, having previously obtained admission into Lyon's Inn. When on his trial for treason in 1603, he solemnly protested that he had never read a word of law in his life. This may have been true, although neither on this, or any other occasion, is it safe to take his word with absolute literalness; for many young men entered the Inns for fashion's sake, as they did in after times, and he may well have become a member of Middle Temple in order to be near the Court, and to have an ostensible career. His brother, Humphrey Gilbert, had in 1572 commanded the English contingent in the service of the States at Flushing, and before Ter Goes, and Ralegh would appear to have served for a short time in the year 1577 or 1578 in the same service under Sir John Norris; but it cannot have been much more than a flying visit, for during a portion of 1577 he is known to have been in London, leading—if Aubrey is to be believed—a somewhat free and riotous life about the Court, apparently with a country retreat at Islington. Nothing is known of his means, but even already he must have moved in good society, to which, moreover, his relationship to the Champernouns and Gilbert would be a passport. For instance, in 1580, he had a quarrel with Sir Thomas Perrot, and both combatants were lodged in the Fleet for six days for brawling. He must also have managed at this time to fasten himself somehow upon the Earl of Leicester—probably he wore his colours, for hundreds of aspiring gentlemen nominally entered the household of the favourite, in order to obtain an introduction into the Court, and the support in need of a powerful protector. Thus far Ralegh's life is mostly dim and conjectural, but he soon emerges into the full light of day.

In November 1572, Humphrey Gilbert had returned with his men secretly from Holland, and after seeing the Queen, was told to go through the pretence of arriving publicly, but as if afraid to approach the Court until he had obtained her Majesty's pardon for helping the States without her leave. Her responsibility was thus saved, whilst her end was served. Gilbert was already a notable man on land and sea; and it was fitting that some reward should be given to him. In March 1574, accordingly, he joined with his cousin Sir Richard Grenville, Sir George Peckham, Captain Carlile, and others, in a petition to the Queen begging her 'To allow of an enterprise by them conceived; and with the help of God under the protection of Her Majesty's most princely name and goodness, at their own charges and adventure, to be performed, for discovery of sundry rich and unknown lands, fatally, and it seemeth by God's providence, reserved for England, and for the honour of Her Majesty.' They assure the Queen that they have means easily to carry out their project, and that the profits will be large. Here we have the first practical suggestion for an English colonial empire. It is no longer an expedition for trade, or gold, or negroes, but a proposal to take possession of lands—'by God's providence reserved for England.' The matter was referred to a committee of the Council, who were at length persuaded by Carlile that 'the northern part of America was inhabited by a savage people of a mild and tractable disposition, and of all other unfrequented places the only most fittest and most commodious for us to intermeddle withal.'

Ten years before, Captain Ribaut of Dieppe had sailed with a commission from Coligny, the Huguenot leader, to take possession of Florida, whether in the name of England or France is uncertain, but the Spanish admiral, Menendez de Avila, had landed and hanged every man of them, fastening upon the breast of each a placard, setting forth that they had not been hanged because they were Frenchmen, but because they were pirates. The French had retorted later by landing in the same place and hanging all the Spaniards they found there; 'not because they were Spaniards, but because they were murderers.' Thenceforward no further attempt had been made to settle any part of the continent north of the point of Florida, although the Biscay smacks were already finding their way to the rich fishing grounds off Newfoundland; and the theoretical claim of the Spaniards to the whole of the American continent had never been relaxed by them, nor admitted by the English.

In Gilbert's patent, therefore, which was granted in June 1578, he was authorised to discover and take possession, in the name of England, of 'any remote, barbarous and heathen lands not possessed by any christian prince or people.'

With Humphrey Gilbert in this enterprise Ralegh was associated. By the 23rd September of the same year Gilbert had gathered in Dartmouth ready to sail, eleven vessels victualled for a year, 'and furnished with five hundred choice soldiers and sailors.' But misfortune dogged the enterprise from the first. The Spanish ambassador looked on with jealous eyes, and tried his hardest to obstruct the expedition, which was to be piloted by Simon Fernandez, one of the best of the King of Spain's pilots, who had been drawn away from his service by Walsingham; and an Englishman in Spanish pay accompanied the expedition, unknown to Gilbert, in order if possible to frustrate its objects. Just as the expedition was about to sail it was ordered to delay its departure until some question with regard to the capture of a Spanish ship was settled; but it put to sea all the same, and Ralegh went with it on the *Falcon* as captain. Young Knollys, the son of the Queen's cousin Sir Francis, who owned some of the ships, began to squabble with Gilbert before the contrary winds allowed them to sail, insulted him at table, flouted his knighthood, and otherwise misbehaved himself. Whilst the expedition was beating about

in the Bay of Biscay, Knollys deserted with all the
men he could prevail upon to follow him, and went
his own way.   Then Gilbert had an encounter
with some Spaniards, in which he lost a ship; and
Ralegh was in great danger, many of his company
being slain.   Head winds at last drove them all
back to Plymouth in November, where Ralegh,
with the rest of Gilbert's faithful officers, laid a de-
position before the Mayor against Knollys for his
desertion.

By the summer of 1579 Gilbert was again roving
in the Channel, on the look-out for plunder, when
news came that James Fitzmaurice, the Earl of
Desmond's brother, had started with a Spanish-
Papal expedition to land in Ireland, and Gilbert
was ordered to capture him at sea, if possible.   He
failed; but in revenge he swooped down upon the
coast of Spain, in Galicia, sacked a hermitage, and
committed other damage, and then returned to
England.   Whether Ralegh was with him on this
raid is uncertain, but most probably he was, for
we hear no more of him until the summer of the
following year, 1580, when, for the first time, he
received the Queen's Commission, as captain of one
hundred foot soldiers, raised to fight the Desmond
rebels in Munster.   Gilbert had been President of
Munster in 1569-70, during another attempt at a
rising, which, by the means of the most merciless
severity, he had suppressed in two months.   His

methods were a little too brutal, even for Elizabeth, and he was recalled ; but, as we shall see, his half-brother, Ralegh, fully approved of his way of dealing with the Irish.

Ralegh's pay, as captain, was four shillings a day, 'not leaving him food and raiment,' and the work was hard and little to his taste, for he was ambitious for a larger field. Upon the Irish he had no mercy, and made no pretence of winning by any other means than fear. The Viceroy, Lord Grey of Wilton, was as severe as his young captain ; but Ralegh's immediate superior, the Earl of Ormond, Deputy of Munster, an Irishman himself, was inclined to question the wisdom or justice of his methods. The first public act of Ralegh in Ireland was to join Sir Warham St Leger in trying and executing, at Cork, the unfortunate Sir James Fitzgerald, who was hanged, drawn and quartered in August 1580.

Philip II. had allowed to be fitted out in the Biscay ports an expedition, nominally under the Papal flag and commanded by Italian officers, but consisting mainly of Spanish troops, to aid the Desmond insurgents in Munster. The expedition arrived off the coast in the middle of September, and the men were landed at Smerwick, where they entrenched themselves in a fort they called Ore.

Lord Grey had assumed the Viceroyalty in September, bringing with him as his secretary the poet Spenser, who subsequently became Ralegh's bosom friend. Grey arrived at Smerwick with a few ships under Winter, on the 7th November. He landed his small force of about two hundred men, and some guns, and at once attacked the Papal force. After a few shots only, a parley was called. Grey feared it was a stratagem to delay matters until Desmond came up and attacked them in the rear, and refused to parley until the next day, when Alexander Bertoni, the second in command of the Spaniards, came out to crave quarter. He grovelled at Grey's feet and prayed for life. Grey asked him under whose orders he fought, and he replied, those of the Pope, whereupon the Viceroy answered that he would not treat them as soldiers, but simply as bandits. Grey demanded immediate unconditional surrender, and in his apology he asserts that no conditions were granted; although the besieged and contemporary Irish records assert positively that a promise was given that the lives of the men should be spared. However that may be, as soon as the surrender was effected, and the weapons of the intruders secured, Grey ordered the two officers of the day, Captains Ralegh and Mackworth, to put the whole garrison to the sword. Six hundred poor wretches were slaughtered in cold blood, and only two or three superior officers were held to ransom. Camden says that the slaughter 'was against the mind of the Lord Deputy, who shed tears at the determination'; although, if Grey, and not Ormond, be meant, it is difficult to absolve him from the responsibility.

His gifted secretary endeavours to justify the step in his *View of the State of Ireland*, by pointing out the difficulty of keeping so large a number of prisoners in a hostile country; and it must not be forgotten that the rebel Desmond was only three days' march away with a force greatly superior in numbers to that of the English. In any case, it will not be just to cast blame upon Ralegh for his share of the carnage, although, with his expressed opinions as to the only way to deal with Irish disaffection, there is every reason to suppose that he approved of it. The Queen was, or pretended to be, much displeased; and Grey's many enemies at Court, especially Leicester, made the most of it, and eventually brought about his dismissal.

During the winter of 1580 Ralegh was quartered at Cork. The Desmond rebellion still lingered, and all south-western Ireland outside of the English garrisons was honeycombed with disaffection. Ralegh, at Cork, was in the midst of it, and apparently considered that Lord Grey was not striking at the roots. The young captain was indefatigable, and gave the rebels no rest, night or day. On one occasion he rode to Dublin to urge Lord Grey and his council to allow him to capture David, Lord Barry of Barrycourt, whose loyalty was more than doubtful. He was given a free hand; but spies were everywhere, and Barry was fully informed of Ralegh's project. To anticipate the action of the English, he burnt

his own castle and wasted his lands, and one of
Desmond's vassals, Fitz-Edmond, lay in ambush for
Captain Ralegh at a ford he had to cross between
Youghal and Cork.   Ralegh's escort was a small
one, only six men, most of whom had straggled
when the ford was reached.   Ralegh suddenly found
himself face to face in a dangerous place with a
relatively large force of horse and foot.   Almost
alone, he literally cut his way through to the
opposite bank of the river, accompanied by another
young Devonian named Moyle.   In crossing the
river the latter twice foundered in deep water,
and twice his life was rescued by Ralegh at the
risk of his own.   Then Ralegh, standing with a
pistol in one hand and his iron-shod quarter-staff in
the other, withstood the rebel force until his straggling escort had crossed the stream.   Shortly afterwards, Fitz-Edmond, with other rebels, was present
at a parley with Ormond and Ralegh, and ventured
to speak of his own bravery.   Ralegh told him
flatly that he was a coward, for he himself alone
had withstood him and twenty men.   Ormond,
jealous, apparently, of the imputation upon Irish
valour, challenged Fitz-Edmond, Sir John Desmond,
and any four others to fight him, Ormond, Ralegh,
and four men of their choosing, but the rebels, perhaps wisely, shirked the encounter, and nothing came
of it.   On the retirement of Ormond from the
presidency of Munster in the spring of 1581, the

government of the province was entrusted jointly to Captain Ralegh, Sir William Morgan and Captain Piers. All the summer Ralegh and his little force of ninety men lay at Lismore and in the neighbourhood, scourging the rebels ceaselessly, until in the autumn he was able safely to return to his old quarters at Cork. Desperate as was Ralegh's energy in his service, how little it was to his taste is seen by a letter he wrote at the time to the Earl of Leicester. It has already been remarked that he must have attached himself in some way to Leicester's party during his stay in London. On the 25th August 1581, he wrote to him :—' I may not forgett continually to put your Honour in mind of my affection unto your Lordshipe, havinge to the worlde bothe professed and protested the same. Your Honour having no use of such poore followers, hathe utterly forgotten mee. Notwithstandinge, if your Lordshipe shall please to thinke me your's, as I am, I wilbe found redy, and dare do as miche in your service as any man you may commande ; and do neither so miche dispaire of my self, but that I may be somway able to perform as miche. I have spent some time here under the Deputy, in such poore place and charge as, were it not for that I knew him to be one of yours, I would disdayn it, as miche as to keap sheep. I will not troble your Honour with the bussiness of this lost lande, for that Sir Warram Sentleger can best of any man deliver unto your Lordshipe the good, the badd, the mischiefs, the means to amend, and all in all of this common-wealthe or rather common-woe.'

Sir Warham St Leger had now been appointed Deputy of Munster, and with him Ralegh apparently agreed better than with Ormond or Grey. In February 1581, before Ormond retired, Ralegh had not scrupled to write to Walsingham an impeachment of his general conduct towards his rebel countrymen. Ormond was far too lenient, he thought, and his kinship with many of the disaffected Irish was a danger. 'Considering that this man having now been Lord Generall of Munstre about two yeares, theire ar at this instant a thowsand traytors more than were the first day. Would God the service of Sir Humphrey Gilbert might be rightly looked into, who, with the third part of the garrison now in Ireland, ended a rebellion not miche inferior to this in three monethes.'

Ralegh, indeed, all through his career, seems to have been a difficult man to get on with. Like many men of vast ambitions, great vitality, and conscious genius, he was fractious until stricken with adversity, and even then his finer qualities did not appear until all seemed lost. His service in Ireland gave several instances of his daring. During his march from Lismore to Cork he learnt that Lord Barry was at Clove, with a body of several hundred rebels whom he determined to attack with his own eighty-eight men. He charged and put them to flight.

Thinking he had done with them, he went on his way with only six horsemen, the rest lagging behind, and soon overtook another band of Irishmen greatly superior in numbers to his own. They faced him and fought desperately, five out of Ralegh's six horses being killed. Ralegh being dismounted, was being overborne by numbers, when one of his men, a Yorkshireman named Nicholas Wright, coped with six of his assailants, whilst an Irishman called Patrick Fagan dealt with some more. Whilst still fighting, Ralegh noticed an Irish gentleman, Fitz-Richards, hardly pressed, and told the sturdy Wright to stand by him no longer, ' but to charge above hand and save the gentleman,' which he did.

His surprise and capture of Lord Roche in his own castle, surrounded by disaffection, was also an extraordinary feat. Roche seems to have been merely suspected, with little reason as it turned out, but Ralegh liked to strike terror, and although Fitz-Edmond, with eight hundred men, was, he knew, lying in ambush for him, he gave him the slip, made a night march with marvellous celerity, obtained entrance to the castle of Roche by a stratagem, and safely carried the nobleman and all his family to Cork, through a country swarming with rebels.

These and similar services were by no means kept in the background. On the contrary, Ralegh was very persevering in urging them upon his superiors, and claiming rewards and consideration for them. In

writing on one occasion to the Viceroy, Lord Grey
(1st May 1581), partly with this object, he made a
suggestion, a few words only, upon which, curiously
enough, all his future greatness was to depend. 'If
it please your Honour,' he wrote, ' to give commission,
there may bee another hundred soldier layd uppon the
cuntre heire aboute. I hope it willbe a most honorable matter for your Lordshipe, most acceptable to Her
Majestie, and profitable to the cuntre ; and the right
meane to banish all idle and fruitles galliglas and
kerne, the ministers of all miseryes.'

It is not quite clear what the proposal was, but
from a marginal note of Lord Grey's it was evidently
a plan to force the Irish to find more men and money
for the English service. Whatever it was, Lord Grey
resented it and snubbed his aspiring captain for a time.
By the end of 1581 the rebellion in Munster had been
got under. John of Desmond had been hanged by
the heels at Cork, and his head sent to London ; his
brother, the earl, was a hunted fugitive, and the
terrified kerns had been crushed into sullen resignation
for twenty years to come. Under the circumstances
it was possible to reduce the English garrisons, and
Ralegh's company was disbanded, the captain himself
being sent to London with dispatches in December,
with £20 for the expenses of his journey.

CHAPTER III

RALEGH was now about to enter upon his splendid career as a courtier and statesman. He was thirty years of age, six feet high, his hair and beard dark, bushy, and naturally curling, his eyes steel grey, and very bright, though, to judge from his portraits, rather too close together. 'He had,' says Naunton, 'a good presence in a handsome and well compacted person, a strong natural wit, and a better judgment; with a bold and plausible tongue, whereby he could set out his parts to the best advantage.' Probably his persuasive eloquence was one of his greatest gifts, and his personal fascination must have been marvellous; for when he chose, which in his arrogance he rarely did, he could bring even those who hated him to his side. He took no care, however, to be popular, for he always scorned and contemned the people, and on the death of Elizabeth he was probably the best hated man in England. A good instance of this occurs in a

31

letter from Dudley Carleton to Chamberlain, giving
an account of the condemnation of Ralegh to death
for treason at Winchester in 1603. He says that the
two men who first took the news to the King were
Roger Ashton and a Scotsman, 'whereof one affirmed
that never man spake so well in times past, nor would
do in the world to come; and the other said that,
whereas, when he first saw him he was so led with
the common hatred that he would have gone a
hundred miles to have seen him hanged, he would,
ere he parted, have gone a thousand to have saved his
life. In one word, never was a man so hated and so
popular in so short a time.' What was true of the
matured genius in the moment of his adversity was
equally true of the almost unknown young captain
who came with dispatches from Ireland twenty years
before. His attraction was irresistible. The particular plan which Ralegh had submitted to Lord
Grey for increasing the English forces in Munster
without expense to the Queen has been lost; but,
whatever it was, Captain Ralegh lost no time in
submitting it to the Queen and Council. It appears
in the ordinary course to have been sent to Lord Grey
for his opinion, and the irate Viceroy lost no time in
making clear that he was offended at Ralegh's pre-
sumption. In his letter to Lord Burghley, dated
January 1582, he says, 'Having lately received
advertisement of a plott delivered by Captain Rawley
unto her Majestie, for the lessening of her charges

here in the province of Mounster, and disposing of the garrisons according to the same ; the matter at first, indeed, offering a very plausible show of thrifte and commoditie, which might easily occasion Her Majestie to thincke that I have not so carefully as behoved looked into the state of the cause and the search of Her Majestie's profitt.'   He then goes on to say that he and his council having considered Captain Rawley's plan, have decided that it is inconvenient and impossible.   'I doubt not but you will soone discerne a difference betweene the judgments of those who, with grounded experience and approved reason, look into the condition of things, and those who upon no grownd but seeming fancies, and affecting credit with profit, frame "plotts" upon impossibilities for others to execute.'

To Walsingham at the same time the Viceroy wrote bitterly complaining of the way he was being traduced and misrepresented at Court.   Leicester was a strenuous enemy of Grey, and doubtless was not sorry to bring forward the brilliant handsome captain, just arrived from Ireland, who might be made his instrument for further discrediting the Viceroy.   In any case, although no record exists of it in the Council book, and Naunton's assertion that Ralegh and Grey personally met at the Council table is incorrect, it is certain that Ralegh on this occasion first made his favourable impression on the Queen.   On the reception of Grey's report there would naturally be some

c

sort of consultation, at which Ralegh would be present, and it is possible that Naunton may have referred to such an occasion when he wrote, 'Among the second causes of Ralegh's growth . . . that variance between him and Lord Grey in his descent upon Ireland was a principal ; for it drew them both over to the Council table . . . where he had much the better in telling of his tale ; and so much that the Queen and the Lords took no small mark of the man and his parts.' Afterwards, he adds that, 'Ralegh had gotten the Queen's ear in a trice; and she began to be taken with his elocution, and loved to hear his reasons to her demands ; and the truth is she took him for a kind of oracle, which nettled them all.' Doubtless this is true in the main, as Naunton of course knew Ralegh well ; but it is loosely told, and in detail open to question.

The pretty story about the gallant captain spreading his rich cloak over a plashy place for the Queen to step upon, as told by old Fuller, has no other authority than his upon which to rest, but there is nothing inherently improbable in it. It is quite in keeping with the inflated gallantry of Elizabeth's Court, and with Ralegh's character. He was determined to 'get on.' His ambition we know was boundless ; he could flatter and crawl as abjectly as the basest ; he could hector as insolently as the highest. He had passed six years amongst French gentlemen, bred in the preposterous fopperies of the

Court which Brantome describes so well. The trick
of spreading the cloak was always a favourite one
amongst Spanish gallants, and, of course, was well
known in France, although apparently it never was
acclimatised in England. It was just the thing to
confirm the vain Queen in the good impression which
Ralegh's eloquence and ability had already produced
upon her, and even on Fuller's authority, we may
accept the story for its verisimilitude.

He had not been in England many weeks before
the first sign of royal favour reached him. At the
end of March 1582, only three months after his
arrival in London, he was appointed to the captaincy
of a company in Ireland, of which the captain
(Appesley) had just died; but he was excused from
commanding in person, and was empowered to appoint a deputy. Shortly before this, indeed, he
had been awarded £100 on account of his Irish
services, to be paid out of the funds destined for
the war.

This was gall and wormwood to Lord Grey, who
wrote a vigorous protest to Walsingham in April.
'As for Captain Rawley's assignment to the charge
of Appeslei's band, which in your letter of the 2nd
April you write to be signified to me by a letter
from Her Majestie. I have no letter which specifieth
any such thing to me, and for myne own part, I must
bee plain : I nether like his carriage nor his company,
and therefore other than by direction and command-

ment, and what his right can require, he is not to expect at my hands.'

But Ralegh's foot was well in the stirrup now, and Grey's ire was powerless to hurt him. On the contrary, it is evident from a paper in the Record Office in Burghley's hand, that he was in October of the same year consulted as to the government of Ireland, and the suppression of the rebellion, and his recommendations were submitted to the Queen.

But by this time the Queen's languishing courtiers, who kept up the eternal pretence of being in love with her, had taken fright at the new-comer's good fortune.

For the last few years she had been playing fast and loose with the young Duke of Anjou, and flirting desperately with his egregious representative Jean de Simier, but she was now rid of them. Leicester's marriage, too, had been divulged to her by Simier a year before, and his position towards her in future was changed; but still her faithful 'bell wether,' Hatton, kept the old game going, and began to get jealous of Ralegh. Sir Thomas Heneage, another old flame of the Queen's, who had now dropped out of the active list of lovers, and was Vice-Chamberlain, sided with Hatton; and at the request of the latter handed to the Queen one morning in October (1582) a letter from his friend, just as 'Her Highness was ready to ride abroad in the great park to kill a doe.' With the letter were sent three tokens—a book, a

bucket and a bodkin—presumably meaning that Hatton
swore that if she did not leave Ralegh (whose pet
name was 'water') he would kill himself.   The
Queen took the letter and tokens, and smilingly said,
'There never was such another.'   She seems to have
been too excited and pleased to fix the bodkin in her
hair, as she tried to do, and gave it and the letter back
to Heneage, until she could bring her horse to a stand
still.   'She read it,' says Heneage, 'with blushing
cheeks, and uttered many speeches (which I refer till I
see you), most of them tending to the discovery of a
doubtful mind, whether she should be angry or well
pleased.'   She decided to be pleased, and told Heneage
to answer, 'that she liked your preamble so ill, as she
had little list to look upon the bucket or the book.
If Princes were like gods, as they should be, they
would suffer no element so to abound as to breed
confusion.   And that *Pecora Campi* (Hatton) was so
dear unto her, that she had bounded her banks so
sure, as no *water* nor floods should ever overthrow
them.   And for better assurance unto you that you
shall not fear drowning, she hath sent you a bird that,
together with the rainbow, brought the good tidings
that there should be no more destruction by water.
. . . You should remember she was a shepherd, and
then you might think how dear her sheep was unto her.
. . . To conclude, *water* hath been more welcome
than were fit for so cold a season.'   Three years later,
when Ralegh was in the height of his favour, the

Queen again assured Hatton that Ralegh should not
supplant him.   She told Heneage at Croydon that she
felt Hatton's absence from her side as much as he
did, 'and marvelled why you came not.'   Heneage let
her know that there was no place for him to stay in,
as his lodging had been occupied.   The Queen flew
into a rage at this, and would not believe that anyone
should dare to occupy Hatton's rooms.   She sent to
make inquiries, and found that Sir Walter Ralegh
was lodged in them.   'Whereupon she grew more
angry with the Lord Chamberlain than I wished she
had been, and used bitterness of speech against R,
telling me before him that she had rather see him
hanged than equal him with you, or that the world
should think she did so.'

Even in that age of display no man perhaps was
so gorgeous in his attire as Ralegh.   Jewels, big
pearls especially, were beloved by him, and wonderful
stories were current in the Court as to the fabulous
value of the adornments he wore ; one writer asserting that the gems upon his shoes alone were worth
6600 gold pieces.   No courtier was more gallant
at tourney or masque than he, no poet readier
to turn a stanza in praise of his mistress, or to
devise a far-fetched compliment ; but, unlike the
other butterflies that fluttered round the Queen, he
was far from confining his attention to these trifles.
From the first the Queen had consulted him and
employed him in affairs of State ; great plans for

the founding of an England over the sea were already
working in his brain. He could dangle at Court and
bandy compliments as well as the most empty-headed
fine gentlemen ; but he gave up only five hours of
the twenty-four to sleep, and spent every hour he
could snatch in study. His reading must have been
omnivorous, for his breadth of view, his depth of
knowledge, and his profundity of thought — far in
advance of his contemporaries—prove him to have
been perhaps the most universally capable Englishman
that ever lived—a fit contemporary of Shakspeare
and Bacon.

   We have seen that from his first appearance before
Elizabeth in January 1582, when he defended his Irish
plans, honours and emoluments were showered upon
him. In the beginning of the following month of
February, the Queen had managed, by dint of bribes,
caresses and promises, to induce the Duke of Anjou to
leave England and embark for Flushing, where he was
to receive the sovereignty of the revolted Flemish States.
William the Silent awaited him at the landing-place,
and some of the principal courtiers of Elizabeth's Court
accompanied the new sovereign to his dominions. He
entered the town in great pomp, with William on one
side of him and Leicester on the other, followed by
Hunsdon, Willoughby, Sir Philip Sidney, Sir John
Norris, Ralegh, and many others. When he was
crowned in Antwerp a few days afterwards, Leicester
and the Englishmen were present. Leicester had

tried his hardest through Hatton to avoid the
journey, for he feared that the new sovereign
might detain him against his will, whilst he pursued
his love-making by letter with the Queen, undisturbed by Leicester's presence near her. So immediately the investure was over, whilst the rest of
the company was at dinner, Leicester escaped and
sailed for England, leaving most of his train behind
him. It suited the Queen for the moment to dis-
claim the investure of Alençon ; and Leicester and
those with him were rated as traitors and rogues
for having been present at the ceremony. William
the Silent understood the position ; he knew that
Anjou was a helpless puppet in the Queen's hands ;
and when Ralegh took leave of him he entrusted
him with dispatches for Elizabeth and her Council,
and bade him deliver to her this message—'*Sub
umbra alarum tuarum protegimur.*'

In the following year the Queen granted Ralegh
the use of Durham House in the Strand, conveniently
near to Whitehall and one of the largest of the riverside palaces, which for many years had been used as a
royal guest-house. Here he lived in splendour until
the Queen's death, having, as he subsequently said, a
retinue of forty persons and as many horses always
maintained there. 'I well remember,' says Aubrey,
'his study, which was on a little turret that looked
into and over the Thames, and had a prospect
which is as pleasant as any in the world.' All this

magnificence, however, needed large revenues to keep it up, and the Queen was not fond of rewarding her favourites with direct gifts of money. She had other ways of enriching them, and these she adopted in Ralegh's case. In April 1583, the Queen induced All Souls College, Oxford, to grant him two beneficial leases of some property. In the following month he received a patent to license vintners, by which he was entitled to a half of all fines inflicted and to exact a fee of £1 per annum from every wine dealer in England. There was no pretence at supervision on his part, for he leased his patent to a certain Richard Browne for seven years at £800 a year. Browne was industrious in increasing the number of taverns, and was making a very good thing of it, when Ralegh claimed a larger share of the profits. This Browne refused, and Ralegh being unable to induce him to surrender his lease, he went to the length of getting his own patent revoked, and regranted for thirty-one years. He subsequently drew large revenues from it—he himself stated £2000 a year—but it involved him in constant trouble and litigation, for the patent was an oppressive and unpopular one, and in the case of the University towns interfered with old and powerful vested interests. In March 1584, a license was given to him to export a certain number of woollen cloths, and in subsequent years this privilege was regranted and extended. This again brought him into collision

with merchants and shippers, who innocently, or
otherwise, infringed his patents.   It will be seen,
therefore, that even in the case of a man less
rapacious and extravagant than Ralegh, there was
sufficient reason for his unpopularity, on account of
these patents alone.

In the following year, 1586, the confiscated lands
of the defeated Desmonds in Munster were to be
scrambled for, and Ralegh naturally came in for the
lion's share, although the actual profit to him turned
out in the end to be small.

The province had been harried by fire and sword to
such an extent, and most of the land itself was so poor,
that Hooker speaks of it thus at the time :—' The curse
of God was so great, and the land so barren, both of man
and beast, that whosoever did travel from one end of
Munster . . . to the other, about six score miles, he
should not meet man, woman or child, saving in the
towns.'   The problem therefore was to repeople this
wilderness, and the land—600,000 acres of it—was
partitioned out amongst gentlemen who undertook
to plant thereon a given number of well-affected
Englishmen.   It was enacted that no person was
to have more than 12,000 acres, upon which eighty-
six families were to be settled, but Ralegh and two
nominal associates got three seigniories and a half, of
12,000 acres each, of fine fertile well-wooded land,
stretching on each side of the Blackwater from Youghal.
He also obtained a grant of Lismore Castle from the

Bishop of Lismore at a nominal rent, and possessed
a manor house at Youghal.   Ralegh did his best
with his vast estate, settling it with Cornish and
Devonshire families, and introducing in after years
many improvements in tillage and management, as
well as first planting potatoes, but he met with
constant obstruction and trouble, causing him endless litigation with regard to the estate.   His occupations were many, and he was necessarily, for the
most part, absent from Ireland.   The prohibition
of exportation of timber, pipe-staves, and the like,
hit him especially hard ; for he had counted much
upon the export of casks from Ireland to Spain.
He had many a hard battle before he could get the
prohibition even partially raised.   He was in constant
hot water, too, with his tenants, and with the English
Viceroy, Fitzwilliam, in after years ; he was swindled
by his partners and representatives, and his broad
acres in Ireland brought him little but bitterness and
disappointment.

Even a more important gift was that of the Lord
Wardenship of the Stannaries, which he received on
the death of the Earl of Bedford in 1585.   The
Stannaries Parliament of Devon and Cornish miners
was held on a secluded tor overlooking Dartmoor,
and here the brilliant courtier, the accomplished
poet, the experienced soldier, the subtle statesman,
became the Devonshire squire ; giving laws to his
own people, and settling the disputes of the rough

miners, in their own broad, soft accent, which even at Court he always retained to the day of his death. To this place of dignity was shortly afterwards added that of Vice-Admiral of the West, and, finally, in 1587, he became Captain of the Queen's Guard in succession to the forlorn 'bell wether,' Lord Chancellor Hatton. The post was a valuable one, although no salary was attached to it, except the uniform of 'six yards of tawney medley at 13s. 4d. a yard, with a fur of black budge, rated at £10,' but it kept him near the Queen's person, and gave him opportunities for asking favours for which he probably exacted large payments from the suitors whose causes he pleaded; as did, indeed, all persons in similar position at the time.

A still greater instance of the royal favour even than this came to Ralegh about the same time as the captaincy of the guard, under circumstances which, to say the least, lay him open to the gravest suspicion.

In May 1586, the priest Ballard had been sent by the English Catholics to the Spanish ambassador in Paris, Mendoza, with a proposal for the murder of the Queen, and a Catholic rising in England with Spanish help. The answer was vaguely sympathetic, but it was sufficient for the purpose. In August of the same year Gifford went to Paris with the full plan. They felt, he said, that war with Spain was inevitable, and that Elizabeth's reign was drawing to a close, and in order to avert ruin they had decided to precipitate matters.

For this purpose they had attracted to their side a
large number of supporters who were not Catholics,
but who were anxious for Mary Stuart to succeed. He
gave Mendoza a list of a great number of noblemen
and gentlemen who would welcome a Spanish force,
and raise a revolt the moment the Queen was
despatched ; and said that six of the Queen's servants,
having constant access to her person, had sworn to
commit the deed of murder. This was a repetition of
Ballard's message in May, and when it came in its
more authorative form it was cautiously welcomed by
Philip. It is useless to remind the reader that the main
threads of the conspiracy were all in Walsingham's
hands from the first, and that before Philip's reply
could reach them Babington and his principal associates
were captured and in jail. When Mendoza wrote to
the King, 10th September, that the conspiracy had
been discovered, he says that out of the six men who
had sworn to kill the Queen, and whose names had
never previously been mentioned, 'only two have
escaped, namely, the favourite Ralegh, and the brother
of Lord Windsor.' At the first sight it appears
absolutely impossible that Ralegh can have been
associated with the conspirators to kill the Queen,
unless it were as a spy ; but there are some curious un-
explained circumstances in connection with the matter,
which—like the allegation itself—have not hitherto
been noticed. Morgan, the Queen of Scotland's
agent in Paris, wrote to her in April 1585, saying that

he had made friends with several of the English gentlemen who had come over to Paris with Lord Derby, and
had since continued in secret communication with
them, whereby he hoped to have drawn some secret
service for her Majesty (Mary Stuart); but in the
midst of his negotiations he had been lodged in the
Bastile, and his purpose had been disappointed.
'Amongst those that I mean was one named William
Langharne, secretary to Master Rawley the Quene's
dere minion who daylye groweth in creditt.   The
said secretary is a good Catholic, and his master and
Her Majestie's new hoste Poulett are friends, which
moved me the more willingly to take hold of his pro-
ferred amity.'   It is true that this mysterious action of
Ralegh's secretary does not in any way compromise
his master; but it is certain that the latter was playing a double game at the time, whatever his object
may have been.   In 1586, a ship belonging to him
had captured at sea a Portuguese vessel, on board of
which was Don Pedro Sarmiento de Gamboa, King
Philip's governor of the Spanish settlements in
Patagonia.   He was an important person, and a
famous navigator, and in the ordinary course would
have been held to heavy ransom.   The English
merchants just then were crying out about the ruin
brought to their commerce by the state of war with
Spain, and it suited Elizabeth to sound Philip about
the conclusion of a peaceable arrangement.   It was
therefore settled that Sarmiento should be released by

Ralegh without ransom, and proceed to Spain with offers for peace. He had more than one interview with the Queen, Cecil, and Ralegh, who entrusted him with pacific messages for the King. Sarmiento told Mendoza that he had had many private conversations with Ralegh ; 'and signified to him how wise it would be for him to offer his services to Your Majesty, as the Queen's favour to him could not last long. He said that if he (Ralegh) would attend sincerely to Your Majesty's interests in England, apart from the direct reward he would receive, Your Majesty's support when occasion arose might prevent him from falling. Ralegh accepted the advice, and asked Sarmiento to inform Your Majesty of his willingness, if Your Majesty would accept his services, to oppose Don Antonio's attempts, and to prevent the sailing of expeditions from England. He would, moreover, send a large ship of his own heavily armed to Lisbon, and sell it for Your Majesty's service for the sum of 5000 crowns. In order that he might learn whether Your Majesty would accept his services, he gave Sarmiento a countersign, and wrote to a nephew of his here (in Paris) learning the language, telling him, that the moment I gave him a letter from Sarmiento he was to start with it to England.' Sarmiento was captured by Huguenots on his way through the south of France, and held as a prisoner. Both Elizabeth and Philip were indignant, and made great efforts to procure his release. As soon as Mendoza learned of Sarmiento's capture, he sent word to Ralegh's nephew, who volunteered to start for England at once and inform his uncle. The latter immediately dispatched two of his followers to France to beg Henry of Navarre, in the name of the Queen, to release Sarmiento. They were first to address themselves to Mendoza, who lent them 100 crowns for their expenses on Ralegh's account. On the 18th February 1587, Mendoza writes to Philip:—'I am assured that he (Ralegh) is very cold about these naval preparations (*i.e.*, in England), and is trying secretly to dissuade the Queen from them. He is much more desirous of sending to Spain his own two ships for sale, than to use them for robbery. To confirm him in his good tendency I came to the help of the two gentlemen he sent hither, who asked me for some money. . . . This will give him hopes that Your Majesty will accept his services, and will cause him to continue to oppose Don Antonio (*i.e.*, the Portuguese pretender), who is upheld by the Earl of Leicester.' In response to this, Philip ordered his ambassador to assure Ralegh that 'his aid would be highly esteemed, and adequately rewarded.' But Philip was somewhat suspicious, for in his next letter he says:—'As for his (Ralegh) sending for sale the two ships he mentions, that is out of the question, in the first place to avoid his being looked upon with suspicion in his own country, in consequence of his being well-treated (here), whilst all his countrymen are persecuted; and secondly to guard ourselves

against the coming of the ships under this pretext
being a feint or trick upon us—which is far from
being improbable—but you need only mention the
first reason to him.'

All this may have been perfectly innocent, or more
likely, intended to mislead the Spaniards, but it certainly
establishes the fact that communications between
them and Ralegh were taking place at that time.
And yet in March 1586, when, according to
Mendoza, he was one of the six men privy to the
intention to kill the Queen, he writes thus to the
Earl of Leicester, then in Holland as the Queen's
governor, who had asked him to send over some
English pioneers. He assures the earl of his desire
'to performe all offices of love, honour, and service
towards you.' 'But I have byn of late very pestilent
reported to be rather a drawer back than a fartherer
of the action where you govern. Your Lordship doth
well understand my affection towards Spayn, and how
I have consumed the best part of my fortune, hating
the tyrannous prosperity of that State; and it were
now strang and monsterous that I should becum an
enemy of my countrey and conscience.' Yet, only
a few months afterwards, he was ostensibly offering
his humble services to Philip to hamper English armaments against him, and wishing to sell his two armed
ships to be used against his own country.

However this may be, no sooner was the wretched
Babington condemned, than he founded all his hope

D

of pardon upon Ralegh's action in his favour, and directed his cousin to offer the favourite £1000 for his life. 'Show this note,' he says, 'to young Master Lovelace, and bid him tell Master Flower that, in respect of the service I can do Her Majesty, I desire to speak with his master' (*i.e.* Ralegh). It is fair to say, however, that there is no other known evidence to connect Ralegh with Babington, except the before-quoted assertion of the Spanish ambassador. By Babington's death the favourite's wealth was very largely increased. His own younger son's estate in Devonshire was a small one indeed—only the poor manor of Collaton Ralegh — and his Irish estates produced but little. But now the Queen granted to him nearly every acre of the broad lands in five English counties possessed by the unfortunate Babington, together with all his goods and property of every sort, with the sole exception of a curious clock which Her Majesty kept for herself.

This may be considered as the highest point of Ralegh's power and splendour ; but already a younger rival was in the field, who, by-and-by, was to deprive him of much of the sovereign's personal regard for him. When in 1587 Mendoza had told his master that the reason why Ralegh was opposed to the plans of the Portuguese pretender, Don Antonio, was because the Earl of Leicester favoured them, he was somewhat behind the times. Leicester's influence over the Queen had greatly

decreased; and, in fact, he never was a strong
supporter of Don Antonio, except when he could
get some advantange for himself. The real backer
of Don Antonio was Leicester's turbulent young
step-son, the Earl of Essex, and it is far more probable that Ralegh's approaches to the Spanish interests
were prompted by a desire to check the efforts of
the rising favourite. Essex was only twenty years.
old at the time, and this is what a courtier writes
of his relations with the Queen, who was over fifty.
'When she is abroad nobody is near her but my
Lord of Essex; and at night my Lord is at cards,
or one game or another with her, till the birds sing
in the morning.' But great as was the favour shown
to him, Essex, it was gall to him if 'that knave
Ralegh,' as he called him, shared with him the good
graces of the Queen.

On one occasion (1587) Essex thought the Queen
had slighted him to please Ralegh; 'for whose sake
I saw she would both grieve me and my love, and
disgrace me in the eye of the world. From thence
she came to speak of Ralegh, and it seemed she
could not well endure anything to be spoken against
him; and taking hold of one word "*disdain*," she said
there was no such cause why I should disdain him.
This speech troubled me so much that, as near as I
could, I did describe unto her what he had been and
what he was.'

The insolent young noble little thought, probably,

that his elder rival was not only a fortunate favourite, and the Queen's platonic lover, but a great genius, whose knowledge was already encyclopedic, and whose busy brain was teeming with far-reaching plans for giving England a noble share in the new found lands beyond the sea.

For the present we have done with him in the enervating surroundings of the Court of the virgin Queen, and will now consider him in his capacity of a prime builder of the empire.

CHAPTER IV

SIR HUMPHREY GILBERT AND THE COLONISATION OF
NORTH AMERICA—RALEGH'S PATENT FOR THE
PLANTING OF VIRGINIA—THE FIRST VOYAGE
THITHER—THE SETTLEMENT AT WOKOKEN

THE age was a prodigal and lavish one. The wondrous tales of the gold brought from the Indies by the Spaniards had fired the greed of the English mariners, who were fully conscious now that they and their ships were more than a match for any others that sailed the sea. They exulted in the knowledge, and flinched from no opportunity of proving their metal. The Spaniards had found their way by the Straits of Magellan into the Southern Sea ; the dream of English mariners was to discover a better and nearer road still to Cathay by the north-west, and perhaps find gold on the way. The Cabots, Master Hore, and Sir Hugh Willoughby and others, long before, had essayed it and had failed, but all undismayed the Elizabethan sailors pursued the same phantom. In 1576 Martin Frobisher thought

he had succeeded when he slowly groped his way
into Hudson's Bay.   He had only two tiny craft
of 35 tons each, and had no thought yet of colonisation, but merely of opening up a new way to the
teeming East for trade.   By chance a shining piece
of pyritic ore glittering with metal was picked up
on the shore, and brought to England.   It was
falsely reported to be rich in gold, and the next
year Frobisher went again and brought home three
cargoes of the stuff.   Gilbert himself wrote a treatise,
which was published without his consent in 1576,
demonstrating the probability of a passage being
discovered that way to China.   We have seen how his
and Ralegh's attempt to establish an English settlement
on the North American coast in 1578 had been frustrated, but Gilbert was ever on the alert, and in the
meantime had not been idle.   The pilot, Simon
Fernandez, had, with Walsingham's help, been sent
to the coast of America, and had brought back
glowing accounts of the fertility of the land.   In
the year 1583 David Ingram of Barking, mariner,
allowed his imagination full play in describing the
banqueting houses of crystal, with pillars of gold
and silver, to be found there, and Captain Walker
reported the discovery of a silver mine within the
mystic River Norumbega.   In all these attempts, the
discovery of the north-west passage was the first
object, the finding of gold the second, and only in
Gilbert's case was colonisation aimed at.

But in the meanwhile Gilbert's six years' patent
was running out, and it was necessary for him to
make a serious attempt to effect its object. Drake's
triumphant return from his voyage round the world
in the autumn of 1580 had given an immense im-
petus to the fitting out of expeditions for plunder
and discovery in all directions, but still with no view
to permanent settlements. With Ralegh's sudden rise
at Court in 1582 came his step-brother's opportunity.
The latter had been nearly ruined, 'forced,' as he
wrote to Walsingham, 'to sell his wife's clothes from
her back,' in consequence of his three ships having
been pressed for the Queen's service in Ireland
during the rebellion, whereby he lost £2000, his
ships having been stolen and carried away in his
absence. This was written in July 1581; but by
June 1582 all had changed. Ralegh was then at
the Queen's ear and could do most things; and his
own means were spent without stint on the object
he had nearest his heart, namely, English maritime
and colonial enterprise. The revived project of the
expedition was a patriotic one in two senses. There
was a considerable number of Catholic gentlemen in
England who were heartily tired of the continual
contest with their fellow-countrymen which their
religion forced upon them. They had no desire to
become the tools of Spanish ambition. They desired
to remain Englishmen and yet to retain the exercise
of their faith. These 'Schismatics,' as they were

called by the Jesuits and the extreme Catholics, were
approached by Walsingham with a suggestion that,
if they would provide money for the expedition,
colonies of English Catholics could be planted on the
American coast, where they would remain under the
English flag, but at liberty to govern their own lives
as they pleased. The Spanish party were horrified
at the idea, which they said had been invented by
Walsingham for the purpose of splitting and weakening the Catholic party in the country. This may
well have been the case, though we can afford now
to give him credit for higher and more patriotic
motives. In June 1582, accordingly, two moderate
Catholic gentlemen, Sir George Gerrard and Sir
Thomas Peckham, received power from Gilbert in
virtue of his patent, 'to discover all lands and isles
upon that part of America between Cape Florida
and Cape Breton. Any two out of four islands
discovered by them, or by Gilbert for them, were
to be held by them and their heirs for ever, together with 1,500,000 acres of land on the "supposed
adjoining continent," paying a small chief-rent to
Gilbert, together with two-fifths of all gold and
silver, pearls or precious stones found.' A further
agreement of the same date set forth, 'that for the
more speedy executing of Her Majesty's grant, *and
the enlargement of her dominions,*' Sir Thomas Peckham
is to be entitled to take possession of a further
500,000 acres on the continent.

Shortly before this date the Spanish ambassador had got wind of the project—for he had his spies everywhere reporting upon the movements of English ships—and wrote to his King that, 'when the Queen was petitioned to aid in the expedition, Gilbert was told that he was to go, and when he had landed and fortified the place, the Queen would send him 10,000 men to hold it.'

By the middle of July the matter was settled. The lands were to be held under the crown of England in fee simple. One soldier was to be maintained by the colonists for every 5000 acres occupied, and the best places were to be reserved for building towns, 'with sufficient ground for their commons of pasture rent free, and also some small portion, not exceeding 10 acres, to be allowed for every house built, for the better maintenance of the poor inhabitants, reserving some small rents for the same. All the colonists were to be sent over at the cost of the realm, and each person was to receive a grant of 60 acres of land for three lives, besides common for so much cattle in the summer as they can keep in the winter, with such allowance for housebote, hedgebote and ploughbote as the country may serve.' There were minute conditions for manuring the lands, for the payment of fines and heriots, all of which feudal paraphernalia reads quaintly and curiously, as applying to the boundless continent of America. Every poor

colonist was to take over so much food, and
picks, spades, saws, etc., for the cost of all of
which the colony was to pay the mother country
every third year — 'which can be no loss to
England.'

Every person who paid his own passage, and
brought with him a sword and harquebuss, was
to have six score acres of land, and every gentleman with five followers was to receive a grant of
2000 acres in fee simple, and every adventurer of
£5, 1000 acres. Each parish was to consist
of exactly 3 miles square, with the church in
the midst, the minister to have his tithes, and
300 acres of land free, each bishop 10,000 acres,
and each archbishop 20,000 acres. It will thus
be seen that the project was a large one ; the
intention being really to plant a great England
in North America. The Spaniards fully understood
it in this light. Mendoza wrote to his master on
the day following the signing of the agreement,
from which the above particulars are extracted
(8th July 1582) :—'As I wrote some time ago,
Humphrey Gilbert is fitting out ships to gain a
footing in Florida, and in order to make this
not only prejudicial to Your Majesty's interests,
but injurious to Catholics here, whilst benefiting
the heretics, Walsingham approached two Catholic
gentlemen, whose estate had been ruined, and in-
timated to them that, if they would help Humphrey

Gilbert in the voyage, their lives and liberties might be saved, and the Queen might . . . allow them to settle there in the enjoyment of freedom of conscience, and of their property in England, for which purpose they might avail themselves of the intercession of Philip Sidney. As they were desirous of living as Catholics, without endangering their lives, they thought the proposal a good one. They with other Catholics have petitioned the Queen, and she has granted them a patent . . . to colonise Florida, on the banks of the Norumbega, where they are to be allowed to live as their conscience dictates, and to enjoy such revenues as they possess in England.' The writer then gives an account of the efforts he has made to dissuade the Catholics from the project. He tells them it is only a trick to destroy them, that the country in question belonged to Spain, and they would all be murdered, as Ribaut was, that they were acting against the interests of His Holiness, whose leave should first be asked. Father Allen, at Rome, was warned also to induce the Pope to ban the expedition. But still the project went on, and in the summer two ships were sent to reconnoitre the sites of the intended settlements.

By December 1582, a great company of adventurers was formed to trade with the new colony, most of the principal people in England having shares in it, including all those—Ralegh amongst them—who had been partners in Gilbert's former abortive attempt. For the purpose of taking part in the expedition, of which he was to be Vice-Admiral, Ralegh decided to put into practice some of his advanced theories with regard to naval construction, and built a ship of 200 tons, which he called the *Bark-Ralegh*. The exact construction of this vessel is not known, but it has been usual to confuse her with the much larger vessel called the *Ark-Ralegh*, built by Ralegh in 1587, and employed in the Armada. The larger ship, the *Ark-Ralegh*, was looked upon as a sort of wonder; and Lord Admiral Howard, who had hoisted his pennant on it, calls it the oddest ship in the world, and the best for all conditions.

At length, in the spring of 1583, all was ready for sailing. The Queen had vetoed the going of Ralegh himself; and mindful of Gilbert's former misfortune, endeavoured to restrain him also. He had started first in February, but was driven back and kept at Southampton, and she, or Walsingham for her, sent him word that she wished him to stay at home, 'as a man noted for no good hap at sea.' But he pleaded hard to be allowed to go. He had spent, he said, all his means on the enterprise, had sold his lands, and risked everything. His unfortunate return on the last occasion was only because he would not do, or allow others to do, anything against the Queen's command. The Queen was appeased, and ordered Ralegh to

send to Sir Humphrey a token and the following
letter :—

'RICHMONDE, 17th March 1583.

'BROTHER,—I have sent you a token from Her
Majestie, an anchor guided by a lady as you see ; and
farther, Her Highness willed me to sende you worde
that she wished you as great good hap, and safty to
your ship, as if her sealf were ther in person : desiring
you to have care of your sealf, as of that which she
tendereth ; and therefore for her sake you must provide for it accordingly.

'Further, she commandeth me that you leve your
picture with me.   For the rest I leve till our meeting, or to the report of this bearer, who would needs
be messengre of this good newse.   So I committ
you to the will and protection of God, Who send us
such life or death as He shall please, or hath appointed.
Your treu brother,   W. RALEGH.'

It was the 11th June before the expedition sailed.
The *Bark-Ralegh* of 200 tons was much the largest of
the ships ; but they had hardly got out of the
Channel when she deserted them and came back.   It
was said that a contagious disease had broken out on
board, but evidently Sir Humphrey did not believe, or
was unaware of it, for he wrote angrily to Sir George
Peckham, that she had run from him in fair clear
weather, having a large wind.   'I pray you solicit
my brother Ralegh to make them an example to

all knaves.' With the other four little ships Sir Humphrey sailed west until he reached the coast of Newfoundland. This was not the place it was intended to colonise, but as he was there he took possession of it for the English crown by the quaint ceremony of cutting a sod and accepting a hazel wand. There were thirty or forty fishing boats of various nationalities off the coast, and Gilbert invited the captains on shore to witness the ceremony. Many of them came, and offered no protest. They were peaceful folk, and it was perhaps wise that they did not. The Queen's arms were set up on the shore, and nominal grants of territory were given to the members of the expedition. But they were a lawless lot, and whilst Gilbert was on shore, his crews tried to desert with his ships, failing in which they robbed the fishing boats. Many fell sick and had to be sent home in the *Swallow;* many more died, and the commander, with his remaining three ships, was glad to sail for the more hospitable south, where the new colony was to be founded. They left St John's on the 20th August, and were driven backwards and forwards on the tempestuous North Atlantic until the 20th, when the *Delight* ran on a bank and was wrecked. The other two vessels, the *Golden Hinde,* and a tiny cockboat of 10 tons burden called the *Squirrel,* overladen, crowded with sick, beset by perils, still battled against head winds. Terrible marine monsters were seen ; shoals, storms, and fog took hope and spirit from the men, who prayed Gilbert to abandon the voyage, and set his course to England. When they had arrived at a point north of the Azores, still in fearful weather, it became apparent that the *Squirrel* could not live through the sea. The men on the *Golden Hinde* besought Gilbert to leave the crazy, overloaded boat and go on board the larger vessel, but he resolutely refused. ' I will·not,' he said, ' forsake my little company with whom I have passed through so many perils.' Those on the *Golden Hinde* saw him calmly, with a book in his hand, sitting in the stern of his doomed craft, and as the ships on one occasion came within hailing distance, he cried out to them, ' Be of good heart, my friends. We are as near to Heaven by sea as by land.' A few hours afterwards, on the night of the 9th September, the light of the *Squirrel* was suddenly quenched, and brave Sir Humphrey and his little company were seen no more. He had faced death on the seas a hundred times before, and could look upon it undismayed, as such a hero should. He had risked all he had in the venture, and probably courted death rather than return home with the indelible brand upon him of ' a man of no good hap at sea.'

The *Golden Hinde* found her way into Falmouth on the 22d September, with the dismal news that Gilbert's second attempt to colonise North America for England had failed more disastrously than the first. The great dream of the Gilberts, like that of

Cabot, Willoughby, Frobisher, Davis, and most English seamen of the time, was the discovery of a north-west passage to China ; and to this task the younger of the brothers, Adrian Gilbert, succeeded Sir Humphrey, always with the support and help of Ralegh. But the genius of the latter enabled him to foresee the importance of the still greater work—that of founding an English nation across the sea, as he himself expressed it—and to this idea through evil fortune, and through good, he was true to the rest of his life—even to martyrdom.

On the 24th March 1584, fresh letters-patent were granted, giving to Sir Walter Ralegh, Esq., and his heirs ' free liberty to discover barbarous countries, not actually possessed of any Christian prince and inhabited by Christian people, to occupy and enjoy the same for ever.' The country was to be held by homage to the Sovereign of England, who was to receive the fifth part of all precious metals found. The inhabitants were to ' enjoy all the privileges of free denizens of England,' and Ralegh or his representatives were to have power ' to punish, pardon, govern and rule ' ; the laws to be ' as near as may be agreeable to the laws of England.' Exactly a month after this (on the 27th April 1584) Ralegh dispatched two of his captains, Philip Amadas and Arthur Barlow, under the guidance of the pilot Simon Fernandez, on a reconnoitring voyage to the proposed settlement, which had previously been fixed upon five years before by Fernandez. They wrongly calculated that the current from the Gulf of Mexico would have carried them greatly in a northerly direction, and accordingly set their course far to the south of the point they desired to gain. Touching the Canaries on the 10th May, they reached the West Indies on the 10th June. They then stretched across to the mainland of Florida, which they reached on the 4th July, and thence groped up the coast to the point previously selected by Fernandez, arriving there on the 13th July. In the report furnished by the captains to Ralegh, they describe how they entered the harbour, three harquebuss shots' distance inland, and then landed and took possession for the Queen of England. Grapes in marvellous abundance grew down to the water's edge ; magnificent cedars and other trees abounded, and the soil appeared to them to be of wonderful fertility. On further search, they found the land to be an island, 20 miles long, and about 6 broad, running parallel with the continent, forming part of a chain of similar islands, extending for a distance of 200 miles along the coast. The natives they found unsuspicious of all harm, peaceful, conciliatory and mild. The brother of the King of the country which they called Wingandecoia—the name of the island being Wokeken—came to them with a band of natives who soon became extremely friendly. Skins, coral and pearls were brought freely in exchange for the wonderful treasures of the white man. The King's brother was

E

especially enamoured of a tin dish, which he obtained
and suspended from his neck as a defence against the
darts of enemies. 'He had,' says the captains, 'a
great liking for our armour, a sword, and divers other
things which we had, and offered to lay a great box
of pearls in gage for them. But we refused it for
this time, because we would not make them know we
esteemed thereof, until we had understood in what
places of the country the pearls grew.' A glowing
picture is given of the luxuriance of the vegetation.
Two crops of corn were gathered in the year, and
food, especially fruit, was so abundant, that the
narrators are obliged to confess that surely this was
the best soil under heaven. The elaborate conditions
in the original patent as to the proper periodical
manuring of the land must have struck the discoverers
as strangely unnecessary, now that, for the first time,
their eyes rested upon the teeming virgin soil of the
West. They heard of a great city five days' journey
away, called Sicoak, and themselves visited the next
island of the chain, that of Roanoak ; and then,
bringing away with them two of the mild natives,
Manteo and Wanchese, they sailed to take the news
to Ralegh of the fertile country of which he in future
was to be the lord. The booty they brought with
them was not magnificent, consisting as it did only
of skins and a bracelet of pearls, 'as big as peasen,'
but it doubtless satisfied Ralegh. What he wanted
was a firm foothold for his countrymen on the northern

continent of America, which should balance the over-weening power of the Spaniards in the South.   In after years, it became necessary for him to hold out the bait of gold, in order to attract adventurers to aid his expeditions with funds, but it was never his own prime object, much as he loved the splendour for which it would pay.

The misfortune of the Spanish dominion in the Indies had always been that the main object of the explorers had been gold.   Their first question on landing had been as to its presence and whereabouts ; and the heartrending cruelties perpetrated upon in-offensive natives to extort the disclosure of their supposed treasures had shocked the more humane of the Spaniards themselves.   The capture and sacking of Quito and Cuzco with their countless hoards of gold and gems, the pillage of the Incas with wealth beyond conception, had inflamed the greed of the world ; and the bait which had drawn the earlier English navigators to the West had been a share, either by discovery or plunder, of the golden stream which seemed inexhaustible.

It is to the lasting glory of Ralegh that his clear prescience pierced beyond the momentary advantage of easily gained mineral wealth.   He and his brother Sir Humphrey Gilbert, indeed, were the forerunners of the school of thought which has now grown predominant, namely, that gold itself is only one instrument of commerce, not a substitute for it.

Gilbert in his treatise on the existence of a north-west passage, which was published without authority by Ralegh's friend Gascoigne, and shows unmistak-able signs of Ralegh's own hand, points out the advantage of planting settlements in suitable situa-tions under English rule, as a means of extending and enriching commerce, and of furnishing employ-ment 'to those needy people who trouble the commonwealth through want at home.' Captain Carleill, who was a follower of Ralegh, and Thomas Hariot, the famous mathematician, who was employed by him to report upon the natural productions and commercial capabilities of Virginia, both enforced the principles, then novel, which had been conceived by the master mind, namely, that colonisation, trade, and the enlargement of empire were all more im-portant for the welfare of England than the discovery of gold. Purchas publishes an anonymous treatise written during Ralegh's life—at the beginning of the seventeenth century—which shows how quickly his ideas had taken hold of the more thinking minds of his countrymen. The sound views of political economy expressed therein were practically undreamt of before Ralegh's time. 'The very name of colony,' says the author, 'imports a reasonable and seasonable culture and planting, before a harvest or vintage can be expected. Though gold and silver have enriched the Spanish exchequer, yet their storehouses hold other and greater wealth, whereof Virginia is no less capable, namely, the country's commodities. What mines have they in Brazil and in the islands where yet so many wealthy Spaniards and Portuguese inhabit? Their ginger, hides, tobacco, and other merchandise, it may be boldly affirmed, yield far more profit to the generality of the Spanish subjects than the mines do, or have done this last age. Who gave gold and silver the monopoly of wealth, or made them the Almighty's favourites? That is the richest land which feeds most men. What remarkable mines hath France, Belgium, Lombardy? What this our fertile mother England? Do we not see that the silks, calicoes, drugs and spices of the East swallow up all the mines of the West?'

These or similar ideas were those which animated Ralegh in his first attempts to establish an ' English nation ' on the other side of the Atlantic, and they have been justified by the added experience of three centuries.

The two captains returned to England in September 1584 with their glowing report of the new land they had visited, and with the natives they had brought. Ralegh submitted the information to the Queen, who herself dubbed the new dominion Virginia, and then the favourite set about his colonising plans in earnest. He was chosen one of the members of parliament for Devonshire at the end of the year ; and early in 1585 obtained a parliamentary confirmation of his colonising patent. But the Spaniards were watching him with jealous eyes. Drake was fitting out his expedition to the West Indies to sack and plunder ; Ralegh being one of the shareholders. Under his auspices, and those of Adrian Gilbert, Davis was preparing for another attempt to discover the northwest passage, and English rovers were busier than ever lying in wait for the rich Spanish galleons. The Spanish ambassador had been expelled from England, and a state of war existed between the two countries ; but Mendoza, in Paris, had his spies in every English port, and ceaselessly sent to his master minute accounts of the movements of English shipping. On the 22d Febuary 1585, he writes :—'The Queen has knighted Ralegh, her favourite, and has given him a ship of her own of 180 tons burden, with five pieces of artillery on each side, and two culverins in the bows. Ralegh has also bought two Dutch fly-boats of 120 tons each to carry stores, and two other boats of 40 tons, in addition to which he is having built four pinnaces of 20 to 30 tons each. Altogether Ralegh will fit out no fewer than 16 vessels, in which he intends to convey 400 men. The Queen has assured him that if he will refrain from going himself she will defray all the expenses of the preparations. Ralegh's fleet will be ready to sail for Norumbega at the beginning of next month.' How disturbed the Spaniards were at all these preparations is seen in a letter from Hakluyt, in Paris, to Walsingham on the 7th April. 'The rumour of Sir Walter Rawley's fleet, and especially the preparations of Sir Francis Drake, doth so much vex the Spaniard and his factors, as nothing can be more, and therefore I could wish that although Sir Francis Drake's journey be stayed, yet the rumour of his setting forth might continue.' They had reason to be vexed, for the English 'corsairs' were growing ever bolder, and a few weeks after this was written, a ship called the *Primrose* entered the river at Bilbao, kidnapped the Lieutenant-Governor of Biscay, and a number of his countrymen, and coolly brought them to England for ransom.

Unfortunately the Queen's affection for Ralegh prevented him from personally accompanying his colonial expedition, which was accordingly entrusted to the command of his cousin Sir Richard Grenville. Like most of the men of his stamp and period, he was brave and magnanimous to a fault, but overbearing, proud, and tyrannical. Fight and plunder were what he gloried in, and the far-reaching ideas of his statesman-cousin with regard to the extension of commerce and empire probably appealed to him but little. In any case, he exhibited no tact in carrying them out.

The expedition sailed from Plymouth on the 9th April 1585, and consisted of a smaller number of vessels than that reported by the Spanish ambassador. There was the *Tyger* of 140 tons, the *Roebuck* of 140, the *Lyon* of 100, the *Elizabeth* of 50, the *Dorothy* and two other

small pinnaces, seven sail in all ; and besides Grenville
there were Ralph Lane, one of the Queen's equerries,
who was to be the governor of the new colony,
Captain Amadas, Thomas Cavendish, John Arundell,
Stukeley, Hariot, the Indian Manteo, and over a
hundred colonists. They, too, went a very roundabout
course, arriving at Lanzarote on the 14th April, at
Dominica on the 7th May, and on the 12th landed in
Mosquito Bay, Porto Rico, where they entrenched
themselves and set about building a new pinnace.
This was decidedly against instructions, as they were
not to assail the dominions of any Christian prince,
and the Spaniards were unquestionably in possession
of the island.   After some days of spying upon the
intruders, the Spanish officials came with a flag of
truce and mildly expostulated with Grenville for erect-
ing a fortification on their territory.   With some discussion they were reassured, and they promised a supply
of provisions, which for some reason—Grenville calls
it their 'habitual perjurie'—they delayed or neglected
to bring; 'so we fired the woods all about,' and
sailed away on the 29th.   On the 1st June the
expedition anchored in the Bay of Isabela, in the
island of Hispaniola, after capturing an unoffending
Spanish frigate.   They found the Spanish governor
extremely hospitable and friendly, which attitude they
rather ungenerously ascribed to his fear of their
superior forces.   In any case, his friendship for the
English must soon have received a rude shock when

Drake, a few months afterwards, sacked and plundered the chief town of the island. On the 7th June they took their departure, and sailing along the Bahamas, sighted the mainland of what was then called Florida, but is now the State of South Carolina, somewhere north of the site of the present Charleston, on the 20th June. They were nearly wrecked off Cape Fear three days afterwards, and on the 26th reached \their destination, the island of Wokoken. The entrance they made use of seems to have been the Okeracoke Inlet, and in this entrance they nearly wrecked the *Tyger*, one of their principal ships, on the 29th, by the fault, according to Grenville, of the pilot Fernandez. They lost no time in sending news of their arrival to the friendly chief Wingina on the larger island of Roanoak ; and on the 11th July Grenville, Arundell, Stukeley, Hariot, Governor Lane, and Assistant-Governor Amadas, victualled for eight days, set forth to effect a landing on the continent of North America. They heard rumours of great towns and powerful peoples, all more or less vague, but from the petty chiefs they met they experienced nothing but kindness and hospitality. On their expedition one of the savages stole a silver cup, and a boat was sent ashore to demand the restitution, which was promised by the chief. The promise apparently was not kept, and the whole town was consequently ' burned and spoyled ' in revenge, the first of a series of feuds, which changed the kindly

aborigines into stealthy, cruel enemies of the white men.
The furthest point north reached by the expedition on
this occasion appears to have been Cape Hatteras; and
on the 27th July they again arrived at the site of the
future settlement, on the island of Wokoken.   Houses
having been erected, and stores of all sorts landed, the
first colony of England in the west was formerly in-
augurated, with Ralph Lane as governor, and 107
settlers; and Sir Richard Grenville sailed away for
England on the 25th August.   Governor Lane reported to Walsingham that Grenville had from the
first exhibited intolerable pride and ambition towards
the entire company, and they were probably not very
sorry to see the back of him.   He had left the colonists
sufficient supplies to last them for a year, but faithfully
promised to return before the following Easter with
fresh provisions.   Six days after leaving the settlement
Grenville fell in with a Spanish ship, richly laden, of
300 tons burden.   He had no proper ship's boat, but
was determined not to be baulked of so tempting a
prize as this, so he and his men shifted to board her in
a boat made of sides of provision chests, which with
difficulty could be kept afloat until it was brought
alongside the Spanish ship.   The moment they
boarded the prize their boat went down, but the
poor Spaniards made no resistance and were meekly
carried to England by their captors, arriving in
Plymouth Sound on the 18th October.   On board
the prize the principal treasure was a fine cabinet

of pearls; and much wrangling ensued between the
captors as to their respective shares of the booty.
Sir Lewis Stukeley, who was afterwards Ralegh's jailer
and betrayer, said that Ralegh had charged Elizabeth
with taking all the pearls for herself, 'without so
much as even giving him one pearl'; which, indeed,
was an extremely likely thing for her to do, though it
was unlike Ralegh to talk about it. Amongst the
men who had been pressed in Plymouth to accompany
the expedition was a German shipmaster, who, much
against his will, accompanied Grenville through the
voyage. It was not easy for him to get away from
England when he came back, but eventually he
managed to find his way to Spain, and gave Philip
a long account in Latin of the whole voyage. This
was sent to Philip's ambassador in Paris, and in
reference thereto the ambassador sent his master
some further interesting particulars. He says, 'The
ship which this captain says was captured by Ralegh's
expedition, with so large a treasure in gold, silver,
pearls, cochineal, sugar, ivory and hides was the one
I advised Your Majesty of months ago as having
arrived in England, and that Ralegh himself had
gone down to the port to take possession of her
cargo, so as not to allow it to be distributed amongst
the sailors.' The Queen had granted 70 fresh
letters of marque in reprisal for the embargo placed
on English ships in Biscay ports, and the sea positively swarmed with privateers. Philip and his officers

were in despair, for the command of the sea was even now slipping away from him. The friendly treatment which Ralegh's expedition had encountered at Porto Rico and Hispaniola was reported to the King by the German captain, and excited great indignation against the officials. Spanish settlers were accused even of making signal fires at night to give notice to the English privateers that they were willing to exchange food for merchandise—merchandise which had mostly been stolen from outward bound Spaniards. Matters had reached such a pass, indeed, that it is difficult to blame the settlers. Philip had prohibited all traffic with the Indies except by means of Spanish ships sailing from Seville. These ships regularly took the same course, by the Azores, where they were just as regularly captured by the crowds of corsairs that awaited them ; and storm and punish as Philip and his officers might, it often happened that the only means the Spanish settlers had of obtaining European commodities at all was through the English privateers.

CHAPTER V

MOST of the misfortunes which befell Ralegh's attempt
to settle his new dominion arose from the fact that his
duties near the Queen prevented him from giving it
the benefit of his personal supervision. His power,
prestige, knowledge of men and enthusiasm would
probably have saved the colonists from the insub-
ordination and folly which led to their failure.
Lane manfully did his best, and sent home by Grenville glowing accounts of the country. To Walsingham (12th August 1585) he wrote that they had
'discovered so many rare and singular commodities
in Her Majesty's new kingdom of Virginia, that no
state in Christendom do yield better or more plentiful, and the ship's freight we are sending will prove
I do not lie.' He says that they have named the
three ports, Trinity, Scarborough and Ocana, where
the fleet stuck, and the *Tyger* was nearly lost. The

77

best port, which was discovered by the pilot-major Simon Fernandez, would, he says, be able to resist the whole force of Spain.   He continues, — 'We have undertaken to remain with a good company, rather to lose our lives than to defer the possession of so noble a kingdom to the Queen, our country and our noble patron Sir Walter Ralegh, through whose and your worship's (Walsingham's) most worthy endeavour and infinite charge, an honourable entry is made to the conquest. . . . I am assured that we will by this means be relieved of the tyranny of the Spaniards, and that the Papists will not be suffered by God to triumph. . . . God will command even the ravens to feed us.'

But after Grenville's departure affairs grew less promising, and Lane's position became more difficult. Quarrels soon broke out amongst the settlers themselves, and between them and the Indians, whom the first visitors had described as 'the most gentle, loving and faithful, void of all guile and treason, and such as live after the manner of the golden age.' It is impossible to say now on which side the fault lay, but differences arose between the settlers and the Indians almost as soon as Grenville sailed away.   The settlers ploughed, planted and sowed ; explored for pearl-fisheries and mines ; and Hariot especially was indefatigable in obtaining knowledge of the natural products of the country.   He it was who first tried the native habit of smoking tobacco, and enjoyed it ;

the food value of the potato also appealed strongly
to his practical wisdom, and he urged the experiment
of its cultivation in England.   The governor explored
and took possession of the coast for a distance of 80
miles south of Roanoak and 130 to the north, as
far as the Chesapeake.   In the spring the King's
brother Granganimeo, the friend of the English, died.
Lane in his subsequent apology alleges that the King,
Wingina, then under another name, plotted an in-
surrection against the English, for which he and his
friends were put to death, another chief called Okisa
doing homage to the Queen of England in his stead.

Grenville had promised to return by Easter, but he
came not, and the colonists lost heart.   The provisions
were well nigh exhausted, although the corn was
almost ready for cutting, when, on the 10th June 1586,
a large fleet of ships appeared on the coast.   This
could not be Grenville, they knew, for he would not
come in so strong a force.   Their anxiety was soon
relieved by learning that the fleet was that of Sir
Francis Drake, gorged with plunder from the sack
of Cartagena and Santo Domingo.   The admiral had
bethought him to visit the new colony on his way
home, and it may be imagined how the disheartened
settlers would yearn with homesickness to desert their
savage quarters, and sail in a powerful and prosperous
fleet back again to their native land.   At first they
were appeased by the gift of fresh supplies, ammunition,
and two boats, in which Lane promised them that

they should all return to England in August, unless
Grenville came in the meanwhile with re-inforce-
ments.   But as they were writing letters to their
friends in England for Drake to carry home, a
tempest sprang up and drove many of the ships out
to sea ; amongst them the vessels with the provisions
and pilots destined for the relief of the colonists, with
many of the latter who were on board.   In vain Sir
Francis offered the rest of them another ship and
supplies ; they insisted upon being taken on board
the fleet and conveyed to England.   Drake at last
gave way, and the whole of the remaining colonists
sailed for England on the 19th June.

Even before Grenville had arrived in England,
Ralegh had ordered supplies to be prepared for the
relief of his people in Virginia.   Some slight delay
had taken place in their departure, probably owing to
the dispute about the division of the plunder from the
prize.   A swift vessel, of 100 tons burden, sailed,
however, soon after Easter with all necessary stores
for the colonists.   It arrived at the deserted settlement almost immediately after Drake had sailed, and
after unsuccessfully searching for the settlers, was
forced to return to England with the stores intact.
About a fortnight after she had left, Sir Richard
Grenville himself, with the main relief and some fresh
intended colonists, appeared at Port Ferdinando, as
the settlers called their principal harbour.   He, of
course, was equally unsuccessful in his search for the

colonists, and in his turn had to set sail for England, after leaving 15 new men on the island of Roanoak to continue the possession of the dominion.

On his way home Grenville, as usual, fell to plundering such Spanish ships as came in his way; and the voyage was not an unprofitable one to Ralegh, although the main object had failed.   Ralegh, indeed, was quite largely engaged in the privateering business at the time.   Most of the details of the voyages have, naturally, not been recorded ; they were more or less business enterprises, and were looked upon in a very prosaic light.   But by the industry of a certain John Evesham, gentleman, a musketeer on board of one of Ralegh's two pinnaces *Serpent* (35 tons) and *Mary Spark* (50 tons), we have in Hakluyt an interesting account of the proceedings of the two pinnaces during this summer of 1586.   Sailing on the 10th June, they first captured a barque loaded with shumach, with the Governor of St Michael's on board ; then when off the island of Graciosa they sighted a flotilla of homeward bound Spaniards to windward of them.   Hoisting the Spanish flag, Ralegh's pinnaces gradually crept near their prey.   When they came near enough, down went the false flag and up to the peak went the cross of St George.   The first vessel they overhauled proved to be only a fisherman and not worth the keeping, so she was let go again ; but the delay in taking her had given time for the other richly-loaded ships and a caravel to creep under the

guns of Graciosa. The pinnaces were to leeward,
and could not approach near enough to attack; and
the Spaniards thought themselves safe for the time;
but, says Evesham, we had a small boat called a
lighthorseman in which a musketeer (myself) and
four men with calivers and four rowers entered, and
rowed towards them. The Spaniards were hurriedly
attempting to land their precious cargoes, and there
were 150 musketeers on the beach to protect them,
but the gallant little 'lighthorseman,' with its five
gunners, cut out the Spanish ships from under the
very cannon of the fort, and towed the caravel and her
cargo out to sea. Two more of the ships were then
captured and manned by English sailors, all the
Spaniards being released but those who were worth
ransom, especially the already mentioned Sarmiento
de Gamboa, Governor of Patagonia. These three
rich prizes being sent home, there were left only 60
men on the pinnaces. Thus weakened, they fell in
with two great carracks of 1200 tons burden, ten
galleons, and as many caravels, loaded with treasure.
Nothing daunted, the two tiny pinnaces engaged the
whole fleet for thirty-two hours in succession, and
finally sailed away—without capturing them it is
true, but without the loss of a single man.

ᒷ   The deserting colonists from Virginia arrived at
Plymouth in Drake's fleet at the end of July, and
brought with them into England, probably for the
first time, the habit of smoking tobacco, which Ralegh

himself subsequently made fashionable at Court. The practice met with considerable opposition at first, and a proclamation was issued against it as the imitation of the manners of savage people. Camden says that it was feared that the English would degenerate thereby into barbarism.

The learned Hariot, however, was loud in his praises of the medical virtue of tobacco. The description he gives of the cultivation of the plant by the Indians is quaint. He says that they distinguished it by sowing it apart from all other vegetables, and held it of the highest estimation in all their sacrifices by fire, water and air ; either for thanksgiving to, or pacification of, their gods. 'And as by sucking it through pipes of clay, they purged all gross humours from the head and stomach, opened all the pores and passages of the body, preserving it from obstructions or breaking them, whereby they notably preserved their health, and knew not many grievous diseases, wherewith we in England are often afflicted. So we ourselves during the time we were there used to suck it after their manner, as also since our return, and have found many rare and wonderful experiments of its virtues, whereof the relation would require a volume by itself; the use of which by so many men and women of great calling, as well as others, and some learned physicians also, is sufficient witness.' The 'learned physicians' and others would probably have cried up in vain the virtue of the plant, had not the splendid Ralegh made it fashionable amongst the fine Court gentlemen, who envied, imitated and admired him.

Howell tells the story that Ralegh was descanting to the Queen upon the virtues of the new herb—the use of which had been strongly encouraged in France by her rival Queen Catherine de Medici—when he assured Her Majesty he had so well experienced the nature of it, that he could tell her what weight even the smoke would be in any quantity proposed to be consumed. 'Her Majesty, fixing her thoughts upon the most impracticable part of the experiment, that of bounding the smoke in a balance, suspected that he put the traveller upon her, and would needs lay him a wager that he could not solve the doubt : so he procured a quantity agreed upon, to be thoroughly smoked, then went to weighing, but it was of the ashes, and in conclusion what was wanting in the prime weight of the tobacco Her Majesty did not deny to have been evaporated in smoke, and further said that many labourers, in the fire she had heard of, who turned their gold into smoke, but Ralegh was the first who had turned smoke into gold.'

As is usually the case in similar enterprises, some of the returned colonists sought to cast the blame of their failure upon the qualities of the new country. Fortunately, however, there was at least one man amongst them of advanced, enlightened views and trained intelligence, who published a defence of it in a

⌐ notable treatise published shortly afterwards. This was Thomas Hariot, who had been specially commissioned by Ralegh to report minutely upon the natural products and capabilities of the region, and his work is per- haps the first methodical statistical survey of a country ever published in English. He describes with great care the merchantable products of the country, and the best means for turning the possession to profit.*

'Seeing the air there,' he says, 'is so temperate and wholesome, the soil so fertile, and yielding such commodities as I have before mentioned ; the voyage also to and fro sufficiently experienced to be per- formed twice a year with ease, and at any season ; and the dealings of Sir Walter Ralegh so liberal in giving and granting lands there, as is already known with many helps and futherances else ; the least that he hath granted having been 500 acres to a man only for the adventure of his person, I

* It was published in 1588, and was called *A Briefe and true report of the new found land of Virginia, of the commodities there found and to be raysed, as well marchantable as others for victual, building and other necessarie use for those that are or shall be planters there; and of the nature and manner of the naturall inhabitants discovered by the English Colony there seated by Sir Richard Grenville, Kt., in the yeere 1585, which remained under the government of Rafe Lane, Esq., one of Her Majestie's equerries, during the space of 12 moneths. At the special charge of the Honble. Sir Walter Ralegh, Kt.; directed to the adventurers, favourers and well-wishers of the action of inhabiting and planting there; by Thomas Hariot, servant of the above-named Sir Walther, a member of the Colony, and there employed in the discoverie.* London, 1588.

hope there remains no cause whereby the action should be misliked.'

Doubtless the real reason for the discouragement of the colonists was the absence of gold in the new country. The ideas of Ralegh and Hariot were in advance of the times; the majority of the adventurers had no taste for permanent expatriation and the slow toil of agriculture in a new country. The idea of all such men was to grow suddenly rich by plunder or the discovery of gold, and to return home to spend their wealth; the colonisation of an agricultural country, indeed, was calculated to be of permanent benefit to the nation, but could hardly bring great or rapid riches to the persons who took part in it. Ralegh's perseverance in it at his own expense becomes in this light the more patriotic. He obtained, it is true, vast sums of money, but he spent them lavishly in what he conceived to be the public good. However this may have been ignored by the crowd, with whom Ralegh was always unpopular, it was recognised by the wiser heads of the time. Hooker, in his dedication to him of his Irish History, says, 'It is well known that it had been no less easy for you than for such as have been advanced by kings to have builded great houses, purchased great circuits, and to have used the fruits of princes' favours, as most men in all former and present ages have done, had you not preferred the general honour and commodity

of your prince and country before all that is private,
whereby you have been rather a servant than a
commander of your own fortune.' The cost of the
three previous expeditions to Virginia had already
been enormous, and had been almost entirely defrayed
by Ralegh ; but on the return of Grenville he lost
no time in making another attempt. He selected
150 more men as colonists, with a Mr John White
as governor, with a council of government of 12
associates. These he incorporated under the title
of ' The governor and assistants of the city of Ralegh
in Virginia,' and the expedition sailed from Portsmouth on the 26th April 1587. It suited Elizabeth
for the moment to feign a desire to be friendly
with Spain, and Ralegh was warned that there must
be no attacks upon Spaniards on this occasion ; so
that the expedition made direct for Cape Hatteras,
which was reached within three months. Thence
they went to the fort on the island of Roanoak to seek
the 15 men left there by Grenville the year before,
the intention being to take them off, and establish
the new city of Ralegh in Chesapeake Bay. But
they found Lane's fort and houses on the north
point of Roanoak in ruins and already overgrown
with vegetation, and they subsequently learnt from
Manteo, the Indian who had visited England, that
the little garrison of white men had been treacherously
attacked and most of them murdered, the rest being
carried into the interior. The Indians on the coast

had now grown suspicious of the white men, and stood aloof. To conciliate them, Manteo was solemnly baptised and made lord of Roanoak; forts and houses were again erected, stores landed, and the little colony once more established. But the work of clearing and planting had all to be begun over again, and it was clear that before crops could be produced the stores would be exhausted. The colonists thereupon prayed Governor White himself to return to England in the ships, in order to obtain fresh supplies for them. His daughter, Eleanor Dare, had just given birth to a girl infant, who was christened Virginia—the first child of English blood ever born in North America—and he hesitated to leave his charge and family under such circumstances. After some persuasion, he unfortunately consented to do so, and arrived in England towards the end of 1587, having left in the new colony 89 men, 17 women, and 11 children.

When White arrived in England, the world was ringing with the pompous preparations of the Spaniards for the conquest and domination of England. Philip's ' leaden foot,' after thirty years of hesitancy, had moved at last, and the ' heretic ' Queen and her Counsellors were to be crushed for once and for all. Drake, Hawkins, Grenville, Ralegh and others of the same sort, who knew by experience how the English corsairs had terrorised the Spaniards at sea, were confident of success, if

only Philip's force could be encountered before it
landed. Ralegh wrote that the ramparts of England
only consisted of men's bodies, there were few coast fortresses, and that a fleet could travel more quickly than
an army, and choose its point of attack where the defender was least prepared. The Spaniard, he urged,
must be met and fought at sea. Drake thought so
too, and had in the summer, much to the Queen's
misgiving, suddonly sailed into Cadiz harbour, burnt
and sunk all the ships there destined for the Armada,
and had then quietly sailed out again, without losing a
man or a boat. If gallant Drake had been allowed to
have his way, indeed, unhampered by the Queen's
tricky diplomacy, and by the secret Catholic influence
at Court, he would have made the Armada impossible
at this time. He looked into the Tagus, and could
easily have burnt the unwieldy fleet ; for, as Santa
Cruz confessed, there were no men or guns on
board to resist him. As he came home he captured
one of the richest prizes ever brought into England,
the great East Indian galleon, *San Felipe.* Well
might the mariners be confident, for they knew that
the very name of Drake paralysed the Spaniards on
every sea ; but the men ashore were not so confident.
If Parma and the fierce Spanish infantry, the finest in
the world, once landed, they thought it would go
badly with the hastily raised militia—and they were
probably right. But the government did its best,
and from Berwick to the Land's End warlike pre-

parations went on ceaselessly. As Lord Lieutenant
of Cornwall and Lord Warden of the Stannaries, as
well as a member of the Commission of National
Defence, Ralegh was busy in raising men and
strengthening fortifications; but his main depend-
ence was always, and for the rest of his life, upon
the fleet and the seamen.

Everything that could arouse hatred and indignation against the invader was spread abroad. Ship-
loads of scourges were being sent to score the backs
of free Englishman; all adults, men and women,
were to be killed; and thousands of Spanish wet-
nurses were coming to suckle the orphaned infants.
Nonsense of this sort ran from mouth to mouth and was
implicitly believed; and the English people by the spring
of 1588 had been raised to frenzy. There was no
longer any room for doubt as to Philip's intentions.
Mary Stuart's death had deprived him of the stalk-
ing horse behind which he had worked, and he meant
to assert his own claim by descent to the crown of
England, and make his daughter Queen in his stead.

For years the English exiles in his pay—the Jesuits
and fanatics who swarmed in Flanders, France, Italy
and Spain—had been egging him on to this. The
English, they said, would have no beggarly Scot to
rule over them. England was rich, powerful and
Catholic at heart, and would welcome the Spaniard
with open arms, to save them from the Frenchified
Scotsmen, who would swarm like locusts over the

border. Philip had been told this so often, and so
long, that he had got to believe it ; and at last, even the
Pope and the French understood that the conquest of
England by Philip would mean a Spanish domination of
Europe. In both cases Philip's diplomacy had cunningly
managed to gag them, and they could only look on im-
potently in doubt and disapproval. But tht English
it touched more nearly. The Peace Commissioners,
it is true, were still sitting at Ostend ; and the frugal
Queen had ordered her own warships to be dismantled
and paid off. But everyone in England knew that
war was inevitable, and whatever the Queen might do
with her ships, the privateers and armed corsairs kept
theirs ready for action, for the men on board were
panting to fight a foe they knew they could beat.

When the land militia were called out, nominally
100,000 of them, though only a third of that number
were armed or drilled, Ralegh was commissioned to
raise 2000 men in the west country. He had hardly
set about it when the peace negotiations in Flanders
seemed to hold out hopes of success, and the preparations were suspended. Early in the spring of 1588,
he went to his estate in Ireland, and served the office
of Mayor of Youghal for that year. On the approach
of the Armada, he hurried into the west country again.
He was a member of the special commission for the
defence of the country against invasion, and had some
time before taken a leading part in the construction
of the new fortifications of Portsmouth. He now set

about raising and arming the west country levies, for which he was responsible, and strengthening the defences of the island of Portland.

On Saturday, July 20th, 1588, the 'most fortunate' Armada was collected off the Lizard; and at three o'clock in the afternoon first sighted some of Howard's ships. The next morning the two fleets were face to face, but the superior qualities of the craft and men of the English had given them the wind; and thenceforward for a week the great galleons, as they sailed up the Channel, were 'pestered by the devilish folk,' who hung upon the flanks and rear—the horns of the great half-moon, in which the affrighted Spaniards sailed. What was the use of bravery? Of what service were great towering hulls and mighty armaments; of the thousands of harquebussiers crowding the decks? They could not get near their foe to board him; for the privateers who had carried their lives in their hands for twenty years had been spurred by necessity to invent ships that could sail round the Spaniards, and beat them piecemeal as they did, until dismay and panic turned the great Armada into a hustling mob, with a hostile fleet, fit and confident, to windward, and a shoally coast to lee; and thus the sceptre of the sea passed from Spain to England.

Ralegh's biographers, one and all, assert that he went on board Howard's fleet on the 23d July with other gentlemen volunteers, and witnessed the rest of the fighting in the Channel. This is just possible, but no more. Not the slightest reference to his presence appears in any of the official correspondence, and in any case he had no command and cannot have taken an active part. Whether he was a spectator or not, he thoroughly agreed with the successful tactics pursued by Howard and Drake. The Council sent Richard Drake to ask the Lord Admiral how it was that the Spanish ships had not been boarded, and Ralegh evidently refers to this question in his remarks in the *History of the World.* 'Certainly,' he says, 'he that will happily perform a fight at sea must believe that there is more belonging to a good man of war upon the waters than great daring, and must know that there is a great deal of difference between fighting loose or at large, and grappling. To clap ships together without consideration belongs rather to a madman than to a man of war ; for by such an ignorant bravery was Peter Strozzi lost at the Azores when he fought against the Marquis of Santa Cruz. In like sort had Lord Charles Howard, Admiral of England, been lost in the year 1588, if he had not been better advised than a great many malignant fools were that found fault with his demeanour. The Spaniards had an army aboard them, and he had none; they had more ships than he had, and of higher building and charging ; so that had he entangled himself with those great and powerful vessels, he had greatly endangered this kingdom of England. For twenty men upon the defences are equal to a hundred that

board and enter ; whereas then the Spaniards, contrari-
wise, had a hundred for twenty of ours to defend
themselves withal. But our admiral knew his advantage and held it ; which had he not done he had
not been worthy to have held his head.'

It is to be remembered, that what was acknowledged to be the best ship in the English fleet, the
Lord Admiral's flagship the *Ark-Ralegh*, had been
built by Ralegh on his own plan. It had been
launched the previous year, 1587, and had been sold
to the Queen for £5000 before it left the stocks.
The *Roebuck* also, which Cecil specially praises as a
fine ship, was owned and built by Ralegh, and the
gallant *Revenge*, Drake's flagship, had been partly owned
by him. During the troublous time of preparation to
resist the Armada, all ships on the English coast were
requisitioned for the royal service, and forbidden to leave
port. Grenville was fitting out a large expedition for
the Virginia colony, at Bideford, when he was stopped.
With difficulty Ralegh obtained a release for two ships
bound for the West Indies, on condition of their
taking colonists and stores to Virginia. The masters
took advantage of the release to sail, but with few
stores or settlers, and went on a plundering expedition.
Off Madeira they were assailed by French pirates and
plundered, whereupon, with Governor White on
board, they returned to England, and the colonists for
a time were left to their fate. Much ungenerous and
unthinking odium has been cast upon Ralegh for his

supposed indifference to these unfortunate people, and
Southey is particularly severe upon him for it.
Ralegh had by this time spent £40,000 on the
venture, representing in spending power at least four
times that amount in the present day, and, as Hakluyt
says in a dedication to him at the time, 'it would have
required a prince's purse to have followed it out.'
Great as his resources had been, he had well-nigh
exhausted them. The 'mere adventurers,' as Hakluyt
calls them, did not partake of his far-seeing patriotic
views as to the permanent value of an agricultural
country to be colonised by Englishmen. As soon as
they understood that there were no gold mines, their
enthusiasm cooled, and no money was forthcoming.
Indeed, from their point of view, the speculation was
much less promising than plundering Spaniards or
finding an easy way to the rich commodities of the
East. As a matter of fact, Ralegh for the rest of his
life never ceased in his endeavours to reach the settlers
he had sent out, although after 1589 his own personal
responsibility was a moral one only. In that year he
gave to a company, formed for the purpose, the right
to trade in the colony, and kept for himself only the
fifth of the precious metals, and the chief rents of the
land ; and in pursuance of this transfer, White again
started in August 1589 to relieve the settlers. This
time he arrived at Roanoak, and found the colony had
been transferred to the island of Croatan, 60 miles
further south. White and his expedition set sail for

the place, but were caught in a storm, and once more
driven back to England without reaching the settlers.
Thenceforward the company made no further attempt
to relieve them, nor did the Queen help in any way,
although the plan from the first had been carried out in
the interests of the country, and not in those of the patriotic projector.   At his own cost Ralegh subsequently
sent at least five expeditions to discover the fate of his
people, but always without success.   It was afterwards
learnt that the whole of them had been murdered by
the Chief Powattan, and it was twenty years longer
before a permanent settlement of Englishmen was
fixed on the northern continent.   But no subsequent
events can take away the glory from Ralegh of having
by his patriotism and example secured for the occupation of the English-speaking race the great continent
which now can never be alienated from it, come what
may.   In the dedication to him by Hakluyt of a
narrative of French voyages to Florida, his really
patriotic objects are fully recognised.   'Touching the
speedy and effectual pursuing of your action, I am of
opinion that you shall draw the same before long to
be profitable and gainful, as well to those of our nation
there remaining as to the merchants of England that
shall trade hereafter thither, partly by certain secret
commodities already discovered by your servants, and
partly by breeding of divers sorts of beasts in those
large and ample regions, and planting such things in
that warm climate as will best prosper there, and our

realm standeth most in need of.   Moreover, there is
no other likelihood but that Her Majesty, who hath
christened and given the name to your Virginia, if
need require, will deal after the manner of honourable
godmothers, which, seeing their gossips not fully able
to bring up their children themselves, are wont to
contribute to their honest education, the rather if they
find any towardliness or reasonable hopes of goodness
in them.'   But the Virgin Queen was not a god-
mother of that description, and Ralegh's colony got
no help from her.   Ralegh himself never lost hope or
faith.   'I shall yet live,' he wrote, shortly before his
ruin—'I shall yet live to see it an English nation.'
And so he did, but he was in the Tower a prisoner.
In the meanwhile he had by his enterprise endowed
his country with vegetable products from abroad,
which others had seen and described, but which he
alone had utilised.   He had impressed upon his fellow-
countrymen the indignation which he felt at the
arrogant assumption of the Spaniards to the exclusive
possession of the western world, by virtue of a papal
bull ; he had demonstrated that limitless regions of
fertile land, with untold natural wealth, were awaiting
the benefits of civilisation and Christianity ; he had
sown the seed of English colonial enterprise, and
others were to reap the harvest.

CHAPTER VI

ADVENTURE was in the air. The dramatic and complete catastrophe of the much-vaunted Armada made
Englishmen more than ever confident that at sea
henceforward they were to be paramount. The
thirst for plunder spread, and citizens of all classes
became eager to participate in the rapid gains of
adventures against foes whom they had begun to
despise. As a thorn in the side of Philip, both
Elizabeth and Catharine de Medici in turn had
entertained and encouraged Don Antonio, a pretender to the Portuguese crown, which Philip had
assumed. From Elizabeth Antonio had hitherto got
little but fine words, but the French Queen Mother
had aided to fit out two disastrous naval expeditions
to the Azores. By 1589 most of his jewels—the
crown jewels of Portugal—had been pledged or

wheedled away from him, but he still had what is
now called the Sancy diamond, and this he pledged,
and came again to England. With Elizabeth's aid
and countenance a joint stock company was formed
to invade Portugal in Don Antonio's interest; he
was sure, poor sanguine man, that his countrymen
would acclaim him king the moment he set foot on
shore; and he promised, if he were successful, not
only to reimburse all the cost of the expedition, but
to make Portugal almost a tributary of England,
and above all to deliver the Spanish belongings in
Lisbon to the sack of the men of the expedition.
England was excited for revenge and loot, and
ruffians, high and low, half the idlers of the Court,
the sweepings of the streets, and the scum of the
jails, flocked to take part in what was represented
as being a pleasant excursion on summer seas to a
paradise of plunder.

An army of 16,000 soldiers, with 2500 sailors was
raised; and after much vexatious delay and disappointment, the expedition of nearly 200 sail was ready in
the middle of April. The chief command of the
land forces was held by Sir John Norris, and Drake
commanded at sea. Ralegh was one of the con-
tributors to the adventure, and accompanied the
expedition; but the Queen had peremptorily refused
the Earl of Essex permission to join. In the previous
autumn there had been a squabble between him and
Ralegh, which had led to a challenge, and the inter-

vention of the Privy Council to prevent hostilities. Jealous, doubtless, that Ralegh should take part in the enterprise whilst he was dangling at the skirts of the imperious old lady whom he alone dared to treat insolently, Essex escaped from Court, rushed in disguise to Plymouth, and got on board the *Swiftsure*, in which the chief officer was Sir Roger Williams, the general second in command of the army. Before his pursuers could catch him, the *Swiftsure*, without Drake's orders, put to sea. The Queen was frantic with rage, swore that Drake and Norris were privy to the favourite's escape, and thenceforward she had nothing but hard words and sour looks for the expedition. Sir Roger Williams especially was threatened with instant death on his return—a threat, by the way, of which he took very little notice. The *Swiftsure* joined the fleet after the latter had wasted ten days at Corunna, sacking, burning and plundering, but neglecting the main object of the expedition. When they reached Peniche, Drake, true to his invariable policy of tackling the Spaniards on the water, was for forcing the entrance of the Tagus and sailing up in front of the city. In this he was supported by Ralegh, and if the plan had been adopted the result of the enterprise would probably have been very different from what it was. But Don Antonio, Norris and Essex, who were no seamen, were for marching over land to Lisbon and besieging it. They had no siege guns or paraphernalia, no proper marching gear, no commissariat, and no medical staff, but Antonio was so confident that Lisbon would open its gates to him, that Drake was overborne; and foolish Essex had his way. It happens that all the historians of the unfortunate expedition were with Norris's force, so that we have no details of Drake's movements, except that he went with the fleet to the mouth of the river at Cascaes to await the return of and re-embark the army. No mention whatever is made of Ralegh, but it is certain that he did not go with Norris and Essex on their wild-goose chase. He and Drake were better employed. During the six days they had awaited Norris off Cascaes they had scoured the seas for miles around in search of prizes, and captured 40 German hulks loaded with goods for the Spaniards. Some of these, and the many other prizes taken, had to be abandoned for want of men; for drink, disease and desertion had reduced the English force to about a quarter of its original number; others were surreptitiously run into remote ports of England and Ireland, and the proceeds of them appropriated by their crews, so that the booty to be divided fairly amongst the adventurers was trifling. In one of Ralegh's prizes, some of Williams's men had been placed to escort it to England, and turbulent Sir Roger, who, henchman of Essex as he was, hated Ralegh, claimed the whole value of the prize, which, he said, but for his men, could not have been brought to England.   His claim was disallowed, for the Queen was still in a violent rage with him, and Essex had not yet dared to return to Court.   Ralegh, on the contrary, who had had no share in the failure, was welcomed, and received a gold chain as a new token of the Queen's regard.   Williams thereupon addressed an insolent letter to the Council, saying that he deserved a chain as well as his fellows.   He was probably unaware that only a few weeks before the Queen had peremptorily ordered Drake and Norris to give him a halter.

Before many weeks were over, however, Essex was taken into favour again, and soon made the Court too warm for Ralegh.   'My Lord of Essex hath chased Mr Ralegh from Court, and hath confined him to Ireland' wrote Anthony Bacon's friend, Allen, in August, though it must be remembered that both of them belonged to Essex's party, and would be glad to exaggerate his influence.   Ralegh himself appears to have heard some such gossip, for he wrote, after his return to London in December 1589, to his cousin George Carew, 'For my retrait from Court, it was uppon good cause to take order for my prize.'   He had other reasons for leaving Court.   His great Irish estates were causing him endless worry.   With characteristic energy, he was deep in experimental planting, mining, draining, and disforesting; he was splendidly rebuilding Lismore Castle, and was full of schemes for improving his property.   But Fitzwilliams,

the Viceroy, was apparently his enemy, and favoured
squatters and claimants upon his lands, and generally
hampered him. His reference to Fitzwilliams in the
letter just quoted to Carew (who was then Master of
the Ordnance in Ireland) is interesting as showing
how his proud spirit chafed at the suggestion that he
was a disgraced favourite. 'If in Irlande they thincke
that I am not worth respectinge they shall mich
deccave them sealvs. I am in place to be beleved not
inferrior to any man, to pleasure or displeasure the
greatest, and my oppinion is so receaved and beleved
as I can anger the best of them. And therfore if the
Deputy (*i.e.*, Fitzwilliams) be not as reddy to steed
me as I have bynn to defend hyme—be it as it
may.

'When Sir William Fitzwilliams shalbe in Ingland,
I take my sealf farr his better by the honorable offices
I hold, as also by that nireness to Her Majestye which
still I enjoy, and never more. I am willing to continue towards hyme all frindly offices, and I doubt not
of the like from hyme as well towards mee as my
frinds.'

This letter must have been written from London
after his visit to Ireland and his short retirement from
Court. He was now sure that his transient disgrace
with the Queen had passed, for he had with him a
new suppliant for her favour. 'When will you cease
to be a beggar?' she asked him once. 'When your
gracious Majesty ceases to be a benefactor,' was his

courtly reply.   He was, in fact, never tired of playing
the patron and friend of those who sought Court
favour.   In the spirit of the times in many cases he
took care to be handsomely paid ; but where poets
and men of letters were concerned, his disinterestedness and generosity knew no bounds.   Himself one
of the noblest of Elizabethan courtly singers, rivalling
Sidney, even approaching Shakespeare in his sonnets,
perhaps the greatest service he rendered to English
poetry was in snatching from obscurity the poet
Spenser, and promoting the publication of the *Faerie
Queen*.   It was on the visit to Ireland in the autumn
of 1589 that he renewed his acquaintance with him.
In the rough days of the Desmond rebellion, when
the masterful Captain Ralegh was sweeping the rebels
from Cork by fire and sword, Edmund Spenser had
been the secretary to the Viceroy, Lord Grey, with
whom Ralegh had so many passages of arms.   The
two young men must have known each other then,
for Ralegh had already written poetry whilst he was
at the Temple, and Spenser had published verse ; but
their lives had thenceforward lain in different places.
Spenser had received the estate of Kilcolman, part of
the Desmond forfeitures, and occupied an official post
he had purchased in Cork ; and on Ralegh's flying
visit to Ireland in 1589 they met.   What happened
at the meeting and afterwards, Spenser himself related,
when he returned to Kilcolman in 1591, in his poem
dedicated to Ralegh, called *Colin Clout's come Home*

again. He tells how the 'Strange Shepherd' found him

> ' *Keeping my sheep among the cooly shade,*
> *Of the green alders by the Mulla's shore.'*

and how without envy the two poets compared their songs. Ralegh's contribution to the conversation seems to have been a plaint,— .

> ' *Of great unkindness and of usage hard,*
> *Of Cynthia, the Lady of the Sea,*
> *Which from her presence faultless him debarred.*
> *And ever and anon with singulfs rife*
> *He cried out to make his undersong ;*
> *Ah! my love's Queen, and goddess of my life,*
> *Who shall pity me when thou do'st me wrong ?* '

Much as Ralegh might complain of the unkindness of 'Great Cynthia,' he was confident, as we have seen by his letter to Carew, of his ability to soften her heart ; and he persuaded Spenser to accompany him to Court and present his poem to the Queen. The commencement of the work had been encouraged by Sir Philip Sidney ; it was published by the advice of Sir Walter Ralegh. With the Queen's patronage the first three 'books' were issued soon after the poet's appearance at Court, and by Ralegh's counsel they were accompanied by an explanatory exposition of the meaning of the allegory. This took the form of a letter printed as an appendix, and addressed to the 'Right noble and valorous Sir Walter Ralegh,' in which the poet's obligations to the favourite were

gratefully acknowledged. A pension of £50 a year
was bestowed upon Spenser, which probably was
sometimes paid to him, nothwithstanding Lord
Treasurer Burghley's demur at 'all this for a song?'
and the poet went back to 'Mulla's shore,' to continue his immortal work, a much more important
person than when the 'Shepherd of the ocean' first
found him there. Kilcolman, however, was not much
more advantageous to Spenser than Lismore was to
Ralegh. Disappointment and discouragement came
to both the 'undertakers,' though Ralegh fortunately
sold his vast domain to Boyle, afterwards Earl of Cork,
in whose hands it prospered exceedingly. Spenser
clung to Kilcolman until Tyrone's great uprising in
1598 harried his lands, burnt his home, and broke his
heart.

Of Ralegh's own position as a poet this is not the
place to speak at any length. In a courtly *dilettante*
way he must have written much, and his verse was
held in high esteem by his contemporaries, though
apparently he cared little for its preservation ; perhaps
he almost despised his great poetic gift, for he signed
hardly anything and printed nothing. He was content to receive the applause of the cultured courtiers,
by whom a turn for amorous verse was looked upon
as a necessary accomplishment. In the fine sonnet
addressed to him by Spenser at the end of the
Faerie Queen, a noble compliment is paid to his
poetry.

'To thee that art the summer's nightingale,
Thy Sovereign goddess's most dear delight,
Why do I send this rustic madrigal,
That may thy tuneful ears unseason quite?
Thou, only fit this argument to write,
In whose high thoughts Pleasure hath built her bower,
And dainty love learned sweetly to indite.
My rhymes, I know, unsavoury and sour
To taste the streams, that like a golden shower
Flow from the fruitful head of thy Love's praise;
Fitter perhaps to thunder martial stowre,
Whenso thee list thy lofty Muse to raise.
Yet till that thou thy poem will make known,
Let thy fair Cynthia's praises be thus rudely shown.'

The poem to which Spenser refers in the last two
lines must have been shown or sketched out to him
when Ralegh saw him in Ireland in 1589, as more than
one reference is made to it in *Colin Clout*. The whole
of it was thought to be lost, until recent years, when
a continuation or sequel to it in Ralegh's hand was
discovered at Hatfield, consisting of over 500 lines.
The fragment was published entire in Dr Hannah's
Poems of Sir Walter Ralegh, and it is there assumed
to have been written shortly after the death of the
Queen, to whom, of course, the poem itself must have
been addressed. Mr Stebbing, on the contrary,
supposes that the fragment in question was written
during Ralegh's disgrace between 1592-5, and that
the references to death in it do not apply to the
Queen personally, but to her dead love for him.
With this I am inclined to agree, although it would
be pleasant to think that Ralegh's regard for his

benefactress should have led him to continue to praise her in the time of her successor.   The following are the lines upon which the question turns :—

> *'If to the living were my muse addressed,*
> *Or did my mind her own spirit still inhold ;*
> *Were not my living passion so repressed*
> *As to the dead, the dead did these unfold.'*

Whichever contention may be right, the poem is a stately one, but imbued, like all of Ralegh's verse, with deep melancholy. With the exception of a few lighter verses, the whole of his poems appear to have been written at periods of disappointment and despondency, as if it were only in depression that his mind was diverted from action. Like many sanguine men, Ralegh must have been easily — though perhaps momentarily—reduced to hopeless misery by failure. Some of his poems of discontent, which do not breathe despair and longing for release by death, are full of almost savage resentment, as in the case of *The Lie.*

> *' Go, Soul, the body's guest,*
> *Upon a thankless arrant ;*
> *Fear not to touch the best ;*
> *The truth shall be thy warrant :*
> *Go, since I needs must die,*
> *And give the world the lie.*
>
> *' Say to the court it glows*
> *And shines like rotten wood ;*
> *Say to the church it shows*
> *What's good, and doth no good :*
> *If church and court reply,*
> *Then give them both the lie.*

' *Tell potentates they live*
Acting by others' action ;
Not loved unless they give,
Not strong but by a faction :
If potentates reply,
Give potentates the lie.

' *Tell men of high condition,*
That manage the Estate,
Their purpose is ambition,
Their practice only hate :
And if they once reply,
Then give them all the lie.

Tell them that brave it most ;
They beg for more by spending,
Who in their greatest cost
Seek nothing but commending :
And if they make reply,
Then give them all the lie.

Tell zeal it wants devotion ;
Tell love it is but lust ;
Tell time it is but motion ;
Tell flesh it is but dust :
And wish them not reply,
For thou must give the lie.

Tell age it daily wasteth ;
Tell honour how it alters ;
Tell beauty how she blasteth ;
Tell favour how it falters :
And as they shall reply,
Give every one the lie.

' *Tell wit how much it wrangles*
In tickle points of niceness ;
Tell wisdom she entangles
Herself in over-wiseness :
And when they do reply,
Straight give them both the lie.

' *Tell physic of her boldness ;*
Tell skill it is pretension ;
Tell charity of coldness ;
Tell law it is contention :
And as they do reply,
So give them still the lie.

' *Tell fortune of her blindness ;*
Tell nature of decay ;
Tell friendship of unkindness ;
Tell justice of delay :
And if they will reply,
Then give them all the lie.

' *Tell arts they have no soundness,*
But vary by esteeming ;
Tell schools they want profoundness,
And stand too much on seeming :
If arts and schools reply,
Give arts and schools the lie.

' *Tell faith it's fled the city ;*
Tell how the country erreth ;
Tell manhood shakes off pity ;
Tell virtue least preferreth ;
And if they do reply,
Spare not to give the lie.

' *So when thou hast, as I*
Commanded thee, done blabbing—
Although to give the lie
Deserves no less than stabbing—
Stab at thee he that will,
No stab the soul can kill.'

No wonder that a man full of such bitter thoughts
and words as these—a man, moreover, arrogant, im-
patient and proud—was cordially detested by the
courtiers over whom he trampled roughshod, and by
the people whom he never condescended to concili-

ate—excepting always his own Devon and Cornish
men, who knew and loved him; and this very
poem of *The Lie* brought many retorts from the
author's enemies in similar metre.   An extract of
two stanzas from one of them will show the feeling
against him.

> ' *The Court hath settled sureness*
> *In banishing such boldness;*
> *The Church retains her pureness,*
> *Though Atheists show their coldness;*
> *The Court and Church, though base,*
> *Turn lies into thy face.*

> ' *The potentates reply,*
> *Thou base, by them advanced,*
> *Sinisterly soarest high,*
> *And at their actions glanced;*
> *They for this thankless part*
> *Turn lies into thy heart.*'

The accusation of Atheism against Ralegh, and
also especially against his *protégé* Hariot, was per-
sisted in during the whole of his life, but, so far as
Ralegh is concerned, there does not seem a tittle
of evidence to support it; the whole of his writings,
especially towards the end of his life, breathing the
sincerest devotion.

The following poem called *The Excuse* is a good
specimen of Ralegh's lighter verse.

> ' *Calling to mind my eyes went long about,*
> *To cause my heart for to forsake my breast;*
> *All in a rage I sought to pull them out;*
> *As who had been such traitors to my rest:*
> *What could they say to win again my grace?*
> *Forsooth that they had seen my mistress's face.*

> '*Another time my heart I called to mind,*
> *Thinking that he this woe on me had brought*
> *Because that he, to love, his force resigned*
> *When of such wars my fancy never thought :*
> *What could he say when I would him have slain ?*
> That he was hers—and had forgone my chain.

> '*At last when I perceived both* eyes *and* heart
> *Excuse themselves as guiltless of my ill,*
> *I found myself the cause of all my smart,*
> *And told myself that I myself would kill :*
> *Yet when I saw myself to you was true,*
> I loved myself because myself loved you.'

His reply to Spenser's address to him in the *Faerie
Queen*, quoted above, is extremely dignified, and will
compare with the finest sonnets in the language.

> ' *Methought I saw the grave where Laura lay,*
> *Within that temple where the vestal flame*
> *Was wont to burn ; and passing by that way*
> *To see that buried dust of living fame,*
> *Whose tomb fair love and fairer virtue kept,*
> *All suddenly I saw the Faerie Queen,*
> *At whose approach the soul of Petrarch wept ;*
> *And from thenceforth those graces were not seen,*
> *For they this Queen attended ; in whose stead*
> *Oblivion laid him down on Laura's hearse.*
> *Hereat the hardest stones were seen to bleed,*
> *And groans of buried ghosts the heavens did pierce ;*
> *Where Homer's sprite did tremble all for grief*
> *And cursed the access of that celestial thief.'*

Nothing of Ralegh's verse has remained imprinted
on the mind of posterity ; hardly a word of his
poetry has become blended into the common English
speech and is unconsciously used, as is the case with
certain expressions of Spenser, Sidney, and, above all,

the great Elizabethan dramatists, but curiously enough the rhyme of Ralegh's which is best known is a couplet contained in what were probably almost the first verses he wrote. They are three commendatory stanzas, prefixed to a satirical poem by his Temple friend Gascoigne, called *The Steele Glass*, published in 1576. The middle stanza is as follows, and the last couplet is not infrequently quoted without any knowledge of its origin.

> ' *Though sundry minds in sundry sorts do deem,*
> *Yet worthiest wights yield praise to every pain :*
> *But envious brains do nought, or light esteem,*
> *Such stately steps as they cannot attain :*
> *For who so reaps renown above the rest,*
> *With heaps of hate shall surely be oppressed.*'

This must have been written before Ralegh was twenty-four, when he was quite unknown ; and yet it is extraordinarily prophetic of the hatred and unpopularity which his own eminence brought upon him.

Ralegh, doubtless, looked upon his poetic gift mainly as a solace in moments of disappointment, or as a means of venting his dissatisfaction, but his deeper studies must have been much nearer his heart ; although, with the exception of his great and really extraordinary *History of the World* and an account by him in Hakluyt of the loss of the *Revenge*, none of his prose writings were avowedly published during his life, many profound and advanced treatises have been given to the world since, and prove him to have been in

H

most things far in advance of his age. In his *Select Observations on Trade and Commerce*, he anticipates nearly all the arguments of free traders; in his *Prerogative of Parliaments* he demonstrates, far in advance of his contemporaries, that the power of the Crown is strengthened by the maintenance of the privileges of the House of Commons; his writings on the construction of ships, and naval tactics, addressed to Prince Henry, anticipate many of the conclusions arrived at by scientific sailors of our own times, and his political *Maxims of State*, written whilst he was a prisoner, are full of far-seeing wisdom, and show how unquenchable was still his ambition to direct affairs and men, even from the Tower. This arrogant desire to take the management of everything and everybody was, through his life, the principal cause of his unpopularity. Few men care for another person calmly to assume, as of right, to take the direction of their affairs out of their hands, and this was what Ralegh invariably did in all matters with which he was concerned.

Some of his writings have been lost; amongst them a *Life of Queen Elizabeth*; and several treatises published under his name are almost certainly by other hands; but the undoubted works of his that remain are sufficient in themselves to establish Ralegh's position as one of the greatest literary geniuses that England ever possessed; and this, be it recollected, was a man who was essentially a man of action, who used his literary gifts not for themselves, but for other ends, to advocate policies or actions, or to prove contentions, not for the sake of literary form.   There was, indeed, never a man less vain of literary eminence than he ; so long as his writings produced the effect / he desired, he cared nothing, what became of them.

Of the *History of the World* I shall speak elsewhere, when treating of his life in the Tower, but the vast project of the work, in a literary sense one of the greatest ever conceived, proves the indomitable energy of the man and his confidence in his extraordinary powers.   Even in a book of this character—treating of far distant times—his intense interest in current affairs, and his desire to influence them, are manifest upon almost every page, where apposite illustrations from his own life, or modern instances gathered from his own observation, supply the principal value of the book to modern readers.

His benefactions to, and support of, literary men were endless.   Hakluyt acknowledges gratefully the information, as well as the material aid, he obtained from him.   He defrayed the cost of publication of coloured illustrations of Florida scenery painted by the French artist Jacques de Morgues ; Laudonnière's narrative of the disastrous French attempts to colonise that region was dedicated to him, both in French and English. He bought for £60 the manuscript of Estevao de Gama's voyage to the Red Sea in 1541, and every Spanish book which could be obtained telling of the

continent of the west, was eagerly purchased and avidly
read by him.   But through all his ceaseless activities,
a speculator with shares in every venture, a shipowner
with privateers scouring every sea, an active member
of parliament, an assiduous courtier, a patient student,
a voluminous writer, a great reforming landowner,
chemist, engineer, statesman, official, and much else,
like a golden vein there ran the determination that
his country should oppose the arrogant assumption by
Spain of the unchallenged domination of the new
world.   He knew by this time that the haughty claim
was based upon an insecure foundation ; that without
the empire of the sea, the empire of the lands across
the sea was untenable.   He and his kinsmen had
proved—if any proof beyond the Armada were needed
—that English ships and English seamen were far
more than a match for the Spaniards.   Hollow pride
should be met by pride as haughty but better
founded.   The Spaniard's loudly proclaimed dominion
of the western world must be challenged, and the
challenger must be England.   This was the master
motive of Ralegh's busy life through soorm and sun-
shine ; and however devious were the courses by which
he sought to reach it, his goal was immoveable, and
he held it unto martyrdom.

CHAPTER VII

ON Ralegh's arrival in Court with Spenser early in
1590, he was received once more into his mistress's
good graces, and shortly afterwards the avowal of his
rival Essex's marriage with the widow of Philip Sidney
raised Ralegh again to his position of chief favourite.
The Queen did not fall into ungovernable rage as she
did upon Leicester's marriage with Essex's mother, but
she insulted the bride, and pursued her with a spite
and venom almost incredible, except by those who
have studied closely the strange blending of grandeur
and meanness in Elizabeth's character. During the
short time of Essex's disgrace, and the longer period in
the ensuing year 1591, when he was in France commanding the English contingent in aid of Henry IV.
against Spain, Ralegh was all powerful with the Queen,

and when in the spring of 1591 it was determined to send an expedition to the Azores to intercept Philip's silver fleet from the west, he secured the appointment of Vice-Admiral. It was an enterprise which would, if successful, bring a great profit, and to this Ralegh was never indifferent. The supreme command was to be given to Lord Thomas Howard, and the squadron consisted of five of the Queen's ships, five cargo ships belonging to London, the *Bark-Ralegh*, and two or three pinnaces. But after all Elizabeth could not spare Ralegh; Essex was away in France, and Hatton was dying; and it was hard to have none of the courtier lovers by her; so his appointment as Vice-Admiral was cancelled, and his cousin Sir Richard Grenville appointed in his stead, doubtless to Sir Walter's discontent. The squadron left England in the early spring, but the silver fleet that year was late. It had encountered heavy storms in the Gulf of Mexico, and other mishaps on the American coast, and Howard's fleet lingered on the look out for it all the summer and autumn. This gave time for Philip to send a powerful escort to bring the silver fleet into Seville, and on the 10th September (N.S.) Captain Middleton, who had been cruising on the look out, came to the English fleet which was at anchor off Flores with the news that Don Alonso de Bazan—Santa Cruz's brother—was in the offing with two squadrons of 53 ships. The English fleet was in bad order with its long waiting. Great numbers of the men were down with scurvy and fever, the ships were crank for want of ballast, and many of the crews were ashore securing water. So short of men were they, that the *Bonaventure*, one of the large ships, had not sufficient hands to work her, and a smaller vessel had to be burnt and the crew put on board the *Bonaventure*. The Spanish fleet was fresh, and enormously superior in strength, and Lord Thomas gave the word for the English to get away. So rapidly did the Spaniards come up that some of the English ships had not time to weigh anchor, but had to slip their cables and run. Sir Richard Grenville in the *Revenge* stood by the longest, to take off the men who had gone ashore ; so that whilst the other ships all recovered the wind, and stood off, he found himself jammed between the shore and the Spanish fleet on his weather bow. He still might escape if he set his mainsail, cast about briskly, and showed a clean pair of heels to the foe. His sailing-master advised him to take this course. 'No,' said Sir Richard, 'I would rather die than dishonour myself, my country, and Her Majesty's ship, by flying from Spaniards. I will force my way through both squadrons of them.' Then began that famous fight that great poets have sung and great historians related, a fight that still stands forth as one of the most splendid in the glorious annals of the British navy. No prose story of it is more vivid than that written by Ralegh himself soon after the event. As the undaunted *Revenge* scornfully sailed on, the foremost ships of the Spanish fleet, surprised, perchance, at the audacity of the act, gave way, luffed, and fell astern of the English ship. But the giant *San Felipe*, of 1500 tons burden, one of the biggest galleons afloat, came looming up to windward, her towering hull all carved and gilded, and her spreading sails becalming the little *Revenge*—she was only 500 tons burden—which now lay like a helpless log in the trough of the sea. Then four other great galleons closed around her, two to port and two to star-board, and the *Revenge* was hemmed in; whilst all the navy of Spain stood by in case of need. Grenville was short handed; 90 of his men lay sick and helpless below; he had no regular fighting men on board, whilst the Spanish ships were crowded with trained soldiers. The tactics of the Spaniards had always been to grapple and board their opponents, whilst the policy of the English was to fire low into the hulls of their enemies and disable them. The *Revenge* adopted this course as usual, and at three o'clock in the afternoon sent a broadside of bar-shot from her lowest row of ports crashing into the great round hull of the *San Felipe*, between wind and water. The galleon was too high to train her big guns on to the hull of the *Revenge*, and was fain to sheer out of the fight, other ships of lower build taking her place. The great galleons closed and grappled, storms of musketry swept the decks of the *Revenge* again and

again.   Swarming up the sides came Spaniards by the
hundred, only to be hurled headlong back again into
the sea.   Grinding of timbers, booming of great guns,
patter of harquebusses, rose loud over the shouts of
command and the sobs of the dying : and still hour
after hour the unequal fight went on, till the decks
of the *Revenge* were all bright and slippery with blood,
and encumbered by the fallen.   Grenville, with blazing
eyes and grinding teeth, stood upon the poop of his
ship through it all—some say sorely wounded from the
first, but in any case there he stood.   Once a bold
little cargo ship, the *George Noble* of London, hanging
on the lee of the *Revenge*, came near enough to shout
to Sir Richard that they only awaited his commands
to take part in the contest.   'Save yourselves,' he
answered, 'and leave me to my fortune.'   Through all
the day, through all the night, the death-struggle
raged unceasing.   As fast as one crowd of boarders
were beaten back, fresh masses swarmed up the sides, to
be met and vanquished, steel to steel, by the dwindling
row of heroes that lined the bulwarks of the *Revenge*.
One after the other, the *Revenge* alone had to cope
with 15 great men-of-war, and when the ghastly
dawn came she was a riddled wreck ; her decks a
shambles, her rigging and spars a hideous ruin over
her sides, Grenville mortally hurt, and hardly a man
on board unwounded.   During the 15 hours fight,
the *Revenge* had received 800 cannon shot and had
sunk by her side two of her great assailants.

Then, when all was hopeless, no men, no ammunition, no serviceable arms, Sir Richard ordered the ship to be scuttled and sunk. 'Trust to God,' he said to his men, 'and to none else. Lessen not your honour now by seeking to prolong your lives by a few days or hours.' But most of his men thought they had done enough for honour, and knew that the Spaniards would be as ready to offer terms as they to accept them. So Sir Richard and his master gunner were overborne, and with bared heads the generous and admiring enemies carried the dying hero on to the ships of Spain. All that chivalrous foes could do was done by the Spaniards for the brave remnant of the crew of the *Revenge*. 'Do with my body what thou wilt,' said Grenville, all helpless now as they carried him from the slaughter house on his decks; and after three days he died on board the *San Pablo*, his last words being in the tongue of the victors, 'Here die I, Richard Grenville, with a joyful and quiet mind, having ended my life like a true soldier that has fought for his country, Queen, religion and honour.' In the fight the Spaniards lost 1000 men; and a great storm a few days afterwards sunk the *Revenge*, 15 of the Spanish war ships, and as many of the Spanish Indiamen, with a total of 10,000 men on board, all of whom perished.

Ralegh's eloquent account of this deed of daring, like all of his writings, was evidently written for a purpose. It was, indeed, a vigorous protest—in many

places violent and unjust—against the ambition of
Spain.   'How irreligiously they cover their greedy
and ambitious practices with that veil of piety ; for
sure I am that there is no kingdom or commonwealth
in all Europe, but if reformed they invade it for
religion's sake ; and if it be, as they term, Catholic,
then they pretend title : *as if the kings of Castile were
the natural heirs of the world.*'

Unfortunate as was the attempt to intercept the
silver fleet in 1591, it was not entirely fruitless, for
'a Mr Watt's ship' brought in some prizes, and a
letter from Ralegh to Lord Burghley about the division
of the spoil amongst the 12 adventurers is interesting.
' All of which amounteth not to the increase of one for
one, which is a small return.   Wee might have gotten
more to have sent them a-fishinge.   I assure your
Lordship whatsoever is taken, fifty of the hundred
goes cleare away from the adventurers to the mariners,
the Lord Admiral, and to the Queene ; the rest being
but £14,000 or therabout, is a small matter amounge
twelve adventurers ; and of which £14,000 the setting out cost us very nire £8000.   This is the very
trewth, I assure your Lordship before the livinge God,
as nire as wee can sett downe or gett knowledge of.'

It will be curious to set forth the actual account
of these prizes as rendered, showing, as it does, the
shares received by the respective parties.   'Value of
merchandise, etc., captured, £31,150.   One third for
the mariners, £10,383 ; for my Lord (Admiral) his

tenth, £3015 ; for the Queen's customs, £1600 ; cost of bringing the goods, £1200=£16,198. Rests unto the owners and victuallers to be divided amongst twelve, £14,952.' It will be seen that the business of plunder was organised on a thoroughly commercial system.

However the result of the adventure of 1591 may have discontented Ralegh, he was determined 'to organise a still bolder enterprise for the following spring, and probably his violent diatribe against Spain in his account of the *Revenge* combat was intended to stir up feeling in England, and aid the procuring capital for the adventure. In this enterprise he himself ventured everything he possessed and more, his principal partner being George Clifford, Earl of Cumberland. The design, as before, was to intercept the silver fleet, and also to repeat Drake's famous coup upon Panama. Thirteen well found and manned ships were provided by the adventurers, and two, the *Garland* and the *Foresight*, by the Queen, and Ralegh was to have chief command as Admiral, his Vice-Admiral being Sir John Borough. Ralegh busied himself in his preparations, but before the time came for him to sail, the Queen relented somewhat, and made him promise that as soon as the expedition was well out to sea, he would hand the chief command to Frobisher, whilst he returned to England in the *Disdain*. Frobisher was very unpopular with seamen, and Ralegh did not

like the idea, for, as he reminded Cecil, he had
ventured everything he possessed in the enterprise.
'If I can persuade the cumpanies to follow Sir
Martin Furbresher, I will without fail returne, and
bringe them but into the sea some fifty or three score
leagues . . . which to do, Her Majestie many
tymes with great grace badd me remember, and sent
me the same message by Will Killigrewe, which, God
willinge, if I can persuade the cumpanies I meane to
perform, though I dare not be acknown thereof to
any creature.' This was written from Chatham on
the 10th March 1592, and already there were
rumours of an entanglement or marriage between
the favourite and Elizabeth Throgmorton, one of
the Queen's maids of honour. Ralegh's enemies at
Court were even now whispering that when once his
foot was on the deck of his ship, he would not come
back until the Queen's anger was appeased. Cecil
seems to have hinted to Ralegh that these rumours were
afloat, for Ralegh, in the same letter as that quoted
above, continues, 'I mean not to cume away as
they say I will for fear of a marriage and I know not
what. If any such thing weare, I would have im-
parted it unto yoursealf before any man livinge; and
therefore I pray believe it not, and I beseich you to
suppress what you can any such malicious report.
For I protest before God, ther is none on the face of
the yearth that I would be fastened unto.' Westerly
winds held him in port whilst he grew more and

more despondent. 'More grieved than ever I was in anything of this world for this cross weather.' By the end of May, however, he put to seat, but he had hardly set sail before Frobisher followed him with orders for him to return immediately to Court. Ralegh's heart was set upon the adventure in which his whole fortune was embarked. He had sworn positively—and falsely—that there was no truth in the marriage rumours, and had no relish for going back to Court just then. So he dared to disregard the Queen's positive orders, and went on his way. But discouragement met him. He learnt that no silver ships were to venture out this year; for the Spaniards knew all about his enterprise. Then a great storm scattered his ships off Finisterre.

It was too late in the season now to attempt the attack on Panama, and he therefore determined to leave Frobisher with one squadron on the Spanish coast to divert attention, and send Borough to the Azores to waylay such ships from the Indies as might happen to pass; whilst he, Ralegh, returned home. He arrived in London in June, and was immediately arrested and lodged in the Tower. No reason was ever given for his imprisonment; it is just possible that the ostensible excuse for it may have been his disobedience to the Queen's orders in not returning at once, but it is certain that his real crime was his liaison with Elizabeth Throgmorton. Taking such slight evidence as exists into consideration, it is doubtful whether at this time Ralegh had been secretly married to her, though for the rest of his life she made him a tender, noble, and faithful wife. But the Virgin Queen arrogated to herself an absolute monopoly of love-making in her Court, and looked upon the marriage of her favourites as a personal insult to herself. The friends of Essex were openly jubilant, whilst the Cecils, his enemies, tried their best to soften the fate of Ralegh. Whether it be true that Lady Ralegh herself was imprisoned in the Tower, as stated, is not certain; but in any case the Queen never forgave her whilst she lived, and Ralegh himself, desirous of winning back the Queen's favour, was careful to avoid all reference to the accomplice of his 'crime.' In a letter from the Tower to Cecil, about the payments on account of the uniform of the Queen's bodyguard, he writes in the following inflated strain. The Queen, be it remembered, was then approaching sixty. 'My heart was never broken till this day that I hear the Queen goes so far off—whom I have followed so many years with so great love and desire in so many journeys, and am now left behind her in a dark prison all alone. While she was yet nire at hand that I might hear of her once in two or three days, my sorrows were less, but even now my heart is cast into the depth of all misery. I, that was wont to behold her riding like Alexander, hunting like Diana, walking like Venus, the gentle wind blowing her

fair hair about her pure cheeks like a nymph ; sometimes sitting in the shade like a goddess ; sometimes
singing like an angell, sometime playing like Orpheus.
Behold the sorrow of this world ! Once amiss hath
bereaved me of all. O glory that only shineth in
misfortune what is becum of thy assurance ? All
wounds have skares (scars) but that of fantasie ; all
affections their relenting but that of womankind.
Who is the judge of friendship but adversity ? or
when is grace witnessed but in offences ? There
were no divinity but by reason of compassion, for
revenges are brutish and mortal. All those times past
—the loves, the sighs, the sorrows, the desires, can
they not way down one frail misfortune ? Cannot
one dropp of gall be hidden in so great heaps of
sweetness ? I may then conclude *Spes et fortuna, valete*.
She is gone, in whom I trusted, and of me hath not
one thought of mercy, nor any respect of that that
was. Do with me therefore what you list. I am
more weary of life than they are desirous I should
perish, which if it had been for her, as it is by her, I
had been too happily born. Yours, not worthy any
name or title.—W. R.'

We may be certain that this outburst was not meant
for the eyes of prosaic Robert Cecil alone ; but it was
too early yet to appease the angry Queen. A little
later Ralegh writes to the Lord Admiral Howard, 'I
see there is a determination to disgrace and ruin me,
and therefore beseech your Lordship not to offend Her

Majesty any more by suing for me. I am now resolved of the matter. I only desire that I may be
stayed not one hour from all the extremities that
either law or precedent can avouch.' While Ralegh
was in the Tower under a cloud, and his enemies at
Court and in Ireland striving their utmost, as he says,
to ruin him, his good ship *Roebuck* having escaped
from the Spanish fleet sent out to capture her, fell in,
off Flores, with the great East Indian carracks, bound
to Lisbon. One of them escaped to the shelter of the
land forts, and was burnt, but the greatest and richest
of them all, the *Madre de Dios*, was attacked and
overpowered by Borough's squadron. The poor
Spaniards fought well for three hours, but they were
hopelessly outnumbered, their loss was terrible, and
they surrendered. Traditions have lingered even to
our own days of the excitement in the west country
when this, the greatest prize ever brought to England,
was towed into Dartmouth. The sacredness of the
name of the ship, her great size, and the almost untold wealth contained in her hold, struck the popular
imagination. The statement of her purser sets forth
that she contained '8500 quintals of pepper, 900
quintals of cloves, 700 quintals of cinnamon, 500
quintals of cochineal, and 450 of other like merchandise, with much musk, precious stones worth 400,000
cruzados, and some especially fine diamonds,' and
Hawkins and Ralegh wrote to the Lord Admiral
that the value of the prize would probably turn out

I

to be £500,000, although this was afterwards found to be an exaggeration, but the cargo filled ten English ships to bring it to London, and was worth fully £150,000, besides the precious stones and the ship herself. Pilfering of the valuable cargo began before the ship came into port, each man trying to snatch for himself some share of the great plunder. In vain Borough embargoed it all as the Queen's property, to steal which was treason; pearls and amber, musk and civet were portable, and a competency might be carried away in breeches' pockets. The ship's companies were deeply resentful to hear that their master, Ralegh, was a prisoner, and began to get out of hand. Sir John Hawkins then wrote that Sir Walter was 'the especial man' to bring things to order. By appealing to the Queen's covetousness, Burghley was able to obtain leave for Ralegh to go down to the west, still 'the Queen's prisoner, in charge of Mr Blount,' to arrange matters. Whilst this was being negotiated, Burghley sent his son and successor, Sir Robert Cecil, post-haste to Dartmouth to stop the pilfering. Merchants from the neighbouring towns were already dealing in the rich plunder; every cabin of the carrack had been rifled by the English sailors. Hernando de Mendoza, the captain, said that Sir John Borough got nothing, though the search of his chests told a different story. Cecil found that £28,000 worth of valuables had been filched before he reached Dartmouth. In the trunk

of one English sailor there was found 'a chain of
orient pearls, two chains of gold, four great pearls of
the bigness of a fair pea, four forks of crystal, and
four spoons of crystal set with gold and stones, and
two cords of musk.' The Portuguese on the English
ships bought or plundered priceless gems ; from one
of them being taken as many as 320 diamonds, whilst
another had a bag of diamonds as big as a fist; an
English corporal had a big bag of rubies, and much of
the plunder found its way to the East Coast and to
London. Sir Robert Cecil's letters to his father
(Calendar of State Papers. Dom.) on the subject are
very curious. From Exeter he writes that he stopped
every man he met on the road who had anything
'which did smell of the prizes,' and brought them
back with him. He found the Exeter people backward in revealing the whereabouts of plunder, until
he had clapped a few of them in prison, and this soon
brought things to light ; 'a bag of seed pearls' amongst
others. 'By my rough dealing with them, I have left
an impression with the Mayor and the rest. I have
taken order to search every bag and mail coming from
the west, and though I fear the birds be flown—for
jewels, pearls, and amber—yet will I not doubt but to
save Her Majesty that which shall be worth my
journey. My Lord, there never was such spoil. I
will suppress the confluence of these buyers, of which
there are above two thousand. My sending down
hath made many stagger. Fouler ways, desperate

ways, no more obstinate people did I ever meet with. . . . Her Majesty's captive comes after me, but I have outrid him, and will be at Dartmouth before him.'

Ralegh followed Cecil close, and on his arrival at Dartmouth the latter writes to Heneage, 'I assure you, sir, his poor servants to the number of 140 goodly men, and all the mariners came to him with such shouts of joy, as I never saw a man more troubled to quiet them in my life. But his heart is broken ; for he is very extreme pensive, longer than he is busied, in which he can toil terribly. The meeting between him and Sir John Gilbert was with tears on Sir John's part.   Whensoever he is saluted with congratulations for liberty, he doth answer, ' No, I am still the Queen of England's poor captive. I wished him to conceal it, because here it doth diminish his credit, which I do vow to you before God is greater amongst the mariners than I thought for. I do grace him as much as I may, for I find him marvellously greedy to do anything to recover the conceit of his brutish offence.'

Ralegh, as has already been stated, embarked more than all his fortune in the enterprise, the entire amount contributed by the adventurers, except Cumberland, being £34,000, of which £18,000 had been subscribed in money, and the rest in shipping. The Queen had contributed £1800 in money and two ships, so that her proper share would have been one tenth of the proceeds. She was not satisfied with this and wished to grasp the lion's share. The Earl of Cumberland had contributed £19,000 and was offered £36,000, or a clear profit of £17,000, whilst Ralegh and a few friends had contributed £34,000 and were offered a return of £36,000, out of which they had to pay the city of London and others certain amounts, which left them nett losers of £2200. Ralegh was still the 'Queen's poor captive,' but he would not put up with such injustice as this without a protest; the injustice indeed was so glaring that even Sir John Fortescue, Chancellor of the Exchequer, warned Lord Burghley that the 'adventurers would never be induced to further venture if they were not princely considered of.'

The princely consideration ended in the Queen's keeping half of the great booty for herself, and Ralegh barely got his own back again, but after such a rich haul as this she could hardly send him back to his easy prison in the Brick Tower, and in December we find him once more installed in his own mansion of Durham Place, though for long afterwards he was not allowed to approach the Queen.

Ralegh's release from attendance at Court, however much he may have looked upon it as a crushing disgrace, gave him opportunities for employing his great powers in matters more worthy of him than feigned love-making to the elderly Queen and intrigue against Essex. In the Parliament of 1592-3 he took an active part in the debates. He had already established himself as one of the first authorities on parliamentary procedure and precedents, and his great eloquence and clearness of statement are noticeable, even in the summarised reports of his speeches in D'Ewe's *Journal of the Parliaments of Elizabeth.*

The Spaniards, through the action of the League, had now established a footing in Brittany; and this near neighbourhood caused great anxiety to Elizabeth's government. It became necessary, therefore, to demand considerable grants from Parliament for the defence of the country, and Ralegh took a prominent share in advocating a liberal policy in this respect, not — as he was careful to say — to please the Queen, but because he saw the urgent need of it. He was in favour of dropping the mask and making an open declaration of war. Many persons, he said, considered it wrong to take prizes from the Spaniards under the present circumstances, but if a regular declaration of war was made, no such scruples would exist, and the Queen would have more volunteers at sea to fight the Spaniards than she needed. As usual, in this debate, Ralegh appears as a defender of the privileges of the House of Commons. It had been proposed that the House of Lords should be taken into conference with regard to the granting of the supplies; and this would have been carried but for Ralegh, who pointed out the objections to it. If, he said, the proposal had been for a general conference with the Lords touching the great and imminent dangers of the realm, there would be no objection. The effect would be the same and the privileges of the House preserved. A resolution to this effect was therefore carried.

Ralegh, in this session, spoke strongly in the debate on the question of the alien retailer. It appears that a large number of Dutchmen had established themselves in St Martin's le Grand, which was a sanctuary and extra-municipal, where they carried on a brisk trade as weavers, spinners and retailers of textiles, 'to the great detriment of merchants and regular dealers in our own city, inasmuch that threescore English retailers had been ruined by them since last Parliament.' A bill was introduced to make such alien retail trading illegal, and was supported by Ralegh in a vigorous speech. It was alleged by the opponents of the bill that it was being promoted by 'our mercantile engrossers,' in order that the ruin of the English retail shopkeeper might be imputed to the strangers rather than to the action of what then answered to our modern 'corners' and 'trusts.' The answer to this was that 'engrossing' was quite allowable amongst merchants. 'Others, again, ran upon the more universal topics of charity, in giving shelter and means of getting livelihood to poor, destitute strangers, who fly to us for religion and relief.' Ralegh's reply to the opponents of the bill is extremely curious, touching as it does so closely a burning question of our own day. 'Whereas it is pretended,' he said, 'that for strangers it is against charity, against honour, against profit, to expel them, in my opinion it is no matter of charity to relieve them. For first: such as fly hither do so forsaking their own king; and religion is no pretext for them, for we have no Dutchman here but such as come from where the Gospel is preached. Yet here they live, disliking our church. For *honour:* it is honour to use strangers as we be used amongst strangers, and it is a lightness in a Commonwealth—yea, a baseness in a nation—to give liberty to another nation which we cannot receive again. . . . And for *profit:* they are all of the house of Almoigne who pay nothing; yea, eat out our profits and supplant our own nation. Custom, indeed, they pay—15d. where we pay 12d.—but they are discharged of subsidies. The nature of the Dutchman is to fly to no man but for his profit, and they will obey no man long. . . . Therefore I see no reason that such respect should be given to them; and to conclude: in the whole, no matter of honour, no matter of charity, no profit in relieving them.' The bill for the disestablishing the retailing 'Dutchmen' was passed by 162 votes against 82.

Sir Walter, on the other hand, threw cold water on a bill in the same Parliament for the suppression or

expulsion of the dissenting sect called Brownists. He
had, he said, no sympathy with the sect, but pointed
out the practical difficulties in the way of their expulsion,
and the hardship it would bring about. In this case
the bill was referred to a select committee, of which
Ralegh was chairman, and eventually passed in a
very modified and innocuous form.

Just before his disgrace, whilst he was in high
favour with the Queen, he had obtained, after much
intrigue and importunity, the fine estate of Sherborne,
in Dorsetshire. The estate belonged to the See of
Salisbury, which had been vacant for three years,
having been twice refused because a condition was
attached to the acceptance, that Sherborne Castle was
to be surrendered. At length Ralegh got hold of a
pliant cleric named Coldwell, and gave the Queen a
jewel worth £250 to appoint him to the bishopric. No
sooner was Coldwell appointed than he leased Sherborne
to the crown for 99 years at a rent of £260, which
lease was almost immediately transferred to Ralegh.
This beautiful domain became henceforward for the
next ten years the best beloved abode of Ralegh and
his wife. Deep in his books, his mind full of vast
projects which should bring wealth to himself, and
honour to his country, he passed here much of the
three years following his so called disgrace; and
notwithstanding the heartbroken plaints contained
in the fragment of ' *Cynthia*,' written at the time,
to which reference has been made, it is questionable

whether this period was not really the happiest in his
life. His wife and he were devotedly attached to
each other and to their picturesque home; he had a
son born to him in 1594; and his building, planning
gardens, and planting copses, kept him busy whilst
there. His occupations away from Sherborne were
still numerous, and prevented him from rusting; if,
indeed, such a thing was possible to his keen mind.
He still discharged his important duties as Lord
Warden of the Stannaries, he was intensely absorbed
in his plans at Lismore, in the misgovernment of
Ireland, and in the pipe-stave enterprise on his Irish
estates; and his palace of Durham House was still
filled by his family and a splendid train of followers
at least once every year. While at Sherborne he
kept up a close correspondence with Sir Robert Cecil,
and other friends at Court; he generally had some
claim to forward, or some *protégé* to help; and despondent as his verses are with the perfunctory sorrow
considered becoming on such occasions, there is no
sign in his letters that Sir Walter had changed from
the keen, active, ambitious, brilliant gentleman he
had ever been; though doubtless his pride suffered at
the knowledge that, at last, his enemies at Court, who
for so long had scoffed at him as a 'jack,' a 'knave,'
and an 'upstart,' had prevailed over him. The one
thing they dreaded was that he should again obtain
access to the Queen, and permission to perform his
duties as captain of the guard. Sir Robert Cecil and

the old Lord Treasurer Burghley, against whom Essex was for ever railing, cautiously did what they could for Ralegh, and at one time, after his views on the severe suppression of disaffection in Ireland had been submitted to the Queen, it looked as if he might be recalled to Court and made a Privy Councillor.   One of Essex's friends wrote at this juncture, 'It is now feared of all honest men, that Sir Walter Ralegh shall presently come to Court, and yet it is well withstood. God grant him some further resistance; and that place he better deserveth, if he had his right.'

CHAPTER VIII

GUIANA—THE FIRST EXPEDITION THITHER

It must have become evident to Ralegh in his comparative seclusion, that if ever he was to regain his influence over the Queen it could only be done by some bold and successful action, which should completely throw his rivals into the shade. The vast plunder from the carrack had done something to rehabilitate his name; but it had not gained him access to the sovereign. As we have seen, the main idea which had run through all the actions of his life had been to prove the impotence of Spain upon the sea, and to assert the claims of England to a share in the territory of the new world. The lukewarmness of 'capitalist adventurers' in his Virginian plans had caused the comparative failure which had attended his efforts. The promptness of the colonists to abandon the settlements, and return to England, as soon as they understood that there was no opportunity of acquiring sudden wealth by plundering or discovering gold, had convinced Ralegh that mere extension of territory for England was a motive not powerful enough to unbutton the pocket of investors, accustomed to the great, if uncertain, profits of piracy, or to induce men to risk their bodies in the adventure. He himself had spent the enormous sum of £40,000 on the Virginian enterprise, but neither the Queen nor the bankers would risk a shilling, and it was clear that the promise of gaining of vast and sudden wealth must be held out as a bait in future ventures of the same sort. Ralegh's own ideas, moreover, were extremely lavish and extravagant. He never hoarded money, and though his revenues must have been very large, his expenditure was still larger. His train was as numerous and splendid as that of the greatest nobles in England, whilst the value of his own attire and adornments were incomparably more costly than any. His buildings at Lismore and Sherborne, his experiments in forestry, agriculture, and industry, were all expensive, and unless he was to fall off and become an admittedly decayed and discarded courtier, against which his pride rebelled, it was necessary that he should somehow obtain the control of vast wealth. If he could at the same time perform some brilliant service to the country and his sovereign, then all might be well, and Essex placed in the background.

He had always been a student of Spanish accounts of exploration and travel. He wanted to learn the methods by which the Spaniards had arrived at success, and the reasons why, in some places, they had failed. 'There was,' says Lloyd, 'not an expert soldier or seaman but he consulted, not a printed or manuscript discourse of navigation or war but he perused, nor were there exacter rules or principles for both services than he drew up; so contemplative was he, that you would think he was not active; so active that you would think he was not prudent.' By Ralegh's own remarks in the *History of the World* we know that he ascribed the success of the Spaniards to their dogged perseverance in the face of repeated failure, and to their sowing dissension amongst the various tribes of natives; whereas he attributes their failures to disunion and jealousy amongst themselves.

Gold and territory were therefore the talismans that in Ralegh's eyes were to restore him to the first place in Elizabeth's favour. He knew full well that, as she would not make a formal declaration of war, no permanent occupation of territory in which the Spaniards were established would be permitted, even if it had been possible, and the problem, for Ralegh, was to find a place in which Spain had no footing, and yet where the existence of gold in great quantities was notorious, as a bait for capitalists and adventurers. It is hard to see where Ralegh could cast eyes except upon what was called the great empire of Guiana, the mysterious virgin land of gold, which had for fifty years filled the credulous minds of men with dreams of wealth beyond human computation. Thousands of men, expedition after expedition, had set out to follow the glittering mirage, but it had always receded as they had advanced. Through dense tropical swamps, through trackless virgin forests, dark at noonday, over savage mountains and boundless savannahs, men had vainly sought the fabled city of burnished gold, on the brink of its inland sea. Pestilence and famine, savages and wild beasts, fatigue and accident, had stricken down the gold-seekers before they came within sight of the prize. Now and again a famished straggler came back, distraught perchance by his sufferings, with wondrous tales of the marvels his eyes had seen, or his ears had listened to, and the golden fables were sent on their rounds again, to inspire fresh expeditions and renewed sacrifice of human life. And yet, withal, in 1594 the great empire of Guiana was still virgin, awaiting the coming of its captor. Knowing what we do of Ralegh's character and circumstances, it is not wonderful that he was convinced that fate had reserved for him the honour of casting into his offended mistress's lap riches that should satisfy even her craving, and of endowing his country with an empire which should enable her to lower the pride of Spain.

Everyone in England had heard of the land that had come to be called El Dorado, 'the gilded.' Fable had been mixed with fact in such a way that the idea of where, or exactly what, it was must have been hazy, but the name was one that appealed to the imagination, and Englishmen were eager for further knowledge. The story went that one of the Inca princes of Peru, the kinsman of the murdered sovereign Atahualpa, had fled before the Spanish persecutors, across the Andes with some thousands of Peruvians and vast treasures, and had conquered the empire of Guiana, making himself Emperor, with his capital Manoa on a supposed inland sea 600 miles long, the whole empire extending from the Amazon to the upper Orinoco. There seemed nothing intrinsically improbable in these glowing stories to generations that had seen or heard of the sacking of Quito, Cuzco and Mexico; and Ralegh's anticipations as to the natural riches of Guiana itself, for which even Sir Robert Schomburgk thought it necessary to apologise, are now turning out to be well justified. There is not the slightest ground for the assumption that Ralegh deliberately invented the stories about the abounding gold in Guiana, as David Hume and others would infer. The stories told by those who had seen it seemed convincing enough. Robert Dudley, who went up the Orinoco shortly after Ralegh's first voyage, said that he had found gold, and that the natives had brought him plates of the metal. A Spanish soldier asserted on his death-bed that he had lived for seven months in

Manoa, which city was so large that it took him thirty hours to travel from the outskirts to the centre, and that when he departed the Emperor gave him as much gold as he and several carriers could convey. The Indians on the Orinoco were all anxious to send the greedy white men farther on, and ever farther on, with golden fables either out of the usual savage desire to surprise and delight their interlocutors, or else to save their own tribes from plunder. Ralegh must therefore be acquitted of a fraudulent desire to deceive. What he did was to place the getting of gold in the forefront of the enterprise, because he knew by experience that that was the only inducement which would lead men to take part in it.

The most recent attempt to open up Guiana had been made by Antonio de Berreo, who had married the daughter or niece of Hernan Perez de Quesada, who had attempted the task many years before, and was the founder and governor of the kingdom of New Granada. He, Berreo, told Ralegh that he had spent 300,000 ducats on his expeditions. He had started from New Granada with 700 horsemen, 1000 oxen and many Indians, and travelled 1500 miles before he could get within touch of Guiana. He appears to have gone down the Rio Negro into the Orinoco, down which river he also went, but for a whole year could hear no tidings of the great empire of Guiana, his company meanwhile dwindling fearfully with sickness and the attacks of the Indians. At last he came to a country called Amapaia, where, after much fighting and many months of residence, he obtained news of Guiana from the natives, and acquired ten images of fine gold, plates, crescents, etc., 'which, as he swore to me and divers other gentlemen, were so curiously wrought, as he had not seen the like in Italy, Spain, or the Low Countries.' These he sent by his colonel, Domingo de Vera, to Philip II. After many fruitless attempts to reach Guiana, of which he heard much from an aged river chief called Carapana, Berreo, with the few survivors left to him, was forced to go down the river to Trinidad ; of which island he was made Governor. From there he kept up his attempts to obtain communication with Guiana, and as a preliminary to a systematic attempt at conquest, took possession of the River Orinoco for the King of Spain in April 1593. With the encouragement and help of the home government he was preparing for fitting out a strong new expedition for annexing Guiana to Spain, at the same time that Ralegh had determined, if possible, to capture it for England.

Ralegh's project for a great expedition to Guiana met with opposition from many quarters. He had powerful enemies, and his character did not stand high amongst the people at large. There were persistent rumours that he was either going on a piratical expedition, or else to offer his services to Spain in revenge for his disgrace, and adventurers still fought shy of embarking in his risky enterprises.

His devoted wife, moreover, woman-like, was full of forebodings, and sought to divert his mind from the project. There is a curious letter at Hatfield from her to Sir Robert Cecil (8th February 1594) begging him to dissuade Ralegh from the Guiana enterprise. The orthography is so curious that, as a specimen, it may be given as written by Lady Ralegh. 'Now Sur, for the rest I hope for my sake you will rather draw Sur Watar towardes the est, then heulp hyme forward toward the soonsett, if ani respecke to me or love to him be not forgotten. But everi monthe hath its flower and everi season his contentment, and you greate counselares are so full of new councels, as you ar steddi in nothing, but wee poore soules that hath bought sorrow at a high price desiar, and can be pleased with the same misfortun wee hold, fering alltarracions will but multiply misseri, of wich we have allredi felt sufficiant. I knoo truly your parswadcions ar of efecke with hyme and hild as orrekeles tied to them by Love ; therfore I humbelle besiech you rathar stay hyme then furdar hyme. By the wich you shall bind me for ever.'

During his preparations also other mariners with small forces thought they could forestall him. In a letter to Cecil at the end of December 1594, he urges that an embargo should be placed on shipping. 'For if Eaton's shipps go, who will attempt the chiefest places of my enterprise ? I shall be undun ; and I know they will be beaten and do no good. From

Alresford this Saturday after I left you with a hart half broken.'

As a preliminary to his own expedition, Ralegh sent his old captain, Jacob Whiddon, in 1594, to reconnoitre the delta and entrances of the Orinoco. Whiddon seems to have been a brave, simple-minded sailor, who was beguiled by Berreo, Governor of Trinidad, into giving him a full account of Ralegh's intentions, and he returned home at the end of the year with vague rumours of the golden wonders of Guiana, but with but little topographical information.

On the 6th February 1595, Ralegh sailed out of Plymouth, his expedition consisting of five ships and some boats for river exploration. The list of officers who were to accompany him, as given by Ralegh himself, mentions Captain George Gifford as second in command, with Captains Caulfield, Amiotts Preston, Thynne, Laurence Kemys, Eynos, Whiddon, Clarke, Cross, and Facy; but in the account of the voyage, he says that Howard's ship, the *Lion's Whelp*, and Captain Amiotts Preston's ships failed to join them, and were left behind. Amongst other gentlemen present there seem to have been 'my cousin Butshead Gorges, my nephew John Gilbert, and my cousin Grenville.' Altogether it is stated that there were a hundred men in the expedition, exclusive of the mariners, and from the letter above quoted from Ralegh to Cecil (December 1594) he appears to have again employed the whole of his resources in the preparations. He had obtained a royal patent, addressed drily to 'our servant Sir Walter Ralegh,' authorising him to 'offend and enfeeble the King of Spain, and to discover and subdue heathen lands not in possession of any Christian prince, or inhabited by any Christian people, and to resist and expel any persons who should attempt to settle within 200 leagues of the place he fixed upon for the settlement.'

By the time he arrived at Trinidad, 22nd March, the only ships he had were his own vessel and a small bark of Captain Cross's. With these he remained five days off point Curiapan, the south-west point of Trinidad, now called Hicacos, but could gain no speech of the natives, who were in fear of the Spaniards. Ralegh himself, in his barge, coasted close in shore, surveying every cove and harbour, and describes oysters growing on the mangrove trees, and the great pitch lake of Trinidad, familiar now to all travellers, but then new and marvellous. At what is now called Port of Spain, Ralegh found his missing ships; and a party of Spaniards drawn up on the shore. The latter made signs of amity and of a desire to trade, 'more for doubt of their own strength than for aught else'; and Captain Whiddon was sent on shore to parley with them. After dusk a small Indian canoe stole alongside Ralegh's ship with a chief and another man on board, who had known Whiddon on his former voyage, and desired to give the Englishmen information of the strength and whereabouts of the Spaniards, and especially of the Governor Berreo. The Spaniards, however, who visited Ralegh's ships for trade, or out of curiosity were hospitably received, and from them much knowledge was gained of Guiana. 'For these poor soldiers having been many years without wine a few draughts made them merry, in which mood they vaunted of Guiana, and of the riches thereof, but I bred in them an opinion that I was bound only for the relief of those English which I had planted in Virginia.' On the occasion of Whiddon's previous voyage, Governor Berreo had, it was said, treacherously enticed eight of his men ashore and murdered them, and Ralegh had determined to avenge this injury.   He now learned from a friendly Indian spy that Berreo had sent to Margarita and Cumana for some more soldiers to surprise the expedition. The Indians, moreover, stole on board every night with hideous stories of the tortures Berreo was inflicting upon them. 'So as both to be revenged of the former wrong, as also considering that to enter Guiana by small boats, to depart 400 or 500 miles from my ships, and to leave a garrison at my back interested in the same enterprise who also daily expected supplies out of Spain, I should have savoured very much of the ass ; and therefore taking a time of most advantage, I set upon the *Corps de Garde* in the evening, and having put them to the sword, sent

Captain Caulfield with 60 soldiers, and myself
followed with 40 more, and so took their new city
of San Joseph by break of day; they abode not any
fight, after a few shot, and all being dismissed but
only Berreo and his companion, I brought them with
me aboard, and at the instance of the Indians I set
their new city of San Joseph on fire.' It would
perhaps be unjust to judge this entirely unprovoked
slaughter of Spaniards by the standard of morality
existing in our own day, but it will be readily understood that the fact would be treasured up in the minds
of their countrymen, as was the capture of the great
carrack, and that when Spain had an opportunity of
injuring Ralegh it was quite natural that revenge
should be indulged in to the utmost.   Before Ralegh
left Trinidad, carrying Berreo with him, he assembled
the Indians and told them that he was 'the servant of
a Queen who was the great cacique of the north and
a virgin, who had more caciques under her than there
were trees in the island, that she was an enemy of the
Castellanos in respect of their tyranny and oppression,
and that she delivered all such nations about her as
were by them oppressed, and having freed all the
coast of the northern world from their servitude had
sent me to free them also, and withal to defend the
country of Guiana from their invasion and conquest.
I showed them Her Majesty's picture, which they so
much admired and honoured as it had been easy to
have brought them idolatrous thereof.   The like and

more large discourse I made to the rest of the nations
both in my passing to Guiana and to those of the
borders, so as in that part of the world Her Majesty is
very famous and admirable.'

Berreo made the best of matters, and gave Ralegh
much information about Guiana, amongst other things
that it was 600 miles further from the sea than
Whiddon had reported; a fact which was carefully
concealed from the men on the expedition, 'who
else would never have been brought to attempt the
same.'

The *Lion's Whelp*, and Captain Kemys's ship, which
had been lost sight of early in the voyage, having
joined, and the expedition being complete, except
for Preston's vessel, preparations were made for the
river voyage.   Ralegh thought that if Preston had
come, and they had entered the river ten days earlier,
before the floods, they might have reached Manoa,
or near it.   He was convinced, he said, that 'whatsoever prince shall possess it (Guiana) he shall be
lord of more gold and a more beautiful empire, and
of more cities and people than either the King of
Spain or the great Turk.'

The ships were left at anchor in the Gulf of
Paria, and the main exploring party embarked in
an old 'gallego, which I caused to be fashioned like
a galley, and in one barge, two wherries and a ship's
boat of the *Lion's Whelp* we carried 100 persons and
their victuals for a month in the same, being all

driven to lie in the rain and weather in the open
air, in the burning sun, and upon hard boards, and
to dress our meat, and to carry all manner of furniture
in them, wherewith they were so pestered and unsavoury, that, what with victuals being most fish, with
the wet clothes of so many men thrust together and
the heat of the sun, I will undertake there was never
any prison in England that could be found more
unsavoury and loathsome, especially to myself, who
had for many years before been dieted and cared for
in a sort far differing.'

Before Ralegh started he had obtained from Berreo,
and from the Indians that could give information,
such particulars as would guide him in his search
for the golden city.   It might be reached, it was
said, from the point on the Orinoco belonging to
the aged King Carapana, or from another point
higher up called Morequito, where an expedition previously sent by Berreo had been murdered, except
one man, after approaching the confines of Guiana.
Plates and crescents of gold, we are told, were possessed in great quantities by the Indians all along the
coasts, and even up the Amazon—obtained by trading
with the Guianans; and the oft-told stories of the
men who covered their naked bodies with gold dust
during their drunken orgies, and of the riches, in
comparison with which the treasures of Peru were
insignificant, were all set forth again to the delight
of the English explorers, eager now to start on

their quest. When Berreo learnt that Ralegh's object after all was to take possession of the golden land for England, 'he was stricken with great melancholy and sadness, and used all the arguments he could to dissuade me, and also assured the gentlemen of my company that it would be labour lost; and that they should suffer many miseries if they proceeded.' No entrance, he said, could be obtained by the rivers, which were full of shoals; no Indians would approach the English, but would fly before them; the way was long, the winter at hand, the floods near; and all the chiefs on the borders of Guiana had decreed that no trade for gold should be carried on with Christians. This, and much else of the same sort, failed to move Ralegh, who had gone too far to recede, and was in higher hope now than ever.

An unsuccessful attempt having been made to enter with the ships various branches of the Orinoco, Ralegh determined to trust entirely to the poor boats already described. In a heavy sea they crossed the bay of Guanipa, opposite Trinidad, and entered a river which ran into it. Their pilot was an Indian called Ferdinando from the River Barima, south of the Orinoco, who knew but little of the intricate network of rivers on the north of the delta, 'and if God had not sent us another help we might have wandered a whole year in that labyrinth of rivers ere we had found any way out or in. All the rivers and islands, he says, are

alike, bordered with huge trees ; and for many days
they wandered backwards and forwards hopelessly
astray ; until at last, in a river which Ralegh calls ' Red
Cross River,' on the 22nd May, they providentially
fell in with and captured a canoe with three Indians.
' The rest of the people, shadowed under the thick
wood on the bank, watched in doubtful conceit what
might befall those three we had taken. But when
they saw we offered them no violence . . . they offered
to traffic with us for such things as they had . . .
and we came with our barge to the mouth of a little
creek, which came from their town into the great
river.' The Indian pilot and his brother who went on
shore had a near escape from death as a punishment
for bringing a strange people thither, and in reprisal
Ralegh seized a very old man of the tribe, and forced
him to guide them into the great Orinoco. A good
description is given by Ralegh of the Indians of the
delta, whom he calls Tivitivas, ' a very goodly people and
very valiant, and have the most manly speech that ever
I heard.' They lived, it appears, on the ground in the
summer, and in houses built in the trees when the floods
of the Orinoco drowned their islands every winter.*

* In Captain Thompson's map of the coast of Guiana, 1783, the
north of the delta of the Orinoco traversed by Ralegh is thus described :
' Orinoko islands, covered with palm trees, and overflowed from the
end of January to the middle of July. Inhabited by Guaraunas or
Tivitivas, whose houses are built on piles or among the branches of the
trees.' This description, it will be observed, exactly confirms that given
by Ralegh. Thompson's map has been reprinted by the English Gover-
ment in the supplement to the Venezuelan Blue Book.

'They never eat anything that is set or sown,
but only that which Nature without labour
bringeth forth.   They use the tops of palmitas for
bread, and kill deer, fish and pork for the rest of their
sustenance.'   On the third day after leaving the Indian
town, Ralegh's boats ran aground, 'stuck so fast, as
we thought, that our discovery had ended there, and
that we must have left sixty of our men to have
inhabited like rooks upon the trees with these nations.'
The shoals and rapids were a constant danger to them,
the dense forests on the banks shut them out from air
and prospect, and in the heat and gloom of the apparently endless network of streams, the spirits of the men
sank lower and lower.   Then, when they at length
reached a wider river, the Amana (Manamo), the ebb
and flow of tides abandoned them, and all day they
had to struggle against the rapid current, 'or to return
as wise as we went out.'   The men were assured every
day that two or three days more would bring them
to their destination ; and the gentlemen, to encourage
them, shared their spells at the oar.   At last the
companies began to despair, food ran short, the air
bred faintness, the work was hard.   The pilots were
ordered to assure the men that every reach of the river
was the last before the destination, where food in plenty
would be found, whereas to return meant starvation.
The gorgeous tropical birds and flowers, even the
luscious fruits, had ceased to attract the weary rowers,
when the old pilot suggested that the galley should be

anchored in the stream, and the other boats ascend a
branch, where, he said, there was a village of Araucan
Indians from whom food could be obtained.   He
assured Ralegh that they could return to the galley
before night, and the suggestion was joyfully adopted.
But hour after hour passed and the promised town did
not appear, until, as night came on, the English were
convinced that they were being betrayed.   The pilot
assured them that the place was only four reaches
farther, but four, and another four, having been
passed, 'our poor watermen even, heartbroken and
tired, were ready to give up the ghost, for we had
now come from the galley near 40 miles'; and it was
decided to hang the pilot.   But then came the thought
that they should never find their way back without him.   The river was so narrow and the vegetation
so thick, that they had to hew their way through with
their swords; it was eight o'clock at night, pitch dark,
and their stomachs were empty, and yet the poor
old Indian kept urging them to row just one reach
farther.   At last at one o'clock in the morning they
reached the village, where after a night's rest they
obtained food and returned to the galley.   As they
came down the river by daylight with lighter hearts
now, they saw that the country around them had
changed.   There were no more dense darkling woods
such as for weeks past had closed them in, but flat rolling
savannahs, as far as the eye reached.   Fine short grass
fed great flocks of deer as tame as if in an English park,

thick flights of birds hovered over the banks, and vast
quantities of fish inhabited the river.   What most
struck the explorers, however, was the enormous
number of alligators, one of which, at the mouth of
the river, devoured Ralegh's negro servant.   In a few
days their provisions were once more exhausted, when
they espied four canoes coming down the river.   Two
of the canoes in despair ran ashore, and the men in
them escaped, but the boats were full of cassava bread
bound for Margarita, to be bartered to the Spaniards.
In the small canoes that escaped were several Spaniards,
who were apprised of Ralegh's treatment of their
countrymen in Trinidad, and were trying to get away.
The capture of the bread raised the Englishmen's spirits.
'Let us go on! we care not how far,' they cried.   But
more important still, Ralegh, whilst groping about the
underwood on the banks in search of the canoes that
had escaped, discovered a basket containing quicksilver,
saltpetre, and a gold refiner's outfit, and some gold dust.
Some of the Indians that had been taken said that the
small canoes contained much gold, and Ralegh offered
£500 reward for the capture of the three Spaniards, but
without result.   The chief of the Indians was employed
as a pilot and guide, to show him where the Spaniards
had laboured for gold, 'though I made not the same
known to all.'   Tools were required for gold mining,
and tools they had none.   It was considered imprudent to stay long in the neighbourhood of the gold
country, for fear that the crews might mark the spot

their knowledge as soon as they reached a country : 'and all our care taken for good usage of the people been utterly lost by those that only respect present profit.' When Ralegh reached home, he was blamed for not bringing at least a small quantity of ore from the place, but he defended himself in his narrative by pointing out that the river was rising and the currents violent; he had been over a month away from his ships, now 400 miles distant, 'and to stay to dig out gold with our nails had been *opus laboris* but not *ingenii*'; besides which no sufficient quantity of ore could be obtained without the situation of the mines being made known.

Things were looking brighter now. The Indians were propitiated, and promised protection against the injustice and cruelty of the Spaniards; the former pilots were sent away rejoicing with letters to the ships in one of the captured canoes, and the new pilot and guide, the Araucan Indian Martin, installed in their place. After much hardship, on the fifteenth day, the eyes of the explorers were gladdened by the sight of what their guide told them were the mountains of Guiana, and in the early evening they glided, to their great joy, into the main stream of the Orinoco.

Ralegh must have reached the main river by the Manamo, and emerged opposite the island of Tortola, the ranges described as the mountains of Guiana being the Sierra de Piacoa and the Sierra

de Imataca.   They anchored that night nd vast
spot now called Barrancas, and the next ᴸmost
border chief called Toparimaca came down to see
the white men with many followers and presents
of food.   Wherever Ralegh had come within speaking distance of the natives, he had impressed upon
them that he came to deliver them from the
cruelty and oppression of the Spaniards, and
consequently was warmly welcomed.   He was,
moreover, throughout the voyage most careful to
prevent the slightest depredation or molestation of
the Indians by his men, especially in the matter of
native women, who, Ralegh says, were very beautiful, and the ill-treatment of whom by the Spaniards
was a fertile source of irritation.   Toparimaca led
the white men to his town hard by, 'where some of
our captains caroused of his wine till they were
reasonably pleasant, for it is very strong with pepper
and the juice of divers herbs and fruits digested
and purged; they keep it in great earthen pots of
ten or twelve gallons, very clean and sweet, and
are themselves at their meetings and feasts the
greatest carousers and drunkards in the world.'   Leaving here, the expedition passed the island of Tortola,
which Ralegh calls by the native name of Assapana,
and came to anchor at a place which was understood
to be one of the principal entrances to the empire
of Guiana.   The province had been ruled by a
great border chief called Morequito, whose name

it bore as well as Aromaia, but Morequito himself
having been killed by Berreo, in revenge for the
murder of a Spanish expedition, had at the time of
Ralegh's visit been succeeded by Topiawari. Two
Guianans, who had been staying in Toparimaca's
town, were sent forward by Ralegh to a vassal chief of
Topiawari to give notice of his coming, and the next
few days were passed by the Englishmen rowing west-
ward whilst exploring the river and neighbouring
islands, feasting sumptuously the while on turtle eggs,
which they found in abundance on the sands. The
banks rose high, with a blue metallic lustre, which
Ralegh thought was owing to the presence of steel,
and on the north stretched the great plains of Sayma,
far away over the delta towards Venezuela. They
had continued to row gradually up the river until
the sixth day, when they anchored at the port
of Aromaia, the country of Morequito, and on the
following day there came to welcome the white
men the King Topiawari, the uncle of the dead
Morequito. The old chieftain was 110 years old,
and had walked the 28 miles from his town to
the port, with presents of flesh, fish, fowl, pine-
apples—the 'princess of fruits,' says Ralegh—and
much else. Ralegh was gracious and bounteous,
giving full value for everything he received ; he
had come, he said, to deliver the Indians from Spanish
tyranny, his Queen being greater and more powerful
than the King of Spain. The old chief had himself

been the captive of the Spaniards, led by a chain, and had bought his liberty with a hundred plates of gold, so that he listened eagerly to promises of vengeance. The site of the port must have been on the south bank of the river, shortly below the mouth of the Caroni, for the roaring of the falls was audible therefrom; and after much discourse with the ancient chief, in which direct knowledge of Guiana was gained, Ralegh started to explore the interior by the great river Caroni. They thought to have ascended it 40 miles, but so tremendous was the current, though the river was as broad as the Thames at Woolwich, that an eight-oared barge could not gain a stone's cast in an hour, so the attempt had to be abandoned. At last, Ralegh was in touch with the fabled Guiana. Topiawari had told him that his nation, and all those between the river bank and the mountains behind were Guianans, but 'that long, long ago there came a nation from so far off as the sun slept, with so great a multitude as could not be numbered or resisted, who had slain and rooted out as many of the ancient people as there were leaves on the trees, and had made themselves lords of all.' They wore hats and red coats, he said, and lived in houses of many rooms; they had built on the border of their great plain a strong city called Macureguarai, at the foot of a high mountain, and here 3000 soldiers were kept to defend their country. Since the advent of the Spaniards, how-

ever, the Guianans and border people had become
peaceful, and made common cause; except certain
tribes on the Caroni. It was now Ralegh's policy
to reach these inimical tribes, and he sent from
the mouth of the river native messengers in all
directions to call them to a conference with the
enemies of the Spaniards. The chiefs told him of
powerful nations up the river, who were enemies
of both the Spaniards and the Guianans, and who
would help him to cross the mountains, and conquer
the land, 'where we should satisfy ourselves with
gold and all other good things.' In the meanwhile
the floods were coming, and it behoved the boats
to get away; but it was necessary to take something back beyond Indian promises to satisfy the
'adventurers' in England. A Spanish captain, whom
Ralegh had taken at Trinidad, told him of a great
silver mine on the banks of the Caroni, and an
expedition of five officers and thirty men was sent
on foot to explore it, and, if possible, to push
forward to the neighbourhood of the frontier town
of Guiana, whilst Ralegh and a few followers marched
overland to view the strange Falls of Caroni, and the
plains beyond. From a hill several miles off, he says,
there were visible 'ten or twelve overfalls, everyone
as high over the other as a church tower, with that
fury that the rebound of waters made it seem as if
all covered with a great shower of rain.' Ralegh
says he was but a poor footman, and would have been

content with a distant view, but his companions drew him on little by little. The country he describes in glowing words. 'The plains without bush or stubble, all fair green grass, the deer crossing every path, the birds towards evening singing on every tree, with a thousand several tunes; cranes and herons of white, crimson and carnation, perched on the riverside; the air fresh with a gentle easterly wind, and every stone we stooped to take up promising either gold or silver by his complexion.' Many specimens were taken home, 'and yet we had no means, but with our daggers and fingers, to tear them out here and there,' but want of knowledge led to the taking of much glittering stuff, which was worthless marcasite and the like. Crystals of various sorts, and many samples of auriferous quartz, were brought to the boats. Ralegh says that he saw great ledges and hills of this 'white spar' everywhere in the neighbourhood. 'Of this there hath been made trials. In London it was first assayed by Master Westwood, a refiner dwelling in Wood Street, and it held after a rate of £120 or £130 per ton. Another sort was afterwards tried by Master Palmer and Master Dimoke, assay masters, and it held after the rate of £230 per ton. There was some of it again tried by Master Palmer, Controller of the Mint, and Master Dimoke in Goldsmith's Hall, and it held after the rate of £269 per ton.'

It was time now for Ralegh to return to the ships.

The swift torrent of the already flooded Orinoco
swept his boats towards the sea without labour at a
tremendous rate, even against the wind. He called in
again at the port of Morequito, or Aromaia, to see the
centenarian King Topiawari. Once more the English
sailors were gladdened with plentiful and dainty food ;
for Topiawari loaded them with provender. Ralegh
took the King apart and begged him to tell him as
a friend of his nation how he should reach the rich
and civilised regions of Guiana. Topiawari answered
that neither the time of year nor the number of his
forces were fit for an expedition to Manoa ; and
although he, Topiawari, could never hope to look
upon his face again, he warned him that the Inca
Emperor was so strong that it would be folly to
attempt to invade Guiana without a large force and
the co-operation of the inimical border tribes. The
old King begged Ralegh to leave fifty soldiers with
him until his return, but this was impossible, although
Caulfield, Grenville and young Gilbert begged to be
allowed to stay, for Berreo would be sure to come up
the river as soon as possible, and 'I knew,' says
Ralegh, 'he would use the same measure towards
mine that I offered them at Trinidad.' The old
chief, somewhat offended at this refusal, said that as
soon as Ralegh was gone the Guianans would invade
his country, and that the Spaniards also would attack
him ; for they had already baptized and dressed a
member of his family whom they called Don Juan,

and had set him up as a claimant for the throne.   He
therefore begged Ralegh to avoid all further conference with him for that year, though his followers
were anxious for the English to return, and promised
to help them to fight the Guianans and recover the
women they had stolen from them, for they cared
nothing for their gold.   After much consideration it
was decided not to attempt to attack the Guianan
border town that year, but to return with a larger
force; and Topiawari gave Ralegh his only son,
whom they christened Gualtero, to bring to England.
Two Englishmen, Francis Sparry, a servant of Captain
Gifford, who could describe a country with his pen,
and a boy named Goodwin were left behind at their
own request to learn the language; and the former,
if possible, to reach the border town to trade and
observe.   Ralegh then turned his boats towards the
east, and swiftly sped down the river. With much
cunning he had concealed from the credulous Indians
all desire to obtain gold, or dominion over them; or
otherwise, he says, they would think there was little
to choose between the Spaniards and the English; and
he had given 'many gold pieces of the new money of
20s. with Her Majesty's picture for them to wear' more
than he had received value for.   He had, indeed, quite
won the hearts of the simple people, who, long after
he was in the grave, looked for his promised coming
to free them from the cruelty of the Spaniards.   There
went with them from Aromaia a chief called Putijama,

who prevailed upon them to call in at his port some
way down the river, where he told them he would
show them a mountain of stones the colour of gold.
Wherever Ralegh looked he saw assurance of gold.
Auriferous quartz and matrix were scattered on all
the hillsides : plates and ornaments of gold, smelted
from alluvial nuggets and dust, he was told, were
common, though he pretended not to regard them ;
and he felt now that, at last, the golden empire of
Guiana might be had for the grasping.   Ralegh, with
others, started on foot to visit Putijama's gold mine
at Mount Iconuri, apparently near the subsequent site
of Guayana Vieja (old Guiana), but Sir Walter, after
a day's march, gave up the quest, and sent Captain
Kemys instead, with instructions to rejoin him lower
down the river, at the town of a great chief called
Carapana.   From afar off Ralegh says he saw the
great crystal mountain 'like a white church tower of
exceeding height, with a mighty river falling sheer
over it with a terrible noise and clamour, as if 1000
great bells were knocking against another.'

Carapana the chief had fled for fear of them, but
his people were reassured by the English ; and finally,
after much danger and many adventures, Kemys rejoined his leader, and the whole party reached the ships
lying in the Gulf of Paria without losing a man, except the young negro devoured by alligators.

Ralegh's intention had been to call and succour his
colonists on the island of Roanoak, but westerly winds

drove him from the coast and prevented him.   On his way home he called at Cumana, at Santa Maria, and at Rio de la Hacha, Spanish settlements on the Venezuelan coast, to buy provisions.   They were refused him—perhaps naturally—and he retorted by burning and sacking the settlements, though, he says, he found no treasure in any of them.   Touching at the island of Cuba on his way, he arrived home in England in August, having been absent nearly seven months.

CHAPTER IX

THE one thing that could have rehabilitated Ralegh in the eyes of the world was that he should have returned to England loaded with wealth, and it is somewhat difficult to understand the slight attempts he made to obtain any treasure which might give a show of return for the capital that he and his friends had employed in the enterprise. It is true that he explains it as a matter of policy to gain the Indians, by assuming a complete disinterestedness; but he must have known that without some tangible result of his voyage it would be difficult to enlist capitalists in the further exploration of the golden empire; and the neglect of such obvious precautions as the taking of proper boats for river exploration, a few mining tools, and materials for assaying metals, seems to indicate

169

a lack of practical organising power or foresight, which
was even more conspicuous in his subsequent voyage.
Ralegh arrived home at a time when the English
adventurers were out of heart, and the marvellous
stories of Guiana were received coldly and derisively.
The tales of a nation of men with their faces in their
breasts, of the savage Amazonian women, of the
golden palaces of the Incas, and the diamond mountain,
were sneered at by Ralegh's enemies as so many old
wives' tales.   They said that the ore brought was not
from Guiana at all, but from Africa; that he himself
had been hiding in Cornwall, and had not gone with
the expedition.   Ralegh's answer was the publication
of his vivid *Discoverie of Guiana,* from which the
above particulars of the voyage have been taken.   In
it he vigorously defends himself against his detractors.
In his dedication of the narrative to his principal supporters, Lord Admiral Howard and Sir Robert Cecil,
he indignantly denies that he has been hiding in
Cornwall or elsewhere, or that he had ever intended
to become a servant of the King of Spain ; 'and the
rest were much mistaken who would have persuaded
that I was too easeful and sensual to undertake a
journey of so great travail.   For myself, I have
deserved no thanks, for I am returned a beggar, and
withered ; but that I might have bettered my poor
estate, it shall appear by the following discourse if
I had not respected only Her Majesty's future honour
and riches '; but he says it would ill have become

the honourable offices he held to run from cape to
cape in search of prizes. To those who said that he
had only brought marcasite from the Orinoco, and
that the other ore was from Africa, he replied, 'Surely
the singularity of that device I do not well compre-
hend; for my own part, I am not so much in love
with these long voyages as to devise thereby to
cozen myself, to lie hard, to fare worse, to be subject
to perils, to diseases, to ill savours, to be parched and
withered, and withal to sustain the care and labour
of such an enterprise, except the same had more
comfort than the fetching of marcasite in Guiana or
buying of gold ore in Barbary.'

But for all his eloquent pleading, the capitalists, and
even the Queen, remained cold. His friend Cecil,
who got no return for his capital, was dubious, and
thought Ralegh over sanguine. When it became
evident that the money for a great expedition to
conquer the empire of Guiana for England could not
be obtained, Ralegh advocated another policy. He
drew up a plan, not for conquering the Inca, but for
entering into alliance with him against the Spaniards,
and making him a tributary to England. He proposed
to arm the natives, and with the assistance of 400 or
500 men from England, including armourers, artificers
etc., to keep the Spaniard busy, who 'would not threaten
us with any more invincible Armadas.' The Incas
should be encouraged to attack the Spaniards in Peru ;
they should be shown how rich and powerful England

was, should be introduced to our commodities; a certain number of them every year should be brought to England to educate and civilise, married to English women, and sent back to instruct their fellows. It was proposed 'that they should pay a tribute, and assign to the crown some rich mines, and rivers of gold, pearls, silver, rocks of precious stones, with some large fruitful countries for the planting of colonies of Englishmen.' Ralegh had no doubt, he said, that after the country had been colonised for a year or two, he should see in London 'a contraction house of more receipt for Guiana than that of Seville for the West Indies.'

'The object of the voyage to Guiana,' he says, 'is to subdue and annex it to the crowne imperiall of this Realme of England,' and he proceeds to show that the enterprise would be honourable, profitable, necessary, and cheap. 'The Queen's dominions may be exceedingly enlarged, and this realm of England inestimably enriched.' But though Elizabeth was willing enough to be inestimably enriched by the efforts and expenditure of others, not a ship nor a ducat would she contribute herself.

The Spanish government, slow as it usually was, did not take the matter so coolly. The slaughter at Trinidad and the kidnapping of Governor Berreo had aroused much indignation, and immediate attempts were made to forestall Ralegh's return to Orinoco. Berreo had been landed at Cumana, a settlement on the Venezuelan mainland, Trinidad being left entirely in the hands of the Indians. Soon after Ralegh's departure there arrived Colonel de Vera, whom Berreo had sent to Spain with the golden images obtained from Guiana, and the wonderful stories the Spanish expedition had heard of the wealth of the interior. De Vera had managed to enlist the interest both of the Spanish Government and the merchants of Seville, and returned with a formidable expedition of five or six ships and 2000 men, for the purpose of taking possession of Guiana. In the meanwhile, the Governor of Cumana, Roque de Montes, on hearing Berreo's tale of Ralegh's attack, sent Captain Felipe de Santiago to fix a new Spanish settlement in Trinidad, and then to go up the Orinoco, and report upon the best sites on the river for the establishment of Spanish forts. His reports to his chief, and those of the latter to the King of Spain, are now in the Archives of the Indies at Seville; and prove how jealous the Spanish Government was of Ralegh's attempt to establish the English power in the region. Writing on the 2nd November 1595, describing the mouths of the Orinoco, he says, 'There is another mouth called the Manamo, by which it is known that the Englishman, Guaterral (*i.e.*, Walter Ralegh), entered the Orinoco in the present year 1595, after having caused much trouble and injury to the Isle of Trinidad and its inhabitants. He left two young Englishmen in the Orinoco for the purpose of learning the language and obtaining all information of the country, for on his departure it is said he left with the intention of returning hither.' The report of this captain (De Santiago) with regard to the wealth of Guiana in gold is more glowing even than that of Ralegh, though he says that the Indians 'are very watchful, and always endeavour to conceal it for fear of the Spaniards, whom they fear and dislike, and much dread they may settle there.' He recommends the establishment of the first Spanish post about six miles above Morequito's town, not far from the mouth of the Caroni, the place apparently where subsequently the *original* town of San Thomé stood. It will be necessary to bear well in mind the exact position of this post, as the final accusations against Ralegh largely turned upon the question. The Governor of Cumana, a few months afterwards, writing to the King, says, 'I also instructed him (De Santiago) to apprehend two Englishmen whom Guaterral left there last year, 1595, with the intention of returning, and settling it, for the purpose of their becoming acquainted with the country and its best sites, and learning the language of the natives. I also instructed the captain to advise the chiefs of Indians on the bank not to receive any strangers in their territories, except Spaniards in Your Majesty's service.' It appears from the Governor's report that Santiago had captured in Morequito's country the man Francis Sparry, and had learnt that the other lad had been devoured by a tiger.*   This latter was not the case, as Ralegh's second expedition in 1617 found the lad Goodwin, though he had almost forgotten his own language. Sparry was kept prisoner by the Spaniards until 1602, when he returned to England, and gave a glowing account, quoted by Purchas, of the abundance of auriferous quartz in the country.

On his way up the Orinoco, Santiago met Berreo with the new Spanish expedition ; and they immediately came to loggerheads about the resettling of Trinidad. Berreo said that he had been appointed Governor of the island by the King, and the Governor of Cumana had no business to interfere, but it was eventually decided that Santiago should return to Trinidad and build the new settlement, whilst Berreo remained on the Orinoco.   The Governor writes then to the King, 'It is of the utmost importance to Your Majesty's service that the banks of the Orinoco should be settled, and I have considered well to push the matter forward, and in like manner the navigation for trade, both to New Granada and Trinidad, up and down the river.   Particularly is this matter important for the conquest and settle-

---

* Oldys must have gathered the information that Goodwin had been devoured by a tiger from Spanish sources. Recent writers on the subject express curiosity as to where he could have obtained it, but we see by the above letter that the intelligence was sent to the King of Spain, and was doubtless current amongst Spaniards. The tale was evidently invented by the Indians to prevent the capture of Goodwin by Captain de Santiago.

ment of the provinces of Guiana, Caura and El
Dorado; for this is the entry and road to attain
that which those provinces give promise of. Thus
no opportunity will be given to the enemy of settling
it, nor will they have any entry to it by any other
way, for according to the intention of Guaterral,
who surveyed the whole of it last year, he will keep
his promise and fulfil his bad purpose.'

This was written in April 1596. Poor 'Guaterral,'
in the meanwhile, had been almost in despair. He
knew that Berreo, with the new expedition, had
gone up the Orinoco as soon as he had left it;
and he had prayed and besought in vain that
England should not forego the possession of the
rich empire which he held before her. Cecil and
Howard were incessantly importuned, but with all
his efforts he could do no more than fit out two
ships, the *Darling* and the *Discovery*, under Captain
Kemys, laden with 'merchandise to comfort and
assure the Indians,' and persuade them not to make
any arrangement with the Spaniards. If he could
keep them free, he thought, perhaps the eyes and
pockets of England might be opened by his persuasion, and the rich prize fall to his country after
all. Practically all the cost of the expedition was
defrayed by Ralegh and the Cecils, Lord Burghley
contributing £500, and Sir Robert a fully furnished
ship. Kemys left Portland on the 26th January
1596. When he arrived in the Orinoco, he found, as

he says, that Berreo had got the start of him, and
had established the post shortly beyond Morequito
or Topiawari's town, and below the mouth of the
Caroni, a rocky islet in mid-stream having been
made into a fort of refuge in case of need. Kemys
anchored within musket shot of the town, and
learnt that the Spaniards were lying in ambush at
the mouth of the stream, 'to defend the passage to
the mines whence the ore came from last year.'   An
Indian spy in friendly guise came on board and
attempted to frighten the English by exaggerating
the Spanish strength, but at last confessed that
Berreo had only fifty men with him, who had
taken refuge in the woods. Topiawari, he said, was
dead, though this was untrue, and the Indians had
fled and dispersed. Topiawari's son, Gualtero, now
in England, was consequently King of the tribe,
and his people were being led in his absence by
Putijama, who had taken refuge near Mount Aio,
where he had shown Kemys the rich mine in
the previous year. The expedition consequently
dropped down the river again to Putijama's town,
but found the Indians had fled. One that was left
offered to lead Kemys to a very rich mine in a
mountain 15 miles off, so rich that it had
been jealously kept from the Spaniards, and even
the Indians were warned away from the mountains by their chiefs, by fables of devouring dragons
and other terrible tales. The Indian promised that,

if the English would bring a good store of wine, he would exorcise the dragon.   Kemys, however, was afraid of going, for it might open the eyes of the Spaniards ; and the baptised Indian Don Juan, the cousin of Gualtero, who sought to usurp the kingdom, might help them to the possession of the mine.   So Kemys somewhat lamely returned, capturing some Indian emissaries of Berreo's on the way to the coast for reinforcements, and arrived back in England at the end of June.   The news he brought was a bitter disappointment to Ralegh's friends, for the Spaniards had now established a strong foothold near the mouth of the Caroni, one of the principal entrances to the coveted golden empire.   Ralegh himself was away with the fleet at Cadiz when his captain returned, but Lady Ralegh thus wrote to Sir Robert Cecil on the tidings he brought.   'Thus you hear your poor absent friend's fortune, who if he had been as well credited in his reports and knowledge as it seemeth the Spaniards were, they had not been possessors of that place.'   Nothing seems to have rankled in the minds of Ralegh and his wife so much as the sneers of his enemies that he was telling lies about the wealth of Guiana.   He wrote from Sherborne to Cecil shortly before Kemys sailed.   'What becomes of Guiana I much desire to hear—whether it pass for a history or a fable.   I hear Mr Dudley and others are sending thither ; if it be so, farewell all good from thence. For although myself—like a cockscomb—did rather

prefer the future in respect of others, and rather
thought to win the Kings to Her Majesty's service
than to sack them, I know what others will do when
those Kings shall come simply into their hands.'
Ralegh was ahead of his times. He kept sturdily
through all disappointments to his main object,
namely to win a great colonial empire for England,
and it is pathetic to note how he was blindly thwarted
by others, whose only aim, as he says, was their own
immediate profit.

On his return Kemys wrote a narrative of his
voyage, which was as vigorous an appeal to the
patriotism of his fellow-countrymen as that of his
chief had been. 'Look,' he says, 'how eager the
Spaniard is to forestall us in Guiana. He was preparing an expedition of 600 families to send thither,
but the ships were burnt in Cadiz. They are busy
whilst we are idly waiting for news which we straight-
way forget when we have heard them.' Are the
Spaniards, he asks, more able than we? Have they
more men to spare? Do they love their country
more? and he gives a tremendous negative to all
these questions, and urges Englishmen to seize the
opportunity before it is too late. Kemys's final
exhortation is as persuasive as a modern company
prospectus. 'It is fit only for a prince to begin and
aid this worke; the maintenance and ordering thereof
requiring sovereign power, authoritie and command-
ment. The river of Raleana (Orinoco) giveth upon

and free passage, any provision that the Spaniards can make to the contrary notwithstanding (for once a year the lands near the river be all drowned), to convey men, horses, munitions and victuals, for any power of men that shall be sent thither.

'I doe speak it on my soul's health, as the best testimonie that I can in any case yield to averre a truth, that having been now the second time in this countrey, and with the helpes of time and leisure well advised myself upon all circumstances to be thought of, I can discern no competant impediment, but that with a sufficient number of men, Her Majesty may, and her successors, enjoy this rich and great empire; and having once planted there, may for ever (with the favour of God) holde and keepe it *contra Judæos et Gentes.*' He points out that the enterprise might easily be effected by 'adventurers,' but that that course would bring no permanent benefit to the nation, for they, he says, would return home with gold, and care nothing for holding the place as a colony for the English crown.

Kemys's account is prefaced by a long, fervid poem to the same effect, two or three stanzas of which may be quoted to show how earnestly Ralegh desired the Queen to accept Guiana as an English colony, Kemys's narrative, like his voyage, of course, being inspired by his master.

> ' *Guiana, whose rich seat are mines of gold;*
> *Whose forehead knockes against the roofe of stars;*

Stands on her tiptoes at fair England looking,
Kissing her hand, bowing her mighty breast ;
And every sign of all submission making,
To be her sister, and her daughter both,
Of our most sacred maide. . . .

'*Then, most admirèd sovereign, let your breath*
Goe forth upon the waters and create
A golden world in this our yron age.'

A fervent appeal is made to the belief and courage
of prospective adventurers in the golden promises
held out to them, but care is taken to make it
clear that gold is not the only thing to be thought
of, and that work and livelihood await any number
of colonists who may go thither, 'where learning doth
not eat its thriftless books, nor valour consume its
useless arms.'

'*But all our youth take Hymen's lights in hand*
And fill each roofe with honoured progenie.

'*And there do palaces and temples rise*
Out of the earth and kiss enamoured skies,
Where new Britannia humbly kneels to heaven,
The world to her, and both at her blest feet,
In whom the circles of all empires meet.'

But it was all of no avail. Mismanagement and
parsimony had brought to a disastrous end Drake and
Hawkins's last expedition to the West Indies. Both
great sailors had died broken-hearted, and once more
for a brief season it seemed as if the naval supremacy
of Spain was to be reasserted. The operations of the
League had given Philip a footing in northern France,

with possession of the port of Blavet in Brittany, whence the invasion of England might be undertaken. Spanish aid had already been promised to Tyrone in Ireland, and English spies were reporting great naval preparations in various Spanish ports. The capacity for harm of Philip at the time we know now to have been very small indeed, but thanks in part to the bombastic boasting of his own officers, an exaggerated fear of Spain again took possession of the English. For a considerable time the traitor Antonio Perez had been living with Essex, endeavouring to inflame him, and through him Elizabeth, into offensive warfare against his deadly enemy Philip. Essex never required much urging in such a case, but Elizabeth hesitated long before she openly committed herself to a change of policy from that which had served her so well. Ralegh, with Guiana always in his mind, was anxious to cripple Spain to an extent which should make her powerless to send forces to the Orinoco, and this identity of views for once drew the two rivals together. It was decided to fit out a fleet of ninety-six sail which were joined by twenty-four Dutch ships, the number of men being in all 16,600; the Lord Admiral Howard being in supreme command at sea, and Essex on land, an arrangement which very nearly brought about the failure of the expedition, old Howard protesting against it, as he said he was 'only to be used as a drag.' Orders were sent early in April for levies of men to be made in the counties, but the

ink on the orders was scarcely dry before the Queen
changed her mind, and countermanded them, and
thenceforward for weeks hardly a day passed without
some new resolution being arrived at, Essex the while
fuming and raging to an extent which made him lose
respect for the Queen.   Elizabeth, it is plain,
dreaded the capture of any important Spanish city.
This would have been an embarrassment to her, and,
as she pointed out, would not bring her any profit, as
the soldiers would get out of hand and plunder on
their own account.   What she desired, and in this she
was all through earnestly seconded by Ralegh, was to
strike a decisive blow at Spain's navy.   The English
pressed men had no stomach for the job, and it was
only with the greatest difficulty that the force could
be got together.   Ralegh was to organise a squadron
in the Thames, and take it round to Plymouth to join
the rest of the fleet, but was delayed by head winds
and other causes, whereupon, as usual, his enemies
began to cavil.   Anthony Bacon, Essex's hanger-on,
more ungenerous than his master, hinted that Ralegh
was lingering for a dishonest purpose of his own.
Ralegh wrote a letter on the 4th May from North-
fleet to Cecil, in which it is clear that he had heard
these rumours.   'As fast as wee press men one day,
they come away another and say they will not serve.
. . . I cannot write to our Generalls att this tyme,
for the pursevant found me in a countre villag a mile
from Gravesend honting after runaway mariners, and

dragging in the mire from ale-house to ale-house, and could gett no paper, butt that the pursevant had this peece.

'Sir, by the living God, there is nor King nor Queen nor general nor any elce can take more care than I do to be gonn. Butt I humblie pray yow butt to speak with Mr Borrough, and lett hyme be sent for afterward before my Lorde Chamberlayne, that they may hear hyme speak whether any man can gett down with this wind or no ; which will satisfy them of me.'

At length the force was collected and sailed from Plymouth Sound on the 3rd June. There were four English squadrons, one of which with twenty-two ships from the Thames was under the command of Ralegh as Vice-Admiral, the Dutch fleet being under Maurice of Nassau. A council of war was appointed to advise Essex and Howard, consisting of Ralegh and Lord Thomas Howard, for the navy, and Sir Conyers Clifford, Sir George Carew and Sir Francis Vere for the troops. Philip was usually well served by his spies in English ports, but on this occasion they gave him but inadequate and tardy information, for the men on the fleet itself were ignorant of its destination ; and at dawn on the 20th June, the affrighted citizens of Cadiz beheld the fleet in the offing. Cadiz was the richest city in Spain, the port whither the silver ships of the Indies brought their precious freight. The defences of the place were old and

crumbling, the guns obsolete, and the fighting men
few. That the English should await the flotilla
from the Indies, that it should pounce upon the
Azores, was known to be not improbable; but that
an overwhelmingly powerful fleet like this should
come to Cadiz itself had not been anticipated, and
the people were taken by surprise. Under the surf-
beaten walls of the harbour there lay a fleet of eight
war galleys, their prows towards the entrance; further
in there were six great galleons, and eleven frigates
of war, with forty cargo ships behind them loading
for New Spain, with three strongly armed ships to
convoy them on their voyage.

Whilst the main body of the English fleet anchored
in the bay of St Sebastian, a mile and a half from Cadiz,
Ralegh's squadron was sent round the western or Rota
side of the bay of Cadiz to intercept any ships that
attempted to escape either from there or from San
Lucar. In his absence, a council of war was called by
the Lord Admiral, and the movement amongst the
English ships in consequence was construed by the
watching Spaniards into fear of the formidable array
of Spanish ships in the bay. The Lord Admiral,
whose experience of actual warfare was small, was
always on the side of prudence, and apparently was
also undesirous of venturing into the harbour under
the combined fire of the ships and the forts. He
agreed with Essex that the town should be attacked
and captured first, and the shipping dealt with after-

wards. A heavy southerly swell was rolling, and when
Ralegh arrived to attend the council, two hours after
the rest, he found Essex embarking his troops in boats
to land and attack the town on the west side. The
manœuvre was a most dangerous one ; several boat-
loads of men were swamped before they left the side,
and Ralegh was horrified at the blunder which was
about to be committed. To have desisted at his sole
representation after the council of war had decided,
would have looked like fear on the part of Essex.
Rash and injudicious as the latter was, however, he
knew that Ralegh had a greater and more varied
experience of fighting and navigation than all the
rest of the council put together, and agreed that, if
Ralegh came on board his ship and protested formally
in presence of the Colonels against the decision,
giving reasons why the course proposed might lead
to the destruction of the whole force, he, Essex,
would desist. It was all the Lord Admiral's fault,
he said, who would not enter the harbour until
the town had been secured. The experienced
officers on the fleet coincided with Ralegh's views,
and with difficulty the Lord Admiral was at last
persuaded. It was evening now ; and as Ralegh's
barge passed Essex's ship on his way from his
interview with Howard, the young Earl, eager
for action as usual, whether on sea or land,
was awaiting on his deck the news of the chief's
decision. Ralegh shouted in Spanish as he passed

that the fleet was to enter, and Essex, full of exaltation, waved his plumed hat around his head and
cast it into the sea with a cheer of delight.

On land, the women and non-combatants had
crowded into the citadel, and the men who flocked
in from the outskirts were hastily armed. The Duke
of Medina Sidonia, Governor of Andalucia, was at his
house at San Lucar, but was summoned in all haste,
whilst the Admiral in command, Diego de Sotomayor,
put his ships in order of battle. But Philip's rigid
system of centralisation had sapped the initiative
of his officers everywhere. They were so accustomed to be minutely directed from the Escorial,
that when they were thrown upon their own resources
they were at a loss. Medina Sidonia was a broken
reed to lean upon—it was the same poor-spirited
simpleton who had lost the Armada—but even he
was absent until far into the night, and only arrived
in time to record minutely the successive stages of
the disaster.

On the English fleet Ralegh was tacitly admitted
in the moment of danger to be the natural leader.
Both Howard and Essex claimed the honour of leading
the van, and the matter was disputed for hours; as in
the case of Drake and Norris at Lisbon in 1589 a
divided command always led to trouble. At length
it was decided that Ralegh should lead the advance-
guard, despite the protestations of Lord Thomas
Howard. Ralegh's ship, the *Warsprite*, was to be

followed by the *Mary Rose*, under his cousin and
friend, Sir George Carew, the *Rainbow*, under Sir
Francis Vere, the *Lion*, under Sir Robert Southwell,
the *Dreadnought*, under Sir Conyers Clifford, and the
Nonpareil, under Robert Dudley.   Lord Admiral
Howard, Essex, and Lord Thomas Howard were to
command the main body of the fleet in the rear of
Ralegh's squadron, but Lord Thomas was determined
to be first if he could, and during the night induced
Robert Dudley to change ships with him, in the hope
that in the confusion he might push ahead of Ralegh.
The latter was equally determined that he should not ;
and at the first streak of dawn he gave the signal and
got under way with a good start before all the others.
During the night he had sent to the Lord Admiral
his views as to how the attack should be effected.   He
had, as usual, a keen eye to the main chance, and
foresaw that the Spaniards would burn their ships
rather than surrender them, and in order to prevent
this induced the Lord Admiral to appoint two large
fly-boats to board the great galleons, after the big guns
on the English fleet had done their work.   The
entrance to the harbour was commanded by the guns
of the forts, and the galleys were ranged just inside.
The *Warsprite*, well ahead of the squadron, bore the
brunt of the fire, but disdained to notice ' the wasps,'
except by a derisive flourish of trumpets for each discharge.   Metal more attractive than galleys was before
Ralegh's eager eyes.   Straight ahead of him were the

four greatest galleons in Philip's fleet, and foremost of them was that towering *San Felipe* and the *San Andres* that had attacked the *Revenge* four years before. 'The *San Felipe*, the great and famous admiral of Spain, was the mark I shot at . . . being resolved to be revenged for the *Revenge*, or to second her with mine own life.' Gallant Grenville was not forgotten by his kinsman, and the hour of vengeance had come. It had been decided by Sotomayor that, if the English should enter in force, the Spanish war ships should withdraw to the narrow channel between the castle of Matagorda and Puntales, to prevent the English from penetrating the inner harbour of Puerto Real, where there lay the Indian flotilla with cargoes worth eight millions of ducats. It was an unfortunate decision for the Spaniards, adopted at the instance of the representative of the merchants of Seville, to whom the cargoes belonged, for it left the city of Cadiz at the mercy of the enemy. Like a bridge across the channel stretched the four great galleons of Spain, two of Portugal, three argosies and three frigates, the rest of the war-ships being formed in a second line of defence behind them. Straight as a hawk upon its quarry went the *Warsprite* to the *San Felipe*, disdaining to fire a gun at those who sought to stop her. Ralegh anchored on the north or Matagorda side of the galleon, between her and the *San Andres*, the *Lyon* shortly afterwards anchoring close by him, whilst the *Dreadnought* and the *Mary Rose* took up their positions

on the south or Puntales side of the *San Felipe.* Then
for three hours they pounded away point blank at each
other, 'as two butts.' At ten o'clock in the morning
Essex could keep out of the fray no longer, and in
defiance of all arrangements, pushed ahead through the
fleet till he came to Ralegh's side. 'Always,' says
Sir Walter, 'I must without glory say for myself, that
I held single in the head of all.' Meanwhile the fly-
boats for boarding came not, and Ralegh, losing
patience, was determined to wait no longer, but to
board from the Queen's ships, in defiance of his own
plans. But Essex was his senior in command, and he
sought to obtain his permission to do this. He hastily
went on board the *Swiftsure,* the Earl's flagship, for
the purpose. 'It is the same loss to burn or sink,' he
said, 'and I must endure one or the other'—for
the *Warsprite* was riddled with cannon shot. Essex
tried to dissuade him, not very earnestly we may be
sure, but when he found 'it was not in his power to
command fear, he told me that whatsoever I did, he
would second me in person ; upon his honour.' During Ralegh's short absence from his ship jealous Vere
pushed the *Rainbow* ahead of her, and Lord Thomas,
envious in his turn, thrusting forward the *Nonpareil,*
with the Lord Admiral himself on board, tried to get
in front of him. When Ralegh returned to the
Warsprite, 'from being first he found himself to be
but third.' This he could not brook, so, forcing his
ship between the other two, he went right ahead, and

lay across the channel. 'I was very sure that none would outstart me again for that day'—and none did, although Vere made another attempt by secretly fastening a hawser to the *Warsprite's* side, 'when we were all too busy to look behind us,' and began hauling himself abreast of Ralegh's ship; 'but some of my company advertising me thereof I caused it to be cut, and so he fell back into his place. I guarded him, all but his very prow, from the sight of the enemy.' Ralegh was sternly determined that not even Vere should baulk him of his vengeance upon the *San Felipe*. As soon as he was again face to face with his foe, he laid a warp on board of her and began hauling alongside; the *Repulse* on the other side did the same, and the *Nonpareil* likewise. This was the last straw. A hideous panic seized the Spaniards. They slipped their cables, ran on the mud, for the channel is very narrow, and 'tumbled into the sea heaps of souldiers, so thick as if coals had been powred out of a sack, in many ports at once; some drowned, some sticking in the mud.' The *San Felipe* and the *San Tomas* were fired by their crews, the *San Mateo* and the *San Andres* were captured by Ralegh. 'The spectacle,' says Ralegh, 'was a very lamentable one; for many drowned themselves; many, half burnt, leapt into the water; very many hanging by ropes' ends by the ships' side under water, even to the lips; many swimming with grievous wounds, stricken under water, and put out of their pain; and withal so huge a fire and such tearing of the ordnance of the great Philip, and the rest, when the fire came to them, as if any man had a desire to see hell itself, it was there most lively figured.   We spared the lives of all after the victory; but the Flemings, who did little or nothing in the fight, used merciless slaughter, till they were beaten off by myself, and afterwards by the Lord Admiral.'

This is Ralegh's account, and in the main is confirmed by other English and Spanish eye-witnesses.   Medina Sidonia, writing from Puerto Real to the King, says that the engagement lasted four hours, and that the galleons went aground by accident, as they were trying to retire further up the harbour, and this is most likely what happened. The channel, as has been observed, is very narrow, and doubtless Sotomayor would have liked to lure the English out of it on to the mud.

By the early afternoon the bay of Cadiz was won. Such of the smaller Spanish ships as had escaped destruction were taken up towards Puerto Real, burning all the merchant vessels they came across, to prevent them from falling into the hands of the English.   Soon the Spanish crews got out of hand. All discipline was lost; pillage and flight alone occupied their minds, and all thought of further naval defence was abandoned.   In the meanwhile the English troops were rapidly landed to attack the town.   The Spanish regular garrison was a very

small one, only 150 men, but there were 5000
armed citizens fit for fighting, and a body of
600 or 800 horsemen had ridden over from
Jerez to their aid. Essex was the first to land,
and Ralegh, though badly wounded in the leg,
insisted upon being carried ashore, and so quickly
were the boat-loads of eager Englishmen landed and
drawn up, that by the time the cavaliers from Jerez
could muster, Essex's force was too strong to be
repulsed. One charge was attempted, but a volley of
musketry put the Spanish horsemen to flight. Pell-
mell back to the city they fled. The citizens, in a
panic, were afraid to open the gates to them, for
the English followed them hotly. The horses were
abandoned, and the men scaled the outer glacis at
a point where the walls were crumbling and could
be surmounted. If the Spaniards could surmount
them, so could the English lads who were pressing in pursuit, and soon thousands of Essex's troops
were swarming and tumbling over the defences
into the town. The townspeople, such of them as
had not taken refuge in the citadel, were panic-
stricken. A little desultory fighting in the streets
from the flat roofs of the houses and a last tussel
in the market-place, and Cadiz was at the mercy of
Essex and his men. As soon as the fighting ceased,
the Lord Admiral and all the principal officers, with
Ralegh borne in his litter, entered the market-place,
preceded by Sir Edward Hoby, bearing the standard

of England, to receive with Essex the capitulation
of the city. Submission, complete and abject, was
given by the inhabitants. Forty hostages were sent
on board the ships to secure the payment of 120,000
crowns ransom for the lives of the people, which
ransom was never paid, and the poor hostages were
taken to England. All the rich merchandise in the
town, with 40,000 ducats in cash, were to be spoil in
war, and the inhabitants were to evacuate the place
with only the clothes on their back, 'in order that
the sacking might be the more complete.' The
authorities of the city were paralysed. Poor Medina
Sidonia could only wail to far-off Philip of the
completeness of the catastrophe. 'Nor ships, nor
fleet, nor Cadiz remains,' he wrote. All Andalucia
was in danger. There were only 800 men, some
without arms, in Port St Mary's. 'I have 3000
countrymen in Jerez,' wrote the Duke, 'but I have
no arms for them. . . . This is shameful! I said
how necessary it was to send me men and money,
and I have not even received an answer from Your
Majesty, so I am at my wit's end now, and can
only await Your Majesty's orders.' To this had
Philip's life-long attempt to rule the world from a
writing-table reduced the boasted naval supremacy of
Spain. Almost the only man in Cadiz who was equal
to an emergency was the Jesuit Father Quesada.
He organised the exodus of women and children from
the doomed city, clamoured successfully to the victors

for food, help and protection for the nuns and women who were shelterless and starving. Food they could not have, for the victors themselves were well nigh famished, but all else that brave men could do to help the innocent vanquished was done by Essex and his men. The Spaniards themselves bore grateful witness to their moderation. The moment resistance ceased, slaughter also ceased. No woman was molested, no personal insult offered. For two days the citadel held out, its inhabitants living on water alone. The obselete old guns burst at the second or third discharge; help, the defenders knew, could not reach them, and then they gave in. For sixteen days the city of Cadiz underwent a systematic sack. Father Quesada had aided to conceal the valuables of a few churches and private citizens, but apart from that, everything destructible was destroyed, even to the gratings before the windows, and then the city and its cathedrals were burnt, all of them that the flames would consume.

As soon as the city had capitulated on the night of the 20th June, Ralegh, suffering agony from his wound, was carried on board the *Warsprite*. He knew that once the men were allowed to fall to pillage, then all hope of the capture of the rich Indian fleet up the harbour at Puerto Real was gone, and by daybreak the next morning he sent his brother, Sir John Gilbert, and Lady Ralegh's brother, Sir Arthur Throgmorton, ashore, to beg the com-

manders for permission to take his squadron up to
Puerto Real and secure the rich booty—a booty so
rich that it might have induced the Queen to smile
upon his plea for Guiana. But the confusion of
plunder had already begun and the two commanders
hesitated; for the English ships were well nigh
abandoned, and they were not sure of the force that
might yet be brought against them. Whilst they
were hesitating, the opportunity slipped away. In
the afternoon the representatives of the Seville
merchants came and offered a ransom of 2,000,000
ducats for the fleet, which was refused. 'We came,'
said the Lord Admiral, 'to consume, not to compound.' Ralegh would have been willing enough to
compound for a great ransom, but he thought they
would get better terms if they secured the ships
first, before they were burnt by the Spaniards themselves. Essex, for his part, was for capturing Puerto
Real and the ships with his soldiers, for he was no
lover of the sea or sailors. Before they could make
up their minds, Medina Sidonia, with the energy
of despair, ordered every Spanish ship to be burnt.
Such rich merchandise as could be carried ashore
was hurriedly rescued; and then the great Indian
fleet of forty ships, galleons, frigates, argosies and
emigrant ships for Guiana, over fifty sail in all, were
soon a mass of blazing ruin.

Ralegh was discontented, of course, with his share
of the plunder of Cadiz. *Les absents ont toujours tort,*

and his wound kept him prisoner on board of his ship. 'Some' (*i.e.*, English officers) 'had for their prisoners 20,000 ducats, some 10,000, besides great houses of merchandise'—whereas, he says, all his share was a lame leg, and poverty and pain.

As a matter of fact, in the official inventory of the spoil made after the return to England, he appears to have received £1769, whilst Vere got £3628, and of the two great galleons, which he himself captured, Ralegh got no share of prize money. As usually happened when the command was divided, there had been jealousy amongst the officers from the first ; Essex's unjust partiality for the soldiers in the division of the spoil accentuated the differences; and between Vere and Ralegh particularly the bitter feeling continued, though Ralegh's generous tribute to Essex's gallantry and magnanimity in the struggle shows that his great heart could soar above small jealousies.

On the 5th the men were re-embarked on the fleet, and Cadiz was left behind, a heap of ruins. Essex would have retained possession of the place, but cooler heads said no. They knew that the Queen wished to cripple her foe ; but to have held a principal port of enemy's country far away from England would have crippled her. They called into the port of Faro, and, amongst other things, looted, and brought to England, the library of the Bishop of the Algarves, Geronimo Osorio, and then

sailed for England. Ralegh suffered much from his
wound, and a pestilence had broken out on board
of his ship. He therefore hastened back to
Plymouth in advance of the rest of the fleet, and
arrived in England on the 6th August, bringing for
the first time authentic details of the action, which
had made patent to the world that Spain was impotent and that England was mistress of the sea.

When Drake had sailed into Cadiz harbour and
burnt the ships there in 1587, Philip said that it was
not the material loss he cared about, but the daring
insolence of the action. No attempt on that occasion
had been made to land; it was a simple naval *coup de
main* by the greatest sailor afloat. But the sacking
of Cadiz in 1596 was a very different matter. Not
only was the richest port in Spain captured and pil-
laged with impunity, but thirteen of the best ships in
the Spanish navy, and forty laden Indiamen had been
destroyed. There had been hardly an attempt even
at organised defence. The Duke of Medina Sidonia
could only moan helplessly that he had no money,
no arms, no soldiers, and that for months together
his letters to the King remained unanswered. Philip,
old and broken - hearted, was nearing his grave.
Disaster had dogged his leaden footsteps from youth
to age; for the rigid unadaptability of his administration, the fatuous belief that he, a man of
meditation, could move men of action the world
over, like puppets, from his desk, and that events

would stand still whilst he was pondering, had brought his country to the last stage of destitution and impotence. The invincible Armada had succumbed to the incompetence of its leader and the hazard of the winds; the attempt had been a great one, and the loss was not irreparable. But the catastrophe of Cadiz showed to what an extent the country had declined in the intervening eight years. Dry rot had entered into the heart of the nation; its virility had been drained; its vigour was gone, and the sceptre of the sea had slipped from its nerveless grasp. The truth that Ralegh had been dinning into the ears of his countrymen for years was patent now to all the world. English ships and English seamen were more than a match for all the Spaniards afloat.

CHAPTER X

THE EXPEDITION TO THE AZORES UNDER ESSEX—
DISGRACE OF ESSEX—RALEGH'S ACTION WITH
REGARD TO ESSEX—ROBERT CECIL AND ESSEX
—EXECUTION OF ESSEX—CECIL AND RALEGH

RALEGH and Essex arrived in London at about the
same time, but only the latter was admitted to see
the Queen. The populace had once more been
stirred by the stories of the sack of Cadiz, and those
who took part in it, particularly Essex, were made
popular heroes. An enormous amount of unregis-
tered booty had fallen into the hands of officers and
men of all ranks, and tales were rife through London
of the plate and jewels, the bags of doubloons, the
silks, the velvets, and the costly tapestry hangings,
that had been brought home surreptitiously. This
was exactly what the Queen had foretold when she
objected to the capture of any Spanish towns, and
she gave full rein to her greed and ill-humour when
she saw her prediction had come true. At least, she
could claim all the hostages, and the two galleons

brought home. With regard to the first she had a
long and undignified squabble with Essex, in which,
she was, of course, finally victorious ; and with regard
to the prize money for the galleons also she had her
way, though greatly to the indignation of the Lord
Admiral and the rest of the officers whose claims
were thus set aside. She did not scruple to apply
the epithets of 'coward' and 'miscreant' to her great
minister Burghley, the Lord Treasurer, who ventured
to remonstrate with her on the subject.

Though Ralegh, in his despondent fashion, complained that his only reward had been pain and penury
and a lame leg, he had the satisfaction in a few
months of once more being allowed to bask in the
smiles of the goddess, from whose side he had been
banished since his marriage five years before. His
praise of Essex and the reconciliation between the
latter and Sir Robert Cecil, no doubt, greatly pleased
the Queen, though she continued to affect displeasure with her young favourite about the booty of
Cadiz ; and the squabbles and reconciliations between
them were ceaseless. Though he had somewhat
sulkily made friends with him, it is certain that Essex
himself was not anxious for Ralegh to be taken into
full favour again. During May 1597 Ralegh was
daily about the Court, and at last, on the 1st June,
when Essex had gone to Chatham to be out of the
way, Sir Robert Cecil brought Sir Walter into the
Queen's presence. She received him graciously, and

gave him permission once more to perform his duties as Captain of the Guard. He lost no time; it had all been arranged beforehand; he filled up the vacant places in the ranks, once more donning his splendid uniform and silver armour, that same evening he rode by the Queen's side, and thenceforward had the entrance to the privy chamber, as in the days of his highest favour. From his first appearance at Court, Essex had bitterly opposed the Cecils; and after Walsingham's death had persistently urged the Queen to give the post of Secretary of State to that cruelly ill-used man William Davison or to Sir Thomas Bodley. The aged Lord Burghley was determined that the office should fall to his favourite second son Robert Cecil, and during the absence of Essex at Cadiz, Cecil had been appointed. On the return of the young favourite to Court he found the new Secretary all smiles and cordiality, and for months Ralegh, Essex and Cecil were apparently the best of friends. Cecil was a man who was determined to swim, let who would sink. His own keen self-seeking was seconded by the vast experience and great intellect of his father; and it is in the highest degree improbable that his new friendship for Essex, who had always opposed him, had any other object but his own advantage. The pride and obstinacy of the young favourite were deeply resented by the Queen herself, as were his constant and turbulent attempts to drag her into acts of aggression against

Spain. The Cecils had always advocated a policy of moderation, the triumphant policy which had enabled Elizabeth for nearly forty years to bleed her enemy to exhaustion, without once bringing upon her country the united opposition of all the Catholic powers. If Robert Cecil now turned round and did his best to fan Essex's warlike ardour, we may be sure that he did not do so for the advantage of Essex. How far Ceeil's friendship for Ralegh, who had always been on his side, was sincere, we shall have occasion to consider later, but Ralegh, at least, had reason to question it ; and we shall be doing no violent injustice to Cecil's memory if we conclude that the one person intended to be benefited was Robert Cecil himself. Certain it is, that everything that the new Secretary could do to urge upon Essex fresh warlike adventure which should keep him away from Court, and incur expenditure, without return to the Queen, was done. When, therefore, rumours reached England that the King of Spain would make a supreme effort to revenge the insult of Cadiz, both Ralegh and Essex were encouraged in their proposal for once more anticipating the possible blow by striking at Philip's own dominions. We know now that the Spanish King was utterly unable to fit out an expedition to attack England, except in the form of some quite inadequate aid to the Irish rebels ; and probably Cecil was fully aware of this at the time, but public opinion was excited and had no means of gauging exactly the

depth of Philip's purse.   Ralegh wrote a discourse at
the time, called *Opinion upon the Spanish Alarum*, in
which he expressed his incredulity of the probability
of an attack in force from Spain, but still advocated
the advisability of being prepared for the worst, by
providing for the defence of the coasts.   A fleet of
ten ships of war was hastily put into commission, but as
the news came of the great preparations being made at
Ferrol by the Adelantado of Castile to invade Ireland,
the fleet was increased to twenty sail of the Queen's
ships, with a large number of victuallers, and ten
Dutch men-of-war.   Probably no one in England
knew then, as we know now, that the Adelantado was
wearing his heart out in despair at his inability to
get a fit force together, even to help the Irish Catholics.
Hopeless muddle and confusion reigned supreme at
Ferrol and Corunna.   Money, men, arms, ammunition and ships were all lacking ; corruption, inepti-
tude and impotence were everywhere ; whilst the
King, far away in his cell, wrote letters by the hundred
about petty details, and insisted upon the sending to
him of reports, and ever more reports, each one more
bombastic than the last, until the bluff Adelantado
blurted out the truth.   There was no more real
danger to England from Philip now ; only England
did not know it.   It was decided that the English
fleet of about 120 sail in all, with 5000 soldiers on
board, should sail for Galicia, and, if possible, destroy
the Adelantado's fleet.   The Lord Admiral was ill

and sulky at the Queen's conduct about the Cadiz
plunder, and declined the command, which was
given to Essex, with Lord Thomas Howard and
Ralegh, as his Vice and Rear Admirals respectively.
Lord Mountjoy was under Essex to command the
troops, much to the envy of Vere, who fell out with
his patron and chief about it, and swore never again
to serve under him.

The expedition sailed from Plymouth on the 19th
July, but was scattered and driven back by a storm in
the Bay of Biscay in much suffering and danger, and
for the next month it was held wind-bound.   In
the meanwhile, sickness broke out, provisions went
bad, and discontent became rife.   Essex and Ralegh
posted together from Plymouth to London, and the
former used all his persuasions with the Queen to be
allowed to proceed as soon as his ships were refitted
and the wind served.   The season was advanced,
however, the enemy on the alert, and the Queen
refused to have her ships and men exposed to risk.
Only after much hesitation she consented to some
fire-ships being sent into Ferrol harbour, with the
two captured Spanish galleons from Cadiz and some
merchantmen, to burn the Spanish fleet; but on no
account was any attempt to be made upon land, for
the English troops were to be left in England, and,
above all, Essex was made to promise that he would
remain with the Queen's shpis outside, and take no
personal part in the operations.   The daring task was

entrusted to Ralegh. During his absence in London
his famous ship the *Roebuck* ran aground at Plymouth and was disabled, with other vessels, and when
finally, on the 17th August, the fleet sailed, without
the troops, it was much smaller than had originally
been intended. Once more they were caught in a
furious westerly gale in the Bay of Biscay, and both
of the captured Spanish galleons were disabled, the
San Mateo finding her way back to England. The
easterly wind, that finally enabled them to get out of
the bay, prevented them from approaching Ferrol, and
they were driven towards the south, along the coast
of Portugal. All the country was aroused by this
time, for Essex imprudently kept near enough to the
coast to be seen, and the loss of the *San Mateo* had
convinced the officers that the attempt on Ferrol
must be abandoned. Ralegh's ship, the *Warsprite*,
broke her main yard-arm, and was delayed for two
days ; he and the rest of his squadron with the Dutch
soldiers on board went astray from the fleet ; and then
a series of misunderstandings kept him waiting off the
coast of Portugal, whilst Essex and the main body
sailed for the Azores for the purpose of intercepting
the homeward bound Indian fleet. Ralegh's enemies
tried to persuade Essex that he had wilfully deserted
and left him in the lurch ; but to Essex's credit he
refused to listen to the slander, and told Ralegh that
he knew it came ' from their cankered and scandalous
disposition.' At length, greatly to the joy of Essex,

who for several days had been lying off Flores, the
scene of the memorable fight of the *Revenge*, Ralegh
and his ships joined him, and the fleet was re-united.
False information had been conveyed to them that the
Adelantado's fleet had slipped out of Ferrol, and had
sailed for the Azores to escort the Indiamen ; but
they found now that they had been deceived, and it
was proposed to attack and lay waste the various
islands, which were the principal rendezvous for the
Spanish flotillas ; and after they had successfully dealt
with the smaller islands in separate squadrons to
re-unite and attack Terceira, which was notoriously
disaffected to the Spanish garrison. Whilst Ralegh
and several officers of his squadron were making
an excursion in the interior of Flores, and his
men were busy watering the ships, he suddenly received a message from Essex that he was immediately sailing to attack Fayal, and that Ralegh and
his ships were to join them there without loss of
time. Ralegh hurried after his chief, and arrived
off Fayal the next morning, but could see nothing
of Essex. They found the town in a position
of defence, the non - combatants and valuables
being hastily sent into the interior, the forts fully
manned, and the beach lined with soldiers to dispute
a landing. Without waiting for hostilities from
Ralegh, they opened fire upon him, though they did
him but little damage. This was more than English
human nature could well stand, and the men on board

became clamorous to attack the island.   It was clear,
if they were to get any return for the voyage at all,
this was their chance, for the main object of the
expedition had evidently been frustrated.   But still
Essex came not, and Ralegh hesitated to act without
his chief's orders.   Some of Essex's sycophants, like
Sir Gilly Merrick, strongly opposed any action in the
absence of the chief commanders.   On the fourth day
it was decided to land a few boat-loads of men on the
north-west of the island, some miles from the town,
to obtain water, which they had been unable to do in
sufficient quantity at Flores, but a large force of
armed islanders occupied trenches on the shore, and
defied them to land.   Both Ralegh and his men had
lost patience at the undignified position they had
been occupying for the last three days, and he
determined to read the islanders a lesson, ' and either
gain our landing or a beating.'   He therefore decided
to land a force of about 160 sailors and 100 soldiers
from his own ships.   As he and his little force rowed
through his squadron on his way to the shore, his
captains shouted to him to take some of the Dutch
soldiers with him, as his force was too small.   He
replied that he did not know for what service the
Commander-in-chief intended them, and therefore
only took sailors and his own men.   Fully double
the number of enemies awaited them on the beach,
and the landing-place had been fortified by two long
trenches, which enfiladed a narrow passage by which

the assailants had to pass. Ralegh's force ran in
rapidly, under the protection of some artillery which
he had brought on two pinnaces, but at the landing-
place his men blenched. He scornfully shouted a
rebuke to them, and caused his own barge to be
rowed full upon the rocky beach. He and the
gentlemen led the way, breast high in the surf, under
a heavy fire, and successfully stormed the trenches.
Panic seized the defenders, who fled in confusion,
throwing away their arms and seeking refuge in
the woods. Some of Ralegh's men were killed,
more were drowned, and two of his long boats were
sunk ; but his loss was a small one considering the
end effected. Drawing now a larger force from his
ships, he advanced 500 strong to attack the·chief town,
Villa Dorta, four miles off ; Ralegh himself leading,
wearing no armour but a gorget. The place was
defended by a fort, which received them warmly, and
the Dutchmen seemed inclined to waver. Ralegh
and his 40 gentlemen marched on 250 yards ahead,
scaled the slope, and then, seeing the Dutchmen
slowly straggling up, he called out to know whether
' this was the manner of Low Country troops, to show
such base cowardice at the first sight of the enemy ?'
The fort was soon abandoned by the defenders, but
another fort on the summit of a high rocky hill still
existed. Ralegh found none of his men willing to
reconnoitre this place, and indignantly undertook to
do so himself and alone. His cousin, Sir Arthur

Gorges, and about 10 of his personal followers insisted upon accompanying him, and the undaunted dozen toiled up the hill, full in face of the enemy's fire, Ralegh wearing a white scarf, and Gorges a red one. Ralegh's garments were pierced by bullets in three places, Gorges got a shot through his leg, two of the men were killed outright, and several more wounded ; but before a regular attack of the fort could be made, the defenders fled, and the town itself was also found deserted. He was thus master of the whole island, with a loss of 10 men killed and 20 wounded ; and the lesson which he deduces from the action in an episodical reference to it in the *History of the World* is that a country cannot prevent an enemy's fleet from landing its army without as good a fleet to oppose it, a lesson he was never tired of pressing upon his countrymen. The next morning, September 22nd, Essex and his fleet came into the harbour, and the Commander-in-chief was hotly indignant that his subordinate had robbed him of the glory of taking Fayal. Some of the 'cankered and scandalous' sycophants, who surrounded him, urged him to bring Ralegh to a court-martial, and said that he deserved to lose his head. When Ralegh paid his formal visit to Essex to report his proceedings, he was at once charged with a 'breach of order and the articles.' 'I know of no such breach,' replied Ralegh ; and when Essex pointed out that by the instructions no troops were to be

landed without the General's order, Ralegh entered
into a dignified defence of his action, asserting that
the words, 'or other principal commander,' included
himself, and allowed him discretion in such case.
Essex was not implacable. He knew how much
greater was Ralegh's experience and ability as a
commander than his own, but Blount and Merrick
kept the wound open, and it required all Lord
Thomas Howard's diplomacy to prevent Ralegh
from being punished and disgraced. Essex and his
men, after much hesitation, then attacked Villa
Franca in Sᵗ Michael's, and captured the place,
Ralegh's squadron being kept on the other side of the
island until the whole of the booty had been secured
and shipped, in order that he and his men should
have no share of it. Whilst this was passing in the
Azores, the Adelantado had managed to get together
a fleet of a sort, and early in October it sailed for
Ireland, only to be scattered by a storm before reaching
the Lizard, and to be driven back disabled to Spain.

Essex remained at sea for a month longer way-
laying and capturing Spanish ships. He managed
to miss the main body of Indiamen, but took or burnt
such stragglers as he came across, and finally returned
to England at the end of the month with three rich
carracks, and a few merchantmen from Brazil. The
booty was not imposing, hardly covering, indeed, the
cost of the expedition, and the Queen was accordingly discontented. Essex was received coldly, and

found in his absence that he had lost ground at Court. The Lord Admiral had been made Earl of Notting-ham for his services at Cadiz, and had been given precedence over all other noblemen of his rank, and this made the foolish, headstrong young Earl more insolent and presumptuous than ever. He insulted and challenged the Lord Admiral and his sons, feigned illness, and deprived the Queen of his com-pany, until at last she relented, and for the sake of peace—it is said at the instance of Ralegh—made Essex Earl Marshal, with precedence next after Howard, who then in his turn took umbrage and retired from Court. On the other hand, the Queen had received Ralegh with marked favour, and approved of his action at Fayal. Ralegh had never been popular with the crowd, but his new favour with the Queen, to the apparent detriment of Essex, made him more than ever disliked; and as soon as might be, he retired to peaceful Sherborne to rest and recruit his broken health. He was soon busy again on the fortifications of the Cornish coast and in other duties of his offices, as well as in Parliament; and thenceforward for a time the rivalry between him and Essex slumbered. But Essex was rushing upon his destruction. His insolence to the Queen was unrestrained. He sought to interfere with State appointments with which he had no concern, until at last the appointment of a new Viceroy in Ireland brought matters to a crisis, and his boorish rudeness

to his benefactress, and the famous box on the ears
he got from the outraged Queen, laid the foundation
of his ruin.   After a time, with sulky lip-submission,
he came back to Court, ready to quarrel with anyone.   His temper at the time is well shown by his
treatment of Ralegh at a tourney in the tiltyard at
Whitehall on the Queen's birthday, 1598.   It appears
that Essex learnt of Ralegh's intention of appearing
with his train, wearing orange-coloured plumes in
their hats, and orange favours.   Essex thereupon
dressed himself and all his enormous following in
the same colours, so as to appear to absorb Ralegh
and his smaller suite.   This was petty enough ; but
it was by such acts as this that Essex kept the Court
in a turmoil of jealousy and distrust.   He had opposed
Cecil and the Queen in their intended Irish policy.
The English troops had suffered a serious disaster at
the hands of Tyrone's rebels, and vigorous action
was absolutely necessary, in the face of the intimate
relationship which was known to exist between the
Irish insurgents and Spain.   Essex factiously opposed
everything, until at last the supreme command in
Ireland was offered to him.   To leave Court, with
Cecil and Ralegh unrestrained, was a serious step for
him to take, and he hesitated, but he was discontented
and unhappy, yearning for opportunities of gaining
fresh popular applause, and at last he took the plunge,
and assumed the charge that had ruined and broken
the heart of his father.

He had no sooner decided to go to Ireland˙ than he regretted the step he had taken. 'From a mind delighting in sorrow,' he wrote to the Queen, 'from spirits wasted with passion, from a heart torn in pieces with care, grief and travail, from a man that hateth himself and all things else that keep him alive, what service can Your Majesty expect, since any service past deserves no more than banishment and proscription to the cursedest of islands? It is your rebel's pride and succession must give me leave to ransom myself out of this hateful prison, out of my loathed body, which, if it happeneth so, Your Majesty shall have cause to mislike the fashion of my death, since the course of my life could never please you.'

Soon after his arrival in Ireland he wrote to the Queen in bitter jealousy, 'From England I receive nothing but discomforts and soul's wounds. . . . Is it not lamented of Your Majesty's faithfullest subjects both there and here that a Cobham and Ralegh—I will forbear others for their places' sakes—should have such credit and favour with Your Majesty, when they wish the ill success of Your Majesty's most important action, the decay of your greatest strength, and the destruction of your faithful servants?' For the dastardly suggestion directed against Ralegh—and evidently against Cecil—that they wished for the success of Tyrone is absolutely unfounded. There is no hint of such a thing in the correspondence between the Irish insurgents and the Spaniards, as there would

have been if it were true; but there is a statement
made by Tyrone and O'Donnell that Essex himself
was in negotiation with them for joining forces and
holding Ireland until he could have his own way in
England. The Irish chiefs asserted that it was only
Essex's distrust as to their good faith that prevented
him from joining them. Sir Christopher Blount, who
was executed for complicity in Essex's conspiracy,
said that whilst the Earl was in Ireland he consulted
him, Blount, as to bringing in 4000 Queen's soldiers
then under his (Blount's) command, 'with full purpose
to right himself by force of such wrongs as he complained he had received here in his absence.' Blount
on the scaffold asserted that Essex would have raised
the standard of revolt in Ireland, but for the persuasion
to the contrary of the Earl of Southampton and himself. Moreover, at the time, Essex was certainly
carrying on a secret correspondence with James VI.,
with the alleged purpose of counteracting the supposed
acquiescence of Cecil and Ralegh in plots in favour of
the succession of the Infanta; and subsequent to
Essex's return to England and disgrace with the
Queen, his friend, Lord Mountjoy, then about to
start for Ireland as Essex's successor, wrote to James,
proposing that a Scottish army should be placed on
the borders, to compel the Queen to acknowledge
James as her heir, whilst Essex raised the standard in
England, and Mountjoy himself brought over half the
Queen's army from Ireland to join him; and thus to

overawe Elizabeth and her Government for the benefit
of Essex and James.   Accusations, therefore, brought
by such men as these against Ralegh and Cecil must
be scrutinised very closely before being accepted.   We
shall consider in due course what connection, if any,
Ralegh had with the Infanta's party at a later stage, but
it is certain that up to this time he had no share whatever in it, notwithstanding the hints of Essex and
his friends.

Essex began badly in Ireland by dallying in
Munster, when he should have been striking swiftly
and heavily at Tyrone and O'Donnell.   He offended
the Queen by appointing his friend Southampton to
an important command, after Her Majesty had positively forbidden such an appointment.   He then
made a bad matter worse by refusing to dismiss Southampton ; and his friends at Court told him that the
Queen was looking upon his proceedings as traitorous.
He next took the fatal step of rushing over to England,
abandoning his high post, and, all travel-stained as he
was, pushed his way into the Queen's bedroom at
Nonsuch, and knelt at his Sovereign's feet.   Soon
the Court was ostentatiously divided into two factions.
Essex was under arrest and, so to speak, upon his trial
for disobedience, and was supported by the Earls of
Worcester and Rutland, Lords Mountjoy, Rich,
Lumley and Henry Howard, at least three of whom
are known to have belonged to the Spanish Catholic
party ; whilst Cecil had on his side Ralegh, the

Earls of Shrewsbury and Nottingham, Lords Thomas
Howard, Cobham, Grey, and Ralegh's cousin Sir
George Carew. The danger grew ; the crowd was
on the side of Essex, and large numbers of officers
flocked over from Ireland to stand by the side of
the popular Earl, who lost no opportunity of posing
in the eyes of the people as the victim of Cecil and
Ralegh's jealous intrigues, instead of his own folly
and wrong-headedness. It was during this period of
mutual hatred and distrust (the early summer of
1600) that Ralegh wrote his famous letter to Cecil,
which has so frequently been interpreted to the
writer's prejudice. It may be explained that Cecil
had shown no disposition to push matters to an
extreme against Essex, and had caused the Queen
to remove his case from the Star Chamber, where
the punishment would have been confiscation and
perpetual imprisonment, to the Council itself, where
a milder course would be taken.

The following are Ralegh's words to the
Secretary :—

'I am not wise enough to geve yow advise ; butt if
yow take it for good councell to relent towards this
tirant, yow will repent it when it shalbe too late. His
mallice is fixt, and will not evaporate by any of your
mild courses. For he will ascribe the alteration to
Her Majesty's pusillanimitye, and not to your good
nature ; knowing that yow worke but uppon her
humour, and not out of any love towards hyme.

The less yow make hyme, the less he shalbe able
to harm yow and yours.   And if Her Majesty's
favour faile hyme hee will againe decline to a
common person.   For after - revenges, feare them
not ; for your own father, that was esteemed to be
the contriver of Norfolk's ruin, yet his son followeth
your father's son, and loveth him.   Humours of men
succeed not butt grow by occasions and accidents of
time and power. . . .   I could name yow a thousand
of thos ; and therfore after-fears are but profesies—or
rather conjectures from cawses remote.   Looke to
the present and yow do wisely.   His son shalbe the
youngest Earle of Ingland but one, and if his father
be kept down, Will Cecil shalbe abell to keip as many
men at his heeles as hee, and more too. . . .   But if
the father continue, he wilbe abel to break the branches,
and pull up the tree, root and all.   Lose not your
advantage ; if you do, I rede your destiny.—Your's
to the end,   W. R.'

On the margin is written, 'Lett the Q. hold Bothwell while she hath hyme.   He will ever be the canker
of her estate and sauftye.   Princes are lost by security ;
and preserved by prevention.   I have seen the last of
her good days and all ours, after his libertye.'

Most of Ralegh's biographers have considered it
necessary to offer some apology for this bitter letter.
I do not think that any such is required.   Essex was
clearly now a standing danger to the State.   Some of
the best heads of England had fallen for less than a

tithe of his offences, and with the views of the times it was the most natural thing in the world that Ralegh, to whom his triumph would have meant ruin—probably death—should have urged that the usual punishment for treason should be awarded him, or at least, that the leniency of Cecil should not shield him from it. What Ralegh did not know, but was to find out later to his heavy cost, was that the cool, unemotional hunchback Cecil was intent upon playing a double game by which in any case *he* would win. He knew, of course, that Essex was posing to James as the supporter of his claims to the succession, and saw that leniency to the Earl would be well regarded by the man who might probably become his sovereign. Cecil took care a little later himself to convince James that he was his strongest partisan, but was determined that his friend and colleague Ralegh should have no part in the King's good will.

Whilst Essex was chafing in disgrace, Ralegh was advancing in power and favour. The new King of Spain was forced to recognise the fact that his country was well nigh bankrupt and impotent; and peace both with France and England was in the air. English commissioners were sent to Boulogne, but for the time the negotiations came to nothing, so far as England was concerned. During the course of the conferences, however, it became necessary to send a secret mission to Maurice of Nassau, still engaged in trying to relieve Ostend, with many English sym-

pathisers by his side. The Queen had peremptorily
refused to appoint Essex one of the commissioners for
peace, but, as if to emphasise her displeasure with him,
she entrusted Ralegh and Lord Cobham with the
mission to Prince Maurice, and on Ralegh's return
appointed him Governor of Jersey. Essex was now
at liberty, but out of favour with the Queen, to whom
he grew more and more insolent; telling her on one
occasion, according to Ralegh, 'that her disposition
was as crooked as her carcass.' He wrote to James
alarming letters about Ralegh's unrestrained power in
the west country, and now in Jersey. Lord Cobham,
too, was Lord Warden of the Cinque Ports, and the
Cecil party was in possession of all the principal outlets
to the kingdom where a Spanish force might land.
The government of the country, Essex assured James,
was now in the hands of a party who would sell it to the
Infanta the moment the breath was out of the Queen's
body; and although he knew it was untrue, Essex pretended to believe that he had been marked out by
Ralegh and Cobham as the first person to be destroyed.
It was an absolute fiction that either Cecil or Ralegh
was in negotiation with the Infanta's party, but Essex
knew that no more unpopular charge could be brought
against them, and sheltered his own ambitions and
grievances behind it. There is no doubt that Essex's
conspiracy was far more widespread than it was considered wise to bring out at his trial, and that James
himself was deeply implicated in it, as well as many

important persons in England. At length matters
came to a crisis. Essex had been feigning contrition
at his house in the country, until he found the Queen
was obdurate, and that the Cecil party had a firm
grasp of power. Then he returned ostentatiously to
Essex House, and began to show open disaffection.
Sumptuous entertainments were given to his friends ;
the extreme Puritan party was made much of, and the
populace conciliated by denunciations of Spain and
the Catholics. Secret conferences were held at Drury
House (Sir John Danvers's), on the other side of the
Strand, to divert suspicion from Essex House, and a
plot was formed for seizing Whitehall, and forcing
the Queen to dismiss Cecil, Ralegh, the Lord
Admiral, and the rest of them, and then summon
Parliament and settle the question of the succession.
Cecil had his spies everywhere, and knew all about the
silly plan. Essex was summoned before the Council
on Saturday, 7th February 1601, and declined to attend
on the ground of illness. It was clear that the time
for action had come, but the plan of seizing Whitehall
was evidently impracticable now, for the Government
was on the alert, and the guards had been doubled.
Early on Sunday morning Essex's friends, Southampton,
Monteagle, Sandys, Rutland, and 300 gentlemen,
met at Essex House with the intention of riding
into the city hard by, and arousing the citizens with
the recital of the popular Earl's supposed wrongs, and
his danger from Ralegh, of whom the populace were

willing to believe any slander. Whilst they were
assembled Ralegh sent a message to one of them—
a connection of his own—Sir Ferdinando Gorges, to
come and see him at Durham House. Essex consented to his going, if he met Ralegh on the river
but did not enter his house. Ralegh was alone in his
boat when they met, and advised Gorges to escape to
Plymouth, as a warrant was out for him. Gorges said
it was now too late, and that he had gone too far to
draw back. Ralegh then asked what was the matter.
'I told him there were 2000 gentlemen who had
resolved that day to live or die free men.' To this
Ralegh replied that he did not see what they could
do against the Queen's authority. 'It is the abuse of
that authority by you and others,' said Gorges, 'which
made so many honest men seek a reformation,' whereupon Ralegh sternly told him to remember his allegiance and his duty, and returned to Court; whilst
Gorges rejoined the conspirators at Essex House.
Sir Christopher Blount had—according to Gorges—
advised him to kill Ralegh during the interview on
the river, but he refused to do so, although he con-
fesses that one of his reasons for his not doing so
was to establish a claim upon Ralegh's gratitude
in case of failure. Blount himself, however, was less
scrupulous, and sent four men with muskets to follow
Gorges, and, if possible, to murder Ralegh, for which
on the scaffold he begged the latter's forgiveness. A
commission of the Council was sent to Essex House,

to warn those assembled on their allegiance to disperse.
The members of the commission were shut up in the
house, and the infatuated Earl rode through Temple
Bar with his retinue, crying out that Ralegh had laid
an ambuscade for him on his way to Whitehall, and
sought his life.   The church-going citizens flocked
around him open-mouthed and listened, but made no
move in his favour.   To sympathise with a brilliant,
open-handed, popular favourite in disgrace was one
thing, but to take up arms against the State for his
private grievances was another, and soon murmurs of
'treason' in the crowd warned Essex that he had
made a mistake.   He sought to ride back to Essex
House, but he found the city train-band had blocked
his way and Temple Bar was shut.   Galloping down
one of the side lanes off Fleet Street, he cast himself
into a boat and rowed back to his house, only to find it
besieged on the Strand front, and shortly afterwards
beleaguered by water.   After a siege of a few hours,
he surrendered at discretion, and ten days afterwards
was tried and condemned for high treason.   The
principal conspirators, Essex amongst them, vied
with each other in the frankness and thoroughness
of their confessions, though they all tried to throw
the principal blame upon others, but Blount absolved
Ralegh from the accusation of a design to kill Essex,
which he said was only 'a word cast out to colour
other matters.'   During Essex's trial at Westminster,
Ralegh was on duty as captain of the guard, and

also gave evidence as to his conversation with Gorges
on the river. When Ralegh was called, Essex,
insolent to the last, cried, 'What booteth it to
swear this fox'; and, at a subsequent stage, the
Earl sought to justify his statement that Cecil
and Ralegh were arranging to sell the country to
the Infanta, by alleging that he had been told that
Cecil had said to a fellow - councillor that the
Infanta's title was as good as that of any other
person. Cecil immediately challenged him to prove
it, whereupon he appealed to poor weak Southampton,
who stood by his side in the dock, who, in his
turn, named Sir William Knollys. Before the trial
was allowed to proceed Knollys was sent for, and
as he stepped on to the witness-stand the fate of
Essex trembled in the balance. 'Did Mr Secretary
ever use any such speeches in your hearing or to
your knowledge?' was the question asked. 'I
never heard him speak any words to that effect,'
answered Knollys, and the words must have sounded
like a death knell to the doomed man, enmeshed
in the toils he had spun for others. At Essex's
execution, Ralegh, as captain of the guard, was
present in the Tower. He thought that per-
chance the Earl might wish to speak to him, or
ask his forgiveness in his last moments, and at first
took up a position near the scaffold; but the
populace, who hated Ralegh, and had made up its
mind that Essex was being sacrificed to his intrigues,

began to murmur, and Ralegh retired to a distant window of the armoury where he could see without being seen. He afterwards said he was sorry that he had done so, as the Earl had asked for him. The cruel slanders about his indecent rejoicing at the fall of his rival rest upon an utterly discredited foundation—the imagination of the prejudiced crowd and the statements of the vile scoundrel Stukeley, who afterwards betrayed Ralegh. In his own last moments on the scaffold, Ralegh indignantly repudiated the slander. 'True it was, I was of the contrary faction, but I bare him no ill affection, and always believed it had been better for me that his life had been preserved; for after his fall I got the hatred of those who wished me well before, and those who set me against him set themselves afterwards against me, and were my greatest enemies.'

We are told that Ralegh was sad and troubled on his way back to Durham House, after Essex's execution, and well he might be. He was now supreme favourite, with no one to come between him and the Queen. But Elizabeth herself was a setting sun, and the great problem for courtiers was what luminary was to come after her. Essex had been brought to ruin by his own folly, but his descent had been carefully aided by Cecil for years past; and yet Cecil now posed, both to James VI. and to the London mob, as a man deeply injured by Essex, but who had sought to soften the blow which had fallen on the favourite;

whilst Ralegh was, by his own writing to Cecil, made
to appear a vindictive enemy, urging the Secretary to
extreme courses. Before very long Ralegh was to
find, when too late, that Robert Cecil could as ill
brook the rivalry of friends and partisans like himself,
as that of declared opponents like Essex. Hardly
had the head of the Earl been struck from his
shoulders than the secret correspondence which was
to ruin Ralegh was commenced between Secretary
Cecil, Lord Henry Howard and the coming King
James.

Ralegh's multifarious duties did not sit lightly
upon him : he worked laboriously at them all. As
Governor of Jersey, planning new fortifications, sitting
as supreme judge in litigious cases, or abolishing old
abuses ; as Lord Warden of the Stannaries, safeguard-
ing the interests of his tin miners, whilst securing his
own great revenues ; as Lord Lieutenant of Cornwall,
keeping an eye on the important fortresses upon which
the safety of England so largely depended ; as Captain
of the Guard and informal councillor, in constant
attendance upon the Queen and entertaining foreign
diplomatists ; as a great Irish landowner—a quality
he was soon to relinquish by the sale of his estate
—immersed in litigation with his neighbours and
tenants ; as an English country gentleman, deeply
interested in the cultivation of his lands ; as an explorer, continuing to send expeditions to Guiana at
his own expense to maintain the friendly communica-

tions with the natives, and striving, again and again, unsuccessfully, to join hands with his abandoned colonists in Virginia ; and, above all, as a Parliament man, speaking often and weightily. He sat as senior Knight of the Shire for Cornwall in the Parliament of 1601-2. A bill was introduced for the compulsory sowing of hemp by farmers. To this he was strongly opposed. 'I do not,' he said, 'like this constraining of men to manure or use their ground at our wills ; but rather let every man use his ground for that which it is most fit for, and therein use their own discretion' ; and he subsequently went on to condemn the compulsory ploughing of land, which he said the farmers often were too poor to sow, and it was thus made useless even for pasture. He also spoke strongly and patriotically in favour of a generous grant being voted for the defence of the country. The Spaniards had established a considerable army at Kinsale, and had been twice unsuccessful in subsequent attempts to send strong fleets to reinforce it. There was some attempt in Parliament to exempt the 'three pound men,' but Ralegh successfully demanded that there should be no exemptions. He let it be seen, however, that his action was not from any want of sympathy for the poorer taxpayers, but only because the required subsidy could not be raised unless the 'three pound men' were included. The way in which he turned upon such powerful men as Cecil and Bacon, both of whom favoured his own view, in this debate, is a good specimen of the intellectual arrogance which drew so much dislike upon him. Cecil had said, 'Neither pots or pans nor dish nor spoon should be spared when danger is at our elbows. I would not by any means have the "three pound men" excluded, because I would have the King of Spain to know how willing we are to sell all in defence of God's religion, our prince and our country.' And Ralegh answered, ' I like it not that the Spaniards, our enemies, should know of our selling our pots and pans to pay subsidies ; you may call it policy . . . but I am sure it argues poverty in the State.' Francis Bacon had advocated the inclusion of the 'three pound men' on the ground that ' *Dulcis tractus pari jugo.*' 'Call you this "*par jugum*,"' cried Ralegh, 'when a poor man pays as much as a rich one ; and peradventure his estate is no better than it is set at, or but little better ; while our estates are thirty or forty pounds in the Queen's books, and it is not the hundreth part of our wealth ; therefore it is neither *dulcis* nor *par.*'

In his speeches during the session in favour of the repeal of the act for compulsory tillage, his arguments are curiously anticipatory of the free trade views which in our times have become established. ' The Low Countryman and the Hollander,' he pointed out, 'who never sow corn, have by their industry such plenty that they may serve other nations . . . and therefore I think the best course is to set it (*i.e.*, the cultivation of corn) at liberty, and leave every

man free, which is the desire of a true Englishman.'

By more than one little civil passage of arms between Ralegh and Cecil in this session, it is easy to
see that although they were still ostensibly friendly,
the division had already begun. Cecil's letters to
Ralegh's cousin, Sir George Carew, at the same period
tell a similar story.   It is evident from them that
Cecil stood in the way of Ralegh's constant ambition
to be appointed a privy councillor, and that Cecil's
path of selfish statesmanship here separated from that
of his old friend and colleague.

CHAPTER XI

DURING the whole of her reign Elizabeth had vigorously resisted all persuasions to countenance a successor to her crown. By the will of Henry VIII. it devolved upon her death to the descendants of Frances, Duchess of Suffolk, represented at the end of Elizabeth's reign by William Seymour, the grandson of Catharine Grey by the Earl of Hertford, whom she had married in the Tower. James Stuart, as representing the descendants of the elder daughter of Henry VII., Margaret, Queen of Scotland, was held by many jurists to be excluded in consequence of his being an alien; and his cousin Arabella, the daughter of Darnley's younger brother, was considered to have a better claim to the crown. There

were several descendants of the Poles, notably the
Earl of Huntingdon, who were also considered to
have a right to be included in the line of succession,
and who, at various times during Elizabeth's life,
had been taken up by one or another of the political
parties.

Mary Stuart's will, disinheriting her son James in
consequence of his heresy and bequeathing her rights
to the English crown to Philip of Spain, had been
the outcome of long-continued intrigue on the part
of Spanish paid agents; but it was only intended to
give further sanction to Philip's claim as a descend-
ant of Philippa Plantagenet, daughter of John of
Gaunt, which, for some time previously, had been
cautiously and tentatively advanced. There had
long been a bitter feud between the English and
Scottish Catholic exiles with regard to the succession. Most of them were in the pay of Philip;
and the English, with a few exceptions, were strongly
opposed to the accession of a Scottish king to the
English throne. They were ceaseless in urging
upon Philip that the union of the two crowns
would mean the subjugation of England to Scotland,
which the English would never permit; and Philip's
English advisers pointed out to him that a Catholic
revival, which reached them over the Scottish border,
would be resisted on national grounds even by the
English Catholics themselves. On the other hand,
the Guises, the French cardinals at the Vatican, the

Scots, and the Pope himself, who were not anxious to see the Spaniards supreme over England, were in favour of converting James, or, at least, securing from him toleration for Catholics, and helping him to the crown. For years the main intrigue was worked in Rome, where Allen and Parsons, with Philip's ambassador, were ceaseless in their efforts to throw cold water on the suggestion that James might be sincerely converted ; whilst Cardinal Mondovi, Cardinal Sanzio, the agent of the League, and, above all, the Carthusian Bishop of Dunblane, were equally active in an opposite direction. The duplicity of James himself was marvellous. He blew hot and cold with equal facility ; would enter into Catholic plots with Huntly or Claude Hamilton ; would receive and smile upon the Bishops of Ross or Dunblane, discuss religion with the Jesuit priests, ask the Pope and Philip for men and money to protect him against the heretics ; or allow Guise to suggest a marriage between him and the Pope's niece. But he was equally ready to receive a pension from Elizabeth ; and when it suited him, to be as rigid a Puritan as John Knox himself.

As Elizabeth's days began to draw to an end, it became necessary for English statesmen to consider deeply the subject which she herself avoided. The edifice of English greatness had been laboriously built up during forty years of herculean labour and consummate statesmanship ; and it behoved all those

who had taken part in the work, to safeguard it
when the great Queen should fall.   For personal
reasons, and from the Queen's policy, most of the
English claimants had receded into the background
before Elizabeth's death, and Lady Arabella Stuart was
the only person in England of royal descent who had
any probability of success.   She herself was a somewhat unwise and flighty person, who lived principally with her grandmother, the Countess of Shrewsbury — Bess of Hardwick — at one or other of her
great houses, Chatsworth or Hardwick Hall.   Her life
at Court, when she went thither, was an unquiet
one ; she was alternately patronised and snubbed
by the Queen, and as many husbands had been in
turn suggested for her by various political com-
binations   as   for   Elizabeth   herself — Leicester's
base son, James VI., Henry IV., the Archduke
Mathias, and a host of other pretenders, were in
turn mentioned and dropped, until, in the last year
of the Queen's reign, she took the dangerous step
of marrying clandestinely young William Seymour,
the grandson of Catharine Grey.   The combination
thus formed might have been a powerful one, as it
united the two principal English claimants ; and but
for the obscure intrigues which brought Cecil to adopt
James VI., it is quite possible that Arabella Stuart
and her husband might have succeeded peacefully
to the throne.   The question of the succession was
thus an open one, and it involved no disloyalty on

the part of Ralegh, or any other statesman, to examine and discuss the various claims, or to espouse the cause of either of the claimants.

The pamphlets with regard to the right of succession had been numerous. The Scottish-French party had persistently alleged that Mary Stuart and her son were not ineligible for the English throne in consequence of their being aliens; and when the English Catholics had persuaded Philip that the country would welcome him with open arms in place of a Scotsman, and it was determined to assert his own claims, the arguments of the Scottish party were adopted so far as they related to the eligibility of alien princes to succeed. Philip's descent from John of Gaunt was always coupled with the renunciation of Mary Stuart in his favour; and James was excluded by the Spaniards, not for alienage, but in consequence of his mother's will, and because of his heresy, and the kinship of his parents, who had been married without a papal dispensation. At the time of the Armada the Pope had been cajoled into an agreement by which Philip was to have the right of appointing the Sovereign of England when Elizabeth was deposed; but when the Pontiff became restive as to the person to be appointed, he was told that the King did not want England for himself, but that in order to be quite sure of the effectual conversion of the country, the only person he could depend upon would be his daughter the Infanta.

Sixtus did not like the situation, but both he and
the French had been disarmed by the clever prior
diplomacy of Philip, and he was obliged to put up
with it; rejoicing, nevertheless, at its failure when
the disaster of the Armada had made it for a time
impossible. The English Catholics, however, paid
by Philip; Heighinton, Father Parsons (in his
own name and under that of Dolman), Dr Wendon,
Cardinal Allen and others, continued both in speech
and writing to urge the claims of the Spanish King,
and even the Scottish Bishop of Ross (Leslie) and
the Archbishop of Glasgow (Beton) were ultimately
bought over to the same side.

After the failure of the Armada, the English resi-
dents in Spain, the Duchess of Feria at their head,
begged Philip, again and again, to espouse the cause
of the afflicted Catholics in England; the Jesuits were
ceaseless in their efforts to the same end; and when
it became evident that the King himself was too old
and broken to act for himself, he was urged to make
provisions for aiding by arms and money the accession
of his favourite daughter the Infanta when Elizabeth
should die. No prompt action could be got from
him, and beyond his tardy and inadequate aid to the
Irish rebels, he did little but adopt in principle the
prayer of the English exiles that the Infanta should
be their future sovereign.

After Philip's death in 1598, the English Catholics
continued to urge upon his successor the vigorous pro-

motion of the Infanta's claim. Philip III., however, was even in greater penury than his father had been, utterly exhausted by his disastrous attempts to aid the Irish, and for a time no definite answer could be obtained from him. Father Creswell was representing the English Catholics at Madrid and Father Parsons in Rome, urging upon Philip III. continually the need for a prompt decision, and at length, in July 1600, it was decided that the Infanta and her husband, the Archduke, now Sovereigns of the Netherlands, should be adopted formally as the Spanish candidates for the English throne. It had been decided by Philip and his Council that galleys should be sent to Flanders to be in readiness ; but the King was sadly told that there were no galleys available, and the most that could be done was to send thither 200,000 ducats to hold in readiness for instant use when the Queen of England should die. To Father Parsons in Rome was entrusted the task of conveying the intelligence to the English Catholics, but only those in whom implicit confidence could be placed were to be told.

Late in 1602 Creswell presented to the Council in Madrid communications from the Catholics in England saying that the Queen might die at any moment. James's friends were busy, and it was absolutely necessary, if the Catholics were not to be completely outwitted, that a considerable force should be ready to act in the Infanta's favour when the Queen died. They begged that an immediate

answer, yes or no, should be sent to them ; because
if nothing was to be done, they must make the best
terms they could with the new king. In vain, week
after week, Creswell prayed for an answer, until at
last he lost patience and threatened to inform his
principals that he could do no more, and washed
his hands of the business.

The slow and cumbrous methods of infinite consultation introduced by Philip II. always made
prompt decision impossible ; but the reason why
Creswell was kept waiting from November 1602
to March 1603 for a formal answer as to the
Spanish intentions was that when the communications of the English Catholics were laid before the
Council, Count de Olivares had the boldness for
the first time to seize the bull by the horns, and
in a speech of prodigious length and prolixity
placed an entirely new light on the matter. What
was the good, he asked, of talking about imposing
the Infanta on the English people. She and her
husband were elderly and childless, neither of them
cared a straw about the English throne : they had
more than they could do to hold the Netherlands.
The King's exchequer was empty ; he had no ships
or men to spare ; and to assume an endless responsibility in England would probably complete the ruin
of Spain. Let the English Catholics choose one of
themselves, or even a heretic if he would give toleration ; and then the King of Spain might assume the

disinterested *rôle* of the champion of the English candidate, to whom he would transfer his rights, against the alien King of Scots. This was a new view, and the Council was ordered to discuss it fully and exhaustively. It took them three months to do it, but it was at last decided that the Infanta was to be dropped, and the English Catholics informed that the King would aid any candidate they adopted. It was thought that this solution would disarm the King of France and the Pope, the latter of whom was to be tackled by Father Parsons and the Duke of Sessa. Ships were to be fitted out and a fresh supply of money sent to Flanders, the selected candidate was to be recommended to conciliate other pretenders by almost dividing the country amongst them, and the Spanish force to be sent was to request the new sovereign to grant the Isle of Wight as a station, which, once gained, the Spaniards had no intention of giving up. But, above all, the Queen's ministers were to be approached, and convinced that Spain had now no selfish views, and that this was the solution which offered the best prospects both for them and for England. This formal decision was arrived at on the 2nd March 1603, and the matter has been set forth thus at length, as it probably furnishes the key to the mystery which has always surrounded Ralegh's alleged complicity in a plot in favour of the Spanish party.

There is little reason to doubt, however, that, although the official decision of the Spanish Council was not adopted until the beginning of March, its drift was known to the English Catholics by the end of the year 1602 or very early in 1603, and that the person selected by them to be aided by Spanish arms was Arabella Stuart, whose close imprisonment at that time may be thus explained. It had been decided, as has been said, to approach Elizabeth's ministers and enlist them in the new Spanish plans, on the patriotic grounds of excluding the alien Scot; and there is no doubt that the communications known to have passed between Cobham and Ralegh and the Flemish envoy Aremberg were originally to this effect.

In the meanwhile Cecil had established a perfect secret understanding with James, from which Ralegh was excluded. Several weeks after Essex's death, James's envoys, the Earl of Mar and Mr Bruce of Kinloss, arrived in London, too late of course to save the Earl; but their second instructions were cautiously to approach Cecil and offer him the King's favour in return for help to his cause. Their fulfilment of these orders was more prudent than the orders themselves, which had conveyed a threat, on the supposition that Cecil was taking part in the Spanish plans, a belief doubtless conveyed to James by Essex. A secret conference with Cecil soon convinced Mar that this was a mistake, and an arrangement was made for the carrying on of a correspondence between the King and the

Secretary.   Before this, James had been propitiated by
Lord Henry Howard, certainly the basest villain in
the black story of betrayal that followed.   Lord
Henry Howard, long afterwards the murderer of Sir
Thomas Overbury, had been for many years a spy in
the pay of Spain, and was deep in the confidence of
the Catholic party.   Everything that was done in the
interests of the Spanish plans was known to him.
At the same time he was carrying on a confidential
correspondence with James, in which his hate of
Ralegh was indulged in without restraint.   Not only
was Ralegh blackened, but nearly every other statesman but Cecil, upon whom Howard knew he would
have to depend.   Northumberland and Cobham
especially were attacked, as friends of Ralegh.   'Hell
cannot afford such a like triplicity, that denies the
Trinity,' he wrote to James, speaking of these three.
In November 1601, the Duke of Lennox, who had
been sent by James to Henry IV. to ask for his
countenance to his claims—which, by the way, Henry
IV. was not very willing to give—was ordered to
hasten to London whilst Parliament was sitting, to
watch his master's interests.   He was brought into
touch with Ralegh and Cobham, 'those wicked villains,'
as Howard called them.   Several conferences appear
to have taken place at Durham House, at which
Ralegh expressed his devotion to James—this, be it
remembered, was more than a year before the decision
of the Spaniards to support any English candidate

against James. Anything that should bring Ralegh
into friendly contact with the Scottish King was gall
and wormwood to Henry Howard, who at once
sounded an alarm. First he wrote to the Earl of
Mar suggesting that Lennox was busy raising up a
party in opposition to Mar and Cecil; and to James
he continued to repeat that Ralegh and Cobham were
really against him. 'Hell did never vomit up such a
couple,' he said.

But the dastardly scoundrel went further, and put
in writing the heads of a proposed plot, by which
Ralegh and Cobham should be destroyed. It is in the
form of a letter to Cecil now in the Cotton MSS.
First the Queen's mind must be poisoned against
them. 'Hir Majesty must knowe the rage of their
discontent for want of being called to that height
which they affect; and be made to taste the perill
that growes out of discontented minds. . . . She must
know that the blame is only laid on hir. . . . So
that roundly Hir Majestie must daily and by divers
means be let to know the world's apprehendinge hir
deepe wisdome in discerning the secret flawes of their
affections. She must see some advertisements from
forrain parts of the greif which the Queene's enemies
doo take at their (i.e., Ralegh and Cobham's) sittinge
out, hoping that their placing in authority would so
far alienate the people's reverent affection as some
mischief would succeed of it. She must be taught to
see the perill that growes unto princes, by protecting,

countenancing, or entertaining persons odious to the multitude.' One by one the three friends, Ralegh, Cobham and Northumberland, and even Ralegh's wife, are picked to pieces in order that Cecil may show their failings to the Queen. 'Rawlie that in pride exceedeth all men alive, finds no vent for paradoxis out of a Council board . . . and inspireth Cobham with his own passions. His wife as furious as Proserpina with failing of that restitution at Court which flatterie had moved her to expect.' All this and much more was to be instilled into the Queen's ear by Cecil, 'that she may be more apt to receive impressions of more important reasons when time serves with opportunity.' And then, 'you must embark this gallant Cobham by your witt and interest, in some course the Spanish way, as either may reveale his weaknesse or snare his ambition.' 'For my own part, I account it impossible for him to escape the snares which wit may sett and weaknesse is apt to fall into.' Howard says that the two friends had planned that Cobham should advocate peace with Spain, whilst Ralegh opposed it, in order that in either case one would succeed and help the other. Inferences were to be drawn from their desire, and toils set for them that they could not escape, and, as we shall see, into which they fell. Cecil, in his first letters to James, strikes the note of detraction of Ralegh and his friends, which was to deepen until they were ruined. Cecil had been

the life-long friend of Ralegh, and their correspondence had been of the most affectionate character,
and yet this is how he writes of him when he is
asking the King not to convey to him, Cecil, any
intelligence of the supposed plots of Ralegh and
his friends, in case any accident should happen to
the letter and he should lose their confidence.

'I do profess, in the presence of Him that knoweth
and searcheth all men's hearts, that if I dyd not
some tyme cast a stone into the mouth of these
gaping crabbs when they are in the prodigall humour
of discourses, they would not stick to confess dayly
how contrary it is to their nature to resolve to be
under your sovereignty, though they confess (Ralegh
especially) that *rebus sic stantibus*, naturall policy
forceth him to keep on foot such a trade against
the great day of mart. In all which light and
sudden humours of his, though I do no way check
him becawse he shall not think I reject his freedom
or his affection, but alwaies (*sub sigillo confessionis*)
use contestation with him that I neyther had nor
ever would *in individuo* contemplate future idea, nor
ever hoped for more than justice in time of change ;
yet, under pretext of extraordinary care of his well-
doing, I have seemed to disswade him from ingaging
himself too farr, even for himself — much more,
therefore, to forbeare to assume for me or my present
intentions.' This friend then begs the King to
believe nothing that Ralegh may say under any

circumstances. But why, he asks, should he trouble
the King with the relation of Ralegh's 'ingratitude'
to him. 'I will leave the best and worst of him to
3 (*i.e.*, Lord Henry Howard) relation, in whose
discretion and affection you may sleep securely.'
Cecil, too, working on James's known theological
bias, revived the old slander about Ralegh's religion,
and calls him 'a person whom most religious men
do hold anathema.' So jealous were Cecil and
Howard, that they went to the length of begging
James to tell them the name of the person who
had introduced Ralegh to the Duke of Lennox, their
evident desire being to mark even the intermediary
down for ruin. James himself knew this, for he
writes that the gentleman was Sir Arthur Savage,
'a verrie honest, plaine gentleman.' 'Not doubt-
ing but that 10 (*i.e.*, Cecil) will conserve this as
a freind's secreate, without suffering the gentleman
to receave hairm thereby — since the gentlemanis
nature appearis to be farre different from Raulies.'
Through the correspondence, both with Cecil and
Howard, James and his ministers, Mar and Bruce,
are extravagant in their professions of love and confidence in Cecil, and in their assurances that Ralegh
shall not be allowed to supplant him. Ralegh's
old friend, Northumberland, must have seen that he
was marked out for disgrace, for even he made haste
to scuttle away from the sinking ship. In a letter
to the King, giving him particulars of the tendencies

of the English courtiers towards the succession, he
says that although Ralegh is opposed to some of
James's friends, yet he knows that he is in favour
of the King's claims. 'The first of these (*i.e.*,
Cobham) I know not how his heart is affected,
but the latter (Ralegh), whom sixteen years' acquaint- .
ance hath confirmed to me, I must needs affirme
Rawliegh's ever allowance of yowr right; and al-
thowgh I knowe him insolent, extremely heated,
a man that desirs to seeme to be able to swaye
all men's fancies, all men's cowrses, and a man out
of himself; when your time sall come will never
be able to do yow muche goode nor hearme. Yet
must I needs confesse what I know, that there is
excellent good parts of natur in hem, a man whose
love is disadvantageous to me in somme sort, which
I cherish rather out of constancie than policie, and
one whome I wish Your Majesty not to lose,
because I woulde not that one haire of a man's
head sould be against yow that might be for yow.'
This was written when Elizabeth was already sicken-
ing for her last illness, and it sets forth the impression of the weak time-server, that the powerful
favourite, the great genius of whom he had been a
satellite for years, was already a man to be damned
with faint praise, to be contemptuously apologised
for, but who henceforward could do neither good
nor harm. To this had Ralegh been brought by
the sneers and slanders of Howard and Cecil, during

eighteen months' correspondence with the suspicious
coming King.   Ralegh's absence in Jersey and the
west country had also been taken advantage of by
Cecil to turn the old Queen's mind against her
favourite, in accordance with the Machiavellian sugges-
tions of Howard already quoted; and in the last
months of the reign, the shadow of disgrace was
already descending rapidly upon him.   When, therefore, on the 24th March 1603, the great Queen
breathed her last, the seed so laboriously and secretly
sown by Cecil had produced its harvest; the new
King was ready to look upon Ralegh as a traitor,
and out of Cornwall hardly a man in England
would say a good word for the erstwhile splendid
favourite.

Immediately the Queen died, a meeting of the
principal public men was held at Whitehall to decide
upon the proclamation of a successor.   Ralegh was
not a privy councillor, but he was summoned from
the country, came and signed the letter of welcome
to the King with the rest.   It is difficult for Englishmen in these times to conceive the distrust and
dislike then entertained for Scotsmen.   They were of
course foreigners, and had for centuries been more or
less closely allied to France, the secular enemy of
England; their country was poor, and a large portion
of it in semi-savagery; and it was an article of faith
with most patriotic Englishmen, that the Scot must
never be allowed to dominate this country.   But the

fates had fought in favour of James. The tardy and
cumbrous methods of Philip's Government, the
attempt of Spain to grasp more than she could hold,
had for forty years frustrated all efforts from that
quarter to re-establish influence in England. When
at last the looked-for day arrived, and the throne of
England was vacant, Spain again was too late. We
have seen that the formal decision to adopt and aid
with men and money any Catholic or moderate candidate who should be chosen by the English themselves
against James Stuart, had only been arrived at on the
2nd March, which—allowing for difference of the
calendars—was only about a month before Elizabeth's
death. There was time for the Catholic and anti-Scots
English party to choose Arabella Stuart as their candidate, but not time for the proposed Spanish support
to be prepared to aid her. There was practically therefore no other candidate than James ready at the
time of the Queen's death, and the best that the
patriotic party could do was to endeavour to limit to
some extent the anticipated ravages of the Scottish
locusts upon the fat pastures of the south. At the
meeting at Whitehall, Ralegh's is said to be the voice
that gave utterance to this feeling. He expressed an
opinion that some limit ought to be placed on the
power of the new King to appoint Scotsmen to
English offices. Doubtless many thought so as
well ; but each man was eagerly looking out for his
own future, and dared not anger the coming King.

The people at large had so long anticipated trouble on the death of the Queen, that they were in a fever of unreasoning rejoicing and loyalty to the man who appeared to be able to save them from the affliction of civil war, and Ralegh's voice, if it gave forth such utterances as those mentioned, found no echo outside. Aubrey says—although it is probably untrue—that at the meeting at Whitehall Ralegh proposed a republic, and gives his words as, 'Let us keep the staff in our own hands, and set up a commonwealth and not remain subject to a needy beggarly nation.' In any case, he lost no time, any more than his colleagues, in trying to curry favour by the most abject flattery with the new King.

James set forth for his new kingdom in the beginning of April. The exodus of courtiers and favour-seekers from London to meet the sovereign threatened to be so great that a proclamation was issued forbidding any person in the public service from resorting to the King ; and Cecil advised Ralegh not to go.   Ralegh, however, held many high offices, which gave him right of access to the royal person, and he disregarded the advice.   He met the King for the first time at Burghley House, his excuse for coming being the need of the King's authority for the continuance of legal process in the Duchy of Cornwall.   Several stories have been told of the words that passed between them ; that the King openly insulted him by telling him that he thought

very 'rawly' of him, a poor pun on his name; and
others of a similar sort; but without giving undue
credit to Aubrey's gossip, it may be safely concluded
that there was no cordiality in the interview.   Ralegh
got the document he wanted as soon as might be so,
that he might have no pretext for staying, and Lake
reported to Cecil that he 'had taken no great root
here.'   Then blow after blow fell upon Ralegh.
Soon after his return to London he was summoned
to the Council Chamber and informed that he had
been deprived of his office of Captain of the Guard,
and that Sir Thomas Erskine had been appointed in
his place.   Rumour in the streets had already anticipated this; as well it might, for Cecil had planned
the dismissal long before.   He had apparently asked
the King for the disposal of the office; as Mr Bruce,
writing to Lord Henry Howard, says (25th March
1603), 'So long as 30 (*i.e.*, King James) sall have
need of a guard, so long sall it be at 10 (*i.e.*, Cecil's)
charge.'

What looked like a favour was granted to Ralegh
soon afterwards, but it was not for his benefit.   His
Governorship of Jersey had been charged with the payment of £300 a year to Lord Henry Seymour, and
he was relieved from this payment, but in less than
two months the Governorship of Jersey itself was taken
away from him.   But a more serious loss preceded this.
Almost the first act done by the new King was to
consider, with a view to their abrogation, the various

monopolies granted by Elizabeth. They were very unpopular, and much of Ralegh's own unpopularity was owing to his tavern licensing patent; it was needful for the new King to please the people, and the monopolies were called in. The petition prompting the measure had been especially aimed at Ralegh, but a question arose as to whether his licensing patent was a monoply at all. It was easy, however, to find a pretext for injuring Ralegh, and his patent was suspended until the question was decided ; and he was thus suddenly deprived of his most profitable source of income. Then came the occupation of the crown house of Durham Place. The house had been formerly the palace of the bishops of Durham, but had been taken by the crown, and for many years had been used as a royal guest-house. The Spanish ambassadors had lived there during the reign of Mary, and part of that of Elizabeth, but from 1583 Ralegh had made it his town residence. The part towards the Strand— stables and offices—had already become somewhat ruinous, and the great hall, which was a common thoroughfare for the neighbours going to get water from the conduit in the inner court, had been injured by fire. The character of the Strand, moreover, was changing, and there is no doubt that Cecil and Ralegh had already discussed the conversion of the stable front into something more fitting to a street which was becoming a principal one. Cecil's own house was only separated from it by the narrow thoroughfare called Ivy Lane, and he had already cast covetous eyes across. Toby Matthew, the Bishop of Durham, had welcomed the King · as effusively as if he had never abused him ; and, of course, at Cecil's suggestion, had begged from James the restitution to him of the ancient palace of the See. Matthew got the palace, but very soon the ramshackle congeries of stables and outhouses on the Strand front were transferred to Cecil, who built the new exchange called Britain's Burse upon the site, to the great advantage of himself and his successors ever since. Ralegh had spent large sums in repairing and partly rebuilding the river front ; he had lived undisturbed in the place for twenty years ; but he was turned out with every circumstance of harshness. The King's warrant to the Lord Keeper and the Judges, dated 31st May 1603, sets forth that the law having decided that the persons 'that now dwell in the Bishop of Duresme's house, called Duresme Place, have no right therein' . . . they are to have notice to quit. Ralegh begged earnestly to be allowed to stay until Michaelmas, which the Bishop thought 'nothing reasonable,' and he was obliged to go by midsummer. He was also forbidden to remove any fixtures, 'which' he wrote to the Lord Keeper Egerton, 'seemeth to mee very strange, seeinge that I have had possession of the howse these xx. yeares, and have bestowed well nere £2000 uppon the same.' He says that the meanest gentleman in England would have had six months'·

notice to quit, and even a poor artificer is entitled to three months' notice from his landlord. He had, he said, laid in provisions and fodder for forty persons, and as many horses, 'and to remove my famyly and stuff in 14 days is such a severe expulsion as hath not bynn offered to any man before this daye.' But there was no consideration for Ralegh now, and he was obliged to go.

Ralegh did not fall without a struggle. He professed the profoundest submission to the King's will. He offered to raise 2000 men with which to fight Spain if the King would strike at the enemy, which was now at the last gasp of exhaustion. He sought to gain the new King's ear with his patriotism and eloquence, as he had won that of his dead mistress. But he had a different sovereign to deal with. The base craven who had succeeded to the grand inheritance was all for truckling, and Ralegh could have taken no course more likely to be unpalatable to the Scottish Solomon than to give him bold and patriotic counsel. But though he tried in vain to win his way back to favour by submission and flattery of the man he must have despised, his proud heart must have raged with fury at the indignity to which he was subjected. The French Ambassador, Beaumont, writes to Villeroy in May that Ralegh had been dismissed. 'Dont le dit Sieur Rallé est en telle furie, que partant pour aller trouver le roy, il a protesté de lui faire declarer et faire voir par ecrit toute la caballe et les intelligences que le Sieur Cecil a dressées, et conduites a son prejudice.' Cecil himself, writing in August to inform Sir Thomas Parry of Ralegh's arrest, says, 'This hath been the cause. First, he hath been discontented *in conspectu omnium* ever since the King came, and yet for those offices taken from him the King gave him £300 a year during his life. Secondly, his inwardness, or rather his governing Lord Cobham's spirit, made great suspicion that in these treasons he had part.' Now we see how the snare referred to by Howard to be set for them had been worked. Cobham was weak, shifty and garrulous; his family had been leaning to the Spanish side for years, and he could easily be led into, or be detected in, a compromising position, whilst Ralegh could be drawn up by the same throw of the net, because of his 'inwardness' with, and influence over Cobham, and yet Cobham was the brother-in-law, and Ralegh the life-long friend of Cecil.

It was not to be expected that the Catholic party in England, which had learnt before Elizabeth's death of the intention of the King of Spain to help with all his might the English candidate they might choose, should calmly settle down to the new order of things which disappointed all their hopes. The decision of Philip III. was adopted too late for the plans to be carried into effect when the Queen died, and it was natural that the ferment of the plot should work to the surface in some form or another before affairs became

normal.   For years disputes had raged in the bosom
of the Catholic party in England, a reflection of those
that existed amongst the exiles.   The Jesuits, with
Parsons in Rome or in Spain, were bound heart and
soul to the Spanish interest, as we have seen.   The
secular priests, on the contrary, had, as time went on,
resented the unquiet and unpatriotic action of the
Jesuits, and had assumed the moderate attitude
advocated by the French party and, generally
speaking, by the Vatican.   They resented the idea
of having a king imposed upon England by Spanish
pikes.   If they could not have a Catholic sovereign
they would put up with a Protestant, if only he
would refrain from persecuting them.   Two of the
leaders of this party of priests—Watson and Clarke
—disappointed that James had not consented to
grant toleration, formed a plan in imitation of
several that had been resorted to during James's
youth in Scotland, of seizing him and extorting
from him a decree of full religious toleration.
Their confederates were few and unimportant, two or
three Catholic gentlemen, Anthony Copley, Sir Griffin
Markham, Lord Cobham's brother George Brooke,
and, at first, Lord Grey de Wilton, who wanted
toleration for the Puritans, but who was deceived
with regard to the real objects of the plot.   Anything which would have the effect of bringing about
religious concord in England was naturally opposed
to the objects' of the Jesuit party, which aimed, at

least, at Catholic supremacy; and some of the Jesuit
fathers who had heard of the plot communicated it
to Cecil. The foolish and ill-considered conspiracy
was called the 'Bye' or Priests' Treason, and there is
no proof of any sort that Ralegh was connected
with it; although Cobham must at least have been
cognisant of it.

Copley was arrested on the 6th July. His declarations caused the apprehension of George Brooke
on the 14th; and orders were given for that of
Markham, Lord Grey and the priests. On the
day before, or the day of Brooke's arrest, Ralegh
was walking on the terrace at Windsor, waiting
to ride in the train of the King, who was going
hunting. Cecil approached him, and said that the
Council wished to ask him some questions. He
attended the chamber, and was asked whether he
knew anything of the plot to surprise and seize the
King, and he replied with truth that he did not.
He was then interrogated as to his knowledge of
plots in favour of Arabella, or of treasonable communications between his friend, Lord Cobham, and
the Flemish ambassador, Count Aremberg. He
professed ignorance of any such plots or communications, and was then allowed to retire. In fact,
George Brooke, while under examination about
the 'Bye' Conspiracy, had opened up a wider vista
than that of the Priests' Treason, by confessing knowledge of a more important plot being hatched between

his brother, Cobham, and Count Aremberg; and on the 19th July Cobham himself was interrogated by the Council, and denied all knowledge of the plot attributed to him by his brother. When Ralegh's interrogations had been concluded, he took a step which, in the obscurity which now surrounds the whole business, seems inexplicable, and which he himself subsequently confessed, brought about the ruin which ensued. Cobham was his friend and close political associate, and any proof of treason against him could hardly fail to affect Ralegh; and yet the latter, after his examination was ended, wrote to Cecil that he suspected that Cobham had intelligence with Aremberg—with whom he had, to the knowledge of the Cecils, carried on a correspondence for years — because after Cobham's visiting Durham House, Ralegh had seen him pass his own water gate at Blackfriars, and row over to St Saviours, Southwark, where there lodged a certain La Renzi, a follower of Aremberg's. This letter of Ralegh's, which was intended to be sent to the Council, was by Cecil's advice withheld. Cecil advised Ralegh not to speak of these suspicions, as the King did not wish to cast odium upon Aremberg, and Ralegh then told Cecil that if he did not lay hands on La Renzi the latter would escape, and the matter would never be discovered, and yet if La Renzi were arrested Cobham would at once suspect something. This was a fatal, and on the

face of it, a foolish thing for Ralegh to do; for it
inferred that he knew much more than he said,
and placed him absolutely in Cecil's power. The
letter he had written was immediately shown by
Cecil to Cobham, who was then under examination.
He fell into the trap, jumped to the conclusion that
Ralegh had betrayed him, flew into a rage and
denounced Ralegh. 'Oh, traitor! Oh, villain! I
will now tell you all the truth,' he cried, and he
then assured his examiners 'that he had never
entered into these courses but by the instigation of
Ralegh, who would never let him alone.' Not
many minutes elapsed, however, before even foolish
Cobham saw the fatal step he had taken in thus
losing his temper; and before he got to the
stairs leading from the chamber he retracted what
he had said in his passion about Ralegh. He
adhered, however, to his previous statement that he
had conferred with Aremberg about procuring a large
sum of money—600,000 crowns, he said—from the
King of Spain, in the interests of peace between England and Spain, but had arranged that nothing further
should be done in the matter 'until he had spoken
to Sir Walter Ralegh for the distribution of the
money to them which were discontented in England.
Cobham was again examined on the 29th July, and
quite cleared Ralegh of complicity in his dealings,
and took the whole of the blame upon himself.
This turn of affairs did not suit Cecil, who, having

R

gone so far, could not stop short now of ruining Ralegh. The latter had been sent to the Tower immediately after Cobham's passionate denunciation of him on the 20th July, and it was easy to investigate any communications that had passed between him and Cobham since then, which might explain the latter's change of tone. After Ralegh's first examination at Windsor, when he professed entire ignorance of Cobham's intercourse with Aremberg, and presumably before he wrote the fatal letter of suspicion to Cecil, he had sent Captain Kemys to Cobham to say that the Council had asked certain questions about Cobham, but that he had cleared him ; and then, unfortunately, Kemys had added an exhortation to Cobham 'to be of good comfort, for one witness could not condemn a man for treason.' Ralegh says he gave Kemys no such compromising message, and this may be true ; but if Kemys invented the words himself he was certainly very badly inspired, for they were reported and made the most of against his master. This, however, was in the earlier stages. Between the 20th and 29th July, when both Ralegh and Cobham were in the Tower, the latter saw from his window young John Peyton, the son of the Governor, in conversation with Ralegh. Some hours afterwards Peyton came to visit Cobham, and the latter mentioned that he had seen him talking with Ralegh. 'God forgive him ! He hath accused me, but I cannot

accuse him.' Peyton replied, 'He doth say the like
of you : that you have accused him, but he cannot
accuse you.'

The only person who seems to have been actively
engaged in the two separate sets of negotiations,
respectively called the Bye or Priests' Treason, and
the Main or Spanish Treason, was George Brooke.
He, Copley, Watson the priest, and Lord Grey, were
examined again and again. Statements wrung out of
one prisoner were artfully dangled before another to
induce further confidences, until each one seemed to
compete with his fellows in his eagerness to make a
clean breast of it. Brooke had been told at the
beginning that the only way to procure favour 'is
to open all that possibly you can.' He began by
saying that 'the Bye Conspirators amongst themselves thought Sir Walter Ralegh a fit man to be
of the action.' This, it was clear, did not implicate
Ralegh; but, as time went on, Brooke, either out
of revenge or hope of favour, became ready to
incriminate both him and Cobham as far as the
examiners might desire. He was ready to drag in
many other names—Sir George Carew, Sir Henry
Brounker and others—but afterwards confessed that
he had only thought they might be likely to be
concerned in anything favourable to Lady Arabella.
In a letter to the Council Brooke plainly indicates
that he has made his reckless statements under
promise of reward. 'Whilst I breathe, if not after,

I shall claime those promises I have receaved both from the King and your Lordships. . . . To object errors committed sure is a frivolous cavilation, seinge I have committed none but for wante of the direction required.' The testimony of this man who, Ralegh said at his trial, 'never loved him,' and 'had been taught his lesson,' was to the effect that his brother Cobham had told him that Ralegh was not in the Bye Plot, but only in the Main, the object of which, he said, was to take away the King and his issue, which *on his conscience*, he thought had been suggested to his brother by Ralegh. Watson the priest deposed that Brooke had told him that Sir Walter Ralegh was upon the Main, the object of which was to destroy 'the King and all his cubs.' Watson also said that he had heard that the disturbances were to begin in Scotland, where he concluded that the Spaniards were to enter ; and Copley testified that Brooke had told him that Ralegh had suggested the commencement of disturbances in Scotland. I have transcripts of original documents in my possession which prove absolutely that this was untrue, so far as regards a project for a Spanish descent upon Scotland. The project had been a favourite one for many years with the Scottish Catholics, and had been embraced by Spain more than once, with the partial connivance of James himself ; but shortly before Elizabeth's death, Francis Stuart, Earl of Bothwell, an exile in Madrid, had presented a complete plan for the introduction

of Spanish troops into England through Scotland, and
the names and particulars of all persons in favour of
such action are given.   The scheme was examined by
Philip III. and his Council, and finally rejected, as
it was considered that it would only benefit James,
whom they could not trust. . The idea of an introduction of a Spanish force through Scotland at the
time in question was therefore absolutely at an end.
La Renzi deposed that Ralegh had been present when
he delivered letters to Cobham from Aremberg, but
he alleged that the sole object of the letters was to
procure peace.   All these odds and ends of more or
less suspicious testimony were carefully pieced together, but even then the evidence was obviously
inadequate upon which to put a great man on trial
for his life.   Cobham had withdrawn his incriminating statement as soon as it was made, and Brooke's
suborned testimony was the only direct evidence against
him.   Cobham's declarations were to the effect that
his interviews and correspondence with Aremberg were
with the object of negotiating for the King of Spain's
providing Cobham with 500,000 or 600,000 crowns,
to be distributed in England in the interests of a peace
between the two countries ; that Cobham was to go
to Spain to discuss the application of the money, and
on his way home was to call at Jersey, and see Ralegh,
further to discuss the same matter, only, Cobham added
during his anger, that he was afraid that if once he
put himself into Ralegh's power in Jersey he might

hand him and the money over to James with an incriminating statement.   Ralegh's own statement to a
certain extent bore out this.   He said that Cobham
had offered him 10,000 crowns of the money for the
furthering of peace between England and Spain ; but
that he had answered, 'When I see the money I will
make answer, for I thought it one of his ordinary idle
conceits, and therefore made no account thereof; but
this was, I think, before Count Aremberg's coming
over.'

Ralegh knew that, with the procedure then adopted
against prisoners for treason, he could hope neither for
fairness nor impartiality on the part of his judges.   He
was keenly conscious of his unpopularity with the
people, the King's dislike of him, and the bitter
jealousy of the nobles, who had always hated him as
an insolent upstart.   It has been remarked that, like
most sanguine and imaginative men, he easily fell into
profound despair.   Only a day after his arrival in the
Tower he attempted to kill himself with a table knife,
but merely inflicted a slight wound.   Although for
the authenticity of the pathetic and beautiful letter
to his wife on the eve of his attempt there is not
sufficient warrant for its reproduction here, there
can be no reasonable doubt of the act itself.   Biographers of Ralegh have sought to explain it according to their bias, some as an evidence of guilt, some
otherwise.   To me it seems that the man who could
fall into the depths of misery expressed in Ralegh's

letters, when the Queen had frowned upon him, would be extremely likely to descend to the level of suicide under the circumstances of utter ruin which faced him now. But this was only a first impulse of despair, and as the toils closed around him his great mind bent to the task of saving himself. He had been compelled to resign the Lord Wardenship of the Stannaries, and had been dismissed the Governorship of Jersey, in which he had been replaced by his late gaoler, Peyton. He was aware that the loose gossip of men like Watson and Brooke would not be sufficient to condemn him, if it were not confirmed by Cobham's declarations. In October Cobham requested the new Governor of the Tower, Sir George Harvey, to be allowed to write a letter to the Council exculpating Ralegh. 'God is my witness,' he said, 'it doth touch my conscience. I would fain have the words that the Lords used of my barbarousness in accusing him falsely.' Harvey concealed this request, and did nothing; desirous, doubtless, of pleasing Cecil. Soon afterwards, Ralegh caused an apple, enclosing a letter, to be thrown into Cobham's window in the Wardrobe Tower, praying him to do him justice, and to confess that he had wronged him by his accusations. Cobham answered this by a letter which did not seem sufficiently explicit to Ralegh, who begged him again to clear him at his trial. Instead of this Cobham wrote a letter including the following lines, which it is difficult to believe are insincere, notwithstanding what followed at the trial, which will be related in the next chapter : 'Seeing myself so near my end, for the discharge of my own conscience, and freeing myself from your blood, which else will cry vengeance against me, I protest upon my salvation I never practised with Spain by your procurement. God so comfort me in this my affliction as you are a true subject for anything that I know. I will say as Daniel : *Purus sum a sanguine hujus.* So God have mercy upon my soul, as I know no treason by you.' This letter was carefully concealed by Ralegh to be produced in due time in his own refutation.

CHAPTER XII

RALEGH'S TRIAL AT WINCHESTER — CONDEMNED TO
DEATH—HIS PRAYERS FOR LIFE—REPRIEVE—IN
THE TOWER

In November 1603 the plague was raging in London
and the law courts were transferred to Winchester.
The indictment against Ralegh was for plotting with
Cobham and Brooke 'to deprive the King of his
crown and dignity; to subvert the Government and
alter the true religion established in England, and to
levy war against the King.' It had been formally
presented at Staines on the 21st September, when the
jury was carefully packed and the proceedings ad-
journed. Early in November Sir William Waad
was instructed to convey Ralegh to Winchester for
trial. The prisoner went in his own coach in charge
of Sir Robert Mansel, 'and,' writes Mr Hicks to Lord
Shrewsbury, 'it was almost incredible what bitter
speeches they, the mob, exclaimed against him as
he went along; which general hatred of the people
would be to me worse than death; but he neglected

and scorned it as from base and rascal people.'
Waad himself reported to Cecil that it was 'touch-
and - go whether Ralegh could be brought alive
through such multitudes of unruly people as did
exclaim against him.' The trial had been postponed
until Aremberg had departed, loaded with presents
and loving messages from James, who tried his
hardest to persuade Beaumont, the French Ambassador,
that Aremberg was quite unconnected with the
affair, even after he had shown him the intercepted
letters which proved his communications with Cobham. There was now nothing to prevent the sacrifice of Ralegh, whom, said Beaumont, James both
feared and hated. The shameful scene took place
in the Palace of the Bishops of Winchester, fitted
up as a Court of King's Bench, and by special commission Ralegh's bitter enemy Henry Howard, his false
friend Cecil, and Sir William Waad, were associated
on the bench with the Lord Chamberlain, the Earl of
Suffolk (Ralegh's old friend Lord Thomas Howard),
the Earl of Devonshire (Blount), Lord Wotton, Sir
John Stanhope, the two chief justices, Popham and
Anderson, and two Puisne judges, Warburton and
Gawdy. The prosecution was conducted by Coke,
the attorney-general, a truculent scoundrel, whose
vile abuse of the prisoner was so scandalous as to be
rebuked even by Cecil; and from the moment that
Ralegh appeared in court the result of the trial
was a foregone conclusion. The general feeling in

England was that he was guilty, but that the evidence was not strong enough to convict him. This latter circumstance, however, did not trouble Coke in the least. Ralegh pleaded Not guilty, and begged, as his health was broken and his memory impaired, that he might be allowed to answer the points of the indictment separately as they occurred ; but Coke objecting, this was only permitted as the proofs were produced, and not as the points were set forth. The particulars of the trial have been so frequently printed that it will not be necessary to reproduce them here, but one or two samples of the mockery of justice may be quoted. With insult and vituperation unexampled in a court of law, Coke set forth the evidence that had been raked together against Cobham, and even against the conspirators of the Bye, in which it was admitted that Ralegh had no part. Ralegh protested that all this did not touch him in the least. He urged that the mere statements of the Attorney-General, without proof, were not evidence against him. 'I do not yet hear that you have spoken one word against me. Here is no treason of mine done. If my Lord Cobham be a traitor, what is that to me?' 'All that he did,' replied Coke, 'was by thy instigation, thou viper! for I thou thee, *thou* traitor. I will prove thee the rankest traitor in all England.' With a wit, readiness and resource, almost marvellous under the circumstances, Ralegh struggled against the inevitable. Whenever he seemed to be gaining a point, or the

Attorney-General's vituperation ran short, Cecil or Henry Howard interposed with a speech as a diversion. None of the ordinary decent etiquette of a court of justice was preserved, even for appearance sake, and the whole proceeding was a tragic travesty. On one occasion Coke shouted, 'Your intent was to set up the Lady Arabella as a titular Queen, and to depose our present rightful King. You pretend that this money was to forward the peace with Spain. Your jargon was peace, which meant Spanish invasion and Scottish subversion,' to which Ralegh replied, 'Let me answer ; it concerns my life.' 'Thou shalt not,' bellowed Coke ; and Popham, the chief justice, bade the prisoner be silent. When Ralegh got his chance at last, he denied, eloquently and fervently, that he had ever entered into any plots with Cobham ; and demanded to be confronted with him. With glowing force he called to witness his past life, his constant struggles against Spain ever since he could bear arms. He knew, he said, how poor, weak and impotent Spain had become. Was he a madman, he asked, to make himself a Jack Cade for the sake of Spain now ? Of what Cobham had done he knew nothing. 'But for my knowing that he had conspired these things with Spain for Arabella against the King, I protest before Almighty God I am as clear as whosoever here is freest. Ralegh begged earnestly, but in vain, to be confronted with Cobham. If he, Cobham, on his honour, said that he had been

instigated by him to treasonable plots in the interests
of Spain, then he, Ralegh, would submit to be dealt
with as the King willed.   Ralegh stood firm in the
possession of Cobham's letter, already quoted, solemnly
absolving him from all share of blame.   It looked
almost as if it would be impossible to convict him
without manifest scandal, when Coke produced his
coup de theatre.   Poor, weak, storm-tossed Cobham
had been 'got at'—Ralegh said, probably with
truth—by his wife, the Countèss of Kildare, who was
a Howard, and persuaded to buy favour by recant-
ing his retractation, and again to accuse Ralegh.
Coke read the letter in triumph.   'I have thought
fit, in duty to my Sovereign,' it said, 'and in discharge of my conscience, to set this down to your
Lordships ; wherein I protest, upon my soul, to write
nothing but what is true.   For I am not ignorant
of my present condition, and now to dissemble with
God is no time.'   Then he tells how Ralegh had
induced him in the Tower to write the letter absolving him ; and how the truth was that Ralegh had
proposed to him to obtain from Aremberg a pension
of £1500 a year from Spain to aid her interests and
to report all that happened in England.   Upon
Ralegh he throws once more the whole blame of
his ruin.   The story of throwing the apple into
Cobham's window was recounted, and Ralegh's
letters to him disclosed ; and then all hope for
acquittal was gone, and Ralegh was found guilty.

Before the verdict was given the prisoner again spoke vigorously of Cobham's instability, and read the letter he had written absolving him, but all to no purpose, for the incriminating letter was later. He solemnly declared that he was innocent of any negotiations with Spain, that he knew nothing of any practices in favour of Arabella Stuart, and that he was ignorant of Cobham's dealings with Aremberg.

Then Popham's turn came, and he made the most of it. Coke's abuse had been virulent, but the Lord Chief Justice, in passing sentence of death, surpassed him in insult; and so one of the most undignified and scandalous pages in English jurisprudence came to a fitting close.

An eye-witness of the trial thus speaks of Ralegh's part in it : 'He did as much as wit of man could advise to clear himself. . . . Sir Walter Ralegh served for a whole act and played all the parts himself. . . . He answered with that wit, learning, courage and judgment, that, save that it went with the hazard of his life, it was the happiest day that he had ever spent. And so well he shifted all advantages that were taken against him, that, were not *fama malum gravius quam res*, and an ill name half hanged, in the opinion of all men, he would have been acquitted.'

Beaumont, the French Ambassador, echoed the general opinion when he said that Ralegh was probably guilty, but had been illegally condemned. It is certain that the evidence produced against

him was absurdly inadequate. It was mostly loose
gossip, depending upon Brooke, whose object in
accusing his brother and Ralegh is difficult to understand, unless it was to save his own life, in which he
failed. On the scaffold he hinted at some mystery
behind it, which would surely come to light, and said
something secretly which greatly alarmed Cecil, but
which was never made public. The whole of the circumstances, however, which surround his evidence deprive it of any weight as against Ralegh. Cobham's
frequent accusations and retractations are so contradic-
tory of each other that it is impossible to arrive at
anything like a final conclusion with regard to them.
The letter, so triumphantly read by Coke in Court,
does not appear, on examination, to be so incriminating
of Ralegh as was hastily assumed at the trial. The
writer asserts that Ralegh had promoted his discontent
at the new order of things, which, if true, was perfectly natural, and certainly not treasonable ; and that
he had asked him to obtain a pension from Spain for
giving information ; and some colour is given to this
by Ralegh's declaration, although, according to Cobham, he had taken no step in the matter. It is quite
probable that this latter accusation was true. During
Elizabeth's reign many of her ministers were constantly in the pay of Spain. Lord Henry Howard,
Ralegh's enemy and judge, had been the chief spy
for years. Cobham's kinsman, Sir Edward Stafford,
the English Ambassador in Paris, had sold to Spain

every secret he possessed up to the time of the Armada. Cecil himself was a Spanish pensioner, and we have seen how Ralegh had offered his services in 1586. The loose political morality of the time made such an offence venial, and there is nothing more likely than that Ralegh did make such a suggestion to Cobham. That Cobham himself was engaged before Elizabeth's death in the arrangement with Spain which I have described in previous pages, I have no doubt—half the nobility of England were so engaged—and it is extremely likely that Ralegh may have been sympathetic after he heard that the Spaniards would help any native candidate that might be chosen against the King of Scots. All this was certainly not treasonable until James had been accepted by the nation as King ; and although Ralegh would naturally be discontented as a disgraced favourite and ruined courtier, there is not the remotest evidence, except Cobham's subsequent unsupported accusations at his (Cobham's) trial, that after the accession of James Ralegh had proposed a plot for the landing of a Spanish force at Milford Haven or elsewhere. The Spanish State papers conclusively prove that no such project was entertained at the time. The whole life record of Ralegh, moreover, was against it. A careful consideration of such documentary evidence as exists convinces me that Ralegh was not a party to any plot to depose James by the help of Spain, but that he was quite willing to accept a pension from the latter ; and that, *before Elizabeth's death,* he belonged to the very large party in England which was opposed to the Scottish domination of their country. When he was approached — as he must have been—shortly before the Queen's death, with the news that the Infanta had finally abandoned her claim, and that Spain would now support any candidate chosen by the English, who would grant toleration and peace, he would no doubt welcome such an apparently safe and patriotic solution of the difficulty ; not that he had any particular sympathy for Arabella, but to prevent the subjugation of the greater country by the lesser. This was probably the foundation of all of Cobham's tergiversation. Ralegh, however, was far too worldly wise and ambitious to oppose established facts ; and I am convinced that, after James' accession, he did not plot to depose him. The doubt expressed by Cobham as to whether Ralegh did not intend to betray him, if he went to Jersey, is unsupported, except by the gossip of Ralegh's enemies. Southampton certainly believed it, as did Bishop Goodman ; but Ralegh's character was considered so unprincipled by his contemporaries that they would be sure to adopt the most ungenerous view of his intentions. Brooke was beheaded in the castle yard at Winchester on the 16th December, full of vague hints of mystery behind his statements ; but he said nothing definite, except to withdraw the words he had attributed to his brother

about the 'fox and his cubs.' The priests, Watson
and Clarke, were submitted to the inhuman torture
imposed for high treason: half-hanged, cut down,
their entrails torn from their living bodies, and their
quarters exposed on the city gates. But James was
not fond of blood. His councillors urged him not to
begin his reign by severity, and his Queen used all
her influence in Ralegh's favour. Peace with Spain,
moreover, was in the air, and James desired it of all
things. Aremberg's reception had encouraged the
coming of a Spanish Ambassador, for the first time
for twenty years. He was that Don Juan Bautista
de Tassis, through whom Mary Stuart had conveyed
her assurance of exclusive attachment to the Spanish
interests. He, too, begged the King to be merciful
to the condemned. It could not be questioned that
their execution would be a jarring note in the concord
which was being so laboriously concluded between the
two countries, and in the interests of which De Tassis
was giving and promising vast sums of money to the
men who surrounded the King. But to all prayers
for mercy James affected to be deaf, and planned a
mystification thoroughly characteristic of him. On
the 8th December he signed the death warrants for
Cobham, Grey and Markham, whose execution was
fixed for the 9th. What followed may be told in
Cecil's own words, written to Winwood, on the
12th December, from Wilton. 'It remaineth that
I tell you what succeeded of the rest; wherein if

you could as well by relation apprehend all the circumstances as we did, you would, equally with us,
admire the excellent mixture of the King's mercy
with justice, for even after he had first absolutely
taught us all our duties, to leave all mediation in this
case (mercy being only his), he signed three warrants
for the execution of the two Lords, Cobham and
Grey, with Sir Griffin Markham, all to be done on
the same day, Friday following, pretending to forbear
Sir Walter Ralegh for the present, until Lord Cobham's death had given some light how far he would
make good his accusation. Which being done (God
of Heaven doth know it), we here at Wilton expected
nothing till Friday at 9 o'clock, to hear from Winchester of their execution : until it pleased the King
that very morning here at Wilton to call his Council
together, and told them what order he had taken ;
to which, upon my credit and reputation, he made
no soul living privy, the messenger excepted, whom
he dispatched the day before with the warrant, written
all in his own hand, which was used in manner following : Sir Griffin Markham, whose turn was first to be
executed, being brought forth upon the scaffold at
the hour appointed, and there having made his prayers
and spoken what else he thought good, prepared himself to lay down his head for the stroke, at which
instant one Mr Gibb, a Scottish gentleman of the
King's bed chamber, who was the messenger, stepped
forth and drew the Sheriff aside, presenting him his

warrant; whereupon the Sheriff (not making any
show at all of what he received, nor giving the least
cause to hope for that which afterwards followed)
turned again to the prisoner, and told him he was
to go forth of the place for a while, causing him to
be led down into the Castle hall, not far from the
place of execution. In the meanwhile, Lord Grey
was sent for, who, doing much as the other had done
before him, with a full resolution to die, after his
prayers ended and his preparation otherwise made,
was commanded likewise to be led down from the
place to the Castle hall, which proceeding of the
Sheriff neither of them apprehended to their least
comfort, but imagined it was for some other purpose.
Now, this being done, the next turn was Lord Cobham's, who was brought forth upon the scaffold, and
there made himself as ready to die as the rest, till the
Sheriff commanded his execution to be stayed for a
while, sending for the other two forth of the hall,
and then, being all three together on the scaffold, he
signified his Majesty's gracious pleasure unto them
all, which was received, as well of themselves as of
all the standers by, with such joy and admiration
as so rare and unheard of clemency most worthily
deserved.'

   Markham, we are told by an eyewitness was 'sad
and heavy, the very picture of sorrow,' although his
demeanour was fearless and dignified. Lord Grey,
devout Puritan as he was, beloved, popular and brave,

was bright and cheerful, surrounded by friends, and fully reconciled to death. He prayed long and fervently in the drizzling rain that fell, and then once again protested the truth, that he had never plotted treason. He had, in fact, been drawn into the Bye or Priests' Conspiracy by misrepresentation, and had retired from it when he understood its scope and objects. 'His going away seemed more strange unto him than his coming thither, for he had no more hope given him than of an hour's respite. Neither could any man yet dive into the mysteries of this strange proceeding.'

Cobham's fortitude on the scaffold was a strong contrast to his demeanour during his imprisonment and trial. It was probably the fortitude of despair. He answered that 'what he had said of Sir Walter Ralegh is true, as he hoped for his soul's resurrection,' but which of the many conflicting statements he had made about him he referred to is not clear. His latest accusation, with regard to the proposal for bringing Spanish troops to Milford, was the most damning; but no dates are given in it, and even if it were true, and referred to a period before the Queen's death, it was not treason against James. Cobham's own letters, indeed, to Cecil, speak of the plans with regard to Arabella as having been abandoned long before, in all probability when James's accession was assured. During all the tragi - comedy of the deferred executions at Winchester, Ralegh had sat at a window in full view of the scaffold. Through the silver veil of fine rain he had watched, with wondering eyes, the successive disappearance of the prisoners from the place of the execution, and the reappearance of them together to be harangued by the Sheriff. He must then have understood, though he was out of earshot, that his companions in misfortune were not to die; and shortly afterwards his own reprieve was communicated to him.

Ralegh's conduct on many occasions prove him to have been a man of undaunted courage. It was common for him in his periods of disappointment and distress to pray and yearn for death; and yet, such is the perversity of human nature, no poltroon could have begged for life more abjectly than he did. To the Lords of the Council, to Cecil, to the King, in turn, he addressed his beseeching letters for bare life. Lord Grey, with greater dignity, was deeply distressed at the disgrace which was to fall upon his illustrious house, but disdained to sue for his life. Ralegh, on the other hand, threw his dignity to the winds, and both he, personally, and his agonised wife, prayed, with a humility that approaches baseness, that his life might be spared on any terms. After his abject letters to the Lords, Ralegh himself appears to have become ashamed of them. He writes to his wife : 'Get those letters, if it be possible, which I wrote to the Lords, wherein I sued for my life. God knows that it was for you and yours that I desired it. But it is true that I disdain myself for begging it.' This letter to his wife was written in December, when he thought all hope was gone, and it is a beautiful specimen of pathetic English. A few short extracts only can be given here. 'You shall receive, dear wife, my last words in these my last lines. My love I send you, that you may keep it when I am dead, and my counsel, that you may remember it when I am no more. I would not with my last will present you with sorrows, dear Bess. Let them go to the grave with me, and be buried with me in the dust. And, seeing it is not the will of God that I shall ever see you in this life, beare my destruction gentlie, and with a heart like yourself. First, I send you all the thanks my heart can conceive, or my pen expresse, for your many troubles and cares taken for me, which—though they have not taken effect as you wished—yet my debt is to you never the less; but pay it I never shall, in this world.' After begging her not to mourn him long, advising her to marry again, and deploring the poor fortune he leaves behind him for her and their son, he proceeds, 'Remember your poore childe, for his father's sake, that comforted you and loved you in his happiest times, and know itt, dear wife, that your sonne is the childe of a true man, who, in his own respect, despiseth death and all his misshapen and ugly forms. I cannot write much. God knowes howe hardlie I stole this tyme when all sleep; and it is time to separate my thoughts from the world. Begg my dead body, which, living, was denied you; and either lay itt at Sherborne or in Exeter Church, by my father and mother.   I can write no more; tyme and death call me awaye.

'The everlasting, infinite, powerfull, and inscrutable God: that Almighty God that is goodness itself, mercy itself, the true light and life, keep you and yours, and have mercy on me, and teach me to forgive my persecutors and false accusers, and send us to meet in His glorious kingdom.   My true wife, farewell.   Blesse my poore boye.   Pray for me. My true God hold you both in His armes.   Written with the dying hand of sometyme thy husband, but now, alas! overthrowne.   Yours that was, but now not my owne.   W. RALEGH.'   This was the true Ralegh, in his better moments, and it is difficult to understand how the fine spirit that prompted such utterances could stoop to address his 'Most dread Sovereigne,' the despicable James Stuart, in such terms as these.   'But the greate God so relieve me and mine in both worlds, as I was the contrary (of discontented), and as I tooke no greater comfort than to behold Your Majesty, and always learning some good, and bettering my knowledge by Your Majesty's discourse. . . .   For myself, I protest before the everlasting God, and to my master and Sovereign, that I never invented treason, consented to treason, nor performed treason against him; and yet I know that I shall fall, *in manus eorum a quibus non possum exsurgere*,

unless by Your Majesty's great compassion I be sustained. . . . I do therefore, on the knees of my hart,
beseich Your Majesty to take counsel from your own
sweet and mercifull disposition, and to remember that
I have loved Your Majesty now twenty years, for
which Your Majesty hath yett given me no reward.
And it is fitter that I should be indebted to my
Sovereign Lord, than the King to his poore vassall.
Save me, therefore, most merciful Prince, that I
may owe to Your Majesty my life itself, than which
there cannot be a greater debt. Lend it to me at
least, my Sovereign Lord, that I may pay it agayne
for your service, when Your Majesty shall please.
If the law destroy me, Your Majesty shall put me
out of your power; and I shall have then none to
fear, none to reverence but the King of Kings—'
and Ralegh signs this 'your penitent vassall.' To
the Council he writes: 'For the mercy of God do
not doubt to move so mercifull a prince to compassion, and that the extremity of all extremities be
not laid on me. Lett the offence be esteemed as
your Lordships shall please in charity to believe it,
and value it; yet it is but my first offence, and my
service to my country, and my love so many years
to my supreme Lord, I trust may move so greate
and goode a kinge, who was never esteemed cruel. . . .
And if I may not begg a pardon or a life, yet lett
me begg a tyme at the King's merciful hands. Lett
me have one year in prison to give to God and to

serve Hyme.   I trust his pitiful nature will have
compassion on my sowle ; and it is my sowle that
beggeth a tyme of the Kinge.'

The arrogant favourite, who, in the days of his
splendour, had ridden roughshod over ancient nobles
who had dared to become his rivals for the Queen's
smile, could fall no lower than this, let the reason
for his supplication have been what it may.

Ralegh and his fellow-prisoners were brought to the
Tower of London less than a week after the farce
on the scaffold at Winchester. Thence they were
conveyed to the Fleet, and so backward and forward,
between the two prisons, several times before Ralegh
finally settled down with his wife and child in the
not incommodious rooms in the Bloody Tower.

His love of life was still strong within him. Whilst
he lived the possibilities of his indomitable energy and
powerful intellect were unbounded, and his busy mind
was full of vast and far-reaching plans. True, he was
a ruined man, and his enemies triumphed over him to
the utmost. All his offices were forfeited. The wine
patent was granted to the Lord Admiral. Sherborne
and the other estates were in the hands of royal commissioners, creditors were clamouring for payment,
rapacious agents were plundering everything they
could grasp, and, for a time, it looked as if beggary
as complete as that which fell upon Cobham, would
afflict Ralegh. But his brave wife struggled hard,
and Cecil did his best to help her. Now that there

was no danger of rivalry from Ralegh in the King's
favour, some of his old friendship came back again.
He had no desire to compass his death or absolute
ruin ; but that Ralegh should ever become the chief
adviser of the new King he was determined at any
cost to prevent. When once this danger was at an
end Cecil had no particular reason for carrying his
rancour to further extremes, and during the rest of
his life remained in friendly communication with Lady
Ralegh. Ralegh had many a hard struggle yet before
he could feel sure that he and his would be saved from
penury. The Sherborne estate, whilst in the charge of
the royal commissioners, had been stripped and rifled ;
his plate was 'all lost, or eaten out with interest,' at
Chenie's the goldsmith in Lombard Street ; his agent
in the patent of wines, Saunderson, made ruinous
claims against him ; and for the first few months of
his imprisonment, sometimes in the Tower, sometimes
in the Fleet, it was a constant struggle to save some
shreds of his wasted fortune. From the first he was
beset with difficulties about Sherborne. In 1602 he
had executed a conveyance of the estates to his son,
subject to a charge in favour of Lady Ralegh, and
his own life interest. By the intervention of Cecil
the interests of the lady and her son were respected
on Ralegh's attainder, and the estates conveyed for
60 years in trust for them. But, by an omission
of the clerk, who engrossed the deed of 1602,
certain necessary words were lacking. The crown

lawyers declared that the deed was void, and that the
estates had consequently been vested only in Ralegh ;
but no fresh action was taken, and here the matter
remained for some years, the revenues, or such of
them as could be rescued from the unjust steward
Meeres, being received and employed by Lady Ralegh
in the maintenance of her husband and family.   When
the prisoner at last settled in the Tower there began
the long battle of the active soaring spirit against the
numbing monotony of a gaol.   Like the seabird dash-
ing itself to death against a lighthouse, the restless
energies of Ralegh beat themselves in vain against
the walls of his prison.   But though his body grew
cold and pulseless, and his hair turned to snow, his
great intellect shone the brighter in the gloom that
surrounded it.

CHAPTER XIII

RALEGH was ever a good suppliant. During the
whole of his life he was begging favours for himself
or others, apparently never contented or satisfied.
When, after the reprieve of Cobham, Grey and Markham, he sent his last prayer for life to the Council,
he wrote : 'The Lord of Heaven doth know that if
it shall pleas my most gracious Lord the King to
geve mee that poore life, that I shall as faythfully
and thankfully serve hyme, eating but bread and
drinking water, as whosoever that hath receved even
the greatest honour or the greatest profyte. For a
greater gift none can geve, none receve, than life. . . .
My Lords, do me this grace to believe, and vouchsafe
to say it for mee to my Soverayne Lorde, that the loss
of my estate, which I have deservedly lost, cannot

make me less faythful or less lovinge both to his
state and person.' But no sooner was his life granted,
and almost blasphemous thanks given for it to the
King, than the prayers for fresh favours became incessant. He wrote to Cecil, praying that his lands might
be restored to him personally, in order that he might
pay his debts and maintain himself in the Tower.
Then he boldly prays the Lord Treasurer for liberty
as the 'Bye' Conspirators had been released; and this
being fruitless, he beseeches the King himself in the
most servile terms to have mercy upon a miserable
prisoner. This was on the 21st January 1604, only
a few weeks after he had been saved from the scaffold,
and Cecil plainly told Lady Ralegh that, 'as for a
pardon, it could not be done.' But still he continued
to beg of Cecil. 'If I may not be here about London
(which God cast my sowle into hell if I desire, but
to do your Lordship some service) I shall be most
contented to be confined within the Hundred of
Sherborne, or if I cannot be allowed so much, I shall
be contented to live in Holland.' His private affairs,
his liberty, his comfort in the Tower, his property,
were all the subjects of unceasing petitions to Cecil,
to his son Lord Cranborne, to the Council, to the
King. His petitions were eloquent, pathetic, plain-
tive, as usual; but it is extremely difficult to reconcile
them with the possession of any real dignity of mind
in the writer. No sooner was one favour wrung
out than another one was prayed for, with the same

lachrymose persistence as the last.   Disappointed
ambition and chafing energy wore out the prisoner's
health.   His apartments in the Bloody, or Garden,
Tower, were large enough for the accommodation of
himself, his wife and son, a second son, Carew, who
was born in the Tower soon after his imprisonment,
Lady Ralegh's maid, and other servants.   He had
the use of a terrace overlooking the Tower-wharf and
the river, and was allowed the occupation of a small
out-house in the garden for his chemical experiments ;
but the place was damp, so near the Thames and the
moat, and almost from the first the prisoner complained that the confinement was killing him. 'He
was in daily danger of death,' he said, ' by the palsy
that afflicted him, and of nightly suffocation by wasted
and obstructed lungs.'   Then the plague broke out
in a neighbouring lodging, and he clamoured for
removal to another place, if he might not be released.
At last, in 1606, the physicians reported that he was
really ill.   The whole of one side of him was cold,
his fingers were contracted, and it was feared that he
was losing the power of speech ; and this report
effected what Ralegh's own prayers had been unable
to obtain, a change in his lodging. He was allowed
to build a little room attached to the out-house in the
garden, and to make it his chamber. Within the
limits of his prison the restless energy of Ralegh at
length found food for occupation which afforded him
solace, and has done much to enhance his reputation

with posterity.   His twelve years of incessant literary
labour in the Tower have left behind him a permanent
memorial of his marvellous and far-reaching powers,
which, but for his enforced seclusion, would, in all
probability, never have been produced, and the extent
of Ralegh's genius would not have been understood.
Such of his servants as could not find room in the
Tower lived hard by, and were in constant attendance
upon him, especially the Indians he had brought from
Guiana with him.   His friends and relatives were
allowed to visit him freely with books and news.   He
frequently dined with Sir George Harvey, the Governor
of the Tower, and in many ways was treated with
leniency.   His chemical and mineralogical researches in
the laboratory at first occupied much of his time, and
in the intervals of labour he was able to satisfy his
vanity by parading on the terrace, splendidly dressed
as usual, in full view of the crowds on the wharf, who
came far and near to see so famous a man ; for there
had been a curious revulsion of public feeling in his
favour after his condemnation.   But Sir William
Waad, who for so many years had been Clerk of
the Council, was appointed to the Governorship of
the Tower in August 1605, and such proceedings
were looked upon suspiciously.   First a brick wall
was built before the Bloody Tower gate ; and then,
in 1608, Waad formally complained to Cecil that
'Sir Walter Ralegh doth show himself upon the wall
of his garden to the view of the people who gaze

upon him, and he stareth upon them. Which he
doeth in his cunning humour, that it might be thought
his being before the Council was rather to clear than
to charge him ' ; and thenceforward whilst Waad was
in command many petty restrictions were placed upon
both Ralegh and his wife—the latter being forbidden
to drive her coach in the courtyard, and the like.
Though he was a close prisoner, it pleased the Government to suspect him of complicity in every seditious
practice.   He was examined about the Gunpowder
Plot, and several times during the next few years, on
the reports of spies, or in the hope of fishing out
some secret, Ralegh was interrogated by the Council.
Once in 1610, on some trifling excuse, he was condemned to close imprisonment for three months, and
Lady Ralegh was excluded from the Tower.

The fame of his chemical experiments, and of
his wonderful curative balsam from Guiana, had
captured the public imagination. He was a necro-
mancer, a show for gaping wonder-seekers ; and the
man whom in his splendour all the world had hated
now became almost a popular hero in his misfortune.

In the midst of his studies and learned seclusion in
1608, a terrible new blow fell upon him. The conveyance by him of the Sherborne estates to his son
and wife in 1602 had been pronounced informal in consequence of the accidental omission of some necessary
words, and the crown lawyers consequently contended
that the King's confirmation of Lady Ralegh and her

T

son's possession of it was invalid, and that the estate was vested in Ralegh himself, by whose conviction it became escheated to the crown. It was proposed to Ralegh that he and his family should join in re-granting the fee-simple of the estates to the King for £8000. Ralegh knew well that such a proposal was a command. In vain he pleaded that the fee-simple did not belong to them, that they would be ruined ; in vain Lady Ralegh and her children cast themselves at the King's feet, and prayed that they might not be despoiled and rendered homeless. Whether James uttered the heartless words, quoted by Carew Ralegh, popularly attributed to him, 'Na ! na ! I maun hae the land. I maun hae it for Car,' be true or not, it is difficult to say ; but, in any case, the shameful favourite, Robert Car, obtained from his master the fine estates of which Ralegh was deprived. The £8000 to be given to Lady Ralegh for her interest was never entirely paid, but henceforward this, and a nominal pension to her of £400 irregularly paid, were the main sources of income upon which they had to depend. Ralegh wrote one of his pleading pathetic letters to the miserable creature Car, but of course in vain. He tells him that, 'after many great losses and many years of sorrow . . . it comes to my knowledge that yourself have been persuaded to give me and myne our last fatall blow, by obtaining from His Majesty the inheritance of my children and nephews, lost in law for want of wordes. This done, ther

remayneth nothinge with me but the bare name of
life; despoiled of all else but the grief and sorrow
thereof.   And for yourself, sir, seinge your daye is
but now in dawne, and myne come to the eveninge,
your own vertues and the King's grace assuringe you
of manye good fortunes and much honour, I beseich
you not to begynne your first buildings upon the
ruyns of the innocent, and that their greifes and
sorrows doe not attend your first plantation.'   Car got
the estates, but an evil fate followed them, and they
changed owners eight times in as many years, until at
last they fell into the hands of the Digbys, as a
reward for Sir John Digby's truckling embassy to
Spain.   Neither spoliation nor imprisonment caused
Ralegh to fall into obscurity.   He was probably never
more talked about than when he was in the Tower.
His past magnificence was exaggerated; his mystic
labours with alembics and retorts were discussed with
bated breath; his distant travels and his Indian
familiars appealed to a wonder-loving generation,
and his 'great cordial,' a panacea to cure all ills, was
eagerly sought for by the highest people in the land.*
From the first, romantic Anne of Denmark had been
fascinated by Ralegh's story, and pleaded hard with the

* No absolutely authentic recipe of the 'great cordial' is known to
exist.   Charles II.'s French physician, Le Febre, by command of the
King, prepared a quantity of the medicine, and wrote a learned treatise
on it, which was translated into English by Peter Belon.   The awesome
preparation as given by Le Febre is bad enough without the two extra
ingredients introduced by the advice of Sir Kenelm Digby, namely, viper

King in his favour. In a great sickness—probably fever—from which she suffered, the 'great cordial,' it is said, saved her life, and thenceforward she became more than ever the prisoner's friend. But she enlisted for Ralegh a much more powerful ally than herself, and one who for a time seemed to hold out promise of renewed fortune and favour to him. The most promising heir to the English crown who ever died prematurely was probably Henry Prince of Wales. Generous, enlightened and broad-minded, the young Prince gave hopes that when in the fulness of time he should succeed to his unworthy father, a new era of dignity and glory should come to England, after its partial eclipse under James. His young imagination had been captivated by Ralegh's romantic story and misfortunes ; and he had carefully examined into the details of his trial. He satisfied himself that the prisoner was no traitor, and joined his mother in constant appeals to the King for Ralegh's pardon and release. But James could be as obstinate in some things as he was weak in others, and the young Prince indignantly, and sometimes imprudently, protested to those around him against his father's treatment of one of

flesh, with the heart and liver, and 'mineral unicorn,' consisting, as it does, of no less than forty herbs, roots, seeds, etc., macerated in spirits of wine and distilled, and then combined with powdered bezoar stones, pearls, red coral, deer's horn, ambergris, musk, antimony, various sorts of earth, white sugar, and much else. It speaks much for the strength of Queen Anne's constitution that this medicament should have cured her.

his greatest subjects. The communication thus set
on foot between the Prince and the prisoner soon
established a feeling of close friendship and confidence,
which must have opened a new vista for Ralegh.
Already, prisoner though he was, and legally dead,
he sought to exert his influence on public affairs.
The Prince was not, like his father, eager for an
undignified alliance with an impoverished and beaten
power like Spain. When in 1611 the proposal was
made to marry the King's eldest daughter to the
Protestant Prince Palatine, the Spanish party endeavoured to counteract it by offering a double
marriage of the Prince and his sister respectively
with a son and daughter of the Catholic and half
Spanish Duke of Savoy. The proposal was dis-
tasteful to the English people and to the Prince
himself, who consulted Ralegh about it. The
prisoner wrote for the Prince's guidance two masterly
State papers setting forth the undesirability of such
alliances, and advocating the Protestant marriage.
Once more he pointed out how Spain had been
beaten into impotence, and how the proposed alliance
would estrange the Hollanders and the Protestant
powers. It was a dangerous line to take, for it was
in opposition to the King's view. Probably Ralegh
had satisfied himself now that he had nothing to
hope from James, and must attach himself to the
heir ; but the vindictive Stuart did not forget it.
The Prince was delighted with the depth of Ralegh's

knowledge, and fascinated by his powerful personality. He discussed shipbuilding with him, and the
prisoner wrote, for his information, *The Discourse of
the Invention of Ships, Observations concerning the
Royal Navy and Sea Service*, and other treatises of a
like nature. The generous young Prince, unable to
obtain his mentor's liberty, prevailed upon the King
to buy Sherborne back again from Car for £20,000,
and grant it to him, Henry, his intention being to
reconvey it to its former possessor; and after an infinity
of appeal he also wrung from his father a promise of
Ralegh's release by the end of 1612. For some
reason not clearly known, probably jealousy of his
influence over the Prince, Ralegh fell into renewed
disgrace with the Council, and Cecil, now Earl of
Salisbury, gravely rebuked him. He was closely
confined for three months, and deprived of the
company of his wife. This was in July 1610, and
Ralegh, referring to his interview with his old friend
Cecil, thus speaks of him, October 1610 : 'I would
have bought his presence at a far dearer rate than these
sharp words and these three months' close imprisonment, for it is in his Lordship's face and countenance
that I behold all that remains to me of comfort, and
all the hope I have.' One year and seven months
after this was written the second great Cecil died, and
the blow to Ralegh's hopes was a heavy one. It is
true that Cecil had been the principal author of his
ruin, and must have known of his innocence, that

he had kept silence when a word would have saved his old friend. But still he had not been absolutely implacable, and he alone probably held the knowledge and power which would have set him free. It may well be that if Ralegh had fallen lower he would have rescued him at last, but the friendship with the Prince raised once more the possibility of Ralegh's becoming his rival, and this perhaps caused the renewed severity referred to in the letter just quoted. Ralegh had no reason to respect the memory of the false friend who had undone him, and he did not do so; but still Cecil's death made his release seem even more distant than it was before. A still greater loss was to follow six months after Cecil's death. Before Prince Henry could convey to Ralegh the estates he had obtained from Car, he fell ill of fever. All England prayed that the life of the young Prince might be spared, and the distressed mother sent to the Tower for a supply of the famous cordial that had saved her own life. It was a simple and natural act for her to do, but the physicians in attendance and the Lords of the Council gravely discussed whether the remedy, coming from so suspicious a source, should be administered. When the patient was speechless, and *in articulo mortis*, the cordial was placed between his lips, and gave him strength once more to speak. But it was powerless to snatch him from the grave, and the Prince finally sank (November 1612). As usual in such cases at that

period there were whispers of poison.   It is evident
now that they were unfounded, but the Queen believed
implicitly in Ralegh, and Ralegh had unfortunately
said that his cordial was sovereign against everything
except poison, and so she thought that her son had
been sacrificed.   There can have been but little love
between the King and her before, but the black
suspicion engendered by these doubts must have
darkened still more the shadow which lay between
them, for James hardly made a pretence of mourning
his son.   To Ralegh the blow was an irreparable
one.   One of the last interests of the Prince's life
had been to plan his restoration to liberty and
fortune, and his death for a time extinguished all
hope.

The vast project of the *History of the World*
throws into prominence perhaps more than any other
thing the splendid confidence of Ralegh in his own
powers.   The earlier stages of the great plan were
discussed with Prince Henry, and the whole work, if
it had been completed, was to have been dedicated
to him.   But with the death of the young patron
despondency seized once more upon the author, and
although the work slowly progressed, it was too
vast in scope, too ambitious in intention, to be carried
to the end, now that the Prince had gone.   There
is a very doubtful story told that a few days before
Ralegh's death he sent for Walter Burr, the book-
seller who had published the first edition in 1614,

and taking his hand asked him how it had sold. The man answered, so slowly, that it had undone him; whereupon Ralegh went to his desk, took out of it the continuation of the *History* to his own times, and said, with a sigh, 'Ah, friend, has the first part undone thee? The second volume shall undo no more; this ungrateful world is unworthy of it,' with which he cast the manuscript into the fire. The story is almost certainly untrue, because during the time that elapsed between the completion of the first part in 1613 and his release from the Tower there was no time for him to have concluded the work on the same scale upon which it had been commenced. There were, however, many other treatises known to have been written by him, and never printed; some of the manuscripts of which he may well have destroyed as described. The *History* itself, as it exists, is probably the greatest work ever produced in captivity, except *Don Quixote*. The learning contained in it is perfectly encyclopedic. Ralegh had always been a collector and lover of books, and had doubtless laid out the plan of the work in his mind even before his fall. He had near him in the Tower his learned friend Hariot, who was indefatigable in helping his master. Ben Jonson boasted that he had contributed to the work, and such books or knowledge as could not be obtained or consulted by a prisoner were made available by scholars like Robert Burhill, by Hughes, Warner or Hariot. Sir John Hoskyns, a great stylist in his day, would advise with regard to construction, and from many other quarters aid of various sorts was obtained. But, withal, the work is purely and entirely Ralegh's. No student of his fine, flowing, majestic style will admit that any other pen but his can have produced it. The vast learning employed in it is now, for the most part, obsolete, but the human asides, where Ralegh's personality reveals itself, the little bits of incidental autobiography, the witty, apt illustrations, will prevent the work itself from dying. To judge from a remark in the preface, the author intended at a later stage to concentrate his history mainly into that of his own country, and that the portion of the book published was to a great extent introductory. Great as were his powers and self-confidence, it must have been obvious to him that it would have been impossible for a man of his age when he began the work (59) to complete a history of the whole world on the same scale, the first six books published reaching from the beginning of the world to the end of the second Macedonian war.

In any case, the book will ever remain a noble fragment of a design, which could only have been conceived by a master mind.

If proof were wanting of how little Ralegh understood the character of James Stuart, it is furnished by the expressions employed in his eloquent preface to his *History*, when speaking of the punishment which inevitably falls upon unjust rulers. The whole of the preface, indeed, is directed to enforcing the lesson of the responsibility of rulers, and in combating the principle for which James lived and his son died. Especially he held up Henry VII. and Henry VIII., from whom James derived the crown, as monsters of iniquity and cruelty; and the same note is struck all through the *History* itself where the tyranny of kings is described. Wrong and injustice to the people may prosper for a season, but surely in the end retribution reaches the evildoer, whatever his power and exaltation. The introductory verses, written by Ben Jonson, but not acknowledged by him at the time, enforce the same lesson. The serious study of history is necessary, we are told,

> '. . . . *that nor the good*
> *Might be defrauded, nor the great secured;*
> *But both might know their ways are understood,*
> *And the reward and punishment assured.*'

No wonder the royal pedant looked sourly upon the book and said, 'It is too saucy in censuring the acts of princes.' Although Ralegh's aim, both in his *History* and in his *Prerogative of Parliament*, dedicated to the King, was to show that the good of the governed must be the supreme end of government, he lost no opportunity of making clear that he was a strenuous enemy of what we now call democracy. His dislike and distrust of the populace were part of his nature, and throughout his life he took no pains to hide them. In the preface to the *History* he compares the multitude to barking dogs 'who accompany one another in clamour,' and, 'who wanting that virtue which we call honesty in all men, and that especial gift of God we call charity in Christian men, condemn without hearing, wound without offence given.' In speaking of the abolition of villainage in England, he says, 'Since our slaves were made free, which were of great use and service, there are grown up a rabble of rogues, cutpurses and other like trades, slaves in nature, though not in law;' and elsewhere, 'There is nothing in any state so terrible as a powerful and authorised ignorance.'

Ralegh, indeed, through all his writings, shows that his ideal of government was a just and benevolent despotism, or oligarchy. He himself was benign and equitable to his dependents, so long as they were absolutely submissive—like his Indian servants by whom he was greatly beloved — but he never wavered in his faith that the chosen few had the right to govern the many for the happiness and well-being of all.

Notwithstanding the King's strictures, the *History of the World* was a great success, especially amongst Puritans and the Protestant party generally. Scholars vied with each other in praising its elegance and erudition, politicians made it a text-book, and divines a basis for their homilies. Its fame and popularity were enhanced rather than diminished by rumours that hidden allusions in it to the King and modern events had caused its suppression. Public curiosity was aroused and people read the book to solve the supposed riddles it contained. A second edition was issued in 1617, and for the next hundred years it was studied as an English classic.

Through all Ralegh's misfortunes, as through his triumphs, in prison and at liberty, there ran the main idea of his life—the Colonial expansion of England. It could only be carried into effect by asserting and maintaining the superiority of England on the sea. He and his had been greatly instrumental in establishing that superiority, and his constant theme now was that the boasted Spanish power was a hollow illusion, and Spain herself a negligable quantity, because she no longer ruled the sea.

He had never lost hope or ceased effort in his colonial ventures. Kemys had been sent to Guiana in 1596, as already related, and had surveyed the coast between the Amazon and the Orinoco, the main entrance to which latter river he had discovered. No sooner had Ralegh returned to England from Cadiz in the same year than he despatched one of his ships, under Leonard Berrie, to the Guiana coast, to keep up communication with the Indians, who were for ever asking for the return of the great white chief, who had promised to defend them against the Spaniards. Again in 1604 Captain Charles Leigh was sent with 50 men to colonise, by the King's authority, some point on the Guiana coast; but the Indians sought to engage them in their inter-tribal wars, and it was considered prudent to return. They begged, however, that missionaries might be sent to teach them to pray. A Captain Harcourt, four years later, actually planted a colony at Wiapoco under the King's license, and he found that the name of Ralegh was still a power through all the region. In 1611 Sir Thomas Roe again explored the coast under the auspices of Prince Henry and Cecil, to the latter of whom he reported that 'the Spaniards were proud and insolent, yet needy and weak, that their power was only in reputation, and that they treated Englishmen worse than Moors.' Harcourt's colonists were by this time tired of their experiment, and returned with Roe. News came that the Spaniards were organising a systematic colonisation of the Orinoco, with the intention of building a great city on the banks to serve as a base for the conquest of the golden Guiana; but, said Roe, withal, 'the Spanish Government there has more skill in planting and selling tobacco, than in planting colonies.' This news redoubled Ralegh's efforts to induce his country to be beforehand with them. He had managed to interest Prince Henry in his project, and with ceaseless persistence he endeavoured from

his prison to enlist the aid of people in authority
for that, or for the Virginian plantation.   In the
latter he was successful, and in 1609 a new charter
was granted to Cecil, Suffolk (Thomas Howard), and
others, under the name of Treasurer and Company of
Adventurers and Planters of the Colony of Virginia,
which, largely by the efforts of Lord Delawarr, ended
in the establishment of the permanent English colony
in North America.   Ralegh himself was in prison,
all his former colonists had been murdered, and he
obtained no benefit under the new charter ; but,
nevertheless, to him is due the undying glory of
having made the great northern continent of
America an English-speaking country.   With him
it was no accident.   The plan sprang fully formed
from his great brain.   He knew that if the claim
of England were not enforced, the whole of the
western world would fall into the nerveless hands
of Spain, and he was determined this should not be
if he could help it.   He was greedy of gain, but he
spent his money like water in this great project.   He
knew full well that there was no gold to reward him ;
that the profit, if any, must be slow, and must accrue
mainly to the nation, and not to an individual ; and
yet he laboured on for thirty years in the face of
defeat, disaster, contumely and disgrace, in full faith
and confidence that the great continent was ‘by
God’s providence reserved for England.’   If Ralegh
had done no more than this he would deserve to be

regarded as one of the great benefactors of the human race, but this was only one of his multitudinous activities.   In his advocacy of the Guiana project he had to appeal to other motives.   Here the hope of rapid gain, of abounding gold, was the bait which was to induce capitalists to adventure their money.

He knew that if gold in large quantities was found, it would be easy for him to establish the claim he had already advanced, that the whole country belonged to England, by virtue of the alleged cession made to him by the Indians in 1595.   Each little expedition that was sent came back with fresh stories of golden wonders.   Of the chiefs who gilded their naked bodies with glittering gold dust from head to foot, of the fabled city of Manoa, virgin yet, with wealth hitherto undreamt of in the world, of mountains of gems, of towering gods of gold.   Ralegh probably believed it all himself, the whole world believed it then and for generations after ; and eager as he was for empire for his country, he knew fully the power of wealth, and he loved power of all things.   So gold was to be the magnet to draw himself, as well as others, to the founding of a great English empire of Guiana. The flat plates of soft gold which were brought back by each expedition were made the most of, the richness of the gold ore smelted and refined over the furnace in the Tower garden, was exaggerated as the talk of it passed from mouth to mouth in Court and city.   To any possible patron who would listen,

Ralegh appealed for help. Cecil had already lost much money in the previous expeditions and was cool. Prince Henry, on the contrary, as impulsive and ambitious for England as Ralegh himself, was sympathetic ; but his hands were tied, for his father was jealous and resented his activity. Ralegh appealed to the Queen in 1611 to patronise an expedition, and to intercede with the King to liberate him for the purpose of commanding it. Cecil was, however, not pleased that the prisoner should possess so much influence with the heir-apparent, and cast doubts upon Ralegh's intentions. It was said that, when once he got to sea he might offer his services to the King of France or the States. Ralegh protested, and proffered the most extravagant pledges for his fidelity ; but for a time without result. Then his patron, Prince Henry, died, and gloom once more temporarily fell upon him. He was old now, and ailing. He plaintively said that he knew he would gain nothing personally, for he was nearing his end ; but for the sake of England he prayed that such a rich inheritance might not be cast aside. He was still persistent and untiring in his petitions, trying to appeal to the weak side of each person he addressed. To Cecil he had held out hopes of boundless wealth, to Prince Henry, dreams of English empire. He now appealed to the Queen's pity, and to the Secretary, Sir Ralph Winwood, who was an advocate of the French alliance, he promised demonstration of the worthlessness of Spain as an ally. But sympathetic and approving as were the Queen and Winwood, they alone were not strong enough to release Ralegh, and a more powerful aid had to be enlisted. The bars that held him in the Tower, however, were weakening of themselves. His venomous foe, Northampton (Lord Henry Howard), was dead, the false friend, Cecil, was gone, and the disgraceful Car was a prisoner for murder, and had been supplanted by another favourite, more brilliant still, and, if possible, more greedy, who was always anxious to wound the Howards.   In 1615, accordingly, the influence of George Villiers, afterwards Duke of Buckingham, was obtained in Ralegh's favour. It was done in much the same way that Ralegh's own aid had been procured in the days of his prosperity. George Villiers's brother, and a kinsman, were paid £750 each, and the favourite soon gained the King's ear to the tales of vast wealth to come to both of them, if Ralegh were allowed to go and re-discover the rich gold mine which Kemys had seen in 1595.

Already, three years before, Ralegh had attempted to bargain for his liberty by proposing to send Kemys to this mine, with instructions to bring away a few boatloads of ore to demonstrate its richness. The prisoner was ready then to stake his liberty and fortune on Kemys's memory. His plans in the meanwhile had developed. He now offered to

realise all his property, the portion of the £8000
paid for Sherborne, and a small estate belonging to
Lady Ralegh at Mitcham, and to induce his friends
to furnish £5000 more; to get together somehow
on his own credit £15,000, and take his expedition
to the mine, coming back loaded with gold, and a
new empire for the King, without assailing the
Spaniards, or encroaching upon their territory.
Bred in the old Elizabethan traditions that success
excused most things, he doubtless held himself but
lightly bound by the last condition; and Sir Ralph
Winwood and other enemies of the Spanish alliance,
would also look upon it as only made for the purpose
of being broken, if necessary. But Ralegh always
failed to understand how mean-spirited was the
man who unworthily sat on the throne of great
Elizabeth, and he was ready to pledge his life and all
he possessed to the fulfilment of this or any other
condition, which should give him the liberty for
which he had yearned so long. Villiers did what
for twelve years others had tried to do in vain.
He aroused James's cupidity, and lulled his fears,
to the extent of obtaining a warrant, dated 19th
March 1616, for Ralegh 'to be permitted to go
abroad to make preparations for his voyage.' The
Tower gates opened, and one of the greatest prisoners
they ever confined stepped out at last upon Tower
Hill a free man, though still with a keeper close by
his side. He was sadly aged and broken by the

twelve years' cruel and unjust imprisonment to
which Cecil's jealousy, Howard's hate, and James's
fears, had condemned him ; but his heart beat high
with hope that a new era of power for himself and
his country was opening to him ; for the sufferings
that had sapped the vigour of his body, had left his
ambition as fierce as ever, and his vast mental
energy unimpaired.

CHAPTER XIV

DIEGO SARMIENTO DE ACUÑA, COUNT DE GONDOMAR
—JAMES'S PROMISE TO HIM, ON HAND, FAITH
AND WORD—POLITICAL INTRIGUES AT COURT—
THE FRENCH AND SPANISH PARTIES—FITTING
OUT THE GUIANA EXPEDITION — SAILING OF
THE EXPEDITION —LANZAROTE, CANARY AND
GOMERA — GONDOMAR'S EFFORTS AGAINST
RALEGH

RALEGH's first enjoyment of his new freedom was to
perambulate London, to note the changes that had
taken place in the physical aspect of the city during
his twelve years' incarceration. He must have seen
much to awaken his admiration and surprise. The
Strand frontage of his old palace at Durham Place was
now a stately new building which rivalled the Royal
Exchange in popularity. Inigo Jones had embellished
Whitehall with the fine banqueting house which still
stands, and the city was growing in wealth and extent
on all sides. But great as may have been the material
changes which met his eyes, they were trifling in com-

parison with the entire political revolution which had
taken place in the respective positions of England
and Spain towards each other. During the whole
of Elizabeth's long reign she had proudly refused to
recognise the pompous claims of superiority put forward by the Spaniards. She had succeeded to the
throne when her country was weak and divided—
when her own position was insecure—but from the
first moment she scornfully rejected the patronage of
Spain. As her position was consolidated, seconded by
Burleigh and her sailors, she played her great game so
well as to sap and paralyse the power, to which from
the first she had disdained to bow, and was able to
treat with hauteur, equal to his own, the King who
had sought to overwhelm her with his might. By
the time she died, the power of Spain was merely
bluster ; and, hector as Philip III. might, he was bound
to sue for peace because he was impotent for war. This
was the position when Ralegh had entered the Tower.
When he came out it was England—or its pusillanimous prince—that was the suppliant. For want
of the dignity which Elizabeth rarely lacked, James
had been driven into the position of taking Spain at its
own valuation, and himself assumed the inferior position, timorously anxious for an alliance with the
House of Spain, which received his advances with
contemptuous coolness. This changed position was
to a certain extent owing to the character of the
Ambassador who represented Spain in James's Court.

Don Diego Sarmiento de Acuña, afterwards Count de Gondomar, was not a haughty Castilian like Feria, Mendoza, or Frias, but one of those crafty Gallegos whose assumed clownishness of speech and boorishness of manner are often made to mask intense earnestness of purpose and boldness of action. He could, and did, play the buffoon to the King's heart's content, but under the clown's motley there was a threatening savagery that frightened James, and a pride that humiliated him. Gondomar knew exactly how far it was safe to go with James at one time. He never went beyond it, but at the next interview he started where he had left off, and carried his point further. James was as cunning and as false as any man of his time, but he was vain of his cunning, and therefore easily circumvented. Gondomar never altered in outward manner from the frank, good fellow, without guile, who said sharp, witty things, out of his abounding simplicity, and never exaggerated the power of his master, because, forsooth, he was too friendly and open to invent anything. The result was that the royal cunning rogue, who could not hide his cunning for vanity, was a simple tool in the hands of the more cunning rogue who could, and by the time that Ralegh was released Sarmiento had King James in the hollow of his hand.

Every shilling that Ralegh could realise of the wrecks of his own or his wife's former fortune was called in for employment on the Guiana expedition,

On his disastrous return he himself expressed wonder at the frenzy that had possessed him thus like a desperate gambler, to stake fortune and life on one cast.   The mine on the Orinoco, it will be remembered, had been shown years before by an Indian chief to Kemys, Ralegh himself never having seen it. But he was ready, nevertheless, to risk everything on its promise of boundless wealth.   His enthusiasm was catching, especially by the idle and adventurous, who were eager to join him.   Most of them, said Ralegh, had never seen the seas or wars, and were a very dissolute and ungovernable crew, 'whom their friends thought it an exceedingly good gain to be discharged of at the hazard of some £40 or £50 pounds, knowing they could not have lived for a whole year so cheap at home.'   But money had to be got together somehow, for Ralegh could only muster £10,000 of his own, and he was in no position to refuse contributions, even if they were hampered with such additions as those stated.   There was much to be done in the first few months of his release, and the talk of the preparations soon reached the ears of Sarmiento.   On the 27th April 1616, one month after Ralegh's release, he sounded his first note of alarm to the King of Spain.   He expresses a wish to go to Spain in order to confer with the King personally with regard to the English maritime designs, 'especially the formation of another company for Guiana and the River Orinoco, which is near Trinidad, the prime

promotor and originator of which is Sir Walter
Ralegh, a great seaman, who took many prizes in the
time of Queen Elizabeth, and who first colonised
Virginia. I am informed that he will sail in the
month of October with six or eight ships of 200 to
500 tons, some belonging to himself, some to his
companions, all well provided. He will also take with
him launches in which to ascend the Orinoco, and he
is trying to get two ships of very light draught to
take them as high up the river as possible. He has
already been in the country, and assures people here
that he knows of a mine that will swell all England
with gold.' This was the first news sent of the
proposed expedition, and with it went the Ambassador's recommendation that a great increase should be
made in the strength of the Spanish navy, and that no
Spanish ship should sail except with a convoy. At
the same time Gondomar promised to exert his influence in London to stop the expedition. He had
means for doing it which must have been staggering
indeed to Englishmen who had lived in the time of
Elizabeth. In his next letter, dated 20th May 1616,
he relates to his King how he had dealt with the
Court of Admiralty, of whose proceedings he dis-
approved. He says that he had complained to the
King, and things were at once reformed, 'not a single
pirate daring either openly or secretly to come to
England.' This is how it was done, according to
Gondomar : 'As the Judge of the Admiralty did not

act properly, the King appointed two adjoints to my satisfaction to attend to the affairs of Your Majesty's subjects. The Judge refused to allow the adjoints to take a seat on the bench, but at my instance the King and the Lord Admiral compelled him to do so. This has caused great annoyance to those who go to Brazil for wood; but I have prosecuted them criminally as disturbers of the peace, and have worried them so that I expect I shall upset all their designs.' And then Gondomar proceeds to say, 'I am trying to do the same with Ralegh, who . . . is secretly fitting out ships and men for an expedition to Guiana . . . but, after all, the sure and necessary thing is for us to increase our naval force, as I recommended before.'

But Gondomar, for his part, did not neglect efforts in England to frustrate Ralegh. There was no man in England now against whom the Spaniards had a deeper grudge; there was no place where the impotence of Spain might be more glaringly demonstrated than in South America, and Gondomar left no stone unturned. Sir Ralph Winwood, the Secretary of State, was warmly in favour of Ralegh's plans; for anything that would convince the King of the worthlessness of a Spanish alliance was welcome to him; but the King was besotted with Gondomar and the Spanish power, Digby and Cottington were humbly negotiating in Madrid for the marriage of the Prince of Wales with the Infanta, and greedy Buckingham was bribed by the Spaniards to his heart's content.

So Gondomar had no difficulty in learning from the King and others the minutest particulars of Ralegh's plans, and taking measures to frustrate them. There had been some hesitation on the part of intended subscribers to the venture, as to the security they would have for receiving their shares of the profits, inasmuch as Ralegh was unpardoned and all his property was attachable by the crown. James was therefore moved to give a commission under the great seal to Ralegh, dated 26th August 1616, authorising him to make the voyage ' to places in South America, or elsewhere, inhabited by heathen and savage people . . . to discover some commodities, etc., profitable for our subjects, and of which the inhabitants make little or no use.' Full power is given to Ralegh to punish, reward and command his force, and to take such arms as may be necessary for defence, and the adventurers are guaranteed that the crown will not interfere with their shares of the profits ; the King reserving for himself only one-fifth of all bullion and precious stones found. Before the King could be induced to grant this patent, he had insisted upon a detailed statement being furnished to him of the exact strength of the proposed expedition, its objects and destination. This information he promised on the ' word of a King' to keep absolutely secret. But it was not easy for him to keep a secret from Sarmiento. The latter assured James that he had discovered the real object of Ralegh. The talk of the mine, he said, was mere moonshine; the real intention was to prevent the close alliance between England and Spain, by attacking and destroying the shipping and possessions of the latter, and by arousing mutual enmity and distrust. James took fright at this, and assured his friend that, if Ralegh dared to attack or plunder any subjects of Spain, he would hand him over on his return to be hanged in the Plaza Mayor of Madrid, and would send every penny of plunder with him. Gondomar said this was all very well, but it would be too late when the damage was done: the force of Ralegh was too great for the mere working of a mine in a savage country, and, indeed, was meant for making piratical war on his master. James swore that it was nothing of the sort, and showed Gondomar Ralegh's secret letter, setting forth the exact number of ships and men, and the precise spot where the mine was situated. This was exactly what Gondomar wanted, and in August, as fast as a courier could speed, went a copy of Ralegh's letter to Madrid. James had insisted upon an assurance being obtained from Ralegh by Winwood, that he would really only go to his proposed gold mine, and would not encroach on the Spanish possessions; but in the patent already quoted, curiously enough, no such condition is imposed, except that the recited intention is to go to parts inhabited only by heathen people. It is not necessary to look very deeply to see here the work of Sarmiento's hand, as also in the erasure of the usual style of 'trusty and well-beloved' before Ralegh's name. Sarmiento boldly and persistently asserted that the whole of the country was Spanish territory, which James could hardly allow, as he had already given licenses for colonisation there in virtue of Ralegh's previous appropriation of it to England. But it is clear that the omission of the words specially warning Ralegh against encroaching upon Spanish territory in South America would have hampered Sarmiento afterwards in his claim that it was all Spanish territory, and in demanding Ralegh's punishment in any case, which was the course he intended to pursue from the first.

It must be confessed that there was a great deal of truth in the assertions of Sarmiento with regard to the underlying objects of Ralegh's expedition. The main article of its leader's political faith was that Spain should not be allowed to revive from the crushing blows she had already suffered, but should be pursued everywhere with relentless animosity, until she was past recovery. The idea of a close alliance with her was anathema to him, and to most of the statesmen who had imbibed the Elizabethan traditions. The French party of James's Court was still a considerable one ; Winwood and Edmonds, Secretary and Treasurer respectively, were strongly in its favour, and all the support which Ralegh received came from the

enemies of the Spanish alliance.   How entirely justified Sarmiento's suspicions were in this respect is seen
by the curious negotiations between Ralegh and the
Savoyard Ambassador, Scarnafissi, with the knowledge
of the King and the intervention of Winwood, during
the period when the expedition was being prepared.
For some years Savoy had been drifting away from
the Spanish interest, to which for two generations it
had been a faithful and ill-requited servitor.   At one
time there had been hopes that the Duke of Savoy
might succeed to the throne of Spain, and at another
that at least he might marry an Infanta, as his father
had done.   But his Spanish hopes had been frustrated,
and the diplomacy of Henry IV. had drawn him away
from his Spanish kinsman by at last ceding to him
the Marquisate of Saluzzo so long in dispute, whilst
the Spanish governors in Italy had, with or without
orders from Madrid, encroached upon his territories,
led him into a war, and caused him endless trouble.
A greater danger than ever threatened the little
potentate now, for the Spanish policy of Marie de
Medici, the Queen-Mother of France, had drawn the
two great rivals together ; and this boded but ill to
their small neighbour.   The Huguenots and Con-
stable Lediguières were favourable to him, and a project was conceived to form a new combination of the
Protestant powers, the Huguenots and Savoy, to withstand the threatening combination of France and
Spain.   In furtherance of this idea, Count Scarnafissi

was sent to England. He was brought into contact
with Ralegh, to whom such a combination would be
sure to appeal, and submitted to James a proposal for
Ralegh's expedition, reinforced by four of the King's
ships and others, to change the route as soon as they
got out to sea, and join a force in the Mediterranean
under the Duke of Montpensier, for the purpose of
surprising and capturing Genoa—which was in the
Spanish interest—for the Duke of Savoy. It was a
bold project, and Winwood and Ralegh approved of
it highly. James pretended to do so ; talked of arming sixteen ships to join Ralegh's eight, and much
more to the same effect, but when matters came to
a point he grew cool, and told Scarnafissi that on no
account would he allow Ralegh to take command, as
he was determined that he should go to the Indies.
The Venetian Ambassador, whose account we are
following, says that the real reasons why the King
would not let Ralegh undertake the enterprise were,
that he did not want to offend the Spaniards, and
because in case of the attempt succeeding he could
not trust Ralegh to give him a fair proportion of the
profits. 'But, I believe,' says the Venetian, 'that as
soon as he (Ralegh) has his ships out of the river, he will
rather go to the Mediterranean than the Atlantic ;
because he has spent 200,000 ducats in fitting out
eight vessels ; he is deeply in debt, and very few people
believe that he means to return to England, but will
take to plundering, perhaps indifferently. He pre-

tends to be willing to obey and go to the Indies, for if he appeared otherwise he would be ruined, but what he will do when he is once out at sea, time alone will show.'   This was at the end of January 1617, and the Genoa enterprise was then seen to be hopeless, as its success depended upon the prompt utilisation of Ralegh's ships.   Ralegh's new flagship, the *Destiny*, was launched in the Thames in January, and for a time was the talk of London, for it was built on his own improved design, and its furnishing was as luxurious and splendid as befitted its owner's tastes. Amongst other persons who went on board to see it was Des Marets, the French Ambassador, to whom Ralegh had already been introduced by Winwood. Des Marets' first visit was in March, and on that day and subsequently he had conferences with Ralegh. It was the ill fortune of the latter, apparently, to impress all contemporaries with his insincerity and want of principle.   He had ventured almost his last penny, had staked his reputation, practically his life, in the Guiana enterprise, to which he had clung for years through all his troubles, and yet there were few people believed that he honestly intended to carry it out.   Des Marets thought that he might be going to aid the Huguenots, who were in open rebellion against the Queen - Mother's Spanish policy, and sought to draw him out for the information of Richelieu, whose public life as minister had just commenced.

Thereupon ensued certain negotiations which have

never yet been satisfactorily explained. Winwood was anxious to combine France with England, and to avoid close union with Spain ; and whatever was done by Ralegh with the French at this juncture must have been known to him, and partly also to James, although Ralegh alone had to suffer for it at a subsequent stage. Des Marets reported that Ralegh had told him that he had a great enterprise in hand, 'which would bring great honour and profit *to the sovereign who shall reap the fruit of his labours*. Seeing himself so badly and tyrannously treated by his King, he had resolved, if God sent him good fortune, to quit his country, and make to the King our master the first offer of that which falls into his hands. . . . I did my best to confirm him in this good intention, and assured him that he could not possibly address himself to any quarter where he would be received with greater courtesy or friendship. I thought best to give him fair words, although, for my own part, I do not expect his voyage will result in much profit.' It does not appear that this alleged strange avowal of Ralegh to the French Ambassador produced any further direct negotiations, although, as we shall see later, one of the officers of the French Embassy was afterwards accused of carrying on communications with Ralegh of a questionable character. It is certain that before he finally sailed Ralegh opened up a correspondence with the Admiral of France, Montmorenci, for the purpose of obtaining a patent allowing him to enter any French ports with whatever prizes he may have captured, and that he made arrangements for a number of French ships to join him on the Orinoco. When Ralegh returned to England, the King told Gondomar that Ralegh asserted that he had taken possession of Guiana by virtue of warrants granted by Queen Elizabeth and Henry IV. of France. It is unlikely that he should have obtained a patent from Henry for his first voyage, so that, if the King (James) told the truth, Ralegh had probably obtained a transfer to him of the patent granted by Henry IV. to Henry Maree de Montbariot and others, many years before, for the conquest of Guiana, or else that he had in some way associated with him the holders of the patent, with whom it is known that he carried on a correspondence. In any case, the best proof that Ralegh never intended to offer his services to France to the detriment of his own country, is afforded by the fact that he actually did return to England, when he must have known that his return meant ruin, and perhaps death, which he could have avoided by taking refuge in a French port. The balance of probability seems to be that Ralegh in this expedition was used merely as a pawn in the game, respectively by the French and Spanish parties in the English Court, with the full knowledge of the King, to be accepted or repudiated, as circumstances rendered advisable. He was a man whom nobody trusted; and yet, such is the irony of events, that he was almost the only man who was perfectly single-hearted and sincere in his intentions for the expedition. Similar expeditions under Elizabeth were often bound by the most stringent conditions from offending Spain, and yet it was perfectly understood that the conditions might be ignored with safety, so long as the nation was relieved of responsibility. Ralegh never doubted for a moment that the same course would be followed now. He knew—everybody knew—that he would probably have to fight the Spaniards before he effected a permanent settlement in Guiana. Gondomar was quite right when he told the King that so large a force could only mean fighting; and he offered that if Ralegh would consent to go unarmed, with two ships only, the King of Spain himself would give him an escort and protect his working of the mine. It suited all English parties that he should go in strength, and be exalted or sacrificed, as might be convenient, on his return; and most men of position saw it but himself. He was too deeply absorbed in the great dream of his life to see anything but the vast golden empire of Guiana beckoning him and his to wealth untold, and to undying fame as a man who had endowed his country with the mighty dominion of El Dorado. By the middle of March 1617, Ralegh's preparations in the

Thames were complete, and a survey of his ships was made by order of the Lord Admiral, of which the following is a copy :—

'The *Destiny* of London, of the burthen of 440 tons, whereof Sir Walter Rauleigh goeth generall, Walter Rauleigh the younger captaine, Robert Barwick master, 200 men, whereof 100 saylers, 20 watermen, 80 gentlemen, the rest servants and labourers, 36 pieces of ordnance. The *Starre*, *alias* the *Jason* of London, of the burthen of 240 tons, John Pennington captain, George Clevingham master, 80 men, 1 gentleman and no more, 25 pieces of ordnance. The *Encounter* of London, of the burthen of 160 tons, Edward Hastings captain, Thomas Pye master, 17 pieces of ordnance. The *John and Francis*, *alias* the *Thunder*, of the burthen of 150 tons, Sir William St Leger Kt. captaine, William Gurden master, 60 souldiers, 10 landsmen, 6 gentlemen, 20 pieces of ordnance. The *Flying Joane* of London, of the burthen of 120 tons, John Chidley captaine, William Thorne master, 25 men, 14 pieces of ordnance. The *Husband*, *alias* the *Southampton*, of the burthen of 80 tons, John Bayley captaine, Philip Fabian master, 25 mariners, 2 gentlemen, 6 pieces of ordnance. The pinnace *Page*, James Barker captaine, Stephen Selbye master, 8 saylers, 3 robinets of brasse.

'Sum total. 1215 tons. Men 431. Ordnance 121 pieces.

'The number of men on the *Encounter* is not stated.'
This report was duly sent to Philip, but one of the
Spanish spies at Plymouth subsequently reported that
when the expedition finally sailed it consisted in all
of 17 ships, 14 of which were armed, carrying a
force of 2000 men. The real strength, however,
that sailed from Plymouth was 14 ships in all, with
about 900 men. Troubles and delays innumerable
occurred before Ralegh could leave England behind
him. He put out of the Thames at the end of
March 1617, and awaited his stragglers at the Isle
of Wight. After he reached Plymouth, the
victuallers refused to supply biscuits for the *Jason*
without payment, and Lady Ralegh in London
was obliged to enter into a bond for the money.
Then Sir John Ferne, the captain of the *Flying
Hart*, could not sail without a fresh supply of
money, and Ralegh had to borrow £200 from two
friends. Captain Whitney's ship, too, ran short
of provisions, and Ralegh's plate was sold to the
Plymouth silversmiths to pay for them; and so
three months wore away in heart-breaking inactivity,
provisions dwindling, money running short and men
grumbling. In May the commander issued a general
order for the government of the fleet, which is curiously reminiscent of the order issued by Medina
Sidonia on the sailing of the Armada, and in parts
is evidently inspired by it. Divine service was to
be performed every morning and evening on all the

ships; there was to be no swearing, blasphemy or gaming on board; landsmen were to learn the names of the ropes, and sailors the use of arms, and so on; but the most important parts for our present purpose are the elaborate directions given for fighting at sea, and the frequent reference to 'the enemy'; quite in the old Elizabethan vein. Considering that England was then ostensibly at peace with all Europe, and the expedition was supposed to be bound for a country to which no nation laid claim but Spain, it is evident that Ralegh had not the slightest doubt from the first that he would probably have to fight, and that the enemy could only be the Spaniards. For James or others to plead ignorance of it was sheer hypocrisy; although the King gave 'his hand, word and faith' to Gondomar that if the Spaniards were assailed in any way Ralegh should die, and exacted heavy sureties from some of his friends in England that he (Ralegh) would return and answer for his conduct of the expedition. Ralegh sailed from Plymouth on the 4th July, but off Scilly was caught in a tempest which sank Chidley's pinnace, and scattered the rest of the fleet. Thereafter for seven weary weeks the unfortunate expedition remained wind-bound in Cork harbour, and on the 19th August, nearly five months after he had left the Thames, Ralegh finally spread his sails to a fair north-east wind, and started on his fateful voyage.

Ralegh's first voyage 1595
Second voyage 1617 ———
River expedition 1617-18 ------

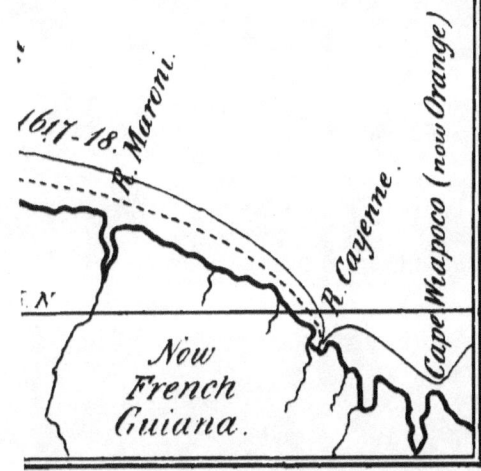

1617-18   R. Maroni.

R. Cayenne.

Cape Wiapoco (now Orange)

N

New
French
Guiana.

On the 30th, 20 leagues from Cape St Vincent, the
expedition fell in with four suspicious French ships,
loaded with fish and train oil.   Ralegh's captains
wanted to persuade him to capture them as pirates,
but he told them it was not his right to examine the
subjects of the French King, and it was legal for them
to capture Spanish ships south of the Canaries and
west of the Azores, and : 'I did not suffer my
company to take from them any pennyworth of their
goods, greatly to the discontent of my company, who
cried out that they were men-of-war and thieves, as
so indeed they were, for I met a Spaniard afterwards
whom they had robbed.'   A pinnace of 7 tons and
three pipes of oil were bought of them for 61 crowns,
and they were, after some prudent detention, sent
on their way unplundered.   On Sunday the 7th
September the   English expedition   anchored off
Lanzarote, one of the Canary Islands.   The Moorish
pirates had recently been in the neighbourhood, and
the people of the island thought that Ralegh's fleet
might be they, so that when some of the Englishmen
landed 'to stretch their legs,' the islanders came
down to the beach fully armed, but carrying a flag
of truce.   When they found that they had to deal
with Englishmen, they requested that two officers,
armed only with rapiers, might be sent to confer with
the Governor.   Ralegh, and an officer named Brad-
shaw, advanced into a plain for the purpose, and the
leader was appealed to by the Governor as to what he

wanted in so poor and barren a place, peopled mainly
by Moriscos. He told him that he had no desire to
injure any of the King of Spain's dominions, having
received from his King express orders to the contrary.
All he wanted was to be allowed to purchase at a fair
price such fresh provisions as the place afforded. The
Governor promised him facility for this. As agreed,
a list of the stores he required was sent on shore, but
Ralegh waited in vain for the provisions to be sent,
the Governor in the meanwhile forwarding to him
fresh promises of immediate supplies. Ralegh says that
he never believed him, for he knew he was carrying
his goods up to the mountains in the interior, and the
English captains were all for attacking the town, but,
says Ralegh, 'I knew it would offend His Majesty,
and the poor English merchant whose goods were in
their hands would have been ruined.' After waiting
for some days, Ralegh sent word to the Governor, that
if it were not that he did not wish to offend the King
of England he would pull him and his Moriscos out
of the town by the ears. It is not surprising that in
response to this the Governor said he knew they were
the same Turks that had been plundering their neighbours, and he would consequently stand on his guard
against them. Even if they were English, he said, he
should be hanged if he helped them, and they should
have nothing except by force. Ralegh, before he
sailed away, sent a curt answer to this, saying that he
took note of the King of Spain's disposition, notwith-

standing the peace with England. The next day the
expedition reached Grand Canary, and Ralegh sent a
copy of his correspondence with the Governor of
Lanzarote to the Governor-in-Chief, and landed a few
of his men to obtain fresh water. Whilst this was
proceeding some of the country people attacked the
English sentries, and in the ensuing skirmish three
of the islanders were killed ; 'which,' says Sir Walter,
'made up for two of his own men' who were killed
in a brawl at Lanzarote.

As we have seen, the long delay in the sailing of
the expedition had given ample time for the Spaniards
to make preparations to frustrate the aims in view.
Several agents of Gondomar had shipped with Ralegh,
in order to report anything which, by any possibility,
might furnish a pretext for demanding of James the
fulfilment of his promise, on 'hand, word and faith,'
to surrender Ralegh if any offence were offered to
Spain, and this landing on the Canaries to water was
thought to be enough. Captain Bailey, with the
Husband, deserted, and flew to England with the
news. He at once sent his statement to Buckingham, as agreed upon, by whom it was handed to the
King, and from him to Fenton for inquiry and report.
In the meanwhile Gondomar was fully informed of
what had passed, and sent the following letter to the
King of Spain (22nd Oct.). As the particulars in it
have not hitherto been published, I have thought well
to transcribe it nearly at length. 'I informed Your

Majesty on the 3rd August that Walter Ralegh had arrived in Ireland short of stores, and that an English baron there had provided him with 100 oxen, etc. He sailed on the 19th August, having added to his fleet there some little craft of 20 or 30 tons each. He is said to have in all 13 or 14 sail, and 900 or 1000 men, soldiers and sailors. I now learn that letters have been received here from some of the men who went with him, and particularly from the chief gunner of his flagship, written from the Canary Islands, where they say he had tried to get some water and stores. I expect he will do more injury than that there if he can. No doubt news of his actions will arrive in Spain more speedily and frequently than here, and as all possible efforts have been made here, without avail, to prevent his voyage, whatever measures Your Majesty may adopt to punish him will be fully justified, and many honourable Englishmen will be very glad of it. Amongst these is Sir John Digby,* for he protested here frequently and vigorously against the evils which would arise to England if Walter Ralegh were allowed to go on this voyage. I have also asked the folks here what right they have to complain of pirates, since they let this man sail, who has no other intention than to be a pirate. If he has stolen so much as a cow at

---

* Sir John Digby, Ralegh's successor in the possession of the Sherborne estate, was sent as English convoy to Madrid to treat of the marriage of Prince Charles and the Infanta. He, Cottington, and Lord Roos ·were ceaselessly urged by Philip and Lerma to write to James I., pressing for the condign punishment of Ralegh.

Canary, it would be well for the Governor to seize
the goods of the first English ship which goes there,
in order to fully satisfy the owners. It would be a
great shame if he did not do so, and tell the captain, if
he complains, that he had better come and recover
the damage from Ralegh's sureties, as it is easier for
an Englishman to make a claim in London than a
Canarian.

'Since writing the above I have received the paper I
enclose. It is from a person very zealous in Your
Majesty's interests, and I also send the paper from
Sir Thomas Lake, who came personally to express to
me the great sorrow of the King and all good people
at what Ralegh has done. The King promises that he
will do whatever we like to remedy and redress it.
Although I judge Lake to be a very honest man, and
sincere in what he says, I look upon it as absurd to
expect that a fitting redress will be afforded here for
so atrocious a wickedness as this, as I clearly foresaw
and foretold what would happen in ample time to
prevent it, and urgently pressed the King and Council
frequently to do so, and also Secretary Winwood, who
really was Ralegh's supporter. One day, when the
King wanted to persuade me of the perfect security
Ralegh was leaving that he would do no harm, I·
said I would call him to witness that if Ralegh sailed
I knew that he would proceed in such a manner as
would force Your Majesty's officers to embargo the
persons and property of Englishmen in your dominions.

He replied that it would be very just to do so if Ralegh did anything wrong, but that I should see that he (the King) would not deceive himself to the extent of imperilling the persons and property of his subjects, or permit Ralegh to go, unless he left security.

Captain Bailey, who has returned from Ralegh, declares that the latter approached Canary, and the Governor sent to say that Your Majesty was at peace with the King of England, and if he required provisions, he could have them and welcome. Seeing that the people there were prepared for him, he went to another island of which the captain is not quite sure of the name, but believes it to be Lanzarote, where he landed 600 men with the intention of fortifying himself, and awaiting the Indian flotilla. The captain says that he had sailed with him, under the belief that his intention was to discover unknown countries, but when he saw his evil objects he returned hither to the Isle of Wight, where he now is, and has sent this news. Ralegh's friends are greatly perturbed, and are trying to find excuses for him. Amongst other absurdities they are saying that he bore a commission from the King of France to make war on Your Majesty at sea.'

Gondomar's urgent advice to Philip then follows. Let the authorities at Seville—as if of their own motion—draw up a statement that an English fleet bearing the King's commission has raided the Canaries, and that, pending Your Majesty's orders, they have

embargoed all English property there (*i.e.*, at Seville).
This, he says, will soon bring James to his knees, but
he will be very insolent if it be not done. 'Pray,' he
says to Philip, 'send the fleet to punish this pirate.'
It will be easy, as his force is small. Every man
caught should at once be killed, except Ralegh and
the officers, who should be brought to Seville, and
executed in the Plaza the next day. It is the only
way to treat such pirates and disturbers, and *it is a
necessary step for the preservation of the peace with
England, France and Holland.* Gondomar also relates
that the Earl of Southampton had received a letter
from Ralegh from Canary, saying that he had decided
that the best thing to do would be to await there the
arrival of the silver fleet, and that he, some French
ships having joined him, is now so strong, that none
of the Spanish ships will escape him. 'I am certain,'
says Gondomar, 'that no redress is to be expected
from here ; because those who might redress the evil
would, in my opinion, rather see the millions of the
silver fleet in Ralegh's hands than in those of Your
Majesty. I have constantly urged upon Your Majesty
the course I think you should take. Ralegh sailed
with the King's commission to command the expedition, in spite of all my remonstrances and protests,
and those of his better councillors, and after he had
often given me his word that Ralegh should leave
such security as would prevent him from injuring any
of Your Majesty's subjects. He sent to tell me this a

hundred times by several councillors and by Sir John Digby. The King should now be made to feel the responsibility. It is certain that the King does not wish for war.'

I have reproduced this letter at length, because it proves beyond doubt that the intention of the Spaniards from the first was to sacrifice Ralegh, and that the moment the King was weak and foolish enough to pledge himself to Gondomar that if the least injury was done to Spanish subjects he should be sacrificed, Ralegh was doomed. Be it remembered that when the above letter was written, no attack whatever had really been made upon Spanish interests, and the Bailey's assertions were absolutely untrue. The letter written by Sir Thomas Lake to Gondomar, enclosed to the King of Spain, in Spanish, contains the following expressions, which display even more luridly the miserable weakness of James, considering that when they were written there was nothing against Ralegh but the utterly false and unsupported suppositions of Captain Bailey. 'I return you the letter you did me the honour of writing to me, and I am glad to be able to transmit to you the account of the matter I have just received in a letter from Viscount Fenton, respecting Ralegh's business, and his action in Canary. He tells me that His Majesty is very disposed and determined against Ralegh, and will join the King of Spain in ruining him, but he wishes this resolution to be kept secret for some little while, in order that, in the interim, he may keep an eye on the disposition of some of the people here. If Your Excellency is willing, I will call and see you to-morrow. 21st October.—THOMAS LAKE.'

The evidence which was enough to make James willing to 'ruin' his most distinguished subject seemed to the English Ambassador, Cottington, in Madrid to need further proofs, and every unbiased person will now come to the same conclusion. The probability seems to be, that James was eager to seize upon the first pretext to sell Ralegh to the Spaniards, in order to curry favour with them.

Captain Bailey and his crew were brought to London, and examined by the King himself, who told Gondomar 'that the statements of one half of them were opposed by those of the other half; some saying that Ralegh had done nothing wrong, whilst others asserted that he was a great pirate, confirming Captain Bailey's own statement. He (the King) told me he wished we had some trust-worthy news from Spain, because he was anxious to proclaim Ralegh at once as a traitor, and pro-ceed against his sureties, and against all those who took part in the voyage. He said that during this week he would make some demonstration, which would please me, and would bridle and alarm his subjects; and that Sir John Digby was the person who had spoken most worthily to him on the matter.

When he was opposing Ralegh's being allowed to sail, he had told him (the King) that if the voyage were not prevented great evils would ensue, and all the world would throw the blame upon the King (James). He (Digby) said, if the King wished to break with Your Majesty, he would undertake to find a pretext of a more honourable description than this. The King said that he saw now that Digby had told him the truth, and he would at once adopt such measures of redress as Your Majesty wished and would convey to him through me.'

These letters, which have never hitherto been published, prove to demonstration James' complaisant baseness in the matter ; and that Ralegh was a doomed man, even if the subsequent events on the Orinoco had never happened. But as month succeeded month, whilst no fresh news came of Ralegh's misdeeds, and the slow administration in Spain took no open measures of retaliation, Ralegh's friends plucked up spirits. They pointed out if Bailey's statements or suppositions had been true the results would have been seen before, and resentment would have been shown in Madrid. In the absence of Gondomar, Father Fuentes writes from London (2nd February 1618), that the King would be very glad now of an opportunity of punishing those who promoted Ralegh's voyage, and the writer recommends that Digby in Madrid be requested to urge the making of some great demonstration in England. 'Digby,' he says, 'would be more delighted than anyone; but as no representations are made in Madrid, Ralegh's friends are saying that nothing wrong has been done, and that Bailey is a liar.'

On the 4th September Ralegh arrived at Gomera, one of the smaller Canary Islands. His men were falling sick with overcrowding, heat, and bad water; and a fresh supply of the latter was of vital necessity. There was only one small landing-place, which a handful of men could defend against a host, and a few shots were fired against the English from the rocks above it. Twenty demi-culverin balls were sent through the houses of the town by the English, just to show that the expedition was well armed, and then Ralegh sent a peaceful message to the Governor, saying he only wanted water, and would do no harm unless attacked. The Governor had been advised that they were Moorish pirates, and hesitated; but some Canarians, whom Ralegh had taken on the coast of Africa, were sent to reassure him, and an agreement was made for a few of the Englishmen to land and obtain a supply of water. Only six men went ashore, but ten of Ralegh's vessels were put broadside on the town, which, he said, he would knock to bits if treachery were practised on his men. He had nothing to fear, however. The Governor's wife was half an Englishwoman—her mother was a Stafford—to whom Ralegh sent six fine handkerchiefs, and six pairs of gloves, welcome, doubtless, in that remote place.   But not more welcome than were her gracious kindly words and presents in return.   It was almost the only pleasant occurrence in this disastrous voyage, this friendly interchange of courtesies at Gomera.   'She sent,' says Ralegh, 'four very great loaves of sugar, a basket of lemons, which I much desired to comfort and refresh our many sick men, a basket of oranges, a basket of most delicate grapes, another of pome-granates and figs, which trifles were better welcome to me than 1000 crowns would have been.'   In reply he sent the Countess '2 ounces of ambergris, an ounce of delicate extract of amber, a great glass of rose water in high estimation here, a very excellent picture of Mary Magdalen, and a cutwork ruff.'   It would perhaps be indiscreet to ask where Puritan Sir Walter had obtained the picture of the Magdalen ; but whatever he may have plundered elsewhere, all things at Gomera were sacred, and he threatened his men with instant death if so much as a pennyworth were taken without due payment.   Before he sailed he received plenty more of refreshing fruit, a basket of fine white manchet (bread), and two dozen fat hens, with a full supply of good water.   'And we departed without any offence given or received to the value of a farthing, whereof the Count sent his friar aboard my ship, with a letter to Don Diego de Sarmiento, Ambassador in England, witnessing how nobly we had behaved ourselves, and how justly we had dealt with

the inhabitants of the island.' The good Governor
little knew that Don Diego and James Stuart between
them had already agreed to 'ruin' the greatest
Englishman afloat for daring to sail the seas at all,
whether his conduct was good or ill. Releasing the
small Spanish prizes he had detained, and recompensing
the masters, he departed from Gomera on the 21st
September, with mutual expressions of kindliness and
goodwill. Head winds and tempests kept him buffet-
ing about in the Atlantic for six weeks, in danger
from shipwreck again and again, with pestilence
raging on his fleet, until it seemed as if ill-fortune
had marked out Ralegh as its own. On his flagship,
the *Destiny*, he had threescore men sick at the same
time, and no less than forty-two died on the terrible
passage. Water fell short, the heat was stifling, and
when the head winds fell, a dead calm held them
motionless on seas like burnished copper ; and then a
mysterious darkness overwhelmed them so that for
two whole days they had to steer by candlelight. At
length, on the 31st October, the leader was aroused
from his sweltering couch by a sudden hurricane, and
rushing on deck, he too caught a chill, and was soon
down with a raging fever. Overwrought with anxiety
and fatigue, he was like to die for many weary days,
sustained only, as he says, by the grateful fruit which
the Countess of Gomera had sent him ; and when at
last, on the 11th November, the welcome cry of
'land' was heard, weak and helpless as a child he

could only gaze sadly from his pallet upon the first promontory of the great empire with which it was the dream of his life to endow the English crown.

CHAPTER XV

RALEGH IN GUIANA — THE RIVER EXPEDITION—
ATTACK ON SAN THOMÉ—DEATH OF YOUNG
WALTER RALEGH—FAILURE AND RETURN OF
THE RIVER EXPEDITION—GONDOMAR CLAIMS THE
FULFILMENT OF THE KING'S PROMISE—HIS CON-
VERSATIONS WITH JAMES

THE point first sighted was Cape Wiapoco—now
Cape Orange—east of the mouth of the Cayenne.
Ralegh's name was well known there amongst the
Indians, one of the chiefs in the neighbourhood,
Leonard, having lived in England with him. Harcourt's company of Englishmen a few years before
had been succoured and aided by the Indians there,
in the belief that they were Ralegh's men. Leonard,
however, was up the country when the expedition
arrived, and Ralegh decided not to seek him, but to
enter the mouth of the Cayenne, where there lived
another chief called Harry, who had passed two years
in the Tower with the leader. Cassava bread, luscious
pines and fresh meat, came in plenty from the devoted
Indians. Ralegh was carried ashore, 'out of the

unsavoury ship, pestered with many sick men, which, being unable to move, poisoned us with a most filthy stench,' and here, sitting under the shade of a tent, he gradually began to gather strength.   His men were landed and refreshed, his boats cleaned, and for a time affairs looked prosperous.   One of his captains, Alley, was troubled with vertigo, and it was decided to send him home with dispatches, giving the good news that the Guiana coast had been reached at last.   Ralegh wrote by him to his wife (14th Nov.).   'Sweetheart, —I can yet write unto you, but with a weak hand, for I have suffered the most violent calenture for fifteen days that ever man did, and lived : but God that gave me strong heart in all my adversities hath also now strengthened it in the hell fire of heat.   We have had two most grievous sicknesses in our ship, of which fourtie-two have died, and there are yet many sick ; but having recovered the land of Guiana this 12th November, I hope we shall recover them.   We are yet 200 men, and the rest of our fleet are reasonably strong—strong enough I hope to perform what we have undertaken, if the diligent care at London to make our strength known to the Spanish King by his Ambassador have not taught the Spaniards to fortifie all the entraunces against us.   Howsoever, we must make the adventure, and if we perish, it shall be no honour for England, nor gain for His Majestie, to loose, among many other, one hundred as valiant gentlemen as England hath in it. . . .   To tell you

that I might be here King of the Indians were a
vanitie; but my name hath still lived among them.
Here they feed me with fresh meat, and all that the
country yields; all offer to obey me.'

Alley arrived at Portsmouth in March, and the
Spanish Ambassador was promptly ready with his
version of the news to send to Madrid. The expedition, he said, was in dire straits, in a port where
the current was so strong that it would be difficult
for the ships to get out. Provisions were running
short, and—which was true—the mortality had been
terrible. 'Most of the men on board are desperate,
and some of them gave letters for their friends in
England to the captain who has come hither. But
Ralegh took the letters, and, amongst others complaining of his proceedings, he opened one from a
gentleman, saying in what misery they were, and
that if things did not improve they had resolved to
throw Ralegh overboard and return to England.
Ralegh attempted to arrest this gentleman, and
showed him his letter; but the rest of them would
not allow it. All those who have come hither agree
that nothing but entire failure can be expected from
Ralegh's voyage, and they think that those who
remain with him will either be lost, or, if they are
able to get out, will turn pirates. I think this is the
most likely.'

After three weeks stay at Cayenne, and great
danger in crossing the bar, Ralegh's ship and the

Jason sailed higher up the coast to the Triangle Isles—or Health Isles, as they are now called. But the rest of his fleet lagged behind on various pretexts. Indeed, though Ralegh himself does not say so, it is plain that most of his men were already sulky and discontented. At the Isles of Health, the expedition up the Orinoco was organised. The chief had again fallen · sick, and could not personally take command; the officers, moreover, were unwilling to leave the body of the expedition on the coast at the mercy of the Spaniards, unless Ralegh himself remained in charge. Sir Warham St Leger, the second military officer, was also down with fever, and the 400 soldiers, with the river force, were placed under the command of Sir Walter's nephew, George Ralegh, with Captains Parker, North, young Walter Ralegh, Thornehurst, Hall and Chudles under him, Captain Kemys, the only man who had seen the mine, having command of the landing in the river. The *Encounter*, the *Confidence*, the *Supply* and two small craft were directed to take these men to the mouth of the Orinoco, calling at the Rivers Surinam and Essiquibo for refreshment on the way, Ralegh and the rest of the fleet directing their course to Trinidad to await the return of the party.

They parted company on the 10th December, the instructions to the river expedition being that, if possible, they were to reach the mine without coming into conflict with the Spaniards. The soldiers were to encamp 'between the Spanish town and the mine if there be any town. So that being secured, you may make trial what depth and breadth the mine holds, and whether or no it answers your hopes. If you find it royal, and the Spaniards make war upon you, you, George Ralegh, are to repel them, if it be in your power, and to drive them as far as you can.'

When James Stuart found it necessary afterwards to make some apology to his indignant people for having sacrificed Ralegh to please the Spaniards, he —or rather, Bacon for him—asserted, untruly, that orders were given beforehand to the exploring party to capture the Spanish town before going to the mine, but all testimony contradicts this; besides which, Ralegh did not know where the town was.

The main fleet, with Ralegh on board, sighted Barima Point, at the mouth of the Orinoco, on the 15th December, and finally came to anchor in the Gulf of Paria, Trinidad, on the last day of the year 1617. On the 19th January an attempt was made to trade with the Spaniards at Port of Spain, but a volley of musketry, and other volleys of stones and oaths from shore, bade the English keep at a distance. The river expedition had taken stores for a month, and when the month of January had passed without news of it, Ralegh began to grow anxious. He had moved up to the north point of Trinidad to await the return of his absent men—for on this occasion the exploration party had entered by the main mouth of the river discovered by Kemys, and not by the Manamo, by which Ralegh had groped his way in 1595—and continued to send scouting parties along the coast to the east to pick up news. At last, from unwilling Indians, vague rumours came that the English had captured a Spanish town in the Orinoco and had slain the officers, the rest of the Spaniards having fled to the woods, two of the English captains also: having fallen. Armed parties were despatched by Ralegh daily to gather news, and gradually, piece by piece, Ralegh, in dire anxiety, began to realise that some great calamity had fallen upon him.

In the meanwhile we will follow, for a time, the fortunes of the river expedition, as told by some of the men who took part in it. Let Captain Parker tell his story first to his old comrade Captain Alley.

'Your departure from us was fortunate for you, as you thereby avoided miseries and crosses unutterable. We left Cayenne for the Orinoco in company with the ships of Captains Whitney and Wollaston, a flyboat and a caravel; the flagship, vice flagship and the other larger vessels directing their course for Trinidad to await our return. We were a month ascending the Orinoco, and at length landed a league from San Thomé. At one o'clock in the morning we delivered our assault, and lost Captain Rauley and Captain Cosmore, although Captain Rauley was killed by his own carelessness and indiscreet rashness, as you will be told, for I wish to give you an account of the order that was observed by us. Captain Cosmore led the forlorn hope with 50 men, I followed with the first companies of musketeers, and Rauley came after me with the pikemen. As soon as Rauley learned that we had delivered the assault, he indiscreetly abandoned his post and command, and came to us, where, unfortunately, he was welcomed with a bullet which left him no time to beg our Almighty Father for mercy for the sinful life he had led. We at once took possession of the town, with only a loss of two of our men, one of whom was Master Harrington, a kinsman of the Countess of Bedford. The Spaniards were not strong, and being suspicious of our force, fled, abandoning their Governor, who is called Don Diego Palomeque de Acuña, with Captain Santo and Captain Abisueto. When we had the town in our hands, Captain Kemys took several gentlemen with him to find the mine, and in this way passed carelessly from one place to another for about twenty days, always holding out hopes to us that he would find it. But at last we discovered that' it was all nothing but lies and deceit, and that he was a mere Machiavel who told the truth to no one; and especially was he hateful and detestable to himself, for with the most roguish cruelty he sought to take his own life and succeeded in killing himself. But now he can do no more wickedness, I will not dwell further upon this man, odious and detestable to God and the world. I will, however, inform you, as well as I can, what those of us who remain may expect. We have already split into several parties. Captains Whitney and Wollaston agree together to sail in company on the seas, to waylay homeward-bound merchant ships; the flagship, vice flagship and Sir John Ferne, are going to Newfoundland to lay in fresh provisions, and thence to the western isles also to watch for homeward-bound ships. As for myself, with God's help, I also mean to make some voyage that will either give me profit or a grave in the sea. Pray, therefore, tell my friends this. I expect by the end of August that we shall have finished our intentions. As I am in port, I cannot write more, and I only pray to God that you may live prosperously. 22d March.'*

This not particularly chivalrous epistle is somewhat in conflict with Ralegh's own accounts, which always represent the Spaniards as the first aggressors. When Kemys had ascended the Orinoco previously (in 1596) he had found the Spanish settlement San Thomé, as already described, somewhat below the mouth of the Caroni, the mine itself being a considerable distance below that point, near Mount Aio. Ralegh had heard from the

* There is copy of Parker's letter in the Harl MSS. xxxix., folio 342, of which the wording varies somewhat from the above, although the sense is of course the same. This is owing to the fact that the above version is a retranslation into English of the Spanish copy sent to Philip III. by Gondomar.

Indians at Cayenne, if not before, that the settlement
had been moved, but appears to have had no exact knowledge of the position of the new town.   His instructions to Kemys before the departure of the expedition
make this clear, as he tells him to land his men and
encamp them between the town and the mine, *if there
be any town near.*   'If you shall find any great number
of soldiers . . . and that the passages are already forced,
so as without manifest peril of my son, yourself, and
the other captains, you cannot pass towards the mine,
then be well advised how you land, for I know (a few
gentlemen excepted) what a scum of men you have,
and I would not for all the world receive a blow from
the Spaniard to the dishonour of our nation.'

Ralegh's own accounts in his *Apology*, and in his
letters to Winwood and his wife, explain the matter in
a different light.   By them it would appear that the
Indians opposite the Isle of Tortola sent word to
the Spaniards of the coming of the expedition; and
that as they approached the new settlement, which
was on the site now called Guayana Vieja, slightly
below the site of the mine, the Spaniards shot at the
boats, 'both with their ordnance and muskets, whereupon the companies were forced to charge them, and
soon beat them out of the town.   In the assault
whereof, my son (having more desire of honour than
of safety) was slayne, with whom to say the truth all
respect of the world hath taken an end in me.'

Ralegh, in the bitterness of his heart, writing this to

Winwood (who was dead when the letter arrived), complains that the King valued him so little as to allow full particulars and charts of his projected voyage to be sent to Spain by Gondomar, and gives particulars of the orders sent from Madrid to America for the attack and defeat of the expedition. 'Lastly,' he says, 'to make an apology for not working the mine, although I know not (His Majesty excepted) whom I am to satisfie so much as myself, having loste my sonne and my estate in the enterprise, yet it is true that the Spaniards tooke more care to defend the passages leading unto it than they did their towne. . . . But it is true that when Kemys found the rivers low and that he could not approach the banks near the mine by a mile, and when he found a descent, a volley of muskets came from the woods upon the boat, and slew two of the rowers, hurt six others, and shot a valiant gentleman Captain Thornix in the head. He (to wit, Kemys) followed his own advice that it was in vaine to discover the mine (for he gave me this for excuse at his returne that the companies of English in their towne of San Thomé were hardly able to defend it against the dayly and nightly alarmes and assaults of the Spaniards, that the passage to the mine was of thick and unpassable woods, that being discovered they had no men to worke it) did not discover it at all. For it is true that the Spaniards having two gold mines near the towne, left them for want of negroes to work them. . . . Whatsoever that braggadochio the

Spanish Ambassador may say I shall prove it . . . and I shall make it appear to any prince or state that will undertake it, how easily those mines and five or six more may be possessed, most of them in places which have never yet been attempted by any enemy, nor any passage to them ever discovered by English, Dutch or French.'

The news which reached the leader, at first by Indian rumour, and on the 14th February by letters, must have seemed to him worse than death itself. The officers wrote that, after receiving the fire from the new town of San Thomé as they passed up the river, they had landed their men on New Year's day, 1618, a league above the settlement; and according to Ralegh himself (although contradicted by the Spaniards and inferentially by Captain Parker), an ambuscade was led against them at nine o'clock in the evening by a Captain Geronimo de Grados. The English rank and file were worthless, and were thrown into confusion, but were eventually rallied, and were led against the town. An untrustworthy story was afterwards told by Ralegh's enemies that young Walter cried out as he advanced, 'Come on, my hearts; here is the mine we must expect. They that look for other mines are fools.' It is, however, an insult to our intelligence to try to persuade us that Ralegh staked his life and fortune, only to take a poor, half-savage town of 130 palm-leaf huts.

In the attack the Governor Palomeque de Acuña

was killed (he is usually called a kinsman of Gondomar by Ralegh's historians, but I can find no evidence that he was so, except his name), and with him fell three or four other Spanish captains. Young Walter died, it is said, crying out to his comrades, ' Go on ! Lord have mercy upon me, and prosper your enterprise.' When the town had fallen, the Spaniards retreated to an island near, from whence they kept up a desultory attack upon the English. Kemys's attempts to find the mine were resisted by them step by step, and once he fell into an ambuscade and lost nine of his men. Lurking in the fastnesses of the woods and creeks with which they were familiar, the Spaniards picked off the Englishmen at their leisure, until 250 of the latter had fallen. The spirits of the men flagged, and disaffection crept through the dwindling ranks of the expedition. Curses and lowering looks followed the unfortunate Kemys in his futile attempts to reach the mine. George Ralegh, hoping against hope, held out as long as he could, and himself explored the near reaches of the river, constantly harassed by the desultory fire of the Spaniards. But a time came at length when it was evident that a further stay would mean extermination piecemeal, for the Indians told them of Spanish reinforcements coming up the river, and there was nothing for it but to re-embark the little force, and on the swift current of the great river sweep down towards the sea, bearing with them the dismal story of failure, which was ruin and death to their leader. With them they took such booty as the poor settlement of San Thomé afforded, and they left buried before the high altar of the plundered church the body of young Walter Ralegh.

The heartbroken leader, on the return of the expedition on the 2nd March, reproached Kemys for the failure. 'For I told him that, seeing my son was lost, I cared not if he had lost a hundred more in opening the mine, so my credit had been saved. I protest before God that if Captain Whitney had not run from me at the Granadas, and carried with him another ship of Captain Wollaston's, I would have left my bodie at San Thomé by my sonne's, or have brought with me out of that, or other mines, so much gold ore as should have satisfied the King that I had propounded no vaine thing. What shall become or me now I know not. I am unpardoned in England, and my poore estate consumed; and whether any other prince or state will give me bread I know not.' Kemys was heartbroken at his chief's reproaches, for he, poor sanguine man, had doubtless done his best, and incontinently retired to his cabin and committed suicide. After his death some of the other officers told Ralegh that, on the way down the river, Kemys had told them that he could have brought them to the mine within two hours' march of the river's side, but as young Walter was killed and Sir Walter still unpardoned, sick, and unlikely to live, he saw no reason why he should open up the mine; either for the Spaniards or the King (of England).   The officers answered that though no formal pardon had been given, yet the granting of the patent under the great seal was tantamount thereto.   Kemys then pointed out that Ralegh was legally dead, and that the patent therefore had no force.   This question of the pardon had been much discussed before Ralegh left England, and Buckingham's kinsmen had offered, for a money payment, to obtain a formal pardon.   It is said that Ralegh submitted the question to Bacon, who told him that money was the main desideratum for his expedition, and he need not waste it on the pardon, now he had the patent under the great seal.   It is evident by the discussion of the matter by the officers as soon as the failure of the expedition was certain, that they foresaw the probability of what afterwards happened.

Deserted by two of his ships, many of his men mutinous, and his officers falling away from him, as from a doomed man, Ralegh groped up the West India islands, sending from St Kits his cousin, Captain Herbert, with the intelligence of his failure.   To his devoted wife he had to send the news, not only of his and her ruin, but of the death of their firstborn, and there are few more pathetic letters than that which he then wrote to his 'dear Besse.'   'I was lothe to write,' he says, 'because I knew not how to comforte you; and God knows I never knewe what sorrow meant till nowe. . . .   Comfort your heart, dearest Besse, I shall

sorrow for us both. I shall sorrow the lesse, because
I have not longe to sorrow, because I have not longe
to live.' After sealing the sad letter to his wife, he
opened it again to write a long postscript, telling her
the story of the expedition and the alleged reasons for
Kemys' failure. 'For the rest,' he says, 'there never
was a poore man soe exposed to slaughter as I was; for
being commanded upon my allegiance to sett downe
not onely the country, but the very river, by which I
was to enter it, to name my shipps, number of my
men and artillery,—this was sent by the Spanish
Ambassador to his master the King of Spaine; and
the King wrote his letters to all parts of the Indies.
. . . If I live, I shall make it known. . . . My
braynes are broken, and I cannot write much. . . .
Whitney, for whome I sold my plate at Plymouth,
and to whome I gave more credit than all my
captaines, ran from mee at the Granadas, and
Wollaston with him; soe as I am now but five shipps,
and one of those I have sent home—my flyboat—with
a rabble of idle rascalls in her which I know will not
spare to wound mee, but I care not. I am sure there
is never a base slave in the fleet hath taken the pains
and care that I have done, hath slept so little and hath
travailed so much. My friends will not believe them;
and for the rest I care not.'

We have seen it asserted by Parker, and it was subsequently reported by others, that Ralegh's intention,
when he realised that the Guiana project had failed,

was to lie in wait to capture Spanish vessels and take
them to France for sale. It may readily be conceded
that he would have had no conscientious scruples in
doing so, for the English, when weak, were always
attacked by Spaniards ; but there were other considera-
tions now which must have weighed with him. He
was ill and heartbroken, his captains had lost faith in
him, and, above all, he had realised that his failure had
been mainly owing to the fact that the Spaniards were
forewarned of all his movements, by the complais-
ance of the King of England. Under his old mistress
he might safely have harassed the Spaniards whenever
he met them on the seas, so long as her responsibility was saved. But King James was made of other
stuff. Base and truckling by nature, and awestricken
at the name of Spaniard, he was willing to descend to
any sacrifice of dignity rather than offend Spain ; and
Ralegh saw that to plunder on the high seas now
would not only have banished his last hope of forgiveness but would have involved his sureties, Lords
Arundel and Pembroke, in his ruin. To them he
had given his word to return to England and answer
for his proceedings, whatever happened. To say that
he was uniformly a truthful man, or had a high sense
of honour, would be untrue, but Ralegh would never
betray a friend who had trusted to his word, and he
determined to return to England, going by way of
Newfoundland for the purpose of obtaining fresh
stores and to careen his ship. Off Newfoundland he

had to deal with a formidable mutiny. His soldiers endeavoured to force him to take to piracy, and he refused; but they made him swear that he would not put into an English port without their leave, or at least without obtaining for some of them who were criminals the King's pardon. Under these depressing circumstances Ralegh finally sailed towards his native land. All through the early months of 1618, Gondomar, in England, was doing his best to magnify Ralegh's guilt at Canary. Bailey's lies and unfounded suspicions, however, were not long in meeting with refutation. The English mariner, Captain Reeks, who had been at Lanzarote when Ralegh was there, returned to his native Ratcliff, and told the true story of what had happened. The old Lord Admiral, enemy of Ralegh as he was, did not love deserters, and had Bailey and his ship placed under arrest. On the 11th January the deserter was brought before the full Council, and was made to tell his story in detail, and produce the journal which he had written. When his assertions were sifted it was seen how unfounded they were, and he was severely reprimanded for desertion and slandering his chief. He had whispered that he could, an he would, 'charge Sir Walter Ralegh and other great ones of treason.' This was serious—for Ralegh still had friends in the Council, Carew, Zouch, Arundel and others, though Winwood was dead — and Bailey was challenged for proof. He broke down, and alleged some hearsay gossip, and was imprisoned. Gondomar, however, worried James into releasing his tool, and with a paltry apology, to the disgust of Ralegh's friends, the slanderer was set free.

Although no news came of Ralegh until the arrival of Herbert late in April, with the letters for Winwood and Lady Ralegh, the fate of the leader was already sealed. Gondomar in March had once more exacted from James a positive promise that Ralegh should be delivered to Spaniards if he did the least harm. The news was received with jubilation in Madrid, and the King's secretary thus writes to Gondomar on the subject (19th April 1618) : 'Your lordship's account of the conference you had with the King, about Ralegh's affair, pleased our people here so much, that they found it almost too sweet. It really seemed too much that Ralegh should have to be sent hither, but with the .choice your lordship has left open to have the punishment inflicted there, they say there never was such an Ambassador before.'

At last, almost simultaneously with the arrival of Ralegh's letters in England, the news reached Madrid from the townspeople of San Thomé. Their story differs somewhat from Ralegh's, but in the main confirms it. They say that the Governor Palomeque learnt of the landing of the English at ten at night, *and made ready to attack them;* but found them too numerous, and retired to the town, followed by the English. A messenger was sent warning the intruders that the town was a Spanish possession, but

nevertheless it was stormed and captured, the public
funds, papers, etc., being plundered, and the outskirts
of the town burnt. Palomeque was missing, and the
townspeople thought he was captured. A Spanish
soldier was sent to interview Ralegh (this, of course,
was George Ralegh, although the Spaniards thought
he was Sir Walter) and to protest against the invasion, and to beg for the return of the Governor, if
a prisoner, or news of his fate, if he were dead. 'Be
content,' the townspeople besought the English commander, 'with the harm you have already done, and
leave us.' The news aroused the greatest indignation in Madrid. Gondomar was about to go home
on leave, but was ordered to stay and see the matter
through. He was instructed 'to exaggerate as much
as you can Ralegh's guilt and try to get the King to
make a great demonstration.' If James wanted the
friendship of Spain, he must wreak prompt and
exemplary vengeance upon those who have done
harm to Spanish subjects. 'Do not,' says Philip,
'threaten him; but make him understand that I am
offended, and that if a proper remedy be not forthcoming at once, we shall make reprisals and seize
English property in Spain.' Before Gondomar received this letter Herbert had brought the news
to England. The story is told that the Spanish
Ambassador hastened to the palace, and demanded
audience of his royal friend. He was told that the
King was engaged. He said he wished but to say

one word, and was admitted on that condition. He
rushed into the royal presence with uplifted hands
and assumed horror in his voice, shouting the word
pirates ! pirates ! pirates ! and the one word repeated
must have been a perfectly intelligible warning to
James that he would be called upon to fulfil the
promise he had made 'on faith, hand and word.'

Ralegh was storm-driven into Kinsale harbour at the
end of May, and there landed the offenders from his
ship ; and shortly afterwards brought the ill-fated
Destiny alone into Plymouth. During the interval,
Gondomar had been busy. Telling his King of the
arrival of the man they had already doomed, he says
(24th June), 'It would take a long "process" to
recount all the efforts I employed with the King and
Council to stay Ralegh's voyage before he sailed ;
and since I had news of his proceedings in Canary,
to have him and his companions proclaimed traitors,
and his sureties escheated. I have recently spoken
most urgently to the King about it, and have also
written him the enclosed letter on the 14th instant,
and another on the 20th, when I heard of Ralegh's
arrival at Plymouth, urging His Majesty to publish
the proclamation which I now enclose.' The proclamation was promulgated on the 11th June, and
pronounces Ralegh to be guilty of 'a horrible invasion
of the town of San Thomé' ; and for 'a malicious
breaking of the peace which hath been so happily
established, and so long inviolately continued.' There

was apparently no need for investigation or defence before condemnation. Ralegh was in the eyes of the world then, as he is to-day, one of the most distinguished of Englishmen, and yet the King of England was willing to forejudge and condemn him unheard, at the bidding of the Ambassador of a power which Queen Elizabeth had defied for forty years, and at a subsequent stage took great credit to himself for doing so. Gondomar continues, 'They have sent to arrest Ralegh and his ships at Plymouth. If he has brought anything of value, it is sure to have been stolen, but I am told he has nothing but some tobacco, and a dish and ewer of silver gilt. It is certain that Ralegh will try to excuse himself, by saying that everything has been done without his orders or knowledge, and thus cast the blame upon the dead, as he and his friends are already doing. But withal, the living bring the plunder, and I think everything possible is being done here in Your Majesty's interest to bring them to signal punishment and restitution. This King gave me his faith, his hand, and his word, that if Ralegh dared so much as to *look* upon any of Your Majesty's territories or vassals, even if he brought back his ships loaded with gold, he would hand all of them with Ralegh himself to Your Majesty, that you might hang him in the Plaza of Madrid. Now that the time has come for fulfilment, and I have reminded him of it, His Majesty has promised that

he will do it as soon as a judicial examination
proves the excesses to have been committed; and
he says that, for his part, he can do no more than
he has done in publishing the proclamation, arrest-
ing the offender, and embargoing his property. He
says that if Ralegh had attempted to sack Madrid
itself he could do no more, and he has sent
Buckingham and Digby to me to say the same,
and to assure me that Ralegh shall be punished
with the utmost severity; these being the words
they used, and that Ralegh's friends and all England shall not save him from the gallows.' This,
however, was not enough for Gondomar, and he
urges Philip almost violently to instruct the
Governors of Canary, Azores, etc., as if of their
own accord, promptly to seize all English property
and persons. 'I also think it will be necessary that
Your Majesty's fleet should attack some English
ships, on the pretence of their being part of Ralegh's
force. The ships and cargoes might be sold promptly,
and the money desposited until things are settled.'
James, he says, wants peace, and must be frightened.
'The English have changed their tone since I came
and have shown them that I will stand no nonsense.'

Whilst this precious letter was being written,
Gondomar had one of his friendly confabulations
with James, who, for a wonder—perhaps for the
purpose of argument only—took Ralegh's part. It
was asserted by him, he said, that he had a commission

from Queen Elizabeth and Henry IV of France to conquer and colonise the Orinoco; and he had done so in 1595. The fortress and town of San Thomé had been constructed since the annexation of the country by England. As it was necessary for the discovery and working of the mine that this town should be taken, Ralegh's men had taken it. Gondomar hit out at this, and gave the King a piece of his mind. 'I told him that Ralegh's annexation of the country was unfounded. If the contention that the conquest of Your Majesty's territory was necessary for the working of the mine furnished a good reason for Ralegh's proceedings, the conquest of England by Your Majesty would be justified for the taking of Holland, which more really belonged to you than the mine belonged to Ralegh. I asked him what he would think if a Spanish fleet were to commit similar hostilities in the ports of Ireland and Scotland.' James's reply to this shows that he was only 'drawing out' the Ambassador. 'The King replied that I had spoken very well, and had cited an excellent parallel. Ralegh, he said, was a thief, and there was no excuse for him. . . . The King assures me that strict justice shall be done, but I feel sure that he will be slack, unless we keep him up to it by taking the course I recommend. Even though the King hang Ralegh and his companions, and restore the plunder, I should grieve that Your Majesty should be satisfied with this for so atrocious a wickedness. These people should be made to suffer by the seizure of their goods in Spain, which would be a warning both to them and to their neighbours. Perhaps such an opportunity will never occur again of asserting ourselves and giving them a lesson. I told the King and Council that Your Majesty's goodness might lead you to pardon offences against yourself; but conscience will not allow you to forgive injuries done to your subjects. They are already saying on 'Change that English ships and property have been seized in Seville and the islands; and well-disposed people rejoice at it, as do some of the councillors, for the good of the King himself, *because, though they know he will not on any account allow war with Your Majesty, they see that he is more confident of peace than is fitting.*' The last few lines probably contain the real key to the exaggerated importance attached by the Spaniards to Ralegh's expedition. The sacrifice of Ralegh was to be made a test point, upon which James was to be frightened, and at the same time an object lesson to the world of the meekness with which the King of England was brought to heel by the Spaniard.

CHAPTER XVI

THE methods employed by Gondomar to effect the
sacrifice of Ralegh for the exaltation of Spain come
out clearly in his letters, most of which now see
the light here for the first time.   On the 14th
June he wrote to James saying that he had always
urged upon him the danger of Ralegh being allowed
to sail with so many ships, his only object being
to rob and lay waste Spanish territory.   'Your
Majesty deigned to reply that, if he committed any
offence against the lands or vassals of my master,
you would deliver him and his companions to me,
to be sent to Spain to be hanged in the Plaza of
Madrid. I urged that prevention was much better
than cure, whereupon Your Majesty replied that
you would insist upon due sureties being given
that Ralegh should do no harm.   I wrote this to
my King, who, in accordance with this assurance,

refrained from sending out his fleet to oppose Ralegh, notwithstanding that he was informed by others of the evil intentions of the latter.   We know now that Ralegh assailed the Canaries, and attacked towns in Guiana, burning churches, and committing irreparable damage.   Captain Bailey left him when he saw what he was about, and came hither to give an account of his proceedings, when he was at once arrested as a traitor, and his goods embargoed, to the great surprise of everyone, especially of myself.   Prompt and severe public action should now be taken against Ralegh, in order that my master may see by Your Majesty's acts that you are really desirous of his friendship.'

A week later, when Ralegh had reached Plymouth, another turn or two is given to the screw by Gondomar, and the threats of reprisals become more insolent.   On the 2nd June the Ambassador wrote to James : 'Ralegh has arrived in Plymouth with all the property he has seized from my master's subjects.   I do not call it stolen, or him a pirate, because, as he returns so confidently to an English port, after all I said to Your Majesty to prevent his sailing, it is evident that those who told my King that Ralegh was going as commander of Your Majesty's fleet, for the purpose of way-.aying and plundering the Spanish flotilla or of conquering my master's territories, will persist in their opinion.   His Catholic Majesty will certainly

see that when I persuaded him that Ralegh would
do no harm, I was deceived — for the facts are
notoriously otherwise. . . . Your Majesty has
so good a memory that you will not forget your
"faith, hand and word," pledged to me. You are
so great a King, and so good a gentleman, that
you will bear me testimony, and admit that all
Ralegh's acts of war and damage were foretold to
you in writing and speech a thousand times by
me . . . and that I never ceased to urge forcibly
that he should not be allowed to sail. Walter
Ralegh has robbed, sacked and burnt, and murdered
Spanish subjects, and has brought back with him
enough wealth to make him and his supporters rich.
I have now only to beseech you to take pity on
my good intentions, in view of the cries and complaints I shall receive in Spain on account of the
damage done by Ralegh, and *of the measures of
redress which I understand will have been adopted
there, as demanded by justice, reason, and my master's
prestige.* For justice demands that Ralegh and all
his companions should be hanged directly they set one
foot on English soil, without waiting for them to set
the other foot. I am quite sure the King, my master,
would treat any of his vassals so if they had commenced
this rupture.' In written letters such as the above
some little diplomatic reserve was necessary ; but in
Gondomar's familiar gossips with James, boasting
threats were hardly even veiled. In one of the

farewell visits to the King, before the Ambassador's projected departure for Madrid, in which there was much embracing and pressing of hands, James was bewailing that the English people were not so generous to him as the Spaniards to Philip III.; and then stopping short, he said, 'Of course I know that, so far as greatness is concerned, the King of Spain is greater than all the rest of us Christian kings put together.' 'This' says Gondomar, 'he repeated six times, praising the grandeur of Your Majesty. When I thanked him, he seized my hand, and held it, pressing it in his, saying that never, in public or in private, would he do, or even think, anything against Your Majesty, but would in all things strive to avoid evil to you. He had, he said, quite banished piracy, and for the last two years no one had dared to bring to England property seized from Spaniards. I should see, he continued, how he would punish Ralegh and his people, and the example would cause his orders in this respect to be better obeyed in future. . . . I replied that no doubt his good intentions had exerted a favourable influence, and I would say as much to Your Majesty; but I wished to point out to him that things were now in a very different condition from what they were in Queen Elizabeth's and Drake's time, for Your Majesty had taken such measures that the most insignificant of your towns was now in a good state of defence . . . and pirates that assailed Your

Majesty's possessions now would catch nothing but
fish. . . .   In talk, the King admitted that if Your
Majesty would be his friend, he needed nothing
else.'

When Gondomar had thus pledged James up to the
hilt to sacrifice Ralegh in any case, and had hectored
him into a due condition of humility, he took his
leave on 26th June, and made ready to start for Spain.
An account of what followed is best told in a selection
of his own words, as written to the King of Spain in a
letter of the 16th July (N.S.), as at the interviews
therein described Ralegh's fate was finally sealed.
Cottington, the English Ambassador in Madrid, had
been bombarded with demands for vengeance and
redress, and with threats of reprisals.   He wrote to
James in a fright, and Gondomar seconded the effect
he produced, by redoubling his own pressure upon the
timid King.   Cynically he thus informs his King of
the fact : 'I have applied the medicines I thought
necessary.   To persons who do not know the constitution of the patient, they may appear violent.   One
of them was to spread a rumour that English property
had already been embargoed at Seville and the islands.
To all inquiries on the subject I reply that, if I were
Your Majesty's Governor there, I should do so ; and
I hoped it was true. . . .   I had taken leave of the
King, and was about to set out for Spain, when, in
accordance with Your Majesty's orders, I deferred my
departure and sent to Theobalds to ask for another

audience. The King, fearing from Cottington's letter that I wished to see him about Ralegh, and wishing to give time for my anger to cool, sent to say that on Monday 2nd he would expect me at Greenwich. I thought I had better see the Council first, and tackle them; so I conferred with Buckingham, who ordered them in the King's name to give me audience whenever I wished. I fixed five o'clock on the 29th June; and on my arrival all the councillors came out to meet me, the Archbishop of Canterbury saying that they had suspended all their business, and willingly attended my orders.' Then Gondomar opened his batteries, and set forth the 'murders, sackings, pillage and burnings' that Ralegh had committed, 'such as never was seen even in time of war.' He said how offended his King was at such insolence. Once more he repeated the story of the sureties, and the King's pledge, on 'faith, hand and word,' to surrender Ralegh and his companions to be hanged in the Plaza of Madrid; on the faith of which alone the King of Spain had refrained from sending out his fleet to attack the expedition. Great complaints were made that Ralegh in his letter to Winwood had set forth the names of the captains who had attacked San Thomé, as if it had been a meritorious action, and once more the threats of reprisals and boasts of his master's grandeur were reproduced for the benefit of the Council. 'If the punishment were not swift and exemplary, Your Majesty had no need of the King of England's friendship, and in future would take good care of your own prestige and the lives and properties of your subjects. With that I took off my hat, calmly said that I had stated my case, and then re-covered myself.' After a little quiet whispering with the other councillors, Bacon replied. They were all very sorry ; but the King should not be held responsible for the excesses of a private person. The Ambassador might be sure that the King would fulfil his promise, and give full satisfaction. Indeed, he had begun already : for he held Ralegh's sureties, and on mere public rumour he had publicly condemned his proceedings. He had, moreover, arrested Ralegh and his ships as soon as he had arrived. It was impossible to do more. 'Then with a great deal of cordiality he expressed a hope that these little accidents would not shake the two firm columns of our amity, for if this, and other like things, were fittingly punished, there was no reason at all for any interruption in friendship. The Archbishop wished to have his say, to prove his sympathy, but also to bring the question into a controversy between two, parties. Doffing his bonnet and bowing his head low, he very artfully said that Ralegh's proceedings certainly deserved exemplary punishment, and he did not know what answer Ralegh could make, thus trying to indicate that it would be necessary to hear him. I stopped him at once, and said that it was no part of my business to act as Ralegh's prosecutor, and this was not a case for

tribunals at all—I had no more to say about it.   The
Treasurer and the Chancellor struck in between us,
saying they hoped I would continue my usual good
offices.   They were all so courteous and flattering,
that I was forced to reply in the same spirit. . . .
I made the most of San Thomé and Guiana, as many
people here think that it is licit to make captures and
conquests south of the line, and that San Thomé
belonged to England.'   On Sunday the 1st July (O.S.)
James arrived at Greenwich, and held a special Council
about Ralegh's affair.   There was much difference of
opinion, for Ralegh had friends present, especially
Carew, but the general agreement was that the most
ample satisfaction should be given to Spain, and Ralegh
and his companions severely punished; and James
made a long speech to the same effect.   Ralegh's
friends endeavoured to cause a diversion by complaining of Gondomar's attitude before the Council.
He had, they said, dared to use expressions such as
no King or Council of England had ever suffered from
a foreign ambassador, and had tried to saddle the
King with the responsibility of Ralegh's acts; saying
that he had given his 'faith, hand and word,' that if
Ralegh did the slightest thing against Spain, he should
be delivered over to be hanged in Madrid, as if, forsooth, England were a tributary to the King of Spain.
This was rather a facer for James, who said that,
though he was a peaceful King, yet he knew how to
defend his rights; and Buckingham, as behoved him,

hotly took up the cudgels. 'Gondomar,' he said,
'was quite right. He had protested from the first,
and had been assured that Ralegh should do no harm.
No wonder he was indignant ; and was very courteous
and kind not to be more violent about it than he was.'
Thus encouraged, James said he had no doubt that
Gondomar was quite right. Would the Council have
him go to war with the King of Spain to defend such
atrocious crimes as those of Ralegh ? What would
the world say if he did ? Working himself into a
passion with his eloquence, the King answered his
own question. 'Where he would show his courage,'
he said, 'was not in warring against the King of Spain,
but against those traitors, who, under cover of gold
mines and bringing treasure to England, and other
false pretexts, had persuaded him to allow Ralegh to
go on his voyage. He (James) was a man of his word,
and had given his pledge to the Spanish Ambassador.
All he wanted the Council's opinion about was whether
Ralegh ought to be punished or not.' Most of the
councillors answered in the affirmative, and Ralegh's
friends refrained from voting. Since, said the King,
they were apparently unanimous, if ever he learnt
that in secret, or in conversation, any of them defended
Ralegh, he should hold them as traitors. Let this,
he added, be a warning to others who wanted to
assail the King of Spain, whose friendship was the most
desirable thing possible for England.

The next afternoon, Monday, 2nd July (O.S.),

Gondomar was rowed down the river to the palace at Greenwich. He tripped laughingly into the King's chamber and said, 'Look how happy I am in England to come back so soon from Spain.' The King hugged him to his breast as usual, and said he wished to God it were so. Then the room was cleared, the doors shut, and the two friends sat side by side. Neither wanted to open the ball, and there was a good deal of friendly sparring. At last James asked what news there was from Spain. This was Gondomar's opportunity, and he launched out in denunciation of Ralegh's crimes, which he said 'were infinitely greater than reported here, and I exaggerated them as much as I could.' James was very humble and apologetic. He had heard so too, and he hoped Gondomar would be satisfied if he saw him doing everything in his power to punish and redress them. Gondomar had been a true prophet, he said, and he (the King) had been grossly deceived. He himself had always doubted about the mine, but he never dreamed that such excesses would be committed. 'But he thought best, even in Your Majesty's interests, that these people should undeceive themselves and suffer the loss, than that he should seem to oppress them. They were undeceived now, and were sending all mines to the devil. As for his pledge to me, he would leave himself in my hands, but he hoped Your Majesty would not ask more in this case, than if Ralegh had sacked a port in England itself; and he could not forget that many persons tried to persuade him that San Thomé belonged to him, and had been annexed by England before the Spaniards came.' Gondomar began to protest violently at this, but the King seized his arm and stopped him by saying that he was only repeating the arguments of Ralegh's friends, and not his own. He was very sorry, and hoped Gondomar would give him credit for good intentions. He had, he said, been examining all that morning and part of the previous day men who had accompanied Ralegh on his voyage. In the main they had confirmed Spanish accounts, except that Captain Kemys was the principal culprit, as he had assured the rest that it was impossible to discover the mine until the Spaniards had been cast out. Seeing that Gondomar was again going to protest, James said that he had replied that Ralegh was in command and must bear the whole responsibility. He (the King) would have justice done, and really hoped that Gondomar would be satisfied. He begged him to send off a courier that very night to Madrid assuring the King of his desire to please him and keep the peace.

When James had run through all the litany of debasement, Gondomar at length got a chance to speak. He said that he must talk plainly. Would the King allow him to speak—as he himself often said—simply as from 'James to James,' forgetting that he was a king, or that the speaker was a poor gentleman?

James was delighted. Of course he would.
Gondomar told him, with refreshing ,frankness, that
he, James, could not be judge of Ralegh's case ; for
the pirate had sailed with his commission, and the
same influence which had secured it might be exerted
for his defence. No wonder that the King of Spain
was being persuaded to take summary vengeance. If
he (Gondomar) had been Governor of Seville or
Canary, he would not have waited for orders, but
would have done it at once. Proclamations were all
very well before the amount of the depredations was
known ; but the time was now passed for papers and
words, for Ralegh and his men were in England and
still unhung, whilst the councillors who had supported
him were not in the Tower.

The King had promised Gondomar that he would
not be angry, whatever he might say ; but he lost his
self-control at this. Snatching off his hat and tearing
his hair, he shouted that that sort of justice might do
for Spain, but not for England, or wherever he reigned.
He never had, and never would, by God's help, condemn anyone without first hearing him in his own
defence, and a proper trial, even though he had killed
his (James's) son. God knew the first fault of Adam,
and yet he did not condemn him unheard.

Yes, replied Gondomar, sarcastically, he saw the
laws of Spain and England were quite different ; for
such men would have been punished in Spain without
all this talk and delay. But in future the laws of

Spain would be changed in accordance. Look ! he
told James, what the King of Spain had done for him ;
and now he took the part of a pirate against his friend.
Gondomar's love for James had forced this out of him,
he said ; for the duty of friendship was to speak the
plain truth. But since that was unavailing, the King
of Spain would now take the matter in his own hands
and defend his honour. This, of course, brought the
King to his knees at once. He begged the Ambassador
to send his peaceful pledges to Spain that very night,
so as to prevent the war party there from having their
way. He would arrange the next day for the Council
to meet on Wednesday and decide upon Ralegh's
condemnation, which, he promised, should be carried
out without delay ; and on Thursday he would see
Gondomar again and take final leave of him with
that assurance. Gondomar, when he wrote this to his
King, did not attempt to conceal his exultation at the
'increased prestige' it would give to Spain to make
the King of England meekly hand over one of his
subjects for punishment in a foreign country. In
his delight he left the King's presence in high good
humour, and went for a walk in the gardens with
the Duke of Lennox. The King sent after him a
basket of fine cherries, which he ate as he walked along.
Presently great shouts of laughter greeted him from
the windows of a summer-house under which he was
passing. Looking up he saw the King. 'Oho !
where is the Spanish gravity gone to now ? ' shouted

the monarch. 'A dignified Ambassador indeed, eating cherries out of a basket !' These were the men,
and these were the methods by which Ralegh's
life was juggled away, each party trying to outwit
the other in the price to be exacted for the sacrifice.

But James did not find it so easy to coerce his
Council into doing a great crime to please the
Spaniards. Carew, on his knees, prayed for mercy
for his kinsman, but James would only promise
that Ralegh should not be condemned unheard. In
the Council on Wednesday, 4th July (N.S.), there
was an almost general opposition to sending him to
Spain to be hanged. But James said he had given
his promise, and could not break it, and Buckingham confirmed this, casting the blame upon some
of his fellow-councillors for assuring the King that
Ralegh would do no harm, so that His Majesty had
thought he was safe in making the promise. Bacon,
though no friend to Ralegh, sought to save the King
from the supreme humiliation of handing him over
to the Spaniards. The more complete the satisfaction given to Spain the better, he said, but the
promise, of which so much was made, was mere
talk, and was never intended to be taken literally,
or to make England a tributary State. James flew
into a passion at this. His promise was not mere
talk, he said, and he would fulfil it, without taking
any more notice of ignorant and ill-disposed persons ;

and with this he rose in a huff, and flung out of the room.

The next day he saw Gondomar again, and positively promised him to fulfil his pledge. He was more affectionate than before : embraced Gondomar again and again, and swore friendship for ever. The Ambassador said that such kindness demanded some return from him, and that he (the King) should dictate the answer that should be written to the King of Spain's dispatch about Ralegh. James jumped at the idea, and at once dictated 'that he had been grossly deceived, and was so horrified at such crimes as had been committed, that he would punish them swiftly and severely, in a way that should fully satisfy the King of Spain.'

This was not what Gondomar wanted ; and he very adroitly said that, as the King had accepted his services as secretary, he ought, as usual, to make him a councillor. 'With all my heart,' said James. 'I then said that the dispatch he had dictated did not satisfy me, and would do no good. He ought, I said, to do as he had promised me, and let me write that, although Ralegh's crimes were worse even than he had expected, he would send him, with all his companions, their ships and booty, prisoners to Spain, in order that Your Majesty might hang the culprits in the Plaza of Madrid. This, I said, would be fulfilling his promise. It was not much to ask him, surely, to send ten or a dozen of the worst of them to be executed in Spain.'

James knew his people would resent this, and tried to temporise ; but Gondomar began to hector again, and the King tremblingly agreed to send Ralegh and the others, in the *Destiny*, to Spain ; and to recover the rest of the damage from Ralegh's sureties to be paid to the Spaniards. Gondomar told him it was the best thing he could do, if he wanted to avoid war ; and then the King called in Buckingham and Digby, both bribed servants of Spain, to hear him repeat his shameful pledge.   In their presence he again assured Gondomar that he would send Ralegh to Spain, no matter what opposition were offered, unless the King of Spain refused to have him, in which case Ralegh and all his companions should be hanged in England.   He left the decision with the King of Spain, and begged Gondomar to write immediately to him to that effect.   But even this feast of humiliation did not satisfy the Ambassador, and he insolently told the King that he could not write any more verbal pledges to his master ; he must have it in writing.   James said that Buckingham should write him a letter embodying the conversation, and then, as if ashamed of the unworthy figure he was cutting, he asked Gondomar if he had ever in his life heard of a king who drafted his dispatches, and adopted resolutions like this, at the bidding of a foreign ambassador. For his part, he had never dreamt of such a thing before, and he did not believe that even the Archduke Albert would be so submissive to the Spanish Ambassador. To this Gondomar replied by asking him, whether he had ever heard of an ambassador consenting to act as secretary to the king to whom he was accredited, and to take his orders as to what he should write to his own king. And so more than half in joke ended the conference, which was enough to make the dead Elizabeth turn in her grave. But the King would not let his friend bid him good-bye until he had button-holed him apart, to tell him 'some familiar domestic things.'

Before Gondomar left London, Buckingham's letter reached him, of which the original was sent to Spain. James had once told Gondomar that 'Buckingham was a greater Spaniard than the Ambassador himself,' and to judge from the wording of this humiliating letter, this can hardly have been an exaggeration. After setting forth the King's sorrow, and the steps already taken against Ralegh, and promising a summary legal process, 'which cannot be altogether avoided,' he says the King will be as severe in punishment as if the attack had been made on an English city, and 'even though Sir Walter Ralegh should have returned with his ships loaded with gold, taken from the King of Spain or his subjects, he would have sent back again both the treasure and the man himself to the King of Spain, to be punished in accordance with the promise given to you (Gondomar), which promise he is still resolved to fulfil punctually against the persons and property of the delinquents, unless he hears that the King of Spain is of opinion that it would be more convenient and exemplary that they should be punished here as severely as their crimes deserved. In this matter His Majesty is fully determined to take the course which may be most honourable to himself, and satisfactory to the King of Spain.' With this humiliating pledge, Gondomar was content, and departed for Spain, certain now that Ralegh was doomed beyond all human aid. But he still urged upon his King the need for the pretended seizure of English ships and property in Spanish ports, in order that, if any delay occurred in the killing of Ralegh, his head might be bought by the release of the embargoed property.

In the meanwhile Ralegh was under arrest at Plymouth. He had, of course, heard on his arrival of the King's proclamation, and knew that he was on his defence. Orders had already been given to Sir Lewis Stukeley, a connection of his own, and Vice-Admiral of Devon, to bring him a prisoner to London, and realise such property as might be on board the *Destiny*, but Sir Lewis did not start for the west until some time after Ralegh had arrived. In the interim it would have been perfectly easy for the latter to

have slipped over to France. He made no attempt to'
do so, but in company with his devoted wife and his
faithful follower, Captain King, remained at Plymouth
winding up his affairs. We have seen by his bitter'
references in his letters to Winwood and Lady Ralegh'
that he knew that he had been betrayed to failure by
the King, and that he was likely to be sacrificed to
political exigencies, but he does not seem to have
realised fully at first how entirely he was doomed
beforehand, and he still had hope. The first thing to
be done was to place his own version of affairs before
the Council, in order that his friends might act in his
favour. On the 21st June he wrote a long important
statement to his true friend, Lord Carew; and as
Mr Edwards has not printed this letter in his complete collection of Ralegh's known letters, I have no
hesitation in reproducing it here, notwithstanding its
length. Gondomar sent it to his King in Spanish,
and it is now translated back again into English from
his version.

'I am sure your Lordship will have received a copy
of my letter sent by Captain North to Secretary
Winwood, of whose death I learnt with great sorrow
in Ireland. By that letter your Lordship will have
learnt the reasons given by Kemys for not discovering
the mine, which could have been done, notwithstanding his obstinacy, by means of a cacique of the country,
an old acquaintance of mine, if the companies had
remained in the river two days longer; inasmuch as

the cacique offered pledges to do it. The servant of the Governor, moreover, who is now with me, could have led them to two gold mines, not two leagues distant from the town, as well as to a silver mine, at not more than three harquebuss shots distant, and I will make this truth manifest when my health allows me to go to London As for the rest, if Whitney and Wollaston had not gone from me at the Granadas, and the rest had not abandoned me in distress at Meny (?) as if they had some great enterprise in hand, I would have returned from Newfoundland to Guiana, and would have died there or fulfilled my undertaking. When I saw that they had deserted me, I resolved to steer for Newfoundland to take in water, and clean the ship, which resolution we had all adopted six days before they left me. But when I was approaching the land I was informed that a hundred of my men had determined to go ashore and join the English settlement, or at all events to do so when the ship was hauled up on the beach for cleaning. Their intention was to board the best ship of the English flotilla at night, and plunder all the friends of England and the Portuguese in these ports, knowing that I should not be able to get the other ship in order under ten or twelve days, and that I had no men to navigate the ship I had left. I thereupon called all the company together and told them that I had no wish to accuse any of them, but as I had been told by some of the masters of the violence they intended to commit, I had decided to return without taking in any fresh provisions, rather than enter in the Newfoundland ports to the great prejudice of my countrymen, and of the fishermen of other nations therein. I then ordered the master to set sail for England; and the conspirators at once discovered themselves, resisting and shouting that they would rather die than return to England. They were the greater number, and some of the best men I had, some of them being gentlemen. All the harquebusses and swords were in the magazine with the armour for cleaning, and the mutineers had taken possession of them, refusing me admission into the magazine. Finding myself in this peril, I gave way to the mutiny for a time, and during that night I set my course again for Newfoundland, treating in the meanwhile with some of the leaders to abandon the mutiny. With great difficulty I persuaded them to do so, on condition that I would not return to England until I had obtained their pardon for some past piracies; and they demanded my oath. At last we all agreed to sail for Ireland, and they chose the port of Killibeg in the north, a miserable place frequented by desperate corsairs. If I had not consented to this they would have murdered me and those who stood by me, or else I should have killed most of them, in which case, as the mutineers were the best of my men, I should have been unable to bring the ship into port. It is true that when they had calmed down, they said that if I returned home poor I should be

despised, and I answered that even if I were a beggar
I would not be a robber, or do anything base, nor
would I abuse the confidence and commission of the
King.   Before doing that, I would choose, not poverty
alone, but death itself.   I am well aware that, with
my ship (than which in the world there is no better)
I could have enriched myself by £100,000 in the
space of three months, and could have collected a
company which would have impeded the traffic of
Europe.   But those who have told the King that I
had feigned the mine, and really intended to turn
corsair, are now mistaken in their malice, for after
failing in the discovery of the mine, by the fault of
another, and after having lost my estate and my son
and being without pardon for myself, or security for
my life, I have held it all as nought, and offer myself
to His Majesty to do with me as he will, without
making any terms.   As for the mutineers, the greater
number of them fled from me in Ireland, and some
have been persuaded to surrender themselves to His
Majesty's mercy.   Since my arrival in Ireland I have
been alarmed not a little, and have been told that I
have fallen into the grave displeasure of His Majesty
for having taken a town in Guiana which was in the
possession of Spaniards.   When they heard this, my
men were so afraid of being hanged, that they were
on the point of making me sail away again by force.
With regard to taking the town, although I gave no
authority for it to be done, it was impossible to avoid,

because when the English were landed at night to en-
sure Kemys's passage, the Spaniards attacked them with
the intention of destroying them, killing several, and
wounding many. Our companies thereupon pursued
them, and found themselves inside the town before
they knew it. It was at the entrance of the town
that my son was killed, and when the men saw him
dead, they became so enraged that, if the King of
Spain himself had been there in person, they would
have shown him but little respect. With regard to
the burning of the houses near the Plaza, they were
obliged to do it, because the people had made loop-holes
in the walls, and kept up so hot a fire through them,
that in a quarter-of-an-hour they would have killed
them all.

'And my Lord : that Guiana be Spanish territory
can never be acknowledged, for I myself took possession of it for the Queen of England, by virtue of a
cession of all the native chiefs of the country. His
Majesty knows this to be true, as is proved by the
concession granted by him under the great seal of
England to Harcourt. Henry IV., also considering it
a country not justly in possession of any Christian
prince, gave it to Montbariot ; and his lieutenant held
it until, for want of support, he was captured and taken
prisoner to Lisbon. Your Lordship has a copy of the
patent that Count Maurice and the States gave to
some Flemings, who held part of the country for ten
years, until by reason of negligence they were sur-

prised and defeated by the Spaniards. They are now again beginning to settle there. It will thus be seen that His Majesty, in any case, has a better right and title than anyone. I heard in Ireland that my enemies have declared that my intention was to turn corsair and fly ; but, at the manifest peril of my life, I have brought myself and my ship to England. I have suffered as many miseries as it was possible for me to suffer, which I could not have endured if God had not given me strength. If His Majesty wishes that I should suffer even more, let God's will be done ; for even death itself shall not make me turn thief or vagabond, nor will I ever betray the noble courtesy of the several gentleman who gave sureties for me.— Your poor kinsman, W. RALEGH.

' *Postscript.*—I beg you will excuse me to my lords for not writing to them, because want of sleep for fear of being surprised in my cabin at night has almost deprived me of my sight, and some return of the pleurisy which I had in the Tower has so weakened my hand that I cannot hold the pen. 1st (21st) June 1618.'

This important letter, which, so far as I have been able to ascertain, is now printed for the first time, must have been written on the day of Ralegh's arrival at Plymouth, and before his wife left London. It contains the chief points upon which he afterwards depended for his formal defence, and clears up much of the obscurity which has hitherto surrounded his actions. It is evident that he had no idea of the serious light in which it suited the King to regard his proceedings ; but the remark about his sureties indicates that, even if he had known, he would have returned to face the consequences rather than have left them in the lurch. Before the above letter was dispatched, apparently, he received a copy of the allegations made against him by some of his deserting officers, and wrote a second letter to Carew without date, but evidently enclosed with the first. As this letter also is not included by Mr Edwards in Ralegh's complete letters, it is reproduced here in full, translated from the Spanish version sent to the King of Spain by Gondomar.

'Since my arrival here I have had handed to me a copy of the statement given to your Lordship against me. They must say something for themselves. The truth is they all wanted to turn thieves but Warham St Leger, if they had had a chance, but they were obliged to come back. I myself was in manifest peril because I wished to return.

'They say I lingered at Plymouth (*i.e.*, on the outward voyage), but they know I should not have stayed there a day but for Pennington, St Leger, Bailey, Whitney, and Wollaston. I entered Falmouth by reason of head winds, and put into Ireland in consequence of a heavy gale, in which Chidley's pinnace and all her men were lost, and one of my boats driven into Brest. Of the provisions I took in Ireland

they all had their share, although they had credit
there for their requirements. The only things I got
in the Canaries was a basket of oranges and three
loaves of sugar, sent to me by the Countess of
Gomera. Chidley was in no want of provisions, for
he brought a supply for eight months from his home
in England, and the rest of them had great quantities
from Ireland, where I used my influence with Lord
President not to send them prisoners to England, as
he otherwise would have done, and I did not know
what vile accusations they had made against me.
With regard to the sacking of San Thomé, I have
told you the truth in the other letters. I have only
to add these men have not said a single true
word.

   'As to their last accusation, that I was going to
abandon my country and bring them into trouble,
certainly if I had had such an idea I could have carried
it out with their full consent, but I risked my life to
oppose it, and the fact of my having come hither
freely and unconditionally, and cast myself upon His
Majesty's mercy is a sufficient proof of my intention.
If I left here to live elsewhere because I had not a
pardon, why did I come back? I only give your
Lordship a brief answer to the accusations. I hope
to live to answer them to their faces, and prove them
all to be cowards and liars, and, in spirit, thieves. I
write this after having sealed the other letters, and I
pray you give a copy of them to my poor wife, who,

with the death of her son and these rumours, I fear
will go mad.   I forgot to answer the third article, in
which they accuse me of having sacked the town
before seeking the mine.   I have already said that the
men entered the town at night before they were aware
of it, and that they burnt the part near the Plaza to
save their lives, as probably they would not have
willingly done otherwise, because in those houses
everything of value was burnt.   But with regard to
their most impudent assertion, that the entering of the
town and burning the houses was contrary to all my
promises and protestations, I shall be content to suffer
death if I had any part or knowledge whatever of the
burning or sacking.   I knew nothing about it.   It
took place for the reasons already stated, and I could
not, moreover, protest against a thing of which I had
not even thought.

' At the end of the article they say that it was done
without their consent ; and it is true that it was
never proposed.   But their desire to appear ignorant
of the enterprise is imprudent, because I never did
anything without consultation.   Besides Pennington
had a company there (*i.e.*, at San Thomé) under his
lieutenant, and Chidley also obtained a company which
he said he would command himself, but apparently
he did not dare to do so.   St Leger also had his
company there ; so that it is evident that they partici-
pated in the enterprise, and could not be ignorant of it.'

These two letters are of the highest possible import-

ance as evidence in Ralegh's favour. It is undoubted
that he had provided against the possibility of attack
from the Spaniards in his attempt to reach the mine,
and before his departure he made no secret to anyone
of his intention to use force, if force were used against
him. The real point of the accusations against him,
when he returned, were, first that he intended to
turn pirate, and next that he had attacked a territory
already possessed by the Spaniards. That they had a
settlement at the mouth of the Upata, below the
Caroni, seen by Kemys in 1596, he was of course
aware; and also that it had been shifted to some
other place since, but he had no exact knowledge
of its new position, and, from the letters given
above, evidently did not anticipate that it would
be necessary to attack it before he reached the
mine. The establishment, moreover, of one isolated
settlement could not be held to give the Spaniards
dominion over the whole of the Orinoco, and presumably if Ralegh's expedition had landed at any
other place than in the neighbourhood of San Thomé,
even King James must have held him guiltless. It is
conceivable that, if Ralegh had been with the river
expedition, he would have gone elsewhere to explore
on finding that the new town of San Thomé blocked
the mine, and would not have landed. But in any
case, when once the English were first attacked,
as from the convincing statements in the above
letters they evidently were, it was impossible to avoid

a conflict, and it seems unjust and inconsistent to
have punished the absent leader for it. According
to James's view, his crime was for landing in the
place at all, when they found the Spaniards in possession ; but as this latter fact was unknown to
Ralegh, and he was hundreds of miles away, his
personal offence in the matter was certainly not
heinous. With regard to his piratical intentions
on the silver fleet, however much or little foundation there may have been for the accusations against
him in that respect, and they are not unlikely to be
true, for 'no peace beyond the Line' was an axiom
generally accepted by men of his school, the fact
that he attempted nothing of the sort, and exposed
his life at the hands of the mutineers in consequence,
finally returning to England, as he had promised,
should surely have absolved him from blame. But
the point of his guilt or innocence was now of
secondary consideration. We have seen by the letters
of Gondomar that he was condemned before he
reached Guiana at all—indeed, before he left England;
for the extortion of the promise from the foolish King,
upon his 'faith, hand and word,' to send Ralegh to
Spain to be hanged if he 'even so much as looked
upon the territories or subjects of Your Majesty'
was practically a death warrant. James gave to
the Ambassador full particulars and charts of Ralegh's
projected voyage ; and it was intended by Gondomar
from the first that he should be drawn into a conflict,

which would afford a pretext for the Spaniards to
claim the fulfilment of the King's promise. Whatever he did, or failed to do, Ralegh was doomed from
the moment that Gondomar found himself unable to
stop the expedition, and cajoled the King into giving
his fatal pledge upon conditions for the fulfilment
of which the Spaniards could so easily invent a
pretext.

CHAPTER XVII

RALEGH with his wife and Captain King started for London in the middle of July. They had not gone twenty miles on their way before they met Sir Lewis Stukeley coming to arrest Sir Walter, and they had to retrace their steps. Stukeley at once set about realising the contents of the *Destiny*. He was a kinsman of Ralegh and affected friendship with him, but events proved him to have been as black-hearted a traitor as ever lived. Whilst he was busy with the ship, Ralegh was simply placed under nominal arrest in the house of a private gentleman. It was

three weeks since the *Destiny* had arrived, and during
that time, as we have seen, the leader had learned
to the full the accusations against him. He had,
however, made no attempt to escape from the
country; although in King James's 'declaration' or
apology for his judicial murder, written by Bacon,
the contrary is falsely asserted. But now Lady
Ralegh's entreaties prevailed upon her husband to
seek to avoid the plots which she knew were laid
for his destruction. By the aid of King a boat was
hired to carry him to France, and it lay out of
gunshot in the harbour. At night Ralegh entered
a boat to board her, and had gone a quarter of a mile—
had practically, indeed, placed himself beyond danger
—when the thoughts of his pledge to his sureties,
Arundel and Pembroke, rushed through his mind,
and he insisted upon returning. Lady Ralegh
was in despair, but she could not move him. He
would face his accusers and justify himself.

Stukeley and his charge, with Lady Ralegh, Captain
King, and a French doctor named Manourie, whom
Stukeley had engaged to spy upon Ralegh, started
for London on the 25th July. Manourie talked
chemistry with his patient, and wormed himself
into his confidence. On reaching Salisbury, Ralegh
hinted to him that he had reasons for wishing to
delay on the journey, in order that his friends in
London might have longer time to work on his
behalf, and asked him to administer an emetic, or give

him other means to feign sickness. Manourie consented to do so, and it was agreed that Lady Ralegh
and King should go forward to London, whilst their
chief found means to stay at Salisbury. King had
never ceased to bewail the lost opportunity of escape,
and had broached to Manourie a plan for another
attempt, in which the doctor pretended to associate
himself, and Ralegh himself consented. A ship was
to be placed in the Thames in waiting for an opportunity for flight to France. Suddenly, after Lady
Ralegh and King had gone, Stukeley was horrified to
find that his charge had apparently lost his reason, and
was gnawing the rushes on the floor and behaving like
a wild animal. An ointment provided by Manourie,
moreover, had covered him with a fearful purple
eruption which was thought to be the plague, and
the emetic had rendered him deathlike in appearance.
The device was an undignified one, and did nothing
to improve his case when the trick was divulged ; but
it gave Ralegh during his few days' delay time to write
his *Apologie for the Voyage to Guiana*, upon which
his formal defence rests, and which will always remain
the best record of the events of the expedition, taken
in conjunction with the diary of the first portion of
the voyage up to the 13th February. James was on
a progress through the southern counties at the time,
and arrived at Salisbury whilst Ralegh was there, as
the prisoner doubtless had foreseen and intended.
The King was scandalised at the delay, and per-

emptorily ordered Stukeley to conduct his charge to
London.   This was on the 1st August, and if
Manourie is to be believed — which is extremely
doubtful — through all the rest of the journey to
London, Ralegh was speaking disrespectfully of the
King, and talking of the plans of escape.   The
Frenchman says that he offered him £50 a year
for life for his aid.   At Staines, he asserts that Ralegh
gave him a splendid jewel worth £150, with which
to purchase Stukeley's connivance, which in appearance, at least, was easily obtained.   At Brentford,
Ralegh was met by a French gentleman named
David de Novion, Sieur de la Chesne, the translator
at the French embassy, who managed to tell him
that the French agent had something of great interest
to communicate to him.   On reaching Lady Ralegh's
house in Broad Street, whither he was taken before
going to the Tower, Le Clerc, the French agent, and
La Chesne saw him and said they had made arrangements for his escape, and had a ship waiting to carry
him to Calais.   But King had made arrangements
too, and his ketch was lying in the river.   Ralegh
preferred to escape by means of King, and all arrangements were made.   Stukeley pretended to enter fully
into the plans, but gave reports constantly to Secretary
Naunton, who had succeeded Winwood.   Ralegh was,
indeed, doubly betrayed, for King's boatswain, Hart,
had turned traitor, and it was he who awaited the party
at the stairs to row them down the river to the ketch off

Tilbury. Ralegh, with Stukeley and his son and a page, on the night of Sunday, 9th August, crept out of the house in Broad Street and walked to the Tower Dock, where they found King and his men waiting with two wherries. Before stepping into the boat Stukeley saluted King and asked him whether he had not shown himself an honest man ; to which the captain drily replied that he hoped he would continue so. Before they had gone twenty strokes, the rowers said that they were being followed by Mr Herbert's boat. Ralegh was disturbed, but Stukeley sought to tranquillise him. Then the prisoner did an unfortunate thing. He asked the oarsmen—who, of course, did not know him, for he wore a false beard — whether they would continue to row on, even if an attempt was made to arrest him in the King's name. This thoroughly alarmed the men, who began to cry, and almost stopped rowing altogether. Ralegh said he had had a squabble with the Spanish Ambassador, and offered the men ten pieces of gold to go on, and Stukeley, pretending to be annoyed at his fears, threatened to kill the oarsmen if they tarried. But Ralegh was still full of fears, and could not be convinced by all the protestations and embraces of Stukeley, and on approaching Plumstead peremptorily ordered the boatmen to turn back. Herbert's boat then approached them, and Ralegh saw he was betrayed, but still apparently had no suspicion of Stukeley, whom he begged still to retain him in his custody, and gave him some further present; whilst the traitor hugged him, and pretended to invent plans for his safety. He persuaded his prisoner to land at Greenwich, and the pursuing boat followed them. When they were landed the scoundrel threw off the mask, and handed his prisoner to men from the other boat, wearing the livery of Sir William St John, that kinsman of Buckingham who had received the bribe to get him out of the Tower. 'Sir Lewis,' said Ralegh, when he saw he was betrayed, 'these actions will not turn out to your credit.' Nor did they, for the execrations of all England followed Sir Judas Stukeley, as he was thenceforward called, and he died miserably, ruined and mad, after fruitlessly seeking like the King to free himself from the odium of Ralegh's death.

On the morning of Monday, 10th August, the prisoner once more entered the fortress that had held him so long. The next day, Tuesday, there was held a solemn meeting of the Council of State in far off Madrid, to decide upon his fate; and it was resolved that it would be more convenient that he should be executed in London rather than in Spain. And so the great Englishmen was condemned by a foreign tribunal before even the form of a trial had been gone through in London. Since he had been condemned to death, it was now necessary to search for some plausible legal pretext for killing

him. The Privy Council tried very hard, by frequent interrogatories, to entangle Ralegh himself
into compromising admissions. With regard to his
proceedings on the voyage he was immovable, and
on perfectly firm ground. First, he said, San Thomé,
did not belong to Spain, for he had annexed the
whole region himself in 1595, and had continued
his communications with it ever since : the King
had acknowledged this by granting Harcourt's
patent, and his own; 2nd, what had been done
was in self-defence; and 3rd, the Spaniards had
simply gone there when they were informed of his
project. He contended, moreover, that the common
law of England had no jurisdiction for acts committed out of the realm of England; and the
Admiralty Court must decide in his favour, as what
was done was on territory belonging to King James.

There seemed certainly no sufficient ground for
passing the death sentence for what he had done on
the voyage; but if only he could be convicted of
treasonable practices with the French, a decent reason
for his condemnation could be found. It was not
convenient to probe too deeply his former communications with the French Ambassador, but La Chesne
was a comparatively humble individual, and his offer
to aid an escape was seized upon with avidity. He
was arrested, carried before the Council, and closely
interrogated. At the first few examinations he denied
everything, as did the French agent. The latter was

told that he had abetted the escape of a man he knew was under sentence of death, and would not any longer be considered as a diplomatist, his denials being treated as proofs of the many vague charges of intrigue which were brought against Ralegh. Father Fuentes, a Spanish agent, was told by the King on the 12th October, that he was daily discovering the most extraordinary things about Ralegh. • He (Ralegh) had intended, he said, by means of the French, to oust the Spaniards from America, but that he (James) would prove his friendship for Spain by punishing Ralegh. Shortly afterwards Ulloa, the Spanish Chargé d'Affaires, went to Royston to convey to the King of England Philip's orders that Ralegh was to be executed in England, and James then said that these disclosures about Ralegh had made him lose his friendship for France. The French had tried to attract Ralegh to their country, and Des Marets had been at the bottom of the whole expedition. But Ralegh should be executed and full reparation made for the damage done to Spain. He had only brought back with him two little bits of gold, but they should be given up, as they subsequently were, to Ulloa. To this Ulloa replied, that he (James) was delaying Ralegh's execution longer than was needful: he hoped the matter would be promptly settled, and in the next letter he wrote to Philip (28th October) he enclosed what purported to be a commission given by Admiral Montmorenci to Ralegh before he sailed. Some sort of confession was squeezed out of La Chesne, though what it was is not clear, for all the papers in the case have disappeared; but whatever it was, public opinion was encouraged to believe that it disclosed a deep plot, by which Guiana was to be handed over to the King of France; and the Spanish agent's letters are full of horrified references to the iniquity of it. All through the autumn Ralegh was struggling in the toils, and the Spanish agent reports that in October even bets were being laid at Court that he would escape with his life. The Queen constantly pleaded for him, but her pleading was of little use, for she, too, was fading into her grave, and had lost all influence over the King; and the Committee of the Council, whose duty it was to find some pretext by which Ralegh might 'handsomely' be hanged, could only report to the King that they had not found it easy. Ralegh had foiled them at every turn; and as a last resource, they appointed as a special keeper and spy upon him a certain Sir Thomas Wilson, who for many years had been engaged in services of a like nature, and at once managed to worm himself to some extent into Ralegh's confidence. He promised him the King's forgiveness if he would tell all he knew, he intercepted his letters to his wife, he sought to lure him into compromising admissions about France, and his alleged piratical intentions; but withal little or nothing could be obtained of an incriminatory character. 'I never sought for any French commission nor never had any,' said Sir

Walter, and to this assertion he adhered. Sick and
weak, and in utter despondency, he wrote in October
to Buckingham one of those servile letters which came
from him in moments of profound distress, in which
he seeks to excuse his late attempt to escape, by the
evidently false suggestion that it was prompted only
by a desire to prove to the King that he had been
sincere in the Guiana voyage, by returning thither at
once with one ship, 'being resolved (as it is well
known) to have done it from Plymouth, had I not
been restrained.   Hereby I hoped, not only to recover
His Majesty's gracious opinion, but to have destroyed
all those malignant reports which have been spread of
me.'   The suggestion that he intended to start from
France, even with one ship, to go to Guiana, was an
unfortunate one, and certainly could not be expected
to do him much good with the King.   To Carew,
also, he wrote from the Tower, again vigorously setting forth his view of the case in similar terms to those
in which he wrote from Plymouth.   A famous letter
to the King, which both Mr Edwards and Mr
Stebbing believe to have been written from the
Tower on the 24th September, in which he says,
'If it were lawful for the Spaniards to murder 26
Englishmen tyenge them back to back, and then cutt
theire throates . . . and it may not be lawfull for
Your Majesty's subjects, being forced by them, to
repel force by force, we may justly say, O ! miserable
English,' must have been written from Plymouth soon

after his arrival, as a copy of it—or, as I believe, the original—was sent to the King of Spain on the 16th July. By September he was, as he knew, marked for death in the Tower, he had no spirit for writing such a letter to the King as this. His tone had entirely changed.

At length James began to lose patience. The Spanish agent and Father Fuentes were pestering him constantly about the delay in killing Ralegh, the negotiations about the marriage with the Infanta were at a critical stage, and it became necessary, if they were not to cool, that James should somehow fulfil his promise. Every subterfuge to prove something treasonable against the prisoner had failed, and Bacon and the lawyers of the Crown were instructed to devise some legal fiction by which Ralegh might be sacrificed. His old opponent Coke drew up the opinion at which they arrived. Ralegh, in effect, it said, being now under sentence for high treason, could not be tried for any other crime committed since, because he was dead in law ; and the Committee of Council recommended that the King should issue a warrant for the death sentence of 1603 to be carried out, whilst at the same time publishing for the information of the people an account of his 'late crimes and offences.' By this means it would be made to appear that only respect for the law prevented him from being ostensibly punished for his new 'crimes,' though really he would be so. An alternative plan was suggested, by which he might be judged by a secret sitting of the whole Council and the judges, in the presence only of certain invited noblemen and gentlemen, and charged with his recent offences, whereupon the Council might recommend the King to issue a warrant for his execution on the attainder of 1603, 'in respect of his subsequent offences.' How deep was James's distrust and hatred of Ralegh is seen in his reply to this recommendation. He adopted the second procedure, but with the omission of the judges and the few invited spectators. No sort of publicity, however modified, was to be allowed, because it would make the prisoner too popular, as was found by experiment at the arraignment at Winchester, where by his wit he turned the hatred of men into compassion.

It was therefore decided that the Council should sit secretly as a quasi-criminal court, and advise the King as to whether the new offences committed by Ralegh would justify the execution of the death sentence passed in 1603. That the proceedings of this mock trial were a mere matter of form is proved by the fact that on the 23rd October, the day before the final meeting of the Council, a consultation of the law officers was held as to the way in which the sentence was to be carried out. It was decided that the mere issue of a warrant for execution was not now sufficient, as so many years had elapsed since the trial ; but that the prisoner should be brought up under Habeas Corpus before the King's Bench,

and asked if he had any reasons to allege why sentence
should not be passed, as he might plead that a pardon
had been granted, or that he was not the person
who had been sentenced. This course was decided
upon, and the warrant sealed with the Great Seal
before the proceedings before the Council on the 24th
October. Mr Stebbing, Ralegh's latest biographer,
quotes, as representing what took place on this
occasion, the notes from the Lansdowne MSS. (142
fol. 396) in which the Attorney-General, Sir H.
Yelverton formulated the whole of the charges, and
Ralegh replied to them. I am of opinion, however,
that he is mistaken in this, and that the notes refer
to an early stage of the proceedings, namely, the 17th
August. The records of the sitting of the 24th
October have really been lost, but it is evident that
the prisoner was subjected to another long inter-
rogatory, and that finally Bacon informed him that
the Council would advise the King to order the
sentence of 1603 to be executed. Private as the
proceedings were, however, the Spanish agent, Ulloa,
knew all about them, for he wrote to King Philip on
the 16th November (6th November English style)
saying : 'On Saturday last, the 3rd instant (24th
October), Walter Ralegh was taken from the Tower
to the Council, where they kept him under examination from 3 o'clock in the afternoon until 7 at night.
I understand that the High Chancellor of England
(Bacon) described to him the injuries he had inflicted

upon Your Majesty's subjects and territories ; and how
greatly he had abused the King's permission to discover
the gold mine, of which he had pledged his word he
knew the situation.   When he had finished the
recital, he told Ralegh that he must die.   On hearing
this Ralegh lost consciousness for a time, and on
coming to himself I am told he spoke most wildly.
He was taken back to the Tower and put into another
room.   They changed his clothes and his servant, and
appointed guards to watch him, who were relieved
every hour, never leaving him alone day or night in
order that everything he said might be known.   This
care was also necessary so that he might not put an
end to his life by poison, the knife, or otherwise.   On
Wednesday the 7th he was removed from the Tower
well guarded to the King's Bench, where he found
Sir Henry Montague, Chief Justice of England, and
the Sheriffs.   The Chief Justice notified to Ralegh the
sentence of death, and delivered him to the Sheriff,
who was authorised to execute the King's warrant.
Ralegh wished to speak but was not allowed to do
so, and was conveyed to the Gatehouse prison.'

This relates pretty accurately what really took
place.   Ralegh was aroused from his bed in the
Tower in the early morning of the 28th October to
be taken to the King's Bench.   He was in a burning
fever, and dressed hastily without arranging his curly
white hair.   As he passed through the corridors, an
old servitor pressed forward and reminded him of this :

'Let them kem it that have it,' he replied, and then as
if to bring a smile to the man's woeful face he added,
'Peter, dost thou know of any plaister to set a man's
head on again when it is off?'

On his arrival at the King's Bench, Yelverton, the
Attorney-General, demanded that sentence should be
passed upon him for the conviction of 1603. The
Clerk of the Crown read the records of the previous
trial, and the prisoner was then asked by Montague if
he had anything to urge why sentence should not be
passed.   Ralegh began to defend himself about
Guiana, but was told that was not to the purpose.
'All I can say then,' he replied, 'is that the judgment I
received to die so long since cannot now, I hope, be
strained, for since then it was His Majesty's pleasure
to grant me a commission to proceeed on a voyage
beyond the seas, wherein I had martial power on the
life and death of others, so, under favour, I presume I
stand discharged of that judgment. . . . By that commission I gained new life and vigour ; for he that hath
power over the lives of others must surely be master
of his own.' 'The commission does not infer pardon,'
said Montague, 'because treason is a crime which must
be pardoned by express words, not by implication.' 'If
that be your Lordship's opinion,' replied the prisoner,
'I can only put myself upon the mercy of the King.
His Majesty, as well as others who are here present,
have been of opinion that in my former trial I received
but hard measure. Had the King not been exasperated

anew against me, certain I am that I might have lived
a thousand years before he would have taken advantage of that conviction.' Then he pleaded that he
might be granted some little time to arrange his affairs,
and asked for pens, ink and paper ; for he had something, he said, of which to relieve his conscience, and
to satisfy the King. The plea that his commission
condoned his past treason was his last hope, and that
was now gone. So, calm and smiling, the great
Englishman was led from the Hall to the little prison
of the Gatehouse hard by ; doomed beyond hope now
to be sacrificed for daring to assert the right of
England to conquer and civilise a share of the vast
continent of South America, a martyr to the cause of
a great colonial Britain ; done to death by the basest
King that ever sat on Britain's throne. Not an hour
was to be lost before the shameful deed was consum-
mated. The King had hidden himself in the country
to be out of the way of appeals for mercy, or the
execrations of the indignant populace, and before the
day waned the scaffold was being erected in Old Palace
Yard, where the last scene of the tragedy was to be
enacted. The black deed was to be got through
early ; if possible, before the people were fully astir,
for it was Lord Mayor's day, and all the citizens
would flock to see the brave show which came from
the city. From the moment that all hope on earth
had fled for him, there was no more weak whining, no
more abject servility for Ralegh. Dignified and

cheerful, as in his best moments, without bravado and
without complaint, his last hours vindicated his
character for true courage and nobleness.   On his
way from the Hall to the Gatehouse he met an old
acquaintance, Sir Hugh Beeston, whom he asked
whether he would come to the execution the next
morning.   'I do not know what you may do for a
place,' he added ; 'for my own part, I am sure of one.
You must make what shift you can.'   His kinsman,
Thomas Thynne, came to see him at the Gatehouse,
and seemed to think that he was more cheerful than
was becoming.   'Do not carry it with too much
bravery,' he said ; 'your enemies will take exception
if you do.'   'It is my last mirth in this world,' he
replied ; 'do not grudge it me.   When I come to the
sad parting you will see me grave enough.'   The
Dean of Westminster, who attended him, was struck
with the same idea, and warned him against vainglory.
'He seemed to make so light of it that I wondered
at him.   But he gave God thanks that he never feared
death. . . .   He was the most fearless of death that
ever was known, and the most resolute and confident,
yet with reverence and conscience.'

After nightfall the devoted wife was brought to the
Gatehouse to take a last leave of her husband.   She,
poor soul, had prayed and hoped up to now that he
might be saved.   Her boy, Carew Ralegh, had addressed a passionate appeal to the King for his father's
life, and Lady Ralegh had continued to pray to her

husband's friends and kinsmen on the Council to intercede for him.   But it was all of no avail ; and the only grace she could get was that his dead body should be delivered to her.   In their last hours on earth together he told her he could not trust himself to speak of their dear little son ; it would make the parting only the more bitter for them both ; and as if to divert her own thoughts from her approaching widowhood, he dwelt mainly upon her future vindication of his good name, in case, as he feared, that he might be prevented from himself doing so on the scaffold.   Whilst they were thus communing, the clock of the Abbey boomed out the hour of midnight, and the agonised wife was obliged to tear herself away. ' It is well, dear Bess,' were his last words to her, ' that thou mayest dispose of that dead which thou hadst not always the disposing of when alive.'

Through most of the night the prisoner mused and wrote.   He idrew up notes for his intended speech upon the scaffold ; and at some time during his last hours must have written the verse which was found in his Bible after his death.

> ' Even such is time ! who takes in trust
> Our youth, our joys, and all we have,
> And pays us but with earth and dust :
> Who, in the dark and silent grave,
> When we have wandered all our ways,
> Shuts up the story of our days.
> But from that earth, that grave and dust,
> The Lord shall raise me up, I trust.'

The Dean of Westminster was with him to the last, but from his account of his conversations with the prisoner he would seem to have been more controversial than consolatory. 'After he had received the Communion in the morning,' writes the Dean, 'he was very cheerful and merry, and hoped to persuade the world that he dyed an innocent man, as he sayd. Thereat I told him that in these dayes men did not dye in that sort, innocent, and his pleading of innocency was an oblique taxing of the justice of the realm. He confessed justice had been done, and by course of law he must dye, but yet I should give him leave, he sayd, to stand upon his innocency in the fact. . . . I then putt him in mind of the death of my Lord of Essex: how it was generally reported that he was a great instrument of his death, which, if his heart did charge him with, he should repent and ask God forgiveness. To which he made answer as in the former relation ; and sayd, moreover, that my Lord of Essex was fetched off by a trick, which he privately told me of. . . . He was very cheerful that morning he dyed ; eate his breakfast hertily, and tooke tobacco ; and made no more of his death than it had been to take a journey ; and left a great impression in the minds of those that beheld him ; inasmuch that Sir Lewis Stukeley and the Frenchman grow very odious. This,' adds the Dean, 'was the news a week since ; but now it is blowen over, and he is allmost forgotten.'

As he was about to leave the Gatehouse on his long journey a cup of wine was handed to him, and he was asked whether it was to his liking. 'I will answer you,' he replied, 'as did the fellow who drank of St Giles's bowl as he went to Tyburn, "It is good drink, if a man might but tarry by it."'

On the morning of the 29th October 1618 Sir Walter Ralegh was led forth for the short walk from the Gatehouse to the scaffold in Old Palace Yard.   He wore a black velvet wrought gown over a brown satin doubtlet, with a ruff band and black taffety slashed breeches, with ash-coloured silk stockings.   It was still early—between seven and eight o'clock—but the news had spread that the famous man was to lose his life, and crowds of people had flocked to Westminster to see the sight.   The story is thus told by the Spanish agent, Ulloa, to King Philip, at whose behest the head of Ralegh was to fall. 'They brought him on foot, surrounded by 60 guards, to the square at Westminster, near the palace, where the scaffold had been erected.   When he ascended it he spoke, as I have been told, for three-quarters-of-an-hour, saying that he went to discover that gold mine, hoping to enrich England, and that he had sailed with that intention, but that Captain Kemys, who guided him, had deceived him ; for at his despair at having mistaken the place he had killed himself.   Ralegh said not a word about the atrocities he had committed at San Thomé or elsewhere in the Indies, and denied

everything he had confessed to the King and Council
of his treaties with France, declaring that the French
agent had spoken to him but once out of courtesy.
He excused Lord Carew and Lord Hay, Earl of Doncaster, who were those that aided him in his expedition
to Guiana. He also entreated everyone to believe
that he had not been instrumental in causing the
death of the Earl of Essex, nor had he rejoiced thereat,
as had been imputed to him. On the contrary, he
had regretted it more than his own sins. He declared
that he was not an Atheist, as some thought, but a
Protestant and a loyal subject of the King. When he
ended his discourse, the executioner with his axe
(which Ralegh felt to see whether it was sharp) cut
off his head with two strokes, and held it up to the
multitude. As this happened on Lord Mayor's day,
an immense number of people were present, and the
punishment was consequently the more public.
Although he was sentenced to be hanged, his friends,
who, as I have said, are many and powerful, did their
utmost with the King to obtain his pardon and save
his life (*in cipher*, and the Queen has helped as much
as she could to this end), but the only favour they
could obtain was that he should be beheaded instead
of hanged.

'On the scaffold, near Ralegh, until he was beheaded,
were the Earl of Arundel, the Earl of Oxford, Lord
Chamberlain, and the Earls of Doncaster and Northampton, and several members of the Council

were present at a window, concealed behind the
shutters.   Ralegh's spirit never faltered, nor did his
countenance change.   On the contrary, he was extremely brave through it all.   (*In cipher*.   The
death of this man has produced a great commotion
and fear here, and it is looked upon as a matter of
the highest importance, owing to his being a person
of great parts and experience, subtle, crafty, ingenious,
and brave enough for anything.   His supporters had
declared that he could never be executed. . . .   A
declaration is being drawn up of Ralegh's death,
which the King tells me will soon be made public.' . . .)

This is the testimony of Ralegh's enemies.   His
friends are even more emphatic as to his noble bearing
upon the scaffold.   He had always feared that he
would be secretly put out of the way to prevent his
last public vindication from his own mouth, and his
first exclamation of rejoicing on the scaffold was that
he was brought out in the light to die.   He was weak
with fever, and could hardly be heard by the members
of the Council who sat at a window near, so his
friends Arundel, Doncaster and others came down to
the scaffold and stood by him whilst he spoke.   Most
solemnly, and with convincing eloquence, he told his
story once again.   He called God to witness, with
his dying breath, that he was a loyal Englishman, and
had had no treaties with the French, that he had had
no hand in the death of Essex, and that his action in
the Guiana expedition had been throughout honest and

sincere. He indignantly refuted the lies of Manourie
and Stukeley as to his alleged disloyal expressions and
intentions, and then calmly and cheerfully prepared
for the end. ' I have a long journey to go,' he said, as
he put off his long velvet gown and satin doublet,
and then he asked the headsman to let him see the
axe. 'Dost thou think I am afraid of it.' Then,
smiling as he handed it back, he said to the Sheriff,
' This is a sharp medicine, but it is a sound cure for all
diseases.' When he was asked which way he would
lie upon the block, he replied, 'So the heart be right,
it is no matter which way the head lies.' Then, at two
strokes, the wise white head fell, and one of the
brightest geniuses that England ever saw was offered
up ; a fruitless sacrifice to the cause of an impossible
alliance with the power whose arrogance he had dared
to withstand. He had made the fatal mistake of
supposing that the high-handed traditions of Elizabeth maintained their potency under the sway of
James.

The day after his death Lady Ralegh wrote a sad
little letter to her brother, asking him to allow her
' to berri the worthi boddi of my nobell hosban, Sur
Walter Ralegh, in your chorche at Beddington. . . .
God hold me in my wites ' ; but for some reason, now
unknown, the headless corpse was buried within the
chancel of St Margaret's, Westminster. What ultimately became of the head is uncertain ; but it was
long preserved by Lady Ralegh, and on her death by

her son, Carew, in whose grave at West Horsley in Surrey it is believed it was interred.

A groan had involuntarily burst from the crowd as the axe fell. The groan was echoed all over England as the news spread. The Dean of Westminster was premature when he wrote a week after : 'Now it is blowen over, and he is almost forgotten,' for Ralegh embodied in the minds of the people their long fostered hatred of the Spaniards, and he became in his death far more popular than ever he had been in life. A generation had arisen which knew him not in his insolent splendour ; his long stay in the Tower, and the talk of his mystic and profound activities there, had made him something of a popular hero, even before his death ; and thenceforward the men who had hounded him to his doom were marked down for public reprobation. If the idea of a Spanish match was unpopular before, it became doubly hateful now, and soon James himself saw the mistake he had made. He was cunning and crafty, but he was dealing with a power far more crafty still, and had been bullied into parting with his choicest merchandise before exacting the price. In vain he tried when it was too late to appreciate his wares and exact an equivalent. He told the Spaniards that he had put Ralegh to death principally to give them satisfaction, and they would be looked upon as the most unworthy persons in the world if they did not act sincerely now. He pointed out to them how he had strained the affections of his

people in putting to death a man 'who was so able
to have done him service.   Yet, to give them content,
he hath not spared him, when by preserving him he
might have given great satisfaction to his subjects,
and had at command upon all occasions as useful a
man as served any prince in Christendom.'   But it
was too late for James to praise Ralegh now.   The
Spaniards had gained their point ; the King of
England had admitted that all South America was
sacred to them, had shown to the world that he
accepted an inferior position, had sacrificed one of his
most gifted subjects, and was outwitted in the payment of the price for the humiliation of his country.
This is not the place to recount the ridiculous fiasco
of the Spanish match, which made James and his son
the laughing stock of Europe ; but before the King's
death it must have been patent to him, as it was to all
the world, that Ralegh had been sacrificed in vain,
and that the King's base compliance to arrogant
demands had reduced England again to a secondary
place amongst the nations, from which the genius of
Elizabeth had raised it.

A recent biographer of Ralegh has remarked how
much less considerable were his actual achievements than
his undoubted gifts, that in action he had generally
failed, and that not a single one of the great aims of his
life was successfully carried through by him.   He was,
in truth, a man of the very highest intellectual gifts,
but whose moral nature was infinitely inferior to

them. In this he was typical of the age in which he lived. The great Queen, who struck the keynote of the period, suffered from a similar disproportion of the two sides of her nature, and many of the greatest minds that surrounded her were allied to dwarfed moral attributes. The very intensity and vitality of Ralegh's character exaggerated in him this disparity. He was physically brave beyond compare, and yet he begged for bare life like a very coward. He was insolent, vain and domineering to the last degree, and yet he could cringe and snivel abjectly at the least ill-fortune that befell him. He was greedy, unprincipled and rapacious, and yet he squandered his fortune lavishly on his great patriotic scheme of colonisation, by which he personally could hardly hope to gain. His contemporaries utterly disbelieved either in his honesty or his truth, and yet his noble written protestations seem to bear the absolute stamp of veracity upon them. With all his vast ability, he had not that magnetic moral strength that attracts men to a leader in moments of defeat, and enables him to retrieve reverse by victory. At the moment of failure, in the great crisis of his fortune, during the last Guiana voyage, he crumbled down hopelessly, and could only recriminate and lament, whilst his men fell away from him because he was unable to lead them, and he actually returned home a prisoner in his own cabin.

His great misfortune was that he became a royal

favourite. In the purely intellectual domain he would have been eminent, even in an age which possessed a Shakspeare and a Bacon. The reason why he is so much more popular with posterity than he was with his contemporaries, is that the former judge him chiefly by his writings, the product of his brain, whilst the latter were necessarily more closely in contact with the actions of his life, the outcome of his weaker moral and physical nature.

But judge him how we may, we cannot deny him a commanding place in a grand and spacious age. Even if his faults were greater than they were, his love and faith in the future of England as the mighty mother of empires and the mistress of the seas, demand for him the judgment that he was a towering Englishman, and died for a great ideal.

INDEX

THE END

www.ingramcontent.com/pod-product-compliance
Lightning Source LLC
Chambersburg PA
CBHW031055110726
47900CB00003B/931